THE BESTSELLING NOVELS OF
TOM CLANCY

RED RABBIT

Tom Clancy returns to Jack Ryan's early days—in an extraordinary novel of global political drama . . .

"A WILD, SATISFYING RIDE." —*New York Daily News*

THE BEAR AND THE DRAGON

A clash of world powers. President Jack Ryan's trial by fire . . .

"HEART-STOPPING ACTION . . . CLANCY STILL REIGNS." —*The Washington Post*

RAINBOW SIX

John Clark is used to doing the CIA's dirty work. Now he's taking on the world . . .

"ACTION-PACKED."
—*The New York Times Book Review*

EXECUTIVE ORDERS

A devastating terrorist act leaves Jack Ryan as president of the United States . . .

"UNDOUBTEDLY CLANCY'S BEST YET."
—*The Atlanta Journal-Constitution*

continued . . .

DEBT OF HONOR

It begins with the murder of an American woman in the back streets of Tokyo. It ends in war . . .

"A SHOCKER." —*Entertainment Weekly*

THE HUNT FOR RED OCTOBER

The smash bestseller that launched Clancy's career—the incredible search for a Soviet defector and the nuclear submarine he commands . . .

"BREATHLESSLY EXCITING." —*The Washington Post*

RED STORM RISING

The ultimate scenario for World War III—the final battle for global control . . .

"THE ULTIMATE WAR GAME . . . BRILLIANT." —*Newsweek*

PATRIOT GAMES

CIA analyst Jack Ryan stops an assassination—and incurs the wrath of Irish terrorists . . .

"A HIGH PITCH OF EXCITEMENT." —*The Wall Street Journal*

THE CARDINAL OF THE KREMLIN

The superpowers race for the ultimate Star Wars missile defense system . . .

"*CARDINAL* EXCITES, ILLUMINATES . . . A REAL PAGE-TURNER."
—*Los Angeles Daily News*

CLEAR AND PRESENT DANGER

The killing of three U.S. officials in Colombia ignites the American government's explosive, and top secret, response . . .

"A CRACKLING GOOD YARN." —*The Washington Post*

THE SUM OF ALL FEARS

The disappearance of an Israeli nuclear weapon threatens the balance of power in the Middle East—and around the world . . .

"CLANCY AT HIS BEST . . . NOT TO BE MISSED."
—*The Dallas Morning News*

WITHOUT REMORSE

The Clancy epic fans have been waiting for. His code name is Mr. Clark. And his work for the CIA is brilliant, cold-blooded, and efficient . . . but who is he really?

"HIGHLY ENTERTAINING." —*The Wall Street Journal*

Tom Clancy's
POWER PLAYS

ZERO HOUR

CREATED BY
TOM CLANCY
AND
MARTIN GREENBERG

WRITTEN BY
JEROME PREISLER

BERKLEY BOOKS, NEW YORK

TOM CLANCY'S POWER PLAYS: ZERO HOUR

A Berkley Book / published by arrangement with
RSE Holdings, Inc.

PRINTING HISTORY
Berkley edition / November 2003

ISBN: 0-425-19291-1

BERKLEY®
Berkley Books are published by The Berkley Publishing Group,
a division of Penguin Group (USA) Inc.,
375 Hudson Street, New York, New York 10014.
BERKLEY and the "B" design
are trademarks belonging to Penguin Group (USA) Inc.

PRINTED IN THE UNITED STATES OF AMERICA

10 9 8 7 6 5 4 3 2 1

ACKNOWLEDGMENTS

I would like to acknowledge the assistance of Marc Cerasini, Larry Segriff, Denise Little, John Helfers, Brittiany Koren, Robert Youdelman, Esq., Danielle Forte, Esq., Dianne Jude, and the wonderful people at Penguin Group (USA) Inc., including David Shanks and Tom Colgan. But most important, it is for you, my readers, to determine how successful our collective endeavor has been.

—Tom Clancy

PART 1

Blue Fire

ONE

NEW YORK CITY

THE PREDICTED JANUARY SNOWSTORM HAD AR-
rived as a sloppy mix of rain and sleet, sending local weath-
ermen into a scramble to revise their outlooks. But while
Sullivan was glad they'd finally reported what anyone with
two good eyes could see, he hadn't heard a word about the
treacherous roadway icing over the Jaguar's radio.

It never changed in this city, he thought. Whether the
commotion was about a blizzard, a terrorist threat, or some
hot-ticket Broadway opening. You got the obligatory
buildup, countless gasbag media experts, and in the end
nothing was what they claimed it would be. Unless you
were a complete greenhorn, fresh off a bus from Kansas or
wherever it was the deer and antelope played, you realized
their chatter was so much white noise, hardly different
from the everyday racket on a midtown street.

You knew, you damned well did. And if you were smart
you learned to check your expectations, use common sense,

and hope that the next corner you turned didn't lead under a falling metal construction beam.

As he struggled to maintain his traction on the northbound FDR Drive, heading toward upper Manhattan from East 23rd Street, Sullivan was trying hard to apply that perspective to the deal he was about to clinch. Despite his better instincts, it wasn't easy. He was chasing again, and he knew it. Chasing the *perfect* deal that would put him in a position where money wasn't a constant squeeze. Call it an obsession and he wouldn't argue. But his latest number was special. Unique merchandise, a fat cash earning, and excellent value for his buyer, who stood to make a huge bundle of his own on turnaround.

If that didn't translate into perfection, it very definitely came close.

The Jag's powerful heater had been blasting away for a while now, and Sullivan took one hand off the steering wheel long enough to unzip his Altair ski jacket, a sharp-looking piece of outerwear he'd ordered from Switzerland for a small fortune. Although he wondered if maybe it wasn't the torrent of warm air making him perspire. Maybe he was just kind of giddy. He could imagine the tremendous profits that would be generated down the line—or lines, plural, since his different goods would eventually wind up in different places. Spreading the wealth, sharing his success . . . Patrick Sullivan supposed he'd helped create a whole alternative economy in the past few months; call him an enterprising capitalist. And his latest commodity, well, unlike the storm, it *would* live up to its advance billing. He couldn't downplay its unique worth if he tried.

Tonight was about breaking ties, Sullivan thought. About personal expansion, and taking a giant step to secure his future. And he incidentally might be doing the world a favor in the process. When all was said and done, Hasul the Vampire stood to become the major loser in this whole thing—and that freakish bastard and his night stalkers couldn't very well go looking for help or sympathy from anyone.

But Sullivan refused to be troubled with the broad view. If that qualified him as selfish, so it went. He took pride in being a stand-up businessman, a solid provider. All his customers came away satisfied. The people who depended on him for support were happy and comfortable. He met his financial commitments, looked out for his own, and made sure he lived a little, too. A man ought to keep something on the side, no punishable offense there. Sullivan was doing okay in his mind, maybe better than okay, though he knew some would judge him by a hypocritical and unrealistic standard they would never dream of applying to themselves.

Now Sullivan checked the road sign just ahead and was a bit surprised to see he'd almost reached the East 96th Street exit. With the evening rush hour long past and the weather bad as it was, traffic had been light, and his trip uptown shorter than usual in spite of the slippery conditions that had forced him to stay below the forty-five mph speed limit. Most of the other vehicles on the Drive with him were taxicabs going out to La Guardia for inbound fares, but the airport was certain to be a mess of delays and cancellations, and those poor tired hacks wouldn't have much to show for the fuel they burned.

Approaching 103rd Street, Sullivan glanced up at the footbridge to Randalls Island on the chance he'd see a solitary figure moving across from the esplanade, but its stairs and walkway were deserted. This noted for the record, he went on for maybe a quarter mile, then bore left before the road split and diverted him onto the great beyond of Harlem River Drive. The factories and commercial warehouses of

Queens to his right over the river, he swung onto the entrance ramp for the Triboro Bridge, tapping the brake pedal, slowing to a crawl as he took its long ascending curve to the span.

Sullivan found the deck of the bridge spur crossing the river as clear of traffic as the highway. At the toll plaza he pulled up to the cash-only booth and stopped to pay the transit cop, whose subtle eyeballing gave him a reflexive twinge of paranoia. He could remember a time when the city's toll-booths were manned by ordinary clerks, and hadn't quite grown accustomed to the heightened security that had turned the approaches to New York bridges and tunnels into fortified checkpoints. Nowadays it seemed as if you couldn't go from one borough to the next without passing an armed police guard, welcome to the new millennium.

The barrier lifted and Sullivan went on to merge across several lanes to the Randalls/Wards Island down ramp, pausing briefly to flick on his high beams in the pitch darkness at its bottom. Sleet battered the idling Jaguar's roof and windshield. Rubbish blew over the narrow strip of blacktop, the strong winds pushing it into small, loose mounds against the pylons of the Hell Gate railroad trestle and viaducts to his left.

Sullivan drove slowly forward past old Downing Stadium, his brights glancing off reflectorized signs for the FDNY training school, a drug rehab clinic, a men's homeless shelter, and a high-security state psychiatric center, its grim sprawl of buildings recessed behind a forbidding forty-foot cyclone fence topped with razor wire. A quick left put him onto an access road that led past the Department of Sanitation sewage-treatment plant at the island's eastern fringe, where parked garbage trucks, industrial trailers, and enormous steel Dumpsters jostled together inside another tall, ugly chain-link enclosure.

After a few minutes the access road took him across a murky channel of inlet water and dead-ended on Wards Island. Here a third fence, this one only ten or twelve feet high, measured the boundary of a neglected waterfront park. The entrance gate had been completely torn from its hinges and lay on the ground beside an opening easily wide enough for the Jag.

Sullivan ignored the NO CARS ALLOWED BY ORDER OF PO-LICE DEPARTMENT sign on the toppled gate and rolled through into the park.

He steered across the paved footpaths snaking down a series of gradual slopes to the riverbank, his headlights slipping over dead winter grass, disclosing fresh scabs of ice at the bases of trees and wooden benches. Directly ahead of him in the shadows, a concrete utility building with public restrooms on one side stood just about where the descending paths became too narrow for his tires. He nosed to a halt a few yards uphill of the small, squat structure, and then sat back in his seat, keeping the Jag's lights and wipers switched on, running its engine so the heater would continue to blow. His expensive mountain skiwear notwithstanding, he'd decided the dampness under his arms could only be a result of nerves.

Sullivan waited, staring into the night. He observed no sign of anyone standing near the park house and checked the backlit face of his dashboard clock. A quarter of eleven; he'd arrived for his meet right on the button. If experience was a guide, his man would show. Still, Sullivan felt a mild sort of annoyance. Having already torn himself from the Chelsea apartment's blissful comforts for the unbelievable wind and cold of this stinking island, it wasn't so much the waiting that bugged him. Once he was here, he was here. But other things mattered. Or ought to matter, anyway.

Several minutes ticked by. The gusts blew stiffly off the river, howled around the car, whipped sleet against its roof and windows. Bare treetop branches blew and swayed in the heavy gusts. Sullivan reclined in his seat and thought of the attaché in the rear. He'd brought the special merchandise at serious risk. As usual he'd agreed to a time and place chosen by his buyer. No, he decided, his impatience wasn't unwarranted. He was entitled to get back some of the respect and consideration he gave. . . .

A single, hard rap on the passenger's window jolted Sullivan from his thoughts. He straightened with a sharp intake of breath, then glanced over his shoulder as a black-gloved fist knocked on the window a second time.

The man outside the car was tall, thin, and wore one of those draping Aussie outback coats that flowed down below the knees like a cloak. Combed straight back over his head, his dark hair was soaked, his open umbrella offering limited cover against the slanting wetness.

Sullivan exhaled. His buyer had arrived true to form. The way he'd glided toward the car out of nowhere, moving right up to his window without a sound, you could almost believe he had cats' blood in his veins.

Unlocking the passenger door with his master control, Sullivan leaned across the seat, grabbed the handle, and pushed it open.

"Lathrop," he said. "You'd better get in."

"I've been sitting here a while," Sullivan said.

"That right?"

"Yes. Waiting in this god-awful storm. It isn't something I appreciate."

Lathrop looked at him across the front seat.

"Rough day at the office?" he said.

"I'm serious."

"I know," Lathrop said. "And I'm just trying to understand why you're so irritable. My guess would be you're tired, but the sporty new jacket makes it hard to tell."

Sullivan was in no mood for the sarcasm. "I told you, this isn't a joke—"

"I'll bet the women love your youthful, athletic image."

Sullivan swallowed his frustration. He wasn't sure what that remark was meant to suggest, or exactly how much Lathrop knew about him. But his words had a way of slipping right under the skin.

"Listen, I just wanted to get across a point," he said. "Let's concentrate on what's important."

Lathrop gave him a nod. "Let's."

Sullivan fell silent. After a moment or two he produced a low grunt, reached up, and turned on the roof light. Shifting around behind the steering wheel, he took a hard, flat, black leatherette gemstone case from an inner pocket of his jacket and carefully set it on the armrest between Lathrop and himself.

"Here." Sullivan opened the magnetized latches securing the case's lid and lifted it off. "Check these out."

Lathrop bent over the case to examine its contents.

"That brilliant in the middle's damned sexy," Sullivan said. "Go ahead, hold it up, you'll see for yourself."

Lathrop reached into the case for the stone without removing his gloves, a small magnifying loupe in one hand now. He held it to his eye and slowly examined the stone, turning it under the interior light, giving it a long, discerning look.

"Nice," he said. "Very nice."

Sullivan nodded.

"It was brighter around us, you'd be even more impressed," he said. "The three caraters, they should pull, say, between fifteen and twenty thousand apiece. That's at the Exchange or anyplace else, doesn't matter how or where you move them. But the one you're holding, its size and weight are exceptional. And check out the life in it. The fire. That's *hard-on* sexy. A fifteen-carat Kashmir, top grade, brings in . . ."

"I know what it should bring. Provided I'm able to get certs."

"It's the same quality as everything else you've bought from me. Send it to the AGL for a grading report. Or the Gubelin lab in Switzerland. Whichever you like. The experts can run their usual tests. I guarantee it's going to pass with flying colors."

Lathrop finished his inspection, returned the stone to its foam-rubber compartment, pocketed his loupe.

"Blue, especially," he said. "That right?"

Sullivan smiled faintly at the remark. Some of the edginess had gone out of him.

"Yeah," he said. "You've got it there."

Silence. Lathrop looked at him, water dripping from his slicked-back hair, a splotch of moisture spreading under the tip of the folded umbrella beside his leg.

"What are you asking for the lot?" he said.

Sullivan hesitated a moment. He'd been a salesman his whole adult life and ordinarily wasn't concerned about coming off as overanxious. But tonight it required some effort.

"I figured it would make sense to put together a square package, work out a price—"

"Maybe, maybe not," Lathrop said. "I know I can move the stones. Taking on the other thing is an expensive gamble even if your claims about it are true."

Sullivan shook his head.

"I'm not the type to make up stories," he said. "What I've got with Dragonfly . . . I could sit forever rattling off a list of interested parties. Countries, starting with our own U.S. of A. . . . look at what they've been up to at Los Alamos lately. And on that mountain laboratory in California . . . Livermore, I think it's called. Bring it to the fucking government, you'd rake in a heap. And private outfits, Jesus Christ, they'd do anything to get their hands on it. There's that German megacorp for one. UpLink International's another example. Money up the ass, there, I'm telling you from my own experience. You need more choices, I could reel a dozen of them off the top of my head."

Lathrop didn't answer. He'd suddenly turned toward the windshield and was gazing outside with a distant look on his face, his head tilted sideways, his mouth slightly open, the corner of his upper lip twisting upward in what almost resembled a sneer. Sullivan had noticed these mannerisms before and couldn't quite figure out their significance . . . but they always reinforced his impression of Lathrop as being somehow catlike. It was as if he was tasting the air, his full attention captured by a trail nobody else could detect.

"Those interested parties," Lathrop said after a while. His voice had a slight faraway quality that matched his expression. "Why not take it to them yourself, cut out the middleman?"

"Bad business." Sullivan said, shaking his head. "I know

how far I can push my situation." He shrugged. "It's about feeling a certain level of comfort."

Lathrop kept staring out the ice-crusted windshield toward the blurred black line of the water.

"You brought everything?"

"In that briefcase." Sullivan nodded at the backseat. "It's all inside except the keys."

"So your comfort level doesn't allow for trusting me enough to hand them over tonight."

"Come on," Sullivan said. "As it stands, you'd have the brilliants. That ought to be plenty acceptable."

Lathrop turned to him. "What's your asking price?"

"Five hundred thou, all inclusive. You wire half the money into the usual account. I confirm payment, send you the keys right away. Then you transfer the balance and we're settled."

A pause. Lathrop stretched it out a while before extending his right hand across the seat.

"Okay, we've got a deal," he said. "*Mazel* and *broche*."

Sullivan couldn't help but smile again.

"Is that the expression they use?" he said, accepting the handshake.

Lathrop nodded. "Luck and blessings. Those words are tradition. A seal. Binding as any written contract."

Sullivan was feeling pleased with himself.

"May you live as long as you want, and never want as long as you live," he said. "That's how my Mick ancestors would've spun it."

Lathrop sat there without comment, still shaking Sullivan's hand, clasping it in his own. . . .

And then he abruptly *stopped* shaking it and tightened his grip.

Sullivan lifted his eyebrows in confusion, tried to pull

away, realized he couldn't. Lathrop would not let go. He kept holding on, staring at him across the seat.

Sullivan's grin became a wince of pain. He tried pulling free again without success. Lathrop's hand was a clamp around his knuckles, squeezing them hard, crushing them painfully together.

"Hey," Sullivan said. "What *is* this? You're—"

One glimpse of the pistol Lathrop withdrew from his left coat pocket silenced him. A long-barreled .45 automatic, its muzzle came up fast and pushed into the soft flesh below his ear.

"Open your door and get out of the car," Lathrop said.

"I don't understand. . . ."

"I told you to get out," Lathrop said. "Try to take off, I'll kill you on the spot. You have a problem with those instructions?"

Sullivan swallowed, felt the pressure of the gun against his jaw.

"No," he said. "No, I don't."

Lathrop grinned at him.

"Good business," he said.

Sullivan knew he'd set himself up for a ripoff of monumental proportions and was only hoping that would be the worst of it, praying to Heaven above that would be the worst. How on earth could he have been so careless and stupid?

He stood inside the darkened park house where Lathrop had led him at gunpoint, his back to a cold, graffiti-scribbled concrete wall, his feet awash in crumpled food wrappers, soda cans, tossed syringes and crack vials, and whatever other unnameable filth a scabby parade of junkies and derelict winos had left here over the decades. He was sick to his stomach, overcome with fear and the grossly horrible stink of the place.

Lathrop, meanwhile, seemed unaffected by their blighted surroundings. He faced Sullivan in silence, a small flashlight in one hand, the .45 leveled in his other. His tall form cutting a dark silhouette against the park house's barely open steel door.

"I don't see why you'd want to do this," Sullivan said. "I've always been straight with you. You've got some complaints about money, or my terms, we can work it out."

"Wrong," Lathrop said softly. "We can't."

Sullivan's nausea rose higher in his throat. It occurred to him to remind Lathrop about the Dragonfly keys, but then he realized that would be a severe blunder and flushed the idea in a hurry. If Lathrop had forgotten about the keys, or thought he didn't need them, so much the better. He would learn. And maybe then Sullivan could work them for leverage.

"I won't try to change your mind," he said at last. "Take anything you want. Just don't . . . it would be a mistake for you to get carried away."

"Oh?" Lathrop stepped closer, the gun held in front of him. "Go ahead, Sullivan. You're a salesman. Sell me on it."

Sullivan could hear himself breathing as he tried to collect himself, keep his guts from turning inside out.

"It isn't like I can hurt you," he said, swallowing. "Like I can run to the police. We drive off this garbage heap, go our separate ways, it's over. . . ."

"I don't drive here."

"Whatever." Sullivan stared tensely at Lathrop in the pale glow of the flash. "I'm just saying you wouldn't have to think about me causing problems for—"

"You know I don't drive to these meetings," Lathrop said with a flat, latched-on sort of emphasis. "You've watched me. Last time we were here, for instance."

Sullivan blinked. He felt a penetrating chill that was unrelated to the cold, remembered being sweaty with nerves in his car not half an hour earlier.

Inside out.

"That isn't—"

Lathrop frowned in disapproval, took another step forward, jabbed the gun barrel between his ribs.

"Spare me." He adjusted his flash between them, its beam patching the hollows of his face with light and shadow. "You turned off the FDR on a Hundred and Eleventh and First Avenue, and left your car right outside the playground there. Then you went through the basketball courts, crossed the overpass to the riverside, and walked to that fishing pier about four blocks down. Figured you could wait under the roof in the dark, keep an eye out for me without being spotted. Once you saw me take the footbridge to the island, you went back to the car and followed over the Triboro."

An insistent gust pushed the door a little farther ajar and Sullivan heard sleet crackle on the park house's cement floor. The temperature on the island had crept below freezing, crystallizing whatever rain had been mingled with the icy downpour in the offshore winds.

"All right," Sullivan said. His heart pumped. "I'm not going to lie about it. I won't try denying what I did. But I wasn't intending to cross you or anything . . . I was just taking precautions. Watching my back. Of all people, you should understand—"

"I do," Lathrop said. "The problem is you're an excitable boy, Sullivan. And I can't have that."

Sullivan heard the click of the .45's hammer being cocked, *felt* it against his body, stared at him with helpless terror. "My God, please, what are you doing—?"

"Taking precautions," Lathrop said, and then shot him twice, point blank, in the middle of the chest.

• • •

Lathrop gazed out over the river, catching his breath, black oily wavelets splashing the toes of his rubber boots. He'd dragged the industrial drum liner containing Sullivan's body from the park house, brought it downhill to shove it into the water where the city's Irish mob had dumped their unwanted human meat for generations—and this particular Irishman hadn't been a lean slab by any means.

He stood watching the Hell Gate's current swiftly carry his discarded burden toward the Manhattan-Queens branch of the Triboro and then on under the huge, partially submerged bridge posts to vanish in the turbulent night. He could see the lights beading the span's suspension cables twinkle softly through waves of precipitation. See brighter lights in the windows of the public housing projects on the near Manhattan shore, and, a little farther south, in those of the upscale condominiums . . . so many lighted windows climbing the dark sky in high, even rows.

Lathrop found himself wishing he could hold a lens to all those distant panes of glass, peer into every room of every apartment. From out here in the night, standing at the water's edge, he would explore the raw secrets of the lives being led inside them, probe their guarded intimacies, their appetites, their hidden transgressions.

Of course, he thought, playing with secrets could be a dangerous addiction. One that could kill a man if he didn't have the know-how and constitution to handle them.

Lathrop remained there on the riverbank another moment, staring contemplatively at the lights of the city on the far shore. Then he started back uphill toward the Jaguar, aware he had one final task to carry out before the night was done.

• • •

It was minutes shy of two A.M. when Lathrop pulled the
Jaguar to the curb in front of the middle school on East 75th
Street, stopping a yard or two back from the NO STANDING
sign near its entrance.

Turning off the Jag's motor, he pocketed its keys, inspected the interior for visible trace evidence, and satisfied
himself that everything was clean. Then he reached over the
seat for Sullivan's attaché, patted the gemstone case neatly
tucked away inside his coat, got out, and closed the driver's
door behind him.

The changeover from mixed to solid precip had finally
worked its way over the river to Manhattan, and Lathrop felt
hard pellets of ice rattle his open umbrella as he glanced up
at the NO STANDING sign from the pavement. Violators, it
warned, would be towed and fined on schooldays, account-
ing for the absence of any other parked vehicles on that side
of the block.

When the tow trucks made their first passes for illegally
parked cars around seven o'clock in the morning, their drivers would be quick to spot an expensive British sedan they
could never afford on their workaday salaries, assume it belonged to some privileged Upper East Side scofflaw, and
then put on the boots and cart it across town into impound—
spite and envy being two of the sweetest motivators Lathrop
had found in life's big cookie jar. The Jag would sit there in
the city yard indefinitely among hundreds of other tows until someone noticed it was missing and went through whatever bureaucratic hoops had to be jumped to find and
redeem it. Lathrop suspected that wouldn't happen for several days, perhaps longer, and overnight was really all the
hang time he needed.

Still, he wasn't about to relax. There were moves he wanted to make, and though exactly what they would be depended on circumstances he didn't yet know—and the opportunities he could create within them—it was never too soon to get started.

The attaché in his free hand, Lathrop raised his collar, bent his head low behind his umbrella, and strode off down the empty street in the driving wind and hail.

TWO

NEW YORK CITY / HUDSON VALLEY

"MY HUSBAND'S BEEN MISSING FOR ALMOST A week," she said.

Lenny Reisenberg looked at the woman seated across his desk, thinking this wasn't exactly fast-breaking news to him. He'd known about it since the Nassau County Police detectives arrived only a few days earlier for what they had called an informal chat.

"They tell me you could be the last person who saw him," she said. "That you're the last person he's supposed to have met . . ."

Lenny had also learned that, courtesy of the detectives. His business lunch with Patrick Sullivan on the afternoon he vanished had been Sullivan's final appointment . . . or at least the final appointment reminder Sullivan had entered into his office computer's scheduler program for that particular day. And the two of them had, in fact, connected for a late-afternoon huddle at a down-home Southern restaurant over near the Flatiron Building a few blocks downtown, their shared fondness for sweet-potato fries and corn bread, house specialties, having made it a favorite spot for getting together.

"I'm sorry to bother you, but I wonder . . . I was hoping you could tell me how Pat *seemed* when you met," Mrs. Sullivan went on. "If he acted like anything was wrong. Or gave you an idea where he was heading afterwards. Anything you might have noticed." She cleared her throat. "I need to find out what in the world's happened to him. . . ."

The detectives had been here for the same essential reason, Lenny reflected. But their interest was dryly professional, their questions delivered in courteous matter-of-fact tones. And he guessed that was understandable; they'd seen enough cases of married men going off on prolonged toots. Lenny had gotten the sense they'd believed this case would eventually resolve itself with hubby showing up at his front door, tussled and unshaven, his front shirttail caught in his fly, the business card he'd been handed with a wink at the Mustang Ranch tossed out of his back pocket somewhere en route from Nevada.

Patrick Sullivan's wife obviously felt otherwise. She had come to him in anguish and desperation. This was her husband she was talking about, not a case she'd been assigned by a disinterested squad lieutenant.

Her *husband* was missing.

Almost a full week now.

Lenny wished he could tell her something useful.

He kept looking at Mary Sullivan in the quiet of his office, his morning coffee untouched in front of him. She would not have been mistaken for any of his sophisticated female colleagues here on the top floor of UpLink International's regional shipping headquarters. They knew executive vogue down to the buttons and buckles. But she might have looked right at home behind a reception desk, or at a work cubicle on one of the lower floors where he'd gotten his first break with the company, and maybe his *last* chance at making something of himself, two decades ago. He'd been some piece of work then. A Regent's scholarship winner who'd managed to get booted out of college in his first semester. An aimless young man without self-confidence or any immediate plans beyond making his next month's rent . . . and barely looking that far ahead.

A product of Brooklyn to his marrow, Lenny saw the old and familiar in Mrs. Sullivan's choice of clothes, just as he heard it clearly in her speech. In her late forties or early fifties, she had reddish-blond hair that was a little too sprayed and swept around to look stylish, features a little too blunt to be pretty, and a figure a little too thick around the waist, hips, and thighs to be what most men considered well-proportioned. Everything about her appearance ran true to form. Too much of this, too much of that. Her makeup applied on the heavy side. Her perfume hanging, rather than lingering in that subtle way the most expensive fragrances did. She had professionally manicured fingernails, but they were longer and more brightly polished than women on the Manhattan side of the bridge would envision in their worst nightmares. Her emerald turtleneck sweater and matching scarf were likewise bolder than they should have been, and Lenny thought it kind of a shame. Meant to accent eyes infused with pure Irish green DNA, they accomplished the opposite of what was intended, distracting from her best natural feature through overkill. While the clothes would have designer names attached to them, they were middle of the line, bought at one of those off-price strip-mall outlets. TJ Maxx rather than Bloomingdale's.

Lenny recalled noticing her low-heeled pumps when his

admin had showed her through the door. The uppers were decent leather, but their soles would be rubber, probably synthetic. And significantly, they weren't boots. Manhattan women wore boots on winter days. It was a fashion grown out of practicality. They could usually walk where they were going, and did, and boots kept their feet warm and dry out on the street. Women from the outer boroughs had to ride the distance standing on packed subway cars.

What neighborhood did she come up in? Bensonhurst, or maybe Bay Ridge. One of those blocks of rowhouses along Seventh or Eighth Avenue, Lenny bet. It wouldn't have been far from his own exhausted cradle of origin. The evidence was right there on the surface. Lenny imagined working-class parents, a drab railroad apartment with the heavy scent of Glade in the air, and framed prints of the Madonna covering exposed plaster on the walls. Her tiny bedroom shared with a half dozen brothers and sisters in bunk beds. Five days a week, she would have stepped down off a cracked marble stoop and walked toward the bus stop in her Catholic school uniform, a white blouse and pleated plaid skirt.

Lenny got the *sense* of Mary Sullivan, felt almost as if he'd looked into her sad green eyes before. It made knowing he could only disappoint her that much harder.

"I've been thinking about my lunch with Pat, and nothing odd stands out," he said now. "I usually get business out of the way first, then make with the small talk. Sort of the opposite of most people . . ."

"You want to relax," Mary Sullivan said softly. "Enjoy your food,"

Lenny gave a nod.

"Otherwise I might as well stay in the office and toss down a peanut butter sandwich," he said.

She sat there in silence, waiting.

"I don't know how familiar you are with the technical side of Pat's work, but his company supplies the best optical tubing and wafer on the market," Lenny said. "UpLink uses a whole lot of it."

"For fiberoptics? Is that right?"

"Anything to do with lasers," Lenny said. "Fiberoptics included, right."

Mrs. Sullivan gave him a strained smile.

"Don't ask me any more than that," she said. "An Einstein I'll never be, but I try to learn as I go along."

"Beats most people," Lenny said. "Anyway, your husband's company has a shipload coming to us from overseas . . . Pakistan, for what it's worth . . . and we needed to iron out some particulars having to do with the delivery clearing customs. I think we were already into the kibbitzing when our plates hit the table. Covered sports, kids, our usual subjects . . . Pat told me your daughter Andrea's been having a great school year—"

"Donna, you mean."

"Oh, I could've sworn . . . do you have more than—?"

"Just our one. Her full name is Donna Anne, so that might be why you made the mistake."

"Oh."

"But it'd be just like Pat to brag in advance," she said. "Donna's a midyear entrant at Reed and only started classes there last week."

Lenny tried to hide his embarrassment. Besides fouling up her name, he'd had the distinct impression Sullivan's daughter was in *elementary* school. And maybe seven or eight at the oldest.

"Well, Pat *did* say that he was happy with how she was doing," he said. "With some other things, too. His job . . . I think there were some new accounts that had him excited."

Lenny paused. "I remember us talking hockey . . . guess I don't need to tell you Pat's an Islanders fanatic."

"No," Mrs. Sullivan said. Again with that pale, cheerless smile. "You don't."

Lenny was quiet a moment, searching his memory.

"There was a game at the Coliseum that night," he said. "Your husband told me he was going to stay in the city to watch it at one of those sports bars. The jumbo screen, you know." He paused. "Your house is on Long Island . . . somewhere way out at the end of Nassau County, isn't it?"

She gave an affirmative nod.

"Glen Cove. But it's a corporate condo. We sold our old home last summer, bought some land in Amity Harbor, contracted on a bigger place. The builders fell behind schedule, so Pat's employers arranged for us to stay in their apartment complex until it's finished."

Lenny nearly sighed with relief over getting things *halfway* right this time, though he didn't recall Sullivan having told him anything about the move.

"Pat's mentioned that he uses the railroad to commute," he said. "When he said he wasn't heading straight home, I kidded him about being more of a team booster than I'd realized. Because of the weather, I mean. All week long the city's in a panic over the blizzard that's supposed to be heading our way, and then the forecast changes in a snap, and we're hearing it won't be cold enough for even an inch of snow on the ground. But it was still pretty miserable out, and I could see how there might be icing on the tracks that could make his trip to the Island a stalled mess, and told Pat he might be better off getting his hockey fix on the living-room television set." Lenny shrugged. "I remember he said that he couldn't. That there's a standing appointment with his friend . . ."

"Tony DeSanto," Mary Sullivan said with another nod. "They've been like brothers since they were kids, and going out to watch the games together's a regular thing with them. Every Wednesday without fail, year round. The two of them are real sports fanatics. In the winter it's hockey. The Isles versus the Rangers, you'd think their lives depend on who wins. Then it's springtime and the Mets over at Shea. After that, football season. The Giants. Without fail." Her ample bosom rose and fell as she struggled to contain her emotions. "Tony lives down near Union Square. Every now and then . . . if there's a storm like we had the other night, or the games run late, you know . . . Pat stays over at his apartment . . ."

Mrs. Sullivan let the sentence trail, her eyes filling with moisture, reaching into her bag for a Kleenex before Lenny could awkwardly hold out the box on his desk.

"Can I get you a glass of water . . . something else to drink . . . ?"

"No, no, thank you. . . ."

"You're sure? Hot coffee, maybe? It isn't a problem. . . ."

She shook her head slowly.

"Really, it's all right."

There was a brief silence. Lenny's hands found a stray paper clip on his blotter and began fidgeting with it.

"The police talked about your husband's friend when they showed up," he said. "They didn't say much . . . had no reason, I suppose. But, well, I'd wondered why he wasn't a little concerned when Pat didn't meet him."

"I did, too, at first," Mrs. Sullivan said. "I'd tried reaching Pat on his cell phone around five-thirty, six o'clock that afternoon. So I could fix him some dinner if he canceled his plans. Like you said, it was coming down something awful outside. But he keeps the phone off half the time once he's out of the office . . . or I should say purposely forgets to put it on so his night-owl boss can't drag him back there." She dried her eyes with a tissue. "I called Tony's apartment next. Nobody answered, and to me that meant they went ahead with their plans. I never even thought to leave a message."

"Do you know where Tony turned out to be?"

"Waiting for Pat to show up at one of their haunts." She shook her head again, wiped at a blotch of mascara above her left cheek. "Of course he never did. Tony says he figured my husband just went home, maybe rushed to catch the train because he was afraid of delays. And that he'd hear from him later."

More silence. A question flirted with Lenny's curiosity, but then tailed away as she motioned toward the picture frame on his desk.

"Is this your family, Mr. Reisenberg?" she said.

Lenny nodded. He'd taken reels of photos during their vacation out west last summer. Three days in the Badlands of South Dakota, then on to tour the Black Hills, Deadwood, Custer State Park, and finally Rushmore, which formed the backdrop for the shot that had drawn Mary Sullivan's eye.

"My wife's Janice," he said, and indicated the slender brunette waving at his camera from an observation deck in the loom of Abe Lincoln's chin. "The kids are Max—he's the tall one on the left—then Jake and Sarah." He paused. "And you can call me Lenny, by the way."

"Lenny, you'll probably understand what I'm about to tell you," she said. "Pat's a wonderful husband. I don't make a habit of checking up on him. It's like Pat always says . . . twenty years under the same roof, raising our daughter together, we'd better be able to trust each other. With the amount of traveling he does because of his sales job, there'd be no sense trying to watch his every step, anyway." She shrugged, took a trembling breath. "My point is that he's a grown man. I'm not the sort to harp if he stays out late with his friend once in a while. Usually I'm fast asleep when he comes in from watching his games. That night, though, in that storm, with the terrible wind, it was different. I couldn't shut my eyes. And it bothered me when Pat wasn't back by midnight. Or one in the morning. Around two o'clock, I called Tony's apartment again. That time he picked up his phone, told me he'd walked in an hour before, and we compared notes. The minute I found out Pat hadn't gotten in touch with either of us, I knew something was wrong. . . ."

A sob took hold of her, then another, and she began weeping openly. Lenny studied the paper clip in his hand, waiting as she gradually regained her composure.

"Mrs. Sullivan . . ."

"You can call me Mary."

He looked at her. Saw that faint, sorrowful smile on lips wet with her spilled tears.

"Mary," he said. "Your husband and I . . . we've been doing business a while now. Far's our relationship goes, I feel I know him pretty well." Lenny paused, slid the paper clip under one finger, over another. "I've asked myself if there's anything he might've told me the other day, anything I noticed that seemed different than usual. The truth is, there wasn't—"

"Please help me find out what's happened to him," she said all at once.

Her red-rimmed eyes meeting his own, clinging to his own.

Lenny remained quiet for a moment. His face showed surprise and confusion, and on the outside that was a somewhat authentic reaction. The problem being that it was another matter below the surface. In many respects, he didn't consider himself quick on the uptake. Show him a thousand times where to lay down silverware in a standard table setting, or what food went in the refrigerator's crisper drawer, he wouldn't remember. Explain whether you were supposed to turn a screw clockwise or counterclockwise to loosen it, it would never sink into his brain. Figuring out how ordinary things worked defied him. But ordinary *people* were another story. He got their signals without too much difficulty. It would only take a single gesture to give him a full read on someone's personality, a few words to deliver the message he or she was trying to put across to him.

Right now he knew just where Mary Sullivan was going, and suddenly felt too quick for his own good.

"I don't understand," he lied. "That is, how could I . . ."

She shook her head.

"I wasn't talking about you *alone*, Lenny," she said. "But the company you work for . . . UpLink International. It could help."

Lenny stared at her. His sympathy notwithstanding, he really and truly didn't like the turn their conversation had taken.

"Mrs. Sullivan . . . Mary . . . we're a telecom," he said. "We develop *communications* networks."

"And other things, too. For the military, yes?"

"Well, sure. There are the defense contracts. I suppose it's common knowledge Roger Gordian built our company on them. But that doesn't give us any strings with—"

"I try to follow the news, keep up with the main stories," she said. "None of us in this city will ever forget what happened a few years ago, that terrible time we went through. So many thousands of people killed by those maniacs for no reason. And I remember a report on TV, the program might have been *48 Hours* . . ."

In fact it was *60 Minutes*, Lenny thought without bothering to correct her.

"On that show they talked about the security team Up-Link's pulled together to keep its employees safe around the world," she pressed on. "How it's supposed to be the best. And the part that stuck with me, sticks to this day, is when the police commissioner was asked about Mr. Gordian helping our government find the terrorists who attacked us."

Lenny didn't need to be reminded, having played a relatively minor, tell-me-no-secrets-and-I'll-ask-you-no-questions role in UpLink's investigation and eventual pursuit of the conspirators in four separate countries. The boss had wanted it kept under wraps for a slew of reasons, as had the Feds, and the PC had obliged them all to the extent that he could. But then, maybe six months after the tragedy, a former aide at One Police Plaza gave a videotaped interview—his face an unrecognizable smudge on the screen, his voice electronically wound and stretched to a distorted pitch—in which he'd bared much of a classified department file on UpLink's participation. That had put the commissioner in the hot seat. Rather than offer lame denials, he'd acknowledged the "debt of gratitude," or some such, that New Yorkers and the nation in general owed Gordian and company for their patriotic actions. While his answers didn't completely douse the fire under him, they kept the back of his pants from catching until the press scrambled off after the next headline.

Lenny sat gathering his thoughts. He knew he was about to take his cue from the commish and felt kind of lousy.

"Mary," he said. "When our city got hit, all kinds of volunteers committed to picking us up. I know my boss pitched in, but couldn't say how. The situation back then was so far from normal . . ."

Her eyes flashed, the green irises suddenly bright.

"I'm not trying to compare. Not in the way it might have sounded," she said. "Pat's only one man. His disappearing into thin air isn't a crisis except for his family. But are you telling me *it's* normal? Or not different *enough* . . ."

Lenny shook his head.

"You're going through hell," he said. "I realize that. But I'm a shipping officer. I work with freight forwards, import regulations, customs documents . . . I really don't know what I'd do—"

"Anything you can," Mary Sullivan said. Sounding composed, even resolute now. "It isn't easy for me to come here and ask a favor of you, a person I've never met before. And I wouldn't if I had somewhere else to turn." She paused. "I once read, or heard somebody say, the missing are presumed guilty . . . that when they first drop out of sight, the police treat it like they've run off on their own, and wait too long before they start looking for them. You can see what they're thinking on their faces, tell by their voices. Why waste manpower on an angry wife, or a husband who loses it when the charge cards get run up too high?"

Or who decides he feels like a week of fun and games at the Mustang Ranch, Lenny thought.

He hesitated, returned to playing with his paper clip. He felt a load of compassion for the woman sitting across from him. He liked her husband, thought he was a nice guy, and sincerely hoped he came back to her okay. But it was not his responsibility. She was asking him to become involved in something that was none of his affair. Moreover, she was asking him to ask UpLink's security division to get involved. They would want no part of a missing persons investigation unrelated to their duties on behalf of company interests . . . as he was sure to be reminded if he brought the matter to their attention. And knowing the person he'd have to approach, it would be a snub bordering on ridicule. He had no juice with her. Or close to none. And less than he'd had before at the main office in San Jose, what with all the changes going on there lately. Far too much was being expected of him, and he would have to lay that out to Mary Sullivan as delicately as possible.

He looked down at the clip in his hands. Looked up at her.

And before he could say anything heard a pair of voices in his head, his own and another's, a startlingly clear auditory transmission bursting across a quarter century of time:

"You want bop, there's Ornithology."

"I'll do it with Dizzy if you'll give me Anthropology."

For a second Lenny was rocked by those words from the distant past, warped back to the fluke encounter that had reversed the steady downward slide of his life. It hadn't seemed that way to him then, but he'd been at the edge. The very brink of a dark someplace he would surely have fallen into if one man hadn't held out a line for him to grab.

Damn it, he thought. Damn that stinking memory. Why did it have to come to him now?

Lenny sat in silence a brief while longer, feeling as if he needed to catch his breath. Then he dropped the paper clip into the tray where it belonged.

"No promises, Mary," he said. "But I'll see if I can't get you some answers."

"Forget it," Noriko Cousins said without looking up from behind her computer screen.

Lenny didn't say anything. That had been just the response he'd expected.

"No way," Noriko added.

Lenny was silent. She seemed inclined to give her rejection further embellishment, and he figured he'd wait for it before mounting his comeback.

"There's isn't a chance I'm about to get us embroiled in a situation that has absolutely zero bearing on our corporate interests," Noriko said. "If this woman who came to see you needs somebody to sniff out her wayward spouse, she can check the Yellow Pages for bedroom-peeping gumshoes."

Lenny stood facing her desk with his hands in the pockets of his tweed overcoat, uncertain whether the chill he felt was a result of her brusque reception, the low temperature in the room, or his long walk down to Hudson Street from his midtown office. Hudson was a bitter, blustering channel of wind in January. This building, a converted nineteenth-century meat-packing factory, remained full of cold, slippery drafts that would seep through its redbrick facing despite myriad layers of interior renovation. And Noriko tended to keep the thermostat way down for inexplicable reasons of her own. So maybe it was the physical environment making him want to shake off icicles. But Lenny hadn't found it quite so inhospitable when Tony Barnhart had been running things here at the local headquarters of Sword—the official tag for UpLink's intelligence, security, and crisis-control arm, and a clever allusion to the old legend of Alexander of Macedonia undoing the supposedly undoable Gordian knot with a swift, sure stroke of his blade. Roger Gordian, Gordian knot, decisive and pragmatic solutions to tough problems, *whack!*

Lenny took a deep breath. He had liked Barnhart exponentially more than Noriko Cousins, who'd succeeded him as section chief after wounds he suffered in a gunfight with some lowlife Russian hoods had sent him into early retirement. But the plain truth was that Lenny never felt quite at ease around any Sword personnel. It was their collective attitude, mostly. He could tolerate some remoteness given the perilous nature of their work, safeguarding the lives of Up-Link employees in hot spots around the world . . . and probably an untold number of people who knew nothing about UpLink. Given, also, that they were culled from law-enforcement, covert intelligence, and military special operations groups and thus conditioned to secrecy through years of training and experience. Lenny got that without a problem, *yo comprendo todo y más señoritas y señores*. And yet Noriko was a case apart from the rest. In his opinion she had raised close-mouthed, standoffish impenetrability to a new level.

"Look, I didn't say I'm in love with the idea of getting mixed up in this whole thing," he said.

"Good, great."

"For that matter, I wouldn't *dream* of having us stick our noses in a situation with no connection to UpLink."

Her brown Eurasian eyes remaining on the screen, Noriko swished a hand toward the door in an absent gesture of dismissal.

"It's wonderful we agree—"

"Except in this case it happens there *is* one," Lenny said.

She finally glanced up at him. Tall, slender, athletic, her shoulder-length black hair gelled and tousled around symmetrically fine features, she wore a body-hugging black sweater, black leather miniskirt, black tights, and high-shaft black leather boots for a total effect Lenny had to admit was a draw to the eyes. Still, the good looks didn't *nearly* compensate for her brass.

"I hope you aren't going to tell me it's because we buy components from this Patrick Mulligan—"

"Sullivan," Lenny said.

"Right, excuse me," Noriko said. "But if that's your rationale, you might as well make UpLink responsible for the friendly men and women who sell us light bulbs, keep us in bathroom supplies, and stock our hallway vending machines with bags of potato chips and chocolate kisses."

Lenny shook his head.

"Pat's a salesman for the Kiran Group. And we're probably his biggest account, since we lay out maybe five million bucks a year to Kiran for—"

"Synthetic ruby, I know . . ."

"Laboratory-cultivated sapphire," Lenny said. "Sapphires and rubies are the same mineral. Corundum. The difference is their crystallization pattern. And their properties. It's why we use one and not the other in our laser equipment."

Noriko looked at him.

"I stand corrected again," she said. "I also still don't see any logical reason why that makes Mull . . . ah, *Sullivan*, our concern."

Lenny guessed he didn't either. But it was his pledge to Sullivan's wife that he'd make a go of things, not logic, that had propelled him down here to SoHo on his lunch break.

"I'm busy, Lenny," Noriko said now. "What's your point? The *condensed* version, please."

Lenny shrugged his shoulders.

"Just that we're talking about somebody with ties to our core operations, not the Hershey's chocolate guy," he improvised. "It isn't my job to fill in the blanks."

"And how does it follow that it's mine?"

Lenny shrugged a second time, stuck for a persuasive reply. Trying to get past the interference she threw up was like having to dance between raindrops.

Noriko kept looking at him, her expression openly scornful.

"Six months ago the Kiran Group was bought by Arm-bright Industries, a multinational corporation that happens to be our chief competitor in a dozen areas of tech development," she said. "Armbright has its own internal security to look after its employees."

"Their security isn't Sword by a longshot."

"Not my problem," Noriko said. "Let them allocate a heftier slice of their budget to the division. They've mimicked us in every other way."

Lenny felt swamped with futility. He hated talking to her. *Hated* it.

"You're really catching me on a hectic afternoon," she said. "Is there anything else you want me to consider before we wrap up?"

This time Lenny guessed he might have had an answer, but it stalled short of his lips. What was he supposed to tell her? That he'd related to Mary Sullivan's background without ever asking a word about it, her sorrowful but determined green eyes stirring memories that hadn't occurred to him in years?

"No, nothing else," he said at last. "I'm done."

"Okay," Noriko said with flat disinterest. "Be well, Lenny."

"Yup. I'll see myself out."

Noriko Cousins returned her eyes to the computer screen, both hands on the keyboard even before he left her office.

No sooner had the door closed behind Lenny than her clacking stopped.

She leaned back in her chair, arms crossed, her lips pursed in thought.

This question of Sullivan's whereabouts intrigued Noriko, if only because it coincided with certain other peculiarities about the Kiran Group and its recent exports that

Sword's routine monitoring of the company had brought to her attention . . . including shipments of the cultured sapphire she'd pretended to be vague about. But the mind was always quick to put the odd information it gathered in neat, orderly compartments, sorting things away like someone with a neatness fetish driven to fits by a misplaced article of clothing. Reality was far too disorganized for her to fall victim to that tendency.

No, she'd taught herself to be guided by the facts, and would need to turn up many more of them in her probe of Kiran before she drew so much as a single inference or conclusion.

Tied into knots of frustration that made his back and shoulders ache, Lenny decided he'd stretch his lunch hour and walk a few blocks over to Chinatown to purchase his nerve medicine from Yan.

The Snow Mountain Mart on Canal Street was a multistoried Far Eastern emporium that had been a neighborhood fixture seemingly forever, its shelves, counters, and clothes racks displaying imported goods in astonishing quantities— a wild and colorful diversity of curios, kimonos, furniture, bedding, beaded curtains, bird cages, parasols, Chinese lanterns, enormous ceremonial masks and paper dragons, miniature jade Buddhas and crystal lotus vases, incense and incense burners, chopsticks and chopstick holders, bamboo steamers, electric rice cookers, green tea sold loose by the ounce, soap bars wrapped together in packages of several dozen, folk instruments, electric guitars, harmonicas, noise-makers, nail clippers, nose-hair trimmers, magnifying glasses, portable CD players, personal pagers, radar detectors, cameras, film, generic batteries . . . *lots* of batteries . . .

name the item, there was a decent chance you'd find it somewhere in stock.

Today Lenny had found Yan in his usual spot at the end of
a cluttered aisle of herbal remedies around the corner from
the music and video department. A bald, bespectacled guy in
his seventies, Yan always wore a long white frock unbuttoned over his slight paunch. Lenny had been paying him
occasional visits for maybe five, six years, but wasn't absolutely sure if Yan was his first or last name. Lenny was
likewise unsure whether the white coat signified he was a
doctor or pharmacist, although he didn't find the blurred distinction between those professions in traditional Asian
health care to be problematic. It hadn't been so different in
America once upon a time, when drugstore owners had
maintained a close caregiving relationship with their pa-
trons. They had recommended treatments, prescribed medications and tonics, and compounded dosages by hand with
mortar and pestle. This had eventually pricked the competitive sensibilities of profiteering pharmaceutical companies,
raised jealous territorial growls from the American Medical
Association, and been raw meat for the slavering jaws of
personal-injury litigators. Lenny, for his part, thought the
pressures these interests brought to bear upon the Western
druggist had reduced him to little more than a human pill
dispenser. Nowadays he didn't know one customer from another. He poured brand-name medications from big bottles
into smaller bottles, put the smaller bottles into a bag, sta-
pled it shut, and rang up the sale on the register. *Ka-ching,*
next customer.

When it came to getting relief for minor ails and emotional distress, Lenny preferred taking his chances here at
Snow Mountain. So what if his favorite practitioner was a

Mr. Yan, Doctor Yan, Citizen Yan, or just plain Yan, as he asked to be called? Lenny hadn't the foggiest notion whether he was even licensed. He couldn't for a million bucks have positively identified the ingredients that went into the concoctions Yan formulated behind his counter. But they seemed to work okay. Far as he knew, they hadn't been contaminated with the SARS virus. And at least Yan didn't forget his face between return visits.

"So," Yan said now. He'd gotten up off his stool the moment he saw Lenny arrive and started whipping together his usual preparation, hand-measuring something dried and wrinkled—bark shavings? slivers of aged roots?—into a paper plate from an apothecary jar. "How you feel?"

Lenny considered. Yan demanded honest answers from his patients.

"Doing my best." He nodded at the paper plate. "I'm thinking I need a stronger blend this time around."

Yan glanced at him over the frame of his eyeglasses.

"No," he said.

"Come on, Yan. I've got serious stuff on my mind. Been extra nervous—"

A vehement head shake.

"You always tell me same thing," Yan said. "This strong enough. Put half teaspoon in cup hot water. Three minutes. When water turn color of urine, you sip."

"How about I let it sit a little longer—?"

"Three minutes. Urine color. Sip."

Lenny gnawed the inside of his cheek. Wasn't anybody willing to budge an inch for him today?

"There's light urine and dark urine," he said with a kind of childish defiance.

"Hmmm?" Yan scooped from a second deep glass jar, mixed.

"I'm just saying you never really told me how strong the brew should be." Lenny already felt asinine. "What shade of urine to shoot for—"

"Healthy color urine." Yan didn't look a bit annoyed or distracted. He pulled another apothecary jar from the shelf, reached in for some brown powder, tossed it into the paper plate, added a tacky substance from a drawer below the counter top, stirred the entire preparation with his bare fingers, and then poured it into a Ziploc. "This only let you relax. Not forget."

Lenny's brow wrinkled as Yan passed the plastic bag over the counter.

"What's that supposed to mean?" he said.

"You have problem, better solve it," Yan said.

Her phone rang.

"Hello?"

"Jesus Christ, it's about time you picked up."

"I wasn't here. It makes me crazy, staying home. Staring at the four walls. Waiting. I had to do something."

"Did you check your machine? I must've left half a dozen messages on it this morning."

"I just walked in the door, Tony. I've still got my coat on—"

"You said you did something. Like what? What is it you finally went out and did?"

"Look, I wish you'd give me some breathing room. Maybe try to understand a little of what I'm going through."

"Okay, okay. I didn't meant to jump at you."

"Uh-huh."

"No, I mean it. Honestly. But you have to understand, Pat's like my own brother—"

"That's why you should understand my feelings. You of all people, Tony. None of this is my fault. I love him. I've got a daughter who's asking where he's gone. Try putting yourself in my shoes."

"I'm trying."

"Sure."

"I am, believe me. But when you say you went out to do something, and then don't bother explaining. . . ."

"God damn it, Tony. God damn it. Everything's a vicious circle with you. It's like, 'I'm sorry, fuck you, I'm not sorry.' All in one breath, it comes out of your mouth. You'll say anything to me until you get what you want."

"I'm only trying to find out if you went to the police."

"No. I didn't. Is that enough for you? So I can maybe take my coat off—"

"You need to talk to them."

"Shit. Here we go again."

"Just listen . . ."

"I have. A hundred times. And for the hundredth time, I'm telling you I can't."

"Then what's your plan? To keep checking out that information about towed vehicles on the Internet? You're even too afraid to dial that number where you get a real person on the line. I mean, it's like a compulsion at this stage. The Internet. It doesn't accomplish anything. Nobody's claimed the fucking car after a week, a whole goddamn week, and you have to talk to somebody—"

"I did."

"What?"

"That's where I went, okay? To see someone who can help."

"I . . . why didn't you tell me that in the first place?"

"I would've. If you'd given me a chance. If you'd stopped pressing long enough for me to open the closet and hang my coat."

"If you could manage to answer a simple question, I wouldn't need to—"

"Go screw yourself, Tony."

"What?"

"You heard me. I think you should stick it up your own—"

"Look, let's not argue like a couple of teenagers. We're in this together. We'd better remember it."

"Why? So I can listen to more of your insults and accusations?"

"How about for Pat's sake? So we can find him. You're saying you didn't go to the cops. Okay, fine. Just tell me who . . ."

"No. I won't jump when you snap your fingers. Think whatever you want of me, I'm not going to stand for that treatment. I'm sick of it. I've decided to handle this my way. And right now that means I'm getting off the phone."

"Hold it, you can't—"

"Oh? Keep the receiver up to your ear another second and you'll find out what I can do."

"Wait—"

"My way, Tony. Good-bye."

The receiver slammed down on the hook.

Some thirty minutes after he left Snow Mountain, Lenny Reisenberg found himself seated at the counter in the Second Avenue Delicatessen on East 10th Street, waiting for the corned beef sandwich and kasha varnishkes he'd ordered.

No one could have been more surprised by this than Lenny. His original plan had been to buzz over to Sword HQ, fulfill his promise to Mary Sullivan, grab some take-out on the way back to his office, and eat quickly at his desk. A burger and fries, or maybe a tuna salad from the corner luncheonette . . . bland filler food to carry him until dinner, in other words. Things obviously had not gone as intended. But while his detour to Chinatown may have been unforeseen, Lenny was at least clear about why he'd headed down there. It was simple cause-and-effect. His fast appointment with Noriko Cousins had left him a bundle of tension and he'd resolved to pick up something to help him unwind. Simple. Lenny's peregrinations since that time were harder to explain, however. Those wandering feet of his had taken him crosstown into the East Village instead of uptown to his office, a long journey in the wrong direction. What was more, they'd brought him to a restaurant he only visited when in the mood to indulge his occasional craving for Jewish soul food with delightful abandon, not have an automatic midday fill up akin to putting gas in the car at some roadside service plaza. It seemed to Lenny he'd truly gone a little out of his head. Despite the stacks of paperwork awaiting him at the office, he'd stayed away from it for almost two hours, veering farther and farther off course on his supposed walk back. And although he hadn't felt the slightest bit hungry as he'd left Snow Mountain, or as he hiked here along the Bowery in the cold, or even as his waitress had handed him a menu only two or three minutes earlier, he'd all at once become desperately impatient for a towering heap of cured beef, not to mention that side of pan-fried buckwheat groats and bow-tie noodles. . . .

"Excuse me, is there cheese in the potato *kneeeesh*?"

Lenny momentarily put his thoughts on hold. Or rather, they came to a short stop on their own. The source of that high piping voice—and remarkably screwy pronunciation of "knish"—had been a woman in a window booth to his right, and he couldn't resist tossing an inconspicuous glance over at her.

It took perhaps a second for his curiosity to be satisfied.

Young, blond, and blue-eyed, she was definitely a Gentile, and just as surely an out-of-towner. In fact, she seemed as if she ought to have been wearing a shiny Wisconsin State Fair Beauty Queen tiara on her head. The guy opposite her in the booth had a similar scrubbed, fair-haired look. Together they sort of reminded Lenny of Barbie and Ken.

Their waitress, a thickset Latin woman, was eyeing Barbie over her pad with apparent shock and horror.

"This is a kosher restaurant," she said.

Barbie didn't get it.

"Oh, I see," she said. Her blank stare indicating the contrary. "But is there cheese in the potato *kneeeeesh*?"

The waitress tapped her pen against her pad, rolled her eyes. Surely she'd gotten stuck with a simpleton.

"No cheese with meat," she huffed.

"Oh." Poor squeaky Barbie's confusion had deepened. Could the waitress have misunderstood her question? She glanced down at her menu as if seeking enlightenment there, found none, looked back up. "Does that mean the *kneeeesh* has meat in it? Because I want a potato . . ."

Glad for the distraction from his own problems, Lenny continued to casually eavesdrop above the energetic gabbing and lip smacking of his fellow deli-goers. In this ethnic hodgepodge of a city, you'd have to scour the streets for a month to find a longtime resident unacquainted with the orthodox Jewish dietary prohibition against serving meat and dairy products together in any form, cooking them in the same pots and pans, or eating them with the same utensils. But did Barbie truly deserve to be faulted for her ignorance? Lenny guessed that she typified a form of New York snobbery and felt kind of bad for her. On the other hand, a blind person could have seen the word kosher on the sign above the entrance. How oblivious to other cultural traditions could you be? Maybe it was Barbie who was guilty of being a snob, and the waitress who deserved his sympathy. And so much fuss over an appetizer, how much worse would things get once Barbie got around to selecting her main course? Besides, this couple had "dud" written all over them as far as leaving a decent tip.

It was, Lenny decided, important to look at both sides before jumping to an opinion.

Now he saw the swing doors from the kitchen fly open, watched his own waitress shoulder through, identified his food on the dishes she was carrying, and eagerly waited for her to put them down in front of him—farewell Barbie and company, hello lunch. This suddenly tyrannical appetite of his really was nuts, he thought. But then Lenny wondered if something other than a need to fill his stomach might have awakened it. A different sort of emptiness within him that he'd subconsciously wanted to stifle. He didn't want to go deep into psychoanalysis here, but wasn't that what comfort food was about? He'd slipped into a funk, no question, and it occurred to him there were plenty of contributing reasons. Mary Sullivan's pained features, her struggle to keep from falling apart in his office that morning. Noriko Cousins's unassailable indifference. And then the capper, Yan's sternly uttered words of advice at Snow Mountain. *You have problem, better solve it.* Taken individually or rolled into a ball, these things had been weighing on him to a greater degree than he'd cared to admit.

Lenny lifted the top slice of club roll off his sandwich, reached for the mustard dispenser, spooned, smeared, bit in. Tasty. He forked a couple of kasha varnishkes into his mouth. Delicious. Lenny ate some more, felt the gloom that had been hanging over his head begin to lighten. Barbie and Ken's waitress stormed past him toward the kitchen, grumbling under her breath: "*Kneeeesh, kneeeesh*, why don't she go back to school?" He chewed, swallowed, wondered how the issue of schooling had come into play with her. Well, Barbie *did* look like she could be a college student. Maybe the waitress felt Kosher Laws 101 ought to be a basic curricular requirement. At any rate, it was clear that communications hadn't improved over at the window booth.

Lenny decided his reservoir of sympathy was deep enough for everyone there, and silently wished them well. He ate, savoring each scrumptious mouthful of food. Nothing was as bad as it seemed if you gave it a little consideration. Look at his problem, for example. A few bites of sandwich ago it had looked hopeless. Insurmountable. A few bites later, and he had a feeling he'd come upon a solution.

"Gord," he said to the waitress's wide, receding back. "I'm calling Gordian."

Hasul stood at his office window and watched the Durango enter the parking lot five stories below. The slide of its headlights over the pavement, pale yellow on black, was a small observational pleasure that did not escape his appreciation, as few such pleasures would.

Only the shielding on his plate glass window allowed it.

At this late hour his regular employees were gone, driven off to the comforts of home and family, leaving the expansive lot unoccupied except for a handful of vehicles used by Hasul and his inner cadre. The 4×4 went straight up to where they were lined perpendicular to the building entrance and slipped into the first vacant stall at the end of the row. Then its headlamps went out, a door swung open, and its driver emerged into the blue-white radiance of mercury vapor lights at the far side of the lot. Arranged in a single bank, they shone down from almost a hundred feet in the air like the lights of an outdoor sports arena. With Hasul's direct exposure to them restricted, their height and distance mitigated any threat from ultraviolet emissions.

Out in the lot, the driver leaned against the front of his 4×4 and finished a half-smoked cigarette. Hasul noted how its tip flared orange with his deep inhalations, bright specks of not-quite-spent tobacco scattering into the wind as he tapped at the head of ash.

After a minute the driver flicked his stub to the blacktop, crushed it out with his shoe bottom, took a quick look around, and started toward the building entrance. A tall whip of a man, he moved with loose-legged, almost bouncing strides, his shadow stretched long in front of him.

Hasul did not leave the window at once. Instead he reached out to touch the smooth glass, his fingertips meeting their own faint reflections. Darkness had swallowed the countryside mere yards beyond the paved rectangle illuminated by the arc lights. The ice-chandelier treetops of its surrounding woods, the snow-encrusted ground between them, the roadway that wound uphill toward the building . . . he could see none of them under the starless sky and felt something close to the separation, the otherness that normally marked his daylight periods. It was a drastic contrast from the exhilarated feeling Hasul had known hours before, but as one who fancied himself a collector of rare moments, capturing and preserving them as some did exotic butterflies, he realized the lows that gripped him the hardest were often a price he must pay for his memorable highs.

Hasul kept his fingers pressed against the glass now, remembering his walk beneath dusk's heavy overcast. He had left the office building hooded and gloved, a face guard draping down from bridge of his nose, protective sunglasses with side panels over his eyes. His pulse had raced with expectancy. As he did on the rarest occasions—no more than twice, perhaps three times a year—Hasul had decided in his approximate way to know the world as one who was altogether part of it.

For a while he had paused on a hammock near the edge of the trees and looked west in the direction of the expiring sun. At the distant limit of his vision, the clouds above the mountain humps were stained the color of old bruises. Hasul had seen the vapor of his rapid breaths puff into the winter air through his face guard's mesh ventilation panel, his excitement increasing as the latest precious moment to be caught in hand raced up on him.

It was no sudden urge, that wish to feel the cold against his skin. Indeed, Hasul's earliest memories consisted of the excruciating lessons of impulsiveness. The constant forethought and rigorous preparation for which he was lauded in the scientific research community were not, in his eyes, points of pride but absolute necessity.

As he stood out in the gloaming, Hasul had unclipped his portable dosimeter from his coat pocket, held it before him to determine that the UV level was within a comparably tolerable range, and set its timer function for thirty seconds. Caution relaxing its leash on him just so far, he had worn 100 SPF sunblock makeup tinted to match his flesh tone and applied a thick layer of cream to his lips.

His physicians would have crowed in disapproval regardless, not to fault them. Their job was to butler his health. But Hasul had already given them forty-eight years worth of validation, some of it aided by chance, since it was probable he would have died in childhood had his genetic defect not been the variant type . . . and still that wasn't truly the point. In the end nothing escaped decay, flesh least of all, and he saw human longevity for the illusion it was. The body was perishable; only its spirit was eternal. Five years, fifty, a hundred—the difference between one life span and another did not amount to a murmur in the flowing river of time. Hasul had calculated and been willing to accept that each exposure would have consequences along the way. What mattered was that he remain true to the plan for which he was created, and this he had done, sparing none of his wealth and ability. Following God's will through personal discipline, Hasul was soon to reach the culmination of his purpose in this world.

Today at dusk he had permitted himself thirty seconds of release.

No more, no less.

With a quick motion, Hasul had pulled the guard down below his chin. His head thrown back, arms outspread, he stood on his mound of earth and let the trailing remnants of the sunlight press against his naked face. The sound of blood rushing in his ears had been so loud, a thunderous roar beneath which his awareness had been briefly submerged, swept away like a soul in the eternal river.

And then the warning tones of his dosimeter, sounding into the tide.

Now Hasul stepped back from the window, watched his reflection withdraw into the black of night like a disembodied spirit, staring, its hand extended as if groping for the glass's fixed solidity. He turned away and looked across his desk, his eye catching a slip of movement outside the mouth of an artificial rock cave in the large aquarium tank built into the wall to his right. In the opposite corner of the room, a broad, dark-suited man sat at a closed circuit digital surveillance console, his attention fixed on its flat panel monitor.

Hasul noticed his frown.

"Zaheer," he said. "Something troubles you."

"May I speak freely?"

"Please."

Zaheer nodded toward the display.

"This *kaffir* who comes to see you," he said. His use of the Islamic term for nonbelievers was full of disdain. "I fear his inclusion is a mistake."

Hasul strode up to the console and studied the wide screen image. It showed three men in the ground-floor entry vestibule. Two were members of the Cadre, Aasim passing a handheld weapons detector over their visitor's rangy frame, Qamal standing by in guarded readiness.

"He has proven capable and worthy of his reputation," Hasul said.

"More than any of our own?"

"You know what lies ahead of us," Hasul said. And then inserted the expedient half-truth. "No contribution will be greater than yours in coming days."

Zaheer held stiffly silent, his eyes on the monitor.

Down in the vestibule, Aasim finished wanding the visitor and accompanied him through an inner door into the main lobby. Zaheer pressed a channel-selection key on his digital multiplexer and the CCD-TV screen view shifted to an overhead of the elevator bank, where the two men entered a waiting car.

Hasul glanced down from the monitor and saw the barely restrained skepticism on Zaheer's face. "I think of the street dentists in Islamabad, Peshawar, and Karachi," he said. "I remember their offices are dirty blankets and wooden crates on the open sidewalk. Their tools common pliers, chisels, screwdrivers. They are unlearned, work with grime on their hands, and for anaesthesia plunge needles into one side of the patient's mouth to distract him from the agony of a rotting tooth being chopped and filed on the other." He paused, continued to regard the other man. "Their skills are crude, bloody, and yet indispensable to those that require them."

Zaheer's face remained tight.

"Are we then among the poverty stricken who must turn to such a one in desperation?"

Hasul looked at him. Again, the partial falsehood. "We are for a higher mission, and above the sordid errands the infidel will be turned upon," he said.

Zaheer fell silent, switched the monitor to its picture-in-picture mode. The area directly outside the office suite appeared in its main window. Smaller frames on its right tracked Aasim and the visitor as they rose five levels inside the elevator, exited, and then walked along the bends of the corridor to the suite.

Hasul watched them step into the main screen view, Aasim reaching for the buzzer on the electronic access control box beside his door.

He did not wait for the tone to sound.

"Show Mr. Earl through the reception area," he said. "Then I would meet privately with him."

As he rose from his console, Zaheer made another weak effort at masking his unhappiness. Then he bowed his head in formal deference and went to carry out his instructions.

Hasul was standing behind his desk when John Earl came into the office. Zaheer lingered at the doorway only a moment, then backed out to leave them alone.

Earl waited a step or two inside the closed door. Sandy-haired, blue-eyed, sharp-chinned, his nose long and curved with flaring nostrils that gave him a raptorial look, he wore a black leather car coat, gray muffler, and jeans.

Hasul greeted him with a slight nod.

"You've arrived right on time."

"Always."

"And it is always appreciated."

Earl stepped forward into the room, paused, and glanced over his shoulder at the wall aquarium. Nothing stirred amid the stony hollows and ledge formations of its habitat.

"Our pal Legs okay in there?"

"Yes."

"One of these days he'll have to come out and say hello," Earl said. "I've been here enough so you wouldn't think we'd be strangers."

Hasul looked at him. "The blue-ringed octopus is a dangerous but retiring creature," he said. "Its perception of who is or isn't a stranger may be be different from yours."

Earl grunted, still peering into the tank.

"I think maybe Legs just isn't too fond of the nickname I gave him," he said.

Hasul's smile left a barely perceptible stinging sensation in a corner of his lower lip. He touched it with the tip of his tongue, tasted a fleck of dry ointment. Thirty seconds. Might damage to his skin have resulted from only thirty seconds?

He waved Earl into a seat in front of the desk and then settled into his own chair without betraying his discomposure.

Earl looked across at him and unwrapped his muffler. The smallest portion of a tattoo showed on the right side of his neck—just a stroke of red, the actual markings covered by his collar.

"All right," he said after a moment. "What've you got?"

"Two projects for now," Hasul said. "More accurately, a single project with two distinct and crucial elements."

Earl had become very still.

"Break it down for me," he said.

"One of my dealers vanished a week ago with costly inventory in his possession. He may have abused my trust and stolen it, or he may have come to harm during a transaction that was to take place. In either case, something has gone very wrong."

"His name?"

"Patrick Sullivan."

"What about the party he was showing the goods?"

"A buyer whose name I do not know." Hasul shrugged. "As a rule I distance myself from the market chain at that level."

Earl nodded.

"If your man ran off, you want me take care of him."

"Yes."

"If he was hijacked, you want me to track down whoever did it."

"Yes. I also wish to determine whether the offender was acting independently or on orders . . . and have my inventory returned to me if possible."

Earl tipped his head up and down a second time.

"What's the other part of the job?" he said.

Hasul was quiet a second, his palms flat on his desk.

"Patrick Sullivan's woman," he said. "Whatever the reason for his disappearance, I've learned he has shared extremely sensitive information about my business affairs with her."

"And?"

"Unfortunately, I cannot risk her passing this information along to anyone else."

Earl looked at him with a hint of a smile.

"I'm guessing you know her name," he said.

"Yes."

"Where I can find her."

"Yes."

"Okay, leave everything to me." Earl paused. "That takes care of the 'for now' part . . ."

Hasul raised a hand, offering his own taut smile.

"The later," he said, "is for later."

Silence. They looked across the room at each other.

"Zaheer will give you the pertinent details," Hasul said, then. "Of course you can expect to be well compensated."

"Never would doubt it."

Earl rose from his chair, buttoned his jacket, tugged its sleeves down over his arms.

"Better be on my way," he said.

Hasul stood to show him from the office, but Earl had already started toward the door as he came around his desk, breaking stride for only an instant to have another look at the aquarium.

Its inhabitant remained gathered in its sheltering hole.

"See ya when I see ya," Earl said to the glass front of the tank.

Then he turned back toward the door, opened it, and was gone.

Lathrop had noticed Missus Frakes's waning interest in her ball of yarn for quite some time, but it was just recently that this change of behavior had started to infiltrate his thoughts.

It was another of many signs the coon cat was getting up there in age, signs that were inescapable unless Lathrop deliberately blinded himself to them . . . and he wasn't a believer in papering over reality's moldy walls as if calm pastel colors and landscape prints could stop the decay from spreading underneath, turning it to heaps of dust and rubble. The house hadn't been built to last, and Lathrop could smell its infectious rot every waking minute of his life, penetrating the framework like an incurable cancer of the bones. He supposed his biggest goal was to keep a step ahead of the rest as it fell apart piece by piece, edge beneath the final section of roof to come crashing down. He wasn't sure why he ought to care, but there was a certain appeal to the idea of staying on his own two feet to the bitter end and having a good look around at the wreckage.

Now Lathrop sat watching Missus Frakes from the convertible sofa of his studio apartment on the corner of East 63rd and Lexington, a co-op he subleased for a couple thousand a month, no paltry sum for a single room with a view of the faceless high-rise and twenty-four-hour Gristedes supermarket across the street. The cat was curled on the rug near the radiator, warming herself there, her head tucked into her breast, a half-lidded green eye gleaming out from under one furry paw the only discernable evidence that she wasn't asleep. Nearby lay what used to be her favorite plaything, a ball of brown yarn Lathrop had brought across the thousands of miles he'd traveled with her in the past six years, on the move, always on the move, crossing borderlines he couldn't even remember anymore, slipping through the darkest of cracks and crannies in the slowly disintegrating house that God built.

The coon had belonged to a meth chemist in Albuquerque when Lathrop first made her acquaintance. Half starved, beaten, mean, she'd almost completely reverted to a feral state, living off scavenged trash and whatever rodents she could catch in and around some chicken barn her nominal owner was using as a clan lab. This was when Lathrop was still DEA, still chasing drug peddlers, trying to hold on to the belief that it was possible to keep the house upright, or at least slow its inevitable deterioration with management and control, patching holes with mortar, digging out the fungus that had invaded its timbers. His special agent's badge pushed way up where the sun didn't shine—no decent place to keep it clean—he'd been working deep to bust a relocated

East Coast mafia squealer who'd used witness protection's get-out-of-jail-free card as a ticket to organize a hot meth distribution syndicate out west, turning half the teenage kids in his new neighborhood into strung-out jugglers. That winner ended up in a supermax prison as a result of the sting operation, but before Lathrop called a task force down on the speed factory, he'd rushed to pay an *unofficial* call on the guy with the chemistry set, given him his justs for all the times he'd kicked the cat. Lathrop had tried to be environmentally responsible in his efforts to keep his visit a secret, and figured the pieces of the chemist he'd scattered across the desert might have endured to this day as shriveled droppings in abandoned vulture nests and coyote dens.

It wasn't the first bit of personal justice Lathrop had administered before cutting ties with the agency. Nor would it be the last. But it was the only instance on which he'd gotten a new house pet to compensate for his trouble.

All taken into account, it hadn't been a bad deal.

Lathrop could remember when Missus Frakes had loved going vicious on the yarn. She would attack without any quit, first stalking it, then batting it around with her front paws, then pouncing, tearing at it with tooth and claw until the whole thing unraveled, as if hoping to find some sort of bloody reward in the center, a steaming heart or liver that would satisfy her honed killer instincts.

There had been a time when Lathrop would have needed to rewind the long, scrambled skein of yarn within ten minutes after putting it down on the floor beside her.

The ball had been wrapped tight for days now, untouched, ignored.

Missus Frakes was getting old. Her muscles were stiff at the joints and her hindquarters dragged a little when she walked. She slept most of the day, needing help up onto the high perches she had once been able to reach with supple leaps. She hadn't lost any of the toughness or smarts that had carried her along when she'd adapted to fending for herself, and Lathrop thought she still had what it took to make it on her own, might even hang on to that ability for a while longer . . . but the point always came when the senses dulled, and the reflexes slowed just enough to give an enemy the split-second chance it needed to get in under the throat.

Lathrop leaned forward on the couch, winked at the jade green eye studying him from across the room.

"We make some team," he said, and patted his leg to invite her over. "Fellow travelers, partners in crime."

Missus Frakes dropped her paw from her face, stretched, sat, yawned. Then she sauntered over in her listless, draggy way and came brushing up against his legs.

Lathrop stroked her back, heard and felt her purr, gently massaged the tight, stiffened muscles of her hips.

Suddenly a sharp hiss. She twisted clear of his fingertips and raked the back of his hand with her claws before he could pull away, slashing into it from wrist to knuckle.

Then she stood in front of the sofa, facing him calmly.

The scratches on his hand already burning, Lathrop looked at her and almost smiled. She'd gotten her message across loud and clear.

"That a girl," he said. "You show me where it hurts, I'll be more careful about where I touch."

Missus Frakes watched him, her motor purring again. After a moment she turned into the kitchenette with a noticeable little strut in her gait and sat down near her empty food dish.

Lathrop followed her inside, turned on the cold water, held his bleeding hand under the tap, and dabbed it with a paper towel. The furball had skinned him one good, he thought.

He held the blood-splotched paper towel to his hand a minute and disposed of it. Then he reached into an overhead cabinet for a can of moist cat food, opened the flip top, dropped it onto the trash as well. It occurred to him Missus Frakes had parked herself on potentially millions of dollars worth of high-tech swag. *The cat's ass.* In a safe embedded in the flooring under one of its parquet wood tiles—bolted into the surrounding joists, its composite-steel door panel accessible only by enabling its invisible algorithmic lock with Lathrop's credit card–sized remote control—were the gemstone case, data minidiscs, and hard copied schematics he'd acquired from Sullivan's attaché. He was sure he'd be able to move the stones in a hurry once Avram the broker returned from his trip to the Antwerp bourse. The discs, though . . . what got him about the discs was that Sullivan had been telling the irrefutable truth when he'd insisted they were much more valuable with the keys than without them.

Lathrop reached for the cat's dish, spooned some food into it.

Sullivan had been careful to a degree, but he'd never been as smart or guarded as he thought he was. He'd also had a habit of showing off—his conceit like a thin balloon, overinflated with insecurity, ready to burst at the prick of a pin. Those weaknesses had cost him that night on Wards Island, and maybe there was still a way to exploit them. Dragonfly was the score of a lifetime, and Sullivan had known it. Thought he was clever holding back the keys, too . . . it had been all over him. If he'd had the opportunity to open his mouth about that to someone—in his own mind, safely boast—Lathrop was betting he'd have done it.

He crouched, set the dish on the floor. He pictured the Irishman with his restored hairline, his trendy ski jacket, his top-end Jaguar sports car with its plush interior. All evidence of his vanity, meant to impress.

Who would he most want to dazzle with it . . . and also feel he could trust to hang on to what he'd thought would be a big piece of insurance, something that might bail him out of a jam in the event one of his after-hours transactions went bad?

Lathrop scratched Missus Frakes on the back of her neck, thinking the answer seemed much too easy.

"Pillow talk, Missus Frakes," he said. "Sullivan was going to whisper secrets into somebody's ear, it would have been his old lady's."

The cat bent her head to sniff the food in her dish and, satisfied it was to her liking, started on her meal with relish.

THREE

"**HOW DOES THIS ROCK SEEM TO YOU?**" ROGER Gordian said.

"Wait a second, I'm not sure which you mean."

Ashley released the handles of their wheelbarrow, smacked her hands together to dust off the thick cowhide work gloves she was wearing, and stepped toward him. They were at the bottom of a shallow wash about thirty yards down from where they'd left her Land Rover below a switchback that zigzagged roughly east-west through the Santa Cruz mountains.

"Look over there." Gordian pointed at a scattering of sandstone near the base of the slope. "That rock."

"The round one with that sort of reddish stripe?"

"No, no." Gordian gestured. "The flattish one with those brown patches just to its right."

His wife stood beside him, inspected, considered.

"It would be perfect," she said, and nodded.

"Thought so," Gordian said. "I'll start digging it up."

"Oh no, you won't."

His expression went from pleased to perplexed.

"You just told me—"

"I know what I told you," she said. "But I can see from where we're standing that it's set deep in the ground."

Gordian reached for the long-handled shovel he'd rested against a small, weathered outcrop.

"That's why I brought my friend here."

"Can your friend there dig by itself?"

"Ash—"

"Because I won't let you break your back excavating a rock that probably weighs forty pounds and is going to be a *ton* of trouble to get out."

They stood looking at each other a moment in the bright, warm noonday light. Both had worn jeans, hiking boots, identical heavyweight gloves, and denim jackets to keep the stones they'd come to collect from snagging their shirts. On Gordian's head was a blue-and-white striped railroader's cap meant to likewise protect his scalp, his wispy gray hair offering it scant cover from sunburn these days. Ashley's thick blond locks, meanwhile, were in some kind of elaborate feminine twist-and-tuck under a lilac fashion bandanna.

"You can't build a retaining wall with pea gravel and sand," Gordian said.

Ashley frowned.

"Excuse me, wise guy," she said. "Are you suggesting that's what I've loaded into the wheelbarrow?"

Gordian decided he'd better curb his testiness.

"No," he said.

"Pea gravel?"

"They're nice, good-sized rocks, hon. I mean it."

"I hope so, for your sake—"

"Although I do think we need some larger ones," he said,

scratching his head under the cap with one finger. "Especially for our end stones."

Ashley produced a sigh.

"I don't want you overdoing things, Roger," she said. "On last count, it's been a few years since you've been in your twenties."

Or thirties, or forties, or fifties. Gordian thought with a limp smile.

"We could have bought dressed rocks from a stone yard and had them dropped five feet from my rose garden on a pallet," she said. "If I'd realized you were going to be this stubborn, I might have hired a professional contractor."

Gordian looked at her.

"I know a little bit about putting together a stone wall," he said. "My father owned a construction supply business, don't forget."

"I haven't forgotten."

"You also shouldn't forget your stated aversion to made-to-order retaining walls that look like big piles of potato chips."

Ashley frowned again.

"Fried corn chips," she said. "The comparison I made was to fried corn chips. They tend to be more uniform in shape."

"I stand corrected."

They regarded each other quietly.

"Ash, listen," Gordian said. "I stepped down as chief executive of UpLink so we could finally share the personal life we've always missed. So I'd be able to spend more time doing things with you—and for you— after decades of endless responsibility to a corporation with thousands of employees scattered across every continent on earth. But the key phrase is *doing things*. I'm not a dodderer quite yet. And frankly, I've been bending over backward to show you I'm mindful of my limitations."

Ashley glanced down at the lumpy soil underfoot, scuffed the toe of her boot around in a way that endowed her with an unaffected girlishness. Gordian managed to resist a smile.

"Okay, I concede," she said, after almost a full minute of toe-scuffing had left a swash in the dirt. "With the stipulation that we can revisit this issue the instant I see you bend over backward with a *boulder* in your hands."

"Sounds fair enough to m—"

The oddly distant tweedle of his cell phone interrupted Gordian.

He felt for it on his belt clip, couldn't locate it, glanced down at himself. The phone wasn't there.

It rang again.

Gordian searched the area immediately around him, didn't see it there either, then looked toward the slope where he'd been rock-gathering in a minor panic, positive it must have fallen somewhere among the jumbled chunks of broken hillside.

"Over here, Roger."

He glanced over at Ashley, surprised to see the phone in her hand.

"Where did—?"

"I picked it up off the ground after you dropped it half an hour ago."

Twee-dle!

"You should answer before the caller thinks you've fallen asleep on your rocking chair," she said with a lopsided grin.

Gordian scowled in response to her open amusement, took the phone, flipped up the earpiece.

"Hello?"

"Boss, great, I was getting ready to leave a message."

Gordian opened his mouth, closed it. The two or three seconds it took him to place the voice at the other end of the line had nothing to do with it being unfamiliar to him. Rather, it was the unfamiliarity of the context in which he was hearing it. He supposed it had been years since he'd spoken with Lenny Reisenberg outside a business office, whether in person or long distance.

"Lenny?" he said.

"Yeah, Boss." A pause. "This a bad time to talk?"

"No, no."

"You sure? It should only take a couple minutes, but I don't want to keep you from anything . . ."

"No, really, right now is fine," Gordian said. "It's been a while, Len. How are you?"

"Okay," Lenny said. "Yourself?"

"Working hard at semiretirement."

Lenny chuckled. "You were always so busy running the show at HQ, it must be an adjustment having some time on your hands."

"That's what I expected," Gordian said. "But I've found out keeping busy isn't the tough part."

"Oh?"

Gordian leaned back against the outcrop beside his shovel and glanced over at Ashley. She was reorganizing some of the rocks she'd stacked in their wheelbarrow.

"It's all still about negotiation and compromise," he said. "Just happens to be of a slightly different nature than before."

"You'll have to promise to give me the lowdown on that one of these days."

One of these days, Gordian thought. "What can I do for you, Len?"

There was momentary silence in the earpiece. Then Lenny exhaled.

"A favor, I hope," he said. "I feel awkward even asking . . . guess it's pretty unusual . . ."

"Business or personal?"

"I'm not sure there's a clear line," Lenny said. "Or if there is, it's sort of fuzzy in my head."

"Then I suppose you'd better lay everything out before that fuzziness spreads into mine."

Lenny released another tidal wash of air from his lungs and started to explain.

Gordian listened closely. There was the Kiran salesman, Patrick Sullivan. The Long Island detectives who'd arrived at Lenny's office while investigating his disappearance, followed by Sullivan's wife appearing to solicit his help. His initial unwillingness, and her striking a resonant chord inside him that overcame it. Then his pledge to do what he could, Noriko Cousins shooting him down at Sword HQ, a Chinese herbalist named Yan offering sagacious advice, and an epiphany at a kosher deli triggered in some ambiguous way by a bite, or perhaps several bites, of a pastrami sandwich.

Five minutes later Lenny had almost gotten through his struggle to explain what was weighing on him.

"I wandered around half of Manhattan yesterday telling myself I had no right asking for Sword to meddle in something that's happened to a guy who isn't one of our employees," he said, seemingly out of breath. "That I had to let it go. Hell, I don't even know Sullivan well enough to get his daughter's name straight. Thought she was in first or second grade till his wife mentions she's away at college. But then . . . Boss, you remember the old TV show, *This Is Your Life*? Since Mary Sullivan came into my office, it feels like my brain's been taken over by the spirit of the host . . . what was his name . . . ?"

"Ralph Edwards."

"Right, him, and he's been walking my past out in front of me. And I've got to admit, the one memory that keeps coming out from behind the curtain . . . well, you know the day we met . . . the night, that is . . . it was right here in New York. Times Square . . ."

"How could I forget, Len?" Gordian said. "You were, ah, quite the character. Decent salesman, too."

"I was a screwed-up mess with an attitude, a minimum-wage job in a record shop, and a little knowledge of jazz," Lenny said. " 'You want to bop, there's Ornithology.' Remember?"

A reflective smile touched Gordian's lips.

" 'I'll do it with Dizzy if you'll give me Anthropology,' " he said. "I remember, Len."

"Never can tell where you'll find one of life's little shoehorns."

Gordian considered that one, smiled.

"The crossroads of the world would seem just the right place."

"Yeah," Lenny said. "I suppose it would."

Gordian waited in silence.

"Boss, I don't want to sound sappy," Lenny said after a moment. "But the reason I called . . . I know you trust the people at Sword to decide where and where not to stick our noses. I know Noriko Cousins had solid reasons for taking a pass in this situation, and I don't like making an end run around her. But twenty years ago you turned me around for no good reason *I* could figure, and probably none I deserved. You took a chance on me. And I think what I've carried away from it is that there are times when you've got to reach out just for the sake of helping. Or when something inside a person reaches out to something that's inside *you*, and you know it's only right to help. That if you don't, you're dropping the ball."

Gordian thought in silence some more. It had been six

months since he'd turned the daily responsibilities of running UpLink over to Megan Breen, which meant he probably wasn't up to snuff on the doings of the Kiran Group or its parent company, Armbright Industries. But however unsaintly it might be, one of Sword's regular, necessary functions was to compile and evaluate competitive intelligence on other tech firms . . . in blunter terms, shadow UpLink's market rivals. Gordian was sure he did not need to remind Lenny of this, and wouldn't have discussed it over the telephone anyway. CI was a vital, accepted part of business that every major corporation conducted, guarded against, and artfully pretended to know nothing about. The ethical and legal issues associated with it primarily arose when using information for strategic advantage crossed over to intellectual theft or sabotage, boundaries Gordian had always made sure weren't overstepped.

So here came Lenny wanting Noriko Cousins—and now Gordian himself—to have Sword look into the circumstances surrounding the disappearance of a Kiran employee. Or poke around in a missing-husband case, however you chose to frame it. Either way, the first question that request had provoked in Gordian's head was whether it violated any of his basic tenets for CI activity. And while he'd concluded it might not be a typical recon, it still fell more or less into his definition of what went with the program. Which left Gordian to decide if Lenny's appeal warranted an allocation of corporate resources . . . either because he felt it was in UpLink's best interests, or because he was ready to yield to it out of friendship.

Gordian remained thoughtful, watching Ash continue to shift around the stones she'd gathered inside the wheelbarrow. He wondered in a vague sort of way what was wrong with how they'd been stacked in the first place, then realized all at once that she was only fussing with them to give him a chance to talk on the phone. At about the same instant it struck him how much he wanted to get back to her. Then it occurred to him how much he also liked having to make a determination of some significance that concerned UpLink.

He turned his mind back in the direction of Lenny's request, focusing in on his core justification for wanting Sword involved. What exactly was the point he was making?

That it's the decent thing to do. Pure and simple. When you boil it right down, he hasn't tried to convince me there's any benefit in it for UpLink, or sell me on any other reason besides.

Gordian thought for another minute, feeling the warm sunlight press against his face. Then he nodded to himself and pushed off the outcrop.

"Let me get back to you in a day or two, Len," he said. "I'll make a few calls and start that ball of yours rolling in the meantime."

Pete Nimec opened his medicine cabinet, looked inside, frowned, shut it, studied his bristled cheeks in its mirrored door, sighed, bent to open the cabinet under the bathroom sink, reached in, foraged through it a minute, frowned, shut it, stood to examine his weekend scruff of beard again, sighed, and then reopened the medicine cabinet for his fourth sure-to-be-futile inspection of its variously sized compartments.

Nimec hated having to rush around, and never more than on Monday mornings. Especially when his rushing seemed to lead nowhere.

The knock on his bathroom door came just as his lips started to take yet another stymied downturn.

He tightened the belt on his robe.

"C'mon in."

A moment later Christopher Caulfield stood looking at him from the doorway. A month from his twelfth birthday, all four feet and change of him combed, scrubbed, and dressed, he was eminently ready for school.

Nimec noticed the kid's bright expression, then saw the cell phone in his outstretched hand.

"Hey," he said, his latest frown interrupted in progress. "Where'd you dig that up?"

Chris continued to beam.

"You know mom's old wooden box, or whatever it is, with the drawers?"

"The one near the front door."

"Nope, her other one," Chris said. "On that sort of table thing outside the living room."

"Aaah," Nimec said. "I owe you, skipper."

"Like enough for a half hour up in the dojo later?"

"Like you finish your homework soon's you come home and we make it an hour." Nimec gave his shoulder a squeeze. "Linda getting anywhere with my clean dress shirts?"

"She found a white shirt that only stinks a little in the other bathroom."

"Won't do."

"That's what *I* told her." Chris looked at him. "No razor blades yet, huh?"

Nimec scratched the stubble under his chin with deepening self-consciousness.

"No," he said. "I must've looked everywhere."

Chris motioned toward the sink cabinet. "Down there, too?"

"Everywhere."

"Bad news."

"I know."

"We're gonna be late, Pete."

"Not if we rush we won't." That loathsome word.

Nimec reached for the shelf where he'd put his wrist-watch before climbing into the shower . . . well, technically speaking, where he'd put the WristLink wearable micro-computer that did everything under the sun but find the basic necessities for getting him shaved, dressed, and out of the house in time to drive the kids to their respective schools be-fore heading on to his office at UpLink San Jose, where Nimec presided over the company's welfare as Chief of Global Security, a job he could hopefully carry out with greater success than his latest inexpert shot at solo parent-ing. This while Annie—Nimec's bride of four months, and long-experienced mother of the poor children left in his bumbling care—was off in Houston making men and women into astronauts.

"This contraption says it's a quarter to eight," Nimec said, glancing at the WristLink as he buckled it on. "Still gives us fifteen minutes to get out of here."

Chris checked his own watch.

"Pete, mine says it's almost *five* to eight . . ."

"And mine's synched to radio signals from the Time and Frequency Division of the National Institute of Standards and Technology, which makes it official," Nimec said. "Think yours can beat that?"

Chris looked at him.

"Oh, sure," he said. "And I can beat you at karate."

"Someday you might," Nimec said. "Meanwhile, I need to call your mother."

He took the cellular from Chris, flipped it open, held it up to his cheek.

"An-nnuh-ieee," he mouthed with a dragged-out slowness that made him sound piteously speech-impaired . . . and feel

idiotic since he knew it was unnecessary with advanced voice dial interfaces. Old habits died hard, he guessed.

A ring tone in his ear, and then Annie's name appeared on his caller identification display . . . as he imagined would be true in the reverse.

"Hi, Pete."

Nimec smiled. Hearing her gave him a lift. It also made him feel like a lovesick adolescent. She'd been gone four days, what was that? But to be fair with himself, it had been like this since they got back from their honeymoon. Three or four days a week, every week. The separations demanded by Annie's unfinished job commitments weren't your standard ingredients for newly wedded bliss.

"Annie, you at work?"

"I wish," she said. "Stuck in traffic."

"Where about?"

"Maybe a half mile from the Center," she said, using NASA shorthand for the immense complex of research, operational, training, and administrative office facilities that constituted the Lyndon B. Johnson Space Center between Houston and Galveston. "Routine maintenance. They've closed two lanes on the interstate."

"Lousy timing."

"Couldn't be worse," she said. "Talk about a screw-up, Pete. Orion Three launches in about a month . . ."

Five weeks, two days, he thought. *Then you're finished working, over and out, and we're back in orbit together.*

". . . and we've got the shuttle crew in the last stage of intensive training. Full phase mission sims, a rendezvous and docking run-through this morning. So what happens? Some geniuses on the Texas Highways Board decide *now's* when to repave."

"You'd think they'd have the sense to coordinate with LBJ," Nimec said.

"You sure would . . . and I left the apartment forty minutes early to avoid this jam, if you can believe it." Annie sighed. "Anyway, enough griping. Everything okay at home?"

"Yeah," Nimec said. "Well, pretty much. Got a small problem. Or two. But if you're driving . . ."

"More like staring at the butt end of a tanker truck," she said. "What are 'nonedible animal fat products,' by the way?"

"No idea. Why?"

"Because the term's so disgusting it fascinates me," Annie said. "And because a sign on the truck says it's carrying them and warns not to tailgate."

"Really, Annie, this'll wait until you get off the road. . . ."

"Come on, I'm hands-free with my phone," she said. "What can't you find this morning?"

"How'd you know—?"

"Pete, you have the same problem or two *every* morning," Annie said. "So let's hear."

Nimec cleared his throat.

"Fresh razor blades," he said. "Been looking for them everywhere."

"Did you try your bathroom closet?"

Nimec turned toward the closet door right behind him, raised his eyebrows in consternation.

"Well, no . . ."

"There should be a bunch on the middle shelf."

He went to take a look, found several packages in plain sight beside hefty oversupplies of shampoo and shaving cream.

"See them?" Annie said.

"Yeah, thanks." Nimec reached for a pack and tore open the cellophane. "Could've sworn I had my blades under the sink, though . . ."

"Once upon a time, Pete. Under it, over it, on it. But I've been putting them all in the closet for months."

"That long?"

"Since I came along to impose order on your existence."

Nimec thought a moment.

"Guess we have been over this before," he said.

"Uh-huh," Annie said. "What's next?"

"My dress shirts."

"None in your drawer?"

"Not a single one."

"Then Chloe didn't get around to putting away the laundry on Friday," she said.

"The advantages of our hiring on a housekeeper."

"Come on, Pete. She's only part-time."

"Still, I *used* to know where—"

"The washroom," Annie said. "That wicker basket on the floor next to the machines."

"You sure?"

"Guaranteed. She always stacks them there after picking them up from the dry cleaner," Annie said. "Sorts it with the laundry when she's done so she can put everything away at once."

"Hold it, let me see."

Nimec held the phone away from his mouth, sent Chris on a hurried bee through the condo. A couple of minutes later he reappeared in the doorway, his younger sister scrambling up behind him. Each of them had a folded, banded white shirt held out flat with both hands like a pizza box.

"Pete . . . ?"

"We're good here, Annie."

"Good that you're good," she said. "Traffic's starting to move."

"And we'd better do the same at our end. Call you at the apartment tonight?"

"Make it late if you're going to," Annie said. "I'm in for a long day in Building Five."

Nimec quietly scratched under his ear.

"I love you, Pete. Hugs and kisses to the brats."

"Back at you."

Nimec flipped the phone shut, dropped it into the pocket of his robe, and ordered the kids out of the room while he shaved.

Rushing to finish, he nicked his face badly in several spots.

The trio of battered old coal trucks and their fully laden open-bed trailers had thundered through the Pakistani night under a three-quarter moon, journeying almost a hundred-fifty kilometers northwest from the rail yard in Islamabad toward Chikar, an inkblot-small village with limited overland access amounting to a few lightly traveled ribbons of blacktop that dipped and wove between jagged, snowy mountain peaks.

As he crested a steep rise under a projecting spur of hillside, the lead vehicle's driver puzzled at what his headlights revealed straight ahead.

He glanced at the man dozing beside him, then reached across to shake his elbow. "Khalid, snap to it."

Khalid stirred, his head still nodding against his chest.

"What's the problem?" he said fuzzily.

The driver shot him an annoyed look.

"See for yourself," he said.

Khalid jerked himself erect in his seat. Perhaps fifty or

sixty meters up ahead on his right, he could see a string of electric warning flashers along the roadside, where snow-banks were piled high against the slope. They led toward a portable wooden barricade, casting bright red reflections off the inches-thick sheets of recently fallen cover on the black-top and overhanging rock ledges. A pair of soldiers wearing combat helmets, hooded dun coats, and winter boots stood in front of the barricade, assault weapons slung over their shoulders. Angled crosswise behind it were three jeeps. They idled with their lights on, exhaust wisping from their tailpipes. There were more soldiers inside the vehicles, shadowy outlines in the silver moonlight.

"Maader chud," Khalid swore. His eyes had popped wide open. "Do you think they're regular infantry?"

"Look carefully. Those rifles should give you an answer."

Khalid stared out his windshield at the soldiers and mut-tered another curse. The submachine guns were the H&K G3s issued to border-patrol units.

"Rangers," he said.

"So it seems."

They rolled on in silence a moment

"This could be something routine. A spot check," Khalid said, sounding none too confident. "In any event, Yousaf, we have the proper documents."

The driver inwardly dismissed his weak reassurances. Chikar was twenty-five klicks from the restricted zone en-compassing the western boundaries of Kashmir's Muzaf-farabad and Poonch districts, with their military outposts and heavily guarded refugee camps. It was, furthermore, twice that distance from the Line of Control. In the relative quiet that had held across the frontier over the past six months, Yousaf's team had made runs to the area many times without encountering rangers this far from their forward posts.

The coal trucks rumbled toward the barrier, their tires pressing wide tread imprints into the snow. Yousaf saw the two standing guards move into the middle of the road and wave phosphorescent wands over their heads to bring the procession to a halt.

He tapped his hydraulic brakes and the truck slowed with a hiss.

Khalid lurched in its passenger seat. He, too, had grown increasingly sure of imminent trouble. And wasn't it a fair expectation in these times of bottom-dollar loyalties? His country's president was nothing more than a *bharway,* a pimp, his regular army a stable of debased whores—now on their knees for the Americans, now raising their bottoms to let the Indians have a poke at them. For Khalid and his confederates it had been the ultimate shame when even the Inter-Service Intelligence Directorate began turning itself out for the greenback. Praise be to God, there were yet a few who refused to cheapen themselves.

"Make certain the others are ready," Yousaf ordered now, tilting his head back toward the trucks at his rear. "Use only the beep code."

Khalid looked at him across the cab.

"You think those men can break our encryption?" he said.

Yousaf shrugged, his hands on the wheel.

"Who knows what brought them here," he said. "If they're going to pick up anything, let it be meaningless noise."

Khalid grunted. Again, he saw the wariness on Yousaf's features. And again he understood what was at its root. It wasn't only the army they had to worry about—their Hindu bedmates across the LoC were especially skilled at radio intercepts.

He took his cell phone from inside his coat, switched on its walkie-talkie channel, and used the tone pad to transmit a short series of beeps. A moment later he heard a response sequence in the earpiece and slipped the radio back into his pocket.

Yousaf brought the truck to a full stop as one of the soldiers approached his door, glanced at the painted company name on its exterior, and then motioned for him to roll down his window. He lowered it halfway with his right hand, noticing that the second guard had walked around the front grille toward the passenger side.

"It's a hideous night to be out, my brother," Yousaf said, leaning his head out of the cab. "Has there been some sort of local disturbance?"

The ranger ignored his question, his bearded face showing no flicker of expression. His eyes skimmed the inside of the cab, lingered on Khalid a second, then returned to Yousaf.

"I see you're with Daud Fuel and Energy out of the capital," he said.

"Yes."

"Headed where?"

"The power station at Chikar," Khalid said.

The ranger's eyes were steady on him.

"I'll have a look at your papers, if you please," he said.

Khalid had them ready on a clipboard. He leaned over and passed it out the window.

"Is it not late for a delivery?" the guard said, flipping through the permits and manifests

Yousaf had kept his left hand on the steering wheel. Now he flapped it in a gesture of long-suffering resignation and let it drop onto his seat near the floor-mounted stick shift.

"In winter our rail shipment from Dera Ghazi comes when

it comes . . . and what can we do but wait for our pickup?" he said. "Today a storm in the valley put them—and us—three hours behind schedule."

Silence. The wind blew across the snow-decked summits and ledges of the vast mountain range, swirling shrouds of powder into the air. They drifted under the moonlight and sprinkled crystalline glitter onto Yousaf's hood and windshield.

He glanced into his rearview mirror and watched the second border guard continue down the left side of the truck toward its flatbed. He'd expected the rangers would not leave well enough alone, although his answers to the questions posed him had been verifiable. The shipment's destination, his explanation for its lateness . . . that was all true as far as it went. Daud was a legitimate coal and petroleum company, and nine times out of ten its trucks to points out along the country's eastern and western territories carried only their declared cargo.

Yousaf doubted it was any coincidence that this stop had occurred at the odd trip out. Someone had been clued to something. Presumably something vague and largely dismissed, though. Otherwise there would have been more than a token military presence out on the road.

"Respectfully, might we be allowed to get underway?" he asked. "The drivers are tired, and we still have a distance to travel."

The ranger looked at him.

"I'll let you go as soon as possible," he said. "But my men will need to inspect the back of your trucks."

Yousaf made a surprised face, eased his left hand down into the space between the driver's and passenger seats.

"To what purpose?" he said, and felt his heartbeat quicken. In a moment, he knew, the soldier would radio the jeeps. "Each is carrying upwards of forty-five thousand kilos of coal. It will be this time tomorrow before you're finished."

"Relax, I didn't say we'd have to shovel it all onto the road." The ranger started to pass the clipboard back through the open window. "You have your job, we have ours."

And that was the regrettable catch, Yousaf thought.

With the ranger's arm still inside the cab, holding out the clipboard, Yousaf grabbed his wrist with his right hand to pull him forward and off-balance. At the same instant he brought his knife up from the space behind the clutch with his other hand, swept it in front of and across his own chest, and plunged it into the ranger's throat under the angle of the jaw to penetrate the trachea, sharply turning its serrated blade in the wound, then jerking it to the right to cut a wide horizontal slit that severed both carotid arteries.

The ranger's eyes rolled and he emitted a barely audible sputtering sound. His hot blood steaming in the cold night air, pulsing over Yousaf's hand and arm from the ragged gash in his throat, he slumped forward as Yousaf held on to his wrist to keep his body pressed up against the side of the truck a little longer.

"Khalid, fast!" he rasped.

Khalid had already thrown open the passenger door. Now he whipped his sound-and-flash-suppressed Steyr tactical machine pistol from inside his coat, leaned out, and twisted around at the waist to where the second ranger now stood by the trailer, his back to the truck's cab.

In the loud throbbing of wind between the mountain flanks, the soldier hadn't yet heard anything unusual. Nor did he notice until after Yousaf had released his dying companion to let him hit the ground with the knife buried in his throat, and then clenched the steering wheel in one hand, rammed the truck's gearshift into "forward" with dripping, blood-slicked fingers, and lowered his foot onto the gas pedal.

It was only as the truck lurched toward the barricade that the second ranger looked to see what was happening and was struck by a muffled, flashless volley from Khalid's polymer-skinned weapon. The ranger went down at once, collapsing as if deflated, his legs folding underneath him.

The passenger door still open, Khalid pulled his head back into the cab and faced forward.

Tensing, he dug the fingers of his free hand into the side of his bucket seat, holding the grip of his TMP with the other. The coal truck trundled slowly forward, the barrier growing larger in its windshield. Khalid saw soldiers pour out of their jeeps in disorganized haste, expecting to be rammed broadside, firing at the truck as they split toward the opposite shoulders of the road.

His head ducked low as bullets peppered the windshield, Khalid triggered a return salvo out his wide-flung door and saw one of the evacuating soldiers go down. In back of him the two other coal trucks remained at a complete stop, their doors also thrown open now. The men leaping from their cabs onto the road carried heavier firearms than his own compact machine pistol, Kalashnikov AK-100s with night optics and GP-30 underbarrel grenade launchers.

Shattered windshield glass flying over him, blood streaming into his eyes from cuts on his cheeks and forehead, Khalid fired the Steyr until its clip was spent, then tossed it onto his seat, reached down between his legs, pulled open a camouflaged access panel in the floor of the cab, and extracted an AK-100 from a hidden compartment. A moment later it was stuttering in his hand.

Now a pop from behind, a whistle overhead, and Khalid knew one of his confederates at the rear had sent a 40-mm

VOG projectile arcing over the barricade from his tube. He mentally counted down and heard another streak past him at a level trajectory—this grenade issued from the same weapon, its direction and angle of elevation changed to confuse its targets about their enemy's position. The first airburst round lit the night above the left side of the road where several of the rangers had scrambled for cover, its nose detonated by a timed fourteen-second fuze, pelting the area below with a hail of fragmented metal. The next bounding round exploded an almost imperceptible three seconds later and shredded apart lower to the ground on the right. Khalid could hear high, piercing screams through the blast, punctuated with sharp little *spaks* of shrapnel nicking the parked jeeps behind the barricade.

And then the barricade ceased to exist, Yousaf plowing into its crossbeam with a final surge of acceleration, reducing it to scraps of broken wood. They buffeted the front end of the truck, and jutted from the crashed barricade's toppled uprights in splintery bits and pieces.

Khalid braced in his seat, his upper body jolting against its backrest as Yousaf came to a hard, sudden halt scarcely a heartbeat before they would have slammed into an abandoned jeep.

They sat a moment looking out their partially disintegrated windshield. A wounded ranger lay in the snow near Yousaf's door, clutching his chest and groaning in pain. There was still some light, spotty gunfire coming from the roadsides, and Khalid could see the men who'd sprung out of the trucks at his rear sprint on ahead, fanning left and right in the darkness. It wasn't long before the opposing volleys had been squelched.

"We're wasting time," Yousaf said. "Remove all our papers from the truck and have one of the others help us transfer the component and some spare containers of gasoline into one of the jeeps."

Khalid wiped his bloodied face with his sleeve.

"Do you think there might be others waiting for our trucks farther on toward Chikar?" he said.

"Forget Chikar, we can't take the chance," Yousaf said. "We head north now. I know passes that are rarely patrolled and will take us toward the Neelam Valley crossings."

"Neelam?" Khalid said. His eyes widened. "That's a journey of almost a thousand kilometers. Even should the weather hold, it will take us two days over the mountains—"

"Then we'd best get started, drive on while we can make the most of the darkness," Khalid said. "We'll need to leave the men to clean up here, and travel off-road as much as possible tonight to be safe."

Khalid verged on protest a moment, but then thought the better of it. Yousaf was not one to have his wishes denied.

He nodded and went to follow his orders, his boot-heels sinking deep into the snow as he exited the coal truck.

Then the crack of a single bullet from its driver's side made him stiffen, his breath catching in his throat with a little gasp. He glanced sharply over the hood and saw Yousaf standing over the sprawled body of the ranger, looking down at him, the bore of his Steyr pressed to the middle of his head.

"*Gandu*," Yousaf said, using the Urdu vulgarism for asshole.

He spat on the corpse, straightened, turned to make brief eye contact with Khalid.

"I did the traitor a favor he didn't deserve," he said, holstering his weapon.

•   •   •

His fingers steepled under his chin, Lembock was waiting behind his desk when Delano Malisse arrived for their morning appointment.

"Delano, *hoe gaat het met jou?*" Lembock said in Flemish, offering the customary hi-how-are-you without rising from his chair.

Malisse took no offense. It was not discourtesy, but the depredations of rheumatism and chronic bronchitis that kept him off his feet.

Malisse sat down in front of him and unbuttoned his overcoat. As usual, Lembock had the office's heat turned up suffocatingly high, its steam radiator hissing and clanking. Could this possibly be good for his ailing lungs? *"Goed, bedankt,"* he said. "You're looking much recovered from that last bad spell."

A gracious, soft-spoken man, Lembock smiled with the quiet skepticism of one who was appreciative of the polite words, but might have gently begged to differ. He looked at Malisse, his chin balanced on his hands. The fingers long, tapered, almost spindling, the skin tight and thin over knobby, inflamed joints, they reminded Malisse of the ribbed arches that supported the ceilings of the Gothic churches and palaces at the city's centuries-old heart, seeming almost too delicate to last under the ponderous weight resting upon them. Yet last they did, their stability ever a marvel to him.

Rance Lembock's office was about a mile west of the historic district, on the ninth floor of the Diamantclub van Antwerpen, this first and most prominent of Antwerp's four diamond bourses located in a rather nondescript, even homely, building on Pelikaanstraat, a sidestreet running south from the Central Station rail terminal. Two stories above, on the top floor, was the seat of the Secretariat of the

World Federation of Diamond Bourses, which, as its name indicated, codified and oversaw the rules, regulations, laws, and bylaws observed by every reputable exchange in Europe and beyond, its influence spanning continents, ranging from Tokyo in the far east to New York City in the west.

As chairman of the Diamantclub, Lembock had always seemed to bear the great responsibilities of his position with a kind of dutiful fidelity, like an attentive husband who lifts a heavy bag of groceries from his wife's arms to carry it himself, seeing nothing praiseworthy in the assumption of a task for which his greater strength naturally suits him. But whatever leadership qualities Lembock's solid, stable disposition endowed, Malisse felt it was hard work and experience that had finely honed them into something even his frail health of recent years couldn't diminish.

In his middle seventies, his face deeply lined under a high forehead and thick cloud of white hair, Lembock wore a spread-collar white dress shirt and blue boxcloth suspenders that clipped onto the waistband of his trousers with gilt brass fittings. No tie, no jacket. The shirtsleeves were rolled up midway to his elbows with particular neatness, exposing part of the faded blue ink tattoo on his right inner forearm, a five-digit identification number he'd gotten after his arrival at Auschwitz aboard a cattle car loaded with Jews in 1942. As Malisse understood from stories he'd heard, Lembock had been deemed physically suitable for slave labor rather than extermination by a camp physician, sent to the Political Section to assure he cleared a watch list of potential agitators and Communists, and then passed along to an SS functionary in the Labor Assignment Office, who had imprinted him with the number using a punch-card machine custom-adapted by IBM Hollerith for that purpose. Hands across the water, as the saying went.

Malisse sat in respectful silence. Advanced age and stature entitled Lembock to decide when to launch their conversation. Moreover, it was important to be mindful of fundamental protocols. Lembock was the client, he the hired investigator held on no small retainer. And Malisse did not, at any rate, find it difficult to be still and wait. He could discern the numerals 421 on Lembock's skin, the remaining two digits hidden by his shirt cuff. A precise and exacting man, Lembock always folded his sleeves the same three inches above his wrist, so that he had never seen the final two digits of the slave number exposed. Although Malisse's obsessive hunger for detail often urged him to look for them, he took pains to be inconspicuous when overcome.

Just once, to his knowledge, had Lembock become aware of his interest . . . or if there had been other instances, it was only then that he had commented, speaking before Malisse could become too angry at himself over the uncharacteristic slipup.

"I was seventeen when they gave me this," Lembock had said, touching a finger to the mark. "A boy I knew named Yitzhak . . . we'd lived in Marasesti, a small town in Romania . . . he was next in line to receive his number. His family was more observant than mine, and he worried that marring the body with a tattoo was forbidden, against our religion. That we might someday be refused burial in a Jewish cemetery. I recall thinking we would be fortunate for that to ever become a problem, for it would mean we'd have survived the camps. But to comfort Yitzhak, I told him that when the time came, God would surely take our circumstances into account and make an *oysnem* . . . an exception." Lembock had paused. "Later, we were both sent to the Mittelbau-Dora camp, at Nordhausen, and put to work quarrying out granite from the Peenemunde rocket tunnels, where the Nazis developed the V2 missile. Yitzhak became weak—I believe he must have had the beginnings of typhus—and was shot to death, put down with a bullet to the head like a crippled farm animal. I remember that they threw his body onto the open bed of a truck with a pile of other dead bodies and took them all back to the crematoriums." Lembock had fallen silent again, briefly, watching Malisse. Then he'd produced a deep sigh. "Yitzhak did not have to worry about receiving a Jewish burial," he'd said in the husk of a voice, and after a final pause had changed the subject.

This had been three or four years back, Malisse remembered. Soon after he'd stepped out from the encumbrances of government service. He'd been reporting on a case, the sale of a Dresden Green diamond brooch fraudulently purported to be from the priceless seventeenth-century collection of the Polish king, Frederick Augustus II. His efforts to track down the counterfeiter had been at a preliminary stage—his leads undeveloped, his groundwork barely laid. With little to furnish Lembock besides assurances of eventual success, he'd wearied of his own delivery and let his gaze rest on the tattoo a few seconds too long.

Malisse tried diligently to avoid repeating his mistakes, and had some fair confidence that he'd succeeded in not making that one again.

Now he sat and waited in the stifling office. Although Lembock would have no objection to his lighting a cigarette despite his afflicted lungs, Malisse feared the combination of unventilated heat and tobacco smoke might prove smothering to him. Instead he whittled off several moments letting his gaze drift freely about the room—one never could tell when a worthy surprise would spring out of the familiar to catch the eye like a colorful, never-before-seen bird flashing from an old backyard tree.

Nothing of the sort happened this time. Still, Malisse was always able to appreciate the office's simple and tasteful decor. There were soft leather chairs, a large blond-oak desk. Framed professional certificates hung on the walls, along with photographs of Lembock's late wife, his children, his grandchildren. Other photos as well—Lembock in the company of high-placed professional and political associates.

Outside the windows on Malisse's left, a day of bright, cold sunlight had followed a night of steadily falling snow. Melting frost dribbled down the outer surfaces of panes blasted with overwarmed air from within. As the radiator emitted a high-pitched whistle, Malisse dabbed his wet brow with a handkerchief. He, too, had begun to liquefy.

After a bit, Lembock drew erect in his chair, his fingertips parting ways to settle on the desktop.

"I've asked you here because something has come up," he said. "A potential problem."

The statement hardly rocked Malisse. For all its shared respect, theirs was not a social relationship.

"Fakery?" he said. "Theft?"

"It could be one, the other . . . or, I would wish, neither."

Malisse looked at him.

"I hope my ears are not too visibly perked," he said. "Else the hounds see me for a hare."

"Better the other way around, eh?"

"Best not to be seen at all in my game."

Lembock watched him a moment, then gave a calm little smile.

"I want to tell you what I know," he said, and motioned toward the ceiling with his head. "They are words I haven't yet shared with those above us."

Malisse considered a moment, then shrugged.

"My acrophobia keeps me from getting any closer to the

rooftop than our present height," he said. "This anxiety limits, as well, my direct contact with the Secretariat, and reinforces my choice to keep my professional dealings here at your level."

"So I trust we have an understanding?"

"Clear and absolute, yes."

"Then I'll get straight to it." Lembock inhaled, the everpresent rasp in his breath. "Somewhat over a year ago, a jewelry maker in Tel Aviv acquired a parcel of thirty-eight round-cut Ceylon blue sapphires from a New York broker, a member of the Club. They were small—each about four millimeters in size—but of high quality, weighing approximately a third of a carat each."

"Their GIA gradings?"

"Clarity was rated as VS Type Two . . . nearly flawless to the unaided eye. Color is a deep violetish blue, six-five saturation."

"Enhancements?"

"The typical blow heating done near Sri Lankan mines."

"They are Code E, then?"

"Yes."

"Very nice, if unremarkable," Malisse said. "What did they go for wholesale, do you know?"

"Two thousand five hundred dollars, U.S. currency."

Malisse grunted. Again, that seemed normal.

"You mentioned Sri Lanka," he said. "I would imagine, then, that the sapphires come from Ratnapuran gem mines. . . ."

Lembock shrugged.

"The source wasn't divulged," he said. "Of course, a broker is under no obligation to share that information."

"Understandable," Malisse said. "And a common policy, is it not?"

"Every middleman's worry is to be cut out of the process, their very warranted insecurity premised on being nonessential," Lembock said, nodding. "In the field, they are sometimes joked about in a disparaging way. Called *schnorrers*. Sponging, conniving beggars."

"Because their commission adds to the selling price."

"And on the simple theory that leaving them out of a sale reduces the price," Lembock said. "Most purchasers would rather bargain directly with the manufacturer. There is so much aggressive competition in the marketplace these days, so much pressure to best a rival dealer's lowest markdown, that it is becoming truer and truer to say this is also favored on the supply side . . . although many dealers still prefer to use brokerages."

Malisse thought for a moment, mopping himself with his handkerchief. There were, he knew, different reasons for that preference, all legitimate. Conditions of anonymity stipulated by collectors in antique and estate sell-offs, the simple lack of a sales, marketing, and distribution force by a gem producer . . . to name a couple.

"The sapphire transaction," he said. "What was unusual about it?"

"Nothing," Lembock said. "Aside from the broker being known chiefly as a trader of diamonds."

"Comparably graded merchandise?"

"Very," Lembock said. "Decent, but not close to the best." Malisse looked at him.

"Then there is either more going on than a broker's minor diversification, or you are losing me," he said.

"I'm not sure, Delano, that you are ever lost," Lembock said, and paused. "But I want to move ahead a half year or so to last June. Knowing he had to make a trip to New York, the broker contacts the same buyer to inquire if he is interested in another parcel of small round-cuts similar to the previous stones . . . this time offering several sapphires of a higher grade along with them. Ceylons again. VS Type Two. Again violet-blue, six-five saturation. This time they are between six and eight carat ovals. *No* enhancements . . . their Code N certifications guaranteed in a detailed laboratory report and a second evaluation by a highly accredited gemologist."

"Asking prices?"

"Twenty-five hundred dollars per carat. The largest sold for almost thirty thousand dollars."

"Quite a stride for the broker."

"Yes," Lembock said. "And what if I were to tell you he was also at the Miami bourse earlier that month for a delivery to a regular wholesale customer, his typical parcels of so-so diamonds . . . and that he showed that customer, in addition, a matched pair of blue and pink oval-cut sapphires? Top-notch, Ceylon, six carats each, priced in the neighborhood of two thousand per carat?"

Malisse lifted an eyebrow. "If you were to say that, I would begin to think it less likely our broker had stumbled upon a fluke one-time contact than found a new and steady source of merchandise. I would further have some thoughts about whether his strides, plural, had raised him into an entirely different league."

Lembock nodded.

"The Florida wholesaler reluctantly passed," he said. "Financial constraints prevented him from making the investment on speculation—without a resale to a jewelry maker or retailer lined up—but he was impressed, and asked whether he might keep our seller in mind should he have a need for those sapphires, or sapphires of that caliber, in the future. He offered to tell anyone else who might be in the market about the stones."

"An offer which, I take it, was accepted."

"With appreciation," Lembock said. "And seven months later, earlier this month, he *did* mention the broker to a close friend in Germany, a fellow wholesaler who'd won a high-end designer client with a consistent demand for select goods."

"Such selfless generosity to a competitor."

Another faint smile appeared on Lembock's face, crinkling the lines around his eyes.

"Our trade borders on the incestuous," he said. "Everyone knows somebody, who knows somebody else, who happens to know the first person, and has a fair chance of being married to his or her relative . . . and all this makes for very bankable assets."

"One hand washes the other."

Lembock gave another nod.

"As it turned out in this case, the friend's hand already had been washed."

"He *knew* of the broker?"

"From a common acquaintance, the Tel Aviv buyer I mentioned," Lembock said. "Moreover, our broker had just sold him an exquisite gem . . . one that put the matched ovals to shame."

"Sapphire again."

"*Padparadscha* sapphire," Lembock said. "Cushion-cut. Almost nine carats. Perfect symmetry, intense color saturation."

Malisse's eyebrow, which had remained raised, now bent to a sharply acute angle.

"It must have been worth—what?—fifty, sixty thousand dollars?"

"The stone sold for over *seventy-five*, our broker and purchaser meeting right here in Antwerp only days ago to finalize their deal."

Malisse formed a spout with his lips and exhaled a stream of air.

"How did you learn of it?" he said.

Lembock looked at him.

"The Miami dealer could see how a second-rate broker he'd known for many years might come upon several stones of real worth," he said with another of his dry little smiles. "Even a broker with a long and established *schnorrer* pedigree who had inherited most of his contacts from his father and grandfather, themselves having run a middling brokerage. But it stunned the dealer to hear he'd sold an exceedingly rare Padparadscha, a reaction that was heightened by his discovery of the Tel Aviv connection. And he muttered his disbelief to a colleague, who told his brother-in-law, who happens to be my great-niece's fiancé . . ."

Lembock let the sentence fade, shrugged his rail-thin shoulders. *In this trade everybody knows somebody, who knows somebody else.*

There was an extended silence. Malisse sat in deep thought, attempting to pull together the threads Lembock had dangled as a tease to his inquisitive mind. The radiator knocked insolently, a reminder that it was doing its best to melt him into a pool of sweat.

"The question I originally put to you was whether you'd whiffed fakery or theft," he said at last. "But it would seem impossible these stones could be counterfeit. Not unless their grading reports were forged or otherwise suspect."

"They are legitimate."

"You're convinced of this."

"Absolutely convinced."

"Then the probabilities are narrowed," Malisse said. "It can only be that your broker has found his way into either a trove of outstanding good fortune or the black market. Creating an authentic but *enhanced* sapphire that could slip past laboratory analysis is immensely difficult. All the harder to produce a single outright fake able to escape detection. I don't believe there's yet been a successful attempt, and would think the chances of it being done with multiple counterfeits, sapphires of different types and cuts, would be infinitesimal."

Lembock held up a bony hand to interrupt him.

"As we thought about color-enhancing diamonds until General Electric proved us wrong a decade ago," he said.

Malisse did not answer. Having caught Lembock's point, what could he truly say? Regiments of scientists employed by De Beers had taken five years before they came up with an advanced detection technology to catch up with the high-heat, high-pressure GE/POL enhancement method. Identification involved cryogenics—cooling a diamond to a temperature as close to absolute zero as possible, then, using expensive spectroscopes, looking for lightband shifts under argon and cadmium laser excitation, vacancies within the diamond's structure that contained a *single* nitrogen atom. . . . Malisse had studied the process for a considerable amount of time and hadn't managed to fully grasp what was involved.

He sat there thinking for another few seconds.

"If the client is asking the investigator whether he means to keep an open mind, then the investigator's reply is that he will . . . assuming he is entrusted with the case."

"Does he desire it?"

"Very much so."

Lembock looked at him.

"The broker's name is Avram Hoffman," he said.

"Is he still in Antwerp?"

"He's flown back to New York."

"And my airline and hotel reservations?"

"Have been made for the day after tomorrow," Lembock said.

Tom Ricci's head felt simultaneously light and full, as if his brain had been packed inside a thin foam liner. While he wasn't sure he liked the feeling, it did offer some relief. And Ricci had learned that he could appreciate something he needed, even be very grateful for it, without having to like it very much at all.

He stood under a working streetlight—a rarity on this Northside San Jose street—and studied the row of parallel parked cars along the curb, trying to remember where he'd left the Jetta. To his right, it was down the block to his right. Over by the public mailbox.

Ricci turned toward the car and fished around in a pants pocket for his keys. No footsteps in back of him yet, okey-doke. He was honestly thinking he could duck a confrontation he didn't want, make the night a complete success. And why examine too closely how he felt? Why push it? Too much of the time, far too much, Ricci's thoughts would come raging over the dam he'd built to contain them, and he'd feel a band of pressure spread across his forehead, and a throbbing in his temples, and terrible stabs of pain under the tops of his eye sockets—that pain below the brow radiating up and out to intensify the pressure at the sides of his head and then run multiple paths around the back of his skull to its base. Before long it would seem as if his entire head was locked inside a steel cage from the neck up, its bars red-hot and tight, and Ricci wouldn't know whether to curse his rampant thoughts for having put him in that hateful torture mask, or turn all his anger onto himself for leaving the floodgates unattended in the first place.

But at the moment he was doing okay, his brain nestled in

its soft cushion of foam. So say he felt grateful for that. Say he was relieved his thoughts hadn't rocked him with another agonizing blowout tonight, and then be wise enough to leave well-enough alone. Dig too deep and the poisoned water would come gushing from its reservoir again.

Ricci moved down the sidewalk toward his Volkswagen, the key chain out of his pocket, his finger on the button of its remote door opener. Only now he heard the slap of shoes on the pavement behind him and realized he'd been too confident of having gotten in the free and clear.

They had picked him up. There were dark store entrances along both sides of the street, service alleys, one broken streetlight after another with nothing but shadows underneath them . . . and the dive he'd just left probably had a side or back exit they could have slunk through just as he'd been heading out the front door. They had seemed like regulars, asinine, bored, and pathetic. They would know the shortcuts and places to hide, and see this as a chance to spice their dreary routine with some action. Unlike himself, of course.

Ricci increased his pace slightly, pressed the key-fob remote. His Jetta chirped, blinked its headlights and taillights as the locks and burglar alarm disengaged. He'd had reasons galore for not having taken a walk the moment he noticed a situation brewing. If none occurred to him right now, there must be a reason for that, too. Say he was focused on getting to his car, peeling off into the night with a squeal of tires and blast of tailpipe exhaust.

Ricci reached for the VW's doorhandle, missed, grabbed air instead. What the hell, it was dark out here, easy to short-arm it. He got hold of it on the second try, looked back up the block toward the sound of footsteps. They were coming toward him from maybe twenty feet away, a couple of body-builders with the cliff-top brows and widened jawlines of hardcore steroid abusers. Both of them probably pumped full of Equipoise or some spinoff muscle-mass enhancer formulated for three-thousand-pound farm horses and beef cattle. The tall one with tanning-parlor bronze skin and a mustache, his stockier pal wearing a short-sleeved shirt to display his hairy, bulked-up arms. Suntan was on the curb side of the row of parked cars. Hairy Arms in the street. Subtle tacticians, these guys.

A beater Ford sped past, Latino kids in head scarves hanging out its lowered windows, drumming their palms against its sides to loud pulses of hip-hop on its stereo. Ricci opened his door. The lugs who'd followed him weren't carrying hardware, nothing heavy anyway, or he'd have spotted it under the tight shirts and pants gripping their virile physiques. But a knife was easier to hide. So was a sap, or brass knuckles. Ricci knew he should have checked them out when he first realized they'd be a problem back in the dive, couldn't understand why he hadn't. What the hell.

He looked over his shoulder again, felt a sort of lag as he turned his head. Thick and full, wrapped in foam.

His guys were just a few cars down the curb and moving at a decent trot. No chance to pull away in the Jetta. He would need to scramble just to get behind the wheel before they caught up to him.

Ricci wasn't about to do that.

He held onto the doorhandle as they approached. Suntan sidling around the door to stand in front of him. Hairy Arms stepping around the mailbox onto the sidewalk and then hanging back around the front fender.

"Okay," Ricci said. His eyes on Suntan. "I think we should call it a night."

Suntan shook his head.

"It'll be okay when I decide," he said. "My old lady's no house show, blue boy."

Ricci looked at him. Blue Boy. Now they all had smart little nicknames for each other, though he supposed the guy's darling had coined that one. Blond, a tight figure, she'd slid up next to Ricci while he'd been on his stool waiting for a refill, given him a practiced eyebrow flash, hair swish, and flirty smile. Then she momentarily leaned close, held her arm out next to his, and remarked how his navy-blue shirt matched the shade of her blouse . . . except the word she'd used for the articles of clothing in question was "tops." *Nice how our tops fit together, isn't it?* Swaying her body to the music on the jukebox, moving still closer, her hand brushing Ricci's at the edge of the counter. Her come-on pretend sexy, like an imitation of a bad television acting job.

This was Northside, though. Nowhere to come in search of true romance.

The blonde was good-looking in her overdone way, and it had been a long while for Ricci, and he'd felt an itch to take what she was offering. But he'd remembered seeing her hanging all over Suntan in a booth at the other end of the place, figured her for the type who would thrill on playing guys against each other, and reconsidered. So he just kind of smiled at her, said something neutral—yeah, sure, nice— and went back to leaning over his glass at the counter, assuming that would be the end of it.

Except it wasn't. She had gone out of her way to make eye contact with Ricci later on from over in her booth. More than once. And if he'd been able notice her from across the room, Suntan would have noticed from right alongside her, where he'd had his hand grafted to her breast.

Ricci guessed she'd been better at the game than either of them.

"You don't want to make this mistake," he said now. His tongue had a problem with the s's, stretching them out and running them together. "Don't want to get into it with me."

Suntan's response was to inch closer. Behind Ricci on the pavement, Hairy Arms had done the same to block his retreat, corner him between the side of the car and its partially open door. What was next according to the tired script?

As Suntan bulled forward at the car door, meaning to shove it against him with both outthrust hands, body-slam him with the door, Ricci caught hold of its inner handle, beating him to it by an instant, pushing the door outward with all his strength. Suntan staggered back, hands going to his middle, the wind knocked out of him. Ricci started to slip out of the space where he was wedged between the car and door, wanting to follow through immediately, get on top of Suntan before he could recover. But then he felt a blow on the side of his face under the cheekbone, saw an explosive flash of brightness, and knew through the thunder and lightning that he'd been sucker punched from behind. Hairy Arms, son of a bitch. He'd landed a solid one.

Ricci's mouth filled with the salty taste of blood. Careless, sloppy. Why hadn't he been ready? Goddamned son of a bitch.

Hairy Arms stepped in for another swing, but this time Ricci could see it coming. He dropped his head, turned on him, grabbed his wrist with both hands. Then he jerked it down hard, snapped it up again with an equally sharp twist, moving around behind him, holding on to his wrist with one hand, sliding the other down to his elbow, wrenching his arm high up against his back. Hairy Arms grunted in pain but didn't unclench his fingers. Keeping the guy's body between himself and Suntan, his arm still twisted high, Ricci bent his wrist back as far as he could and, as the fist finally sprang open, pushed him against the mailbox and banged his forehead down twice on its metal hood. Hairy Arms hung half-limp over the mailbox a moment and Ricci drove his head down a third time with the heel of his hand so his whole face smashed into it. The bridge of his nose twisted and gashed, blood streaming from his nostrils, he let out another grunt of pain and then fell forward onto the pavement and didn't move.

With his friend collapsed there in a heap, Suntan came charging around him, chin tucked low behind his club fists. Ricci knew he had room to pivot and kick on several different planes, deliver a snap under his upraised arms to his abdomen, a roundhouse over them to his neck, but there was no steadiness in his legs, no balance, nothing to trust at all, and he realized he'd have to count on the likelihood that Suntan would have similar problems for similar reasons. They'd both spent the last few hours doing the same thing in the same squalid dump.

Ricci stood facing Suntan until his lunge had almost brought them into collision, and then sidestepped at the final instant, grabbing his shirt behind the collar with his right hand, and also somewhere lower down between the shoulders with his left, yanking the material in opposite directions as he got his hip out in front of Suntan's waist, using his own momentum to throw him off his feet. As Suntan bellied down on the pavement, Ricci drove his shoe into his spine right around the small of the back, crouched, flipped him over, and straddled his chest, pounding him on the jaw with a right cross, a left, then bringing up his fist and punching him straight-on in the mouth.

Suntan's head rolled backward on the concrete, his eyes half shut, his upper lip split and bloodied.

Ricci bunched his shirt collar in both hands, hauled his shoulders off the ground.

"Look at me," he said, and shook him hard.

Suntan groaned through lips spattered with red foam, his eyelids still drooping.

Ricci shook him.

"I told you to look at me," he said.

Suntan managed to open his eyes a little wider, bring their pupils into bleary focus.

"I could break you apart right here," Ricci said. "Do anything I want to you."

Suntan looked at him without making a sound.

Ricci pulled him up higher, closer. Pulled him up off the sidewalk until their faces almost touched.

"I'm nobody you ever want to see again," he said. "Nobody."

Suntan's mouth worked, produced an unintelligible sound, blood and saliva spilling down over his chin. At last he quit on trying to form the word and simply nodded.

Ricci stared down at his battered face another moment, his eyes steady. Then he released the front of his shirt to let him drop back onto the pavement, rose, got into his car, and keyed the ignition.

His fingers closed around the steering wheel, jittered around the wheel. A breath, Ricci thought. He just needed to take a breath. He felt dull, nauseous, light-headed. The inside of his cheek was torn where he'd caught the hit from Hairy Arms. He probed the area with his tongue and an upper molar wobbled against its tip.

Ricci sat pulling air into his chest, swallowing it in deep gulps. That didn't make things better. Maybe it was his adrenaline level falling, he didn't know. But it had never happened to him before, not like this. His trembling hands. The weakness. The fog in his head.

Ricci reached for the clutch. He didn't care whether somebody found him sitting where he was and called the cops. Didn't care what they'd make of it at UpLink, especially Rollie Thibodeau and Megan Breen the Ice Queen. Nor did he care whether the two big boppers scraped themselves off the sidewalk and came at him again. But he felt that if he stayed there in the car and didn't move, he would just kind of fade out until he wasn't there anymore. That he would start sinking inward, collapse in on himself without being able to stop.

He had to move, right now, or he wouldn't.

His hands still trembling, Ricci backed up, put the car in drive, and without checking traffic, stepped heavily on the accelerator and pulled away.

FOUR

MEGAN BREEN SHOT OFF A CRISP COMBINATION OF blows. Left jab, right cross, left hook.

"So how'm I doing, Pete?" she said, and took a deep breath.

Nimec looked at her from behind one of the 150-pound heavy bags in his boxing gym, spotting her, holding the bag close to his chest with both hands.

"Sounds like you've got this New York deal on your mind," he said.

Megan pounded the bag with another combo.

"I don't get you," she said.

"The ex-mayor's slogan," Nimec said. " 'How'm I do-ing?' He was famous for it over there."

"I thought his claim to fame was dancing on stage with the Rockettes."

Nimec grunted, unsure. Wasn't that a longstanding tradition in the Big Apple, something like the Hasty Puddings, with those Harvard students putting on skits for each other in drag? But who knew. Showtime politicians tired him, and Ivy Leaguedom was outside his realm. All he could say was that guys strutting around in sequins and hose wouldn't have gone down too well in the South Philly pool parlor where he'd gotten his uncommon version of an education, flashing a cue stick like Paul Newman's fictional Fast Eddie Felson in *The Hustler* . . . absent the Hollywood-idol good looks.

He watched Megan work away in her gloves, pushing tempo. Left hook, right cross, uppercut. Jab, cross, jab. She stood flat-footed while attacking the bag, feinting, bobbing, feeling no need to practice her one-two shuffle for what was mainly a strength and stamina drill.

It was now six-thirty A.M. on Monday morning, and the sun had yet to rise outside the windows of the upper-level rec/training course in Nimec's triplex condo, where Megan had arrived exactly half an hour earlier for the first of her regular twice-a-week sessions. Besides the fully equipped gym with its regulation fight ring, this floor-wide modular facility contained a martial arts dojo, a state-of-the-art computerized shooting range, and, not of the least importance to Nimec, a reproduction of the sordid old pool hall of his memories, accurate to its grimy light fixtures and cigarette burns on the baize.

Pleased by the solid thumping impact of Megan's blows against his body, Nimec glanced at the mirrored wall to their right to check her stance.

"You still have to keep those elbows in closer to your sides, set up quicker for the comeback," he said. "But there's more snap to your punches. You're committing better."

"Being the best Megan I can be," she said with a flicker of eye contact.

"*Those* words unintentional, too?"

"Nope," she said. Cross, hook, cross. "But you wondered what's on my mind this morning, and that's it."

Nimec braced the bag against himself.

"Oh," he said. "Wanting to be the best's a good thing."

Her lips pulling tight across her teeth, the muscles of her neck standing out, Megan slammed in an explosive overhand right that wobbled Nimec back a little. Then she paused in her tank top and workout shorts and gave him a long look, wiping perspiration off her forehead with her arm.

"Quit the knucklehead act, Pete, you know what I mean," she said, breathing hard. "We've come pretty far from where we were, haven't we?"

"With our plans."

"Promises."

Nimec looked at her, nodded.

"So far," he said, "so good."

She smiled at him. He smiled back. And they held an easy silence for a while, attuned to each other's thoughts, sharing a single recollection, these old friends whose unbreakable bond of trust had been forged through painful trial and costly triumph, who had together stood against more dangers than they wished to count, who would lay down their lives for each other without a moment's hesitation.

It had been back in Antarctica, a world removed from where they were now in more ways than could be quantified merely in terms of time, distance, or even environment. An inexpressibly *alien* world. They'd stood outside Cold Corners, the UpLink research station on the ice where Megan had served as base commander, a few days after Nimec and his makeshift rescue team had freed two of its personnel, Alan Scarborough and Shevaun Bradley, from their hostage-takers in a subterranean network of outlawed uranium mines and rad dumps. In the wake of a cosmic disturbance, the southern aurora had been putting on a spectacular display, the heavens awash with color in the polar nightfall.

It was, as Megan put it to him, the solar storm's last hurrah. And although forty-eight hours remained before Nimec would wing back to civilization aboard an LC-130 Hercules transport, leaving Megan behind for the duration of her winter-over stint, it was also when they had exchanged their true farewells, aware their remaining time together would be consumed by operational matters. There had been some preliminary banter, some gazing at the aurora overhead—the lights cascading in sheets of red and orange, wheeling like purple daisies, taking soaring, curling plunges through the atmosphere in peacock-green combers.

"So," Megan had asked. This just moments after she'd informed him of having phoned the airbase in New Zealand to confirm his pickup. "What's first for Pete Nimec when he gets home?"

"A call of his own," he'd said. "And then a ride in his hot Corvette."

"That call . . . would it be to a certain lady astronaut in Houston?"

The lady in question was Annie Caulfield. Once bitten by a failed marriage, twice shy of opening himself to another emotional entanglement, Nimec had foolishly let her slip away from him after the budding weeks of their relationship, and would almost surely never have gotten a second chance were it not for Megan's intervention . . . a bit of artful romantic splicing that she dismissed to this day as having been unintentional, or at least blown out of all proportion.

Standing there layered in extreme-cold-weather garb, Nimec had given her a slow affirmative nod, and then jokingly wondered aloud why she hadn't had any follow-up questions about his car. She'd just shrugged him off and told him she had limited areas of interest, or words to that effect, as if the question of his contacting Annie had been something tangential she'd just happened to wonder about on the spot.

"Okay," he'd said, steam puffing from his nose and mouth. "Your turn. What's next for Megan Breen?"

"A very dark and cold Antarctic winter," she said. "After which she expects to turn the reins of Cold Corners over to her second in command, and resume practicing her fisticuffs with a certain trusted fight guru and best pal in San Jose."

Nimec had kept staring up at the wondrous display in the sky.

"Six more months here for you," he said.

"Yes."

"Seems like a long time."

"Time enough to make myself the best Megan Breen I can be."

"Sounds like an army recruitment commercial."

"A line that works is a line that works, so why feel obliged to be original?"

Nimec had smiled under his balaclava and put his arm around her shoulder. Megan had put her arm around his waist. And they had stood with their eyes raised to the sky as the magical lights had soared defiantly through the falling gloom.

That was over a year and a half ago.

Since then Nimec and Annie had become husband and wife, and Megan had succeeded Roger Gordian as chief executive officer of UpLink International at the urging of no lesser personage than Gordian himself, these transitions unfolding, if not quite in an eye-blink, then faster than either of them would have ever supposed . . . had they been able to imagine them occurring at all.

Now Nimec realized he was still holding the heavy bag in his gym. He let go of it, stepped out from behind, and looked at Megan.

"Things've changed a lot," he said.

"Yes," she said. "*We've* changed."

"You like it where you are?"

Megan looked thoughtful.

"I'm not Gord. I can't try to be. But I'm proud to have his confidence," she said. "Every day's another challenge, and if it wasn't for Antarctica, I'm not sure I'd be prepared. But being there taught me patience. I think it helped teach me how to lead." She smiled. "Those polies were characters. Especially the longtimers. You know what I mean, Pete."

He smiled a little, too.

"Yeah," he said, remembering. "I do."

Megan hesitated.

"Volunteering to live in a freezer box for a year or more isn't for your ordinary man or woman," she said. "Reupping for a second tour, or returning for several . . . you need to be a bird of a different color. It shames me to admit it, but my first impression when I got to Cold Corners was that I'd been shipped off to oversee a colony of two hundred misfits and rejects. That sense of things didn't last long, though. It couldn't. They showed too much heart. Too much goodness. I found them to be an inspiring bunch. True, courageous, resourceful, selfless."

"*And* misfits."

"Boastfully," she said. "That was a lesson right there . . . learning to accept people for who they are and make the most of their differences, rather than judge them by my predetermined expectations. And I really can't say it was the hardest lesson, Pete."

"You want to tell me what was?"

"I could list a few that would rate," she said. "But right up top is that I'd been using myself as a standard for those expectations without examining my own flaws. And realizing I had some very serious ones."

Nimec considered a moment, shrugged.

"Funny," he said. "I always figured you for perfect."

Megan smiled.

"Relax, Pete," she said. "I may have become your boss in title, but you're still my shining knight in fact."

"Sure," he said.

"Sure," she said, looking straight at him.

They stood in silence for a few seconds.

"How about you telling me something now?" Megan said.

Nimec shrugged.

"I suppose it'd make us even," he said. "And get you back to the bag."

"You brought up the New York matter," she said. "I'd like your feelings about it."

Another shrug.

"Ask me after our vid conference with Noriko Cousins in a couple hours and they might be clearer," he said. "We've got somebody who could be a roaming husband, a guy in a jam, or an undiscovered body. Gord wants us to look into it as a favor to his friend Lenny Reisenberg, fine. I know Lenny some and he's okay. If we could check things out for him, pass along a tip or two, I'd be all right with it."

"But you aren't."

"Noriko's got her eye on what could be export violations at Armbright. She feels she's right on track and has concerns about having her wheels knocked off. That *could* happen if we get caught sticking our fingers where they don't belong."

"The Case of the Vanishing Husband, you mean."

Nimec gave her a nod.

"Those briefs she e-mailed over the weekend . . . you have a chance to look at the ones I forwarded?"

"Not enough to sound like an authority," Megan said. "Probably enough to have an idea why Noriko might be uncomfortable. Her intel suggests Armbright's been very aggressive with its high-energy laser development program."

"At least a couple of years ahead of our timetable," Nimec said. "Way ahead of what they've got going at Rheinmetall Weapons and Munitions in Germany, or anything the military's tested at White Sands. But for me the yellow flags aren't only waving on a business front. Armbright's laser research went into overdrive when it bought up the Kiran Group. And Kiran's top man . . . this Hasul Benazir . . ."

"Had some ill-chosen associations when he was younger, I know," Megan said. "Except who hasn't, Pete? They seem to begin and end with his early college days. He's made no secret of them and has a long-term business visa, which wouldn't have been awarded without extensive background checks. Talk about UpLink minding its own affairs, it's not up to us to second-guess the INS. And there are at least two major government regulatory bodies overseeing export controls."

"So you're saying . . . ?"

"Just what I did at the start . . . that I wanted a sense of how you're leaning initially before Noriko gives me an earful at the conference." Megan spread her arms. "It's a sensitive issue. There's no question Kiran's operations warrant continued awareness and review from a purely competitive standpoint, and Noriko's position is that looking for hubby could disrupt her work, or in a worst-case scenario blow things for her. I know she'll oppose it, try to sway us toward backing off, even use stall tactics if I give her the chance."

Nimec gave a nod.

"It'd be like Noriko," he said. "She feels we're going to roll over her, she'll do whatever she can to flatten our tires."

"Which leaves me to figure out how to satisfy Gord *and* address her concerns. Find an approach that makes every-body feel accommodated, if not altogether happy—"

Nimec's WristLink timer beeped, interrupting her. He held up a finger, looked at its display.

It was a quarter to six.

"Ten minutes till I need to get the kids shaking for school," he said. "Want to stick around after your session and have breakfast with us? You can leave your car down in the garage, ride along when I drop them off. Then we can pick up on this subject on our way to the office."

Megan nodded.

"Sounds great," she said. "But please tell me Chris isn't going to ask for my hand in marriage again. Because it's hard to reject a proposal gracefully with bits of scrambled egg caught between my teeth."

"Don't worry, I'm serving buttermilk pancakes." Nimec glanced at the lighted floor indicator above the elevator, then gestured toward its door with his head. "Anyway, you'll have the chance to find if he still loves you in a second . . . looks like the little gym rat's out of bed and coming up to join us."

Lately Avram had been conscious of the hallway mirrors. Conscious of them to an unsettling extreme, and for no rea-son he could figure out. True, they were everywhere around him. They paneled the walls to his left and right as he walked through the building's doors. They hung above the guard platform by the elevators, mounted in the corners of the ceiling, concave, silvery, angled downward like inscrutable metallic eyes. They were kept clean and polished, without the merest trace of smudges, dust, or fingerprints. On cloudless mornings such as this one, they would catch the sunlight that came spilling in from the street and bounce it between them to give the corridor a brighter feel, an illusion of space that made the walls seem less pressing and constrictive than they really were.

First and foremost, Avram realized, the mirrors had been installed for purposes of safety. They aided the steady vigilance of Jeffreys, the ground-floor security man, and allowed those who approached the elevators to see what was going on around them, warn them of anything suspicious at their backs. But the stories above were layered with surveillance mechanisms—overt and circumspect—and Avram couldn't recall a single instance of a serious breach having occurred in the building's long history.

As he passed through the entrance from the sidewalk for what was only his third time since flying back into town, Avram again found himself glancing over the mirrored wall, almost as if it were a new addition to the corridor. It was odd, very odd, and hard to understand. In this fixture of stubborn constancy the slightest change was viewed as a concession, and each step forward brought a dose of the familiar that Avram might have expected would dull him to his surroundings. In recent months, however, things had been just the opposite. Avram had probed his mind for an explanation, focused on the obvious possibilities, and ruled them out. He harbored no guilt over his choices. Not a kernel. None. And he hadn't for a minute. Of course he was only human and couldn't deny his increased stress over the recent gambles he'd taken . . . but in his occupation that went along with the terrain, and Avram thought he was better-than-average at handling it.

This building, this *institution*, was for him associated mostly with feelings of comfort and stability. Connected to his formative memories in a thousand ways, it was an inseparable part of his life, and had been since he'd been brought here on regular childhood visits by his father and uncles. These days, so many years later, he was accustomed to coming four, sometimes five mornings a week. Even diminished, the Club carried an influence that was felt worldwide. What went on within its walls imparted a sense of rock-steady continuity.

Why, then, should even a glance at one or another of the mirrors have such an effect on him? It was incomprehensible. Still, Avram would at times glimpse his reflection and halt in mid stride, pausing to wonder over the expression on his face—how it seemed overtaken by a sort of puzzled, disoriented surprise. At other times he might feel an abrupt reversal of perspective, as if he'd switched places with his mirror image. For a span of several heartbeats, he would *become* Avram the Reflection. Detached, two dimensional, without substance, he would manage to hold on to a vague, nameless recognition of the physical form he'd quit, sharing the intense confusion so evident on its features. That person, if not quite a stranger to this scene, seemed at least of questionable identity, bound to draw attention from Jeffreys, and provoke uncertain, even resentful, looks from members of the crowd gathering by the elevator door. Where was he from? Who did he intend to see? Was he trustworthy? Reliable? Beyond all else, did he *belong*?

Now Avram tore his eyes from the mirror, aware he'd been captured by its brightly gleaming surface again. That he'd lost a few seconds, stopped midway down the hall amid the procession heading toward the elevator. It had happened again, and the jarring realization made his chest feel a little clenched. Could the pressures he was under be taking a greater subconscious toll than he'd suspected? He supposed it was possible. Look at what had been going on with him, his change of fortune. Everything *had* accelerated, gathering a pace and momentum of its own. And there were new risks involved, measured as they might be.

Avram pulled a deep breath through his mouth. Whatever the cause of his episodes, he thought, he'd be okay. Mentally and physically. All things considered, Avram took reasonable care of his health, and at forty-seven years old assumed he'd enjoy many more decades of good living. Anxiety attacks should be the worst of his problems, he'd be back to normal in a minute. Fully Avram the Flesh-and-Blood. And he would go on with his customary routine.

A second inhalation, another, and Avram moved on toward the end of the hallway. He gave old Jeffreys a nod, was wished a good morning in return, approached the elevator. Then he abruptly swung back around to the security platform. He'd almost forgotten to tell the guard about a visitor who'd be coming to see him, and appointments didn't often escape his memory.

Avram supposed he wasn't *quite* himself again. Not yet. Absentmindedness wasn't one of his usual shortcomings.

"What can I do for you today, Mr. Hoffman?" Jeffreys asked pleasantly from his stool.

A light-skinned black man in his sixties who knew most of the regulars waiting outside the elevator by name, and the rest by sight, he'd been at his post more than thirty years, a fixture within a fixture. Avram had been a teenager when they were first introduced, Jeffreys younger in those days than he himself was now.

"I'm expecting an important guest in about an hour. Ten-fifteen, ten-thirty," he said. "Mr. Katari has trouble with the language, and might need help finding his way upstairs to the Club. He's Ethiopian . . . well, an Ethiopian-Israeli. . . ."

Jeffreys offered him a wry wink, a smile, and then pinched the pecan-colored skin of his left wrist with his right hand.

"A little piece'a yours, a little piece'a mine, huh?" he said.

It took Avram a second to catch the guard's meaning. His brief lapse, or fugue, or whatever his breathless spell at the mirror might be called, really had left him out of sorts.

"Right," he said at last, and returned the smile. "That's exactly right."

Jeffreys slipped a pen from the breast pocket of his gray uniform shirt.

"This fella . . . he spell his name K-A-T-A-R-I?"

Avram nodded.

"I'll leave a note right here, see he gets to you 'case I step out for a minute," Jeffreys said, scribbling a reminder in the visitors' book.

Avram thanked him, heard the elevator arrive, and hurried to join the dozen or so men crowding inside. Again, he exchanged familiar hellos.

Then he pressed the tenth-floor button and the car started upward with a bump, creaking on pulleys and hoist cables that had seen better days, but nonetheless continued doing the work for which they were built as if age, wear, and rust weren't actually problems at all.

• • •

His eyes on the floor numbers above the ascending elevator, Jeffreys reached for his phone on the wooden podium that passed for a guard station in the hallway's close quarters. The smile he'd shown Avram Hoffman was gone, but like a strip of tape peeled from his mouth it had left a lingering hurt on him.

He hoped his expression didn't show how much pain he felt inside right now.

Jeffreys had known Avram since he was in school. He remembered his late father, Jacob, bragging about his yeshiva grades, and his scholarship to that big college uptown, Columbia University. He remembered Jacob looking so proud of him all the time, coming in with that stack of photos from his year as an exchange student in Israel. The people in this building, and the ones who belonged to the Club in particular . . . it was fair to say pride was the rack they hung their hats on. What they valued more than anything. Some of them were almost like family to Jeffreys. Sure, there were plenty of characters—the slick, fast-talking millionaires at one end, the crapped-out losers who were always asking favors, riding the backs of their successful friends and relatives at the other. If you got wind of their stories, it could be funny. There was competition, feuds that went on for years. One guy saying another guy's only doing good because he's a rotten conniver, the second guy calling the first guy a jealous nitwit, both of them getting on a third guy's case for whatever reason. He's this, he's that, and did you hear what he did to so-and-so? A real kick, listening to them go at it sometimes. But there were the *serious* stories, too, the ones that'd gotten Jeffreys to truly respect these folks. Stories about what they'd accomplished, how they built something out of nothing. How they'd come to this country as refugees after they were chased from more countries than you could begin to count. Russia, maybe a hundred years ago. Near all of Europe in the Second World War. Generations of them coming to America with just the clothes on their backs, driven from their lands, their homes left behind, everything they'd owned burned, wrecked, or stolen. So many losing their loved ones to the gas chambers and ovens in those Nazi death camps.

Jeffreys respected these people for what they'd made of themselves. Respected how they could keep their own house clean, keep it *right*, and not have to look outside for police, lawyers, and courtroom judges to settle their affairs. If it was going to last, honor and trust had to mean something here. Had to hold on strong here. Those values started to break down, Jeffreys figured the end was in sight. They could take a wrecking ball to the building, fill the dusty hole it left on the street with some modern skyscraper a hundred stories tall, where there'd be room for a proper guard station near the entrance instead of his tight spot atop a riser near the elevator. Because the heart and soul would be taken out of the place, lost, and it'd be nothing but a sad reminder of what it used to be. Part of a story that started with the words *once upon a time*.

Jeffreys liked Avram, knew all his relatives, his wife and kids. He didn't want to cause him any grief. Smile to his face, put the screws into him from behind. But his job wasn't always about sitting on the wooden stool that'd given him so much trouble with bleeding piles and backaches over the years. He shook its tougher responsibilities, Jeffreys figured he might as well apply for retirement benefits. While none of the men who wrote his paychecks had come right out and told him what Avram was up to, or what they thought he might be up to, it was clear they had suspicions he'd got his hands into some bad shit.

Jeffreys sighed and made his call, cradling the telephone receiver between his neck and shoulder.

The Belgian snoop answered on his first ring. Jeffreys tipped the guy off like he'd arranged and hung up, the call taking maybe half a minute, but leaving behind a crummy feeling that would stay with him for a long time afterward.

Bad shit, this was, he thought. Serious bad. And he was afraid there would be a whole pile more in the offing . . . enough to throw its stink around the world and back again before everything was said and done.

Avram wasn't surprised to find himself getting off on the tenth floor alone. In years gone by, the elevator would have emptied out here. But change came to everything, like it or not. No man, no institution, was impervious.

Passing the guard booth with a wave to the two uniformed men behind its bullet-resistant window, Avram turned left, swiped his identification card through the turnstile reader, stepped into a bare entry foyer, and then inserted the card into a second reader to unlock a door bracketed by overhead closed-circuit surveillance cameras.

Once past the door he moved into the main hall, an expansive space with floor-to-ceiling windows facing north and south, and rows of plain cafeteria-style tables extending lengthwise from the walls. Although the loudspeaker was presently silent, and the queue of telephones to either side of the central aisle idle, a handful of men were already scattered about the room, pushing glassine packets at each other across bare tabletops. Others were moving toward the end of the aisle, which split to the left and right beyond a second enclosed booth. Most were thickly bearded Hasidic Jews clad in long black coats and wide black hats. Three or four wore conventional office attire like Avram himself, whose goatee was moderate and stylishly trimmed, and whose only clear outward sign of religious orthodoxy was the small yarmulke clipped to the crown of his head.

Avram started down the main aisle after them. God forbid if those men were ever in positions to judge him. They would be appalled, accuse him of *falsche frumkeit*—false orthodoxy—as he was excoriated for how he'd been carrying on. And his self-righteous uncles would share their condemnation, eyes bulging with blind outrage, words of scorn pouring from their mouths. But what did any of them know? They were complacent, anchored in the past. The small traders in particular. Look at their losses, the hits they'd taken in the market. They had refused to chart its trends, adjust on the move, and instead did nothing but complain. The sight-holders had been undermined by the cartel, they'd blathered. Pipelines were being choked, supplies cut, the middleman shut out.

Avram had heard the dour laments repeated many times over, listened to them blame their predicaments on currents beyond their control, pointing fingers this way and that, even at each other, as their ships took on water and went under—and their fatalistic attitudes had largely carried over to Avram's generation. It was the same in Antwerp. In Tel Aviv. There was no helping any of them. Not while they were governed by a timid unwillingness to deviate from an outmoded, absolutist code.

That was their biggest mistake in Avram's view . . . the attachment to moral and ethical definitions that no longer applied, and probably never had in reality. Morality in business was a joke. A lie of convenience, concocted by the big man to keep the little man down. Business was opportunistic, *amoral*. Where was the inherent virtue in scraping to survive? Since when did failure get anyone respect? Was Avram supposed to believe that every miserable wretch he'd seen patted on the back for his success had some hidden nugget of goodness in his heart? Surrender to the tug of obsolete ways, swallow the lie, and you were guaranteed to fall right on your face. *There* was the most ignoble sin in business. His tapping into a new wellspring of profit would kill no one.

Avram passed the second glass enclosure, an intentional step or two behind the small group of men who'd filed into the hallway branching to its right. For him its separation from the rest of the floor was clear evidence of the dividing line between moral probity and material necessity. Yet he was sure none of them—not a single *one*—shared his appreciation of that symbolism. Avram could only begin to imagine the quakes of scandal that would rock these halls if they somehow learned what he was doing. He'd be expelled, blackballed, his family reputation soiled with disgrace . . . which was why he'd have to make sure they were never obliged with that knowledge.

In the cloakroom, Avram hung his overcoat on the wall and took the velveteen pouch that contained his prayer shawl and set of phylacteries from the shelf above it. Then he went out the door and moved on toward the boxy little synagogue chapel farther down the passage.

As was usual these days, Avram saw barely the minimum ten men required by Jewish law for the commencement of services. At nine-fifteen in the morning, it was still too early for the younger sellers, a majority of whom did not even come to the bourse on a regular schedule anymore. Meanwhile the older men who still did their mingling and dealing in the hall outside were for the most part in no hurry to arrive before noon—and those who were observant could conduct their daily morning prayers in shuls closer to home.

Being a broker, Avram mused, his leanings fell somewhere in between.

Now he draped his prayer shawl over his shoulders and donned the phylacteries, or tefillin—two square leather boxes made from the hide of kosher animals, fastened to black leather straps and containing sanctified parchment scrolls inscribed with verses from the Torah. He put one on the underside of his left arm and the other on his forehead, and then quietly recited the appropriate blessings from memory.

Even as he'd begun to wind the straps around himself in the prescribed manner, Avram had made an effort to push aside the worldly thoughts with which he'd entered the chapel. A reminder of one's dedication to God, binding body and soul to His will, the laying of phylacteries required the commandments associated with it to be fulfilled. But was it worldly to consider that the stone tablets into which Moses chiseled the law of the covenant had been made of sapphire from the top of Mount Sinai? And that, according to Rashi, the most eminent of Biblical commentators, God had given the *p'solet*, castoff chips of the carving, to Moses as a precious gift that would bring him and his heirs lasting wealth? The holiest of artifacts given to man had thus come with considerations of worldly value.

But Avram wasn't a theologian. Bent to his prayers before the Arc, he didn't know whether to oust those thoughts from his mind or ponder them. And yet he wouldn't deny they were there, along with his desire to reconcile his constant fear of Heaven and equally constant hunger for the material.

As with the rest of the goals he'd dared to reach for, Avram was determined to find a way to get everything he wanted, and then live with himself as well as he could.

• • • •

Malisse would have preferred to start with Plan B and move on from there. Not just today, but on every assignment he accepted. Hurried or unhurried, he saw his plan of first resort as nothing more than a necessary stage-setting prelude, a rough draft of a work in progress—and with fair cause. Nine times out of ten, Plan A was either deficient or a complete waste. Over the course of his four years as a private investigator, and his twelve prior to that with the Belgian Secret Service, he'd found out that no matter how much thought and effort one put into it, how assured one felt of its perfection, there would be unforseen impediments, pitfalls that found the feet, mistakes looming around the bend that would be revealed only when stumbled upon and confronted. So strongly did Malisse feel about his creed that he had preached it relentlessly and zealously to the young, inexperienced agents who'd fallen under his tutelage in the *Sûreté de L'Etat*. And always he'd been asked by some callow recruits: If Plan A is a kink in the system, predetermined to go awry, why not skip it altogether, put one's best leg forward, and launch an operation with the honed backup contingency? To which he would point out the question's obvious logical flaw. Things must start at the beginning. The elimination of Plan A would simply move Plan B up in order of commencement, hence virtually damning it to failure by turning *it* into Plan A, Plan C into the new Plan B, and so forth. The wheel turned as it would.

In plotting his investigations, Malisse took a Darwinistic approach; in teaching students how to correctly go about them, his method was Socratic. Would it have been better if the lung arose before the gill? he'd sometimes asked to elicit discourse from the lads. Certainly it was the more efficient breathing organ. But how would the first amphibian have fared had not fish preceded it on evolution's ladder? What could it have done, poor creature, but drown in the salty darkness of some primeval sea? On that sequential glitch, that missed link, as it were, the genesis of terrestrial life would have been brought to a full stop. The frog, the snake, the rodent and higher mammals, none would have ever come into existence. Mankind would have been an undreamt dream. And so it was with the investigative probe: It must proceed in orderly stages or else was destined to falter and fizzle.

Malisse's small minority of sharp-witted, committed freshmen had taken this lesson to heart and remained splendid and miserably underpaid field operatives throughout their careers; the greater percentage of them, scoffing mediocrities, had gotten promotions to comfortable desk jobs in the *Sûreté*'s bureaucratic hierarchy.

To each man, his own rewards, Malisse supposed.

Now he sat by himself in the Starbucks café on West 47th Street off Sixth Avenue, drinking a Caramel Macchiato, dipping and taking an occasional bite of his chocolate éclair, and observing the street outside the window with characteristic diligence, inferior as this spot might be. The beverage had nicely warmed his insides while no doubt further eating away at the already eroded lining of his duodenum, aggravating his peptic ulcers—benign despite their burning pain, his doctors had assured—with its high concentration of sugary syrup and caffeine. But it was nine-thirty in the morning, and Malisse's insatiable sweet tooth awoke when he did at the crack of dawn, as did his craving for tobacco. The latter remained unassuaged, since smokers in America, and this city in particular, were not only stigmatized by their habit, but heavily taxed and penalized, a legal harassment that left them with nowhere to have a cigarette except the streets and, presumably, their own toilets. Saloons, too, were off limits . . . what was the point of ordering a cocktail, he wondered, if not to delight in puffing a Gitanes or Dunhill between swallows? Malisse didn't understand—was he not right now in the celebrated land of the free? He'd even had to settle for a non-smoking room at his hotel, all others having been occupied. Thank heaven for the consolation of his hot beverage, and the éclair, which was his self-prescribed method of soaking up some of its acids.

He sat, sipped, dipped, and watched the early-bird buyers and sellers head toward their retail stores, street-level market booths, and offices here on what was known as Jewelry Way. Hasidic males dominated the center, although not to the exclusion of women or any other group. Sprinkled among them were secular Jews, Asians, Africans, Australians . . . Malisse knew there were traders of every nation, religion, and ethnicity passing between the diamond lampposts at the north and south sides of the block over on Sixth. Might the Katari gentleman of whom he'd been told be among them? Moreover, he wondered, would Katari prove integral or irrelevant to his probe? Time and persistence would tell.

Regarding his main player of interest, Malisse wished he could have found a superior vantage from which to monitor Avram Hoffman's arrival at the Diamond Dealers Club this morning, the third of his open-ended surveillance. In the days since Malisse had followed Hoffman from Antwerp to New York—an affair that entailed some hurried packing, a shaky trip aboard an F50 prop, and a nearly missed connection at Heathrow—what surer formula for jet-lagged exhaustion?—he'd stayed close to the DDC entrance down at the corner of Fifth Avenue, remaining out on the street, browsing storefront displays, dawdling at newspaper stands, and generally weaving his way through and among the crowd. Cold as it was, he'd been able to keep the building's doors in easy sight and incidentally enjoy an occasional cig-arette . . . reminding himself of the murderous heat of Rance Lembock's office whenever his bones protested against the low outdoor temperature. But this was post-tragedy Manhat-tan, where anonymity had come to have a paradoxical down-side. In a city of strangers, unfamiliar faces now took on an air of the conspicuous. Passersby were wary of those who might once have escaped their notice as ignored nonentities, blending in amid the urban multitude. Teams of police offi-cers in flak vests, armed with bullpup submachine guns and accompanied by bomb-sniffing German shepherds, could be seen guarding the entrances to large stores and office build-ings against terrorist strikes. If Malisse were perceived to be loitering about the block, he, the honest investigator, might himself become a target of curiosity or criminal suspicion. And Lembock had been emphatic about keeping the author-ities—and the Secretariat, for that matter—out of this busi-ness at any cost. Worried about a scandal that could soil the reputation of the bourses at a time when some in the trade had already assigned them to the junk bin of antiquated global institutions, he wanted to be sure of knowing the facts before they got out of the bag.

And so Malisse had today migrated from the street to his current unexposed position in the café. While offering the niceties of warmth, a cushioned seat, a steaming drink, and pastries, it hindered his ability to do his work, de-manded a reliance on his informant within the DDC's se-curity detail to keep him notified of Avram's comings and goings, *and*, not inconsequentially, prevented him from lighting up.

Malisse, however, could not complain about Jeffreys. He showed every sign of being a dependable set of eyes and ears, and had been quick to message him with confirmation of Avram's appearance at the club. Everything had so far gone smoothly and according to plan.

Plan A, that was.

Which was why Delano Malisse shied from taking optimism too far. If Avram Hoffman was involved in dealing illicitly obtained gemstones—or wondrous fakes—Malisse was confident he could prove it and track them to their source.

He just had a gut feeling that it wouldn't be as simple as A, B, C, or unfortunately D.

Nimec was watching Megan take a quick turn at the speed bag when he happened to notice Chris out the corner of his eye. A minute earlier the kid had been following Meg's every move. Now he'd suddenly gone wandering over to the plate tree near Nimec's free-weight bench.

Nimec saw him spin one of the large thirty-five-pound weights on its post with both hands, and almost winced as he pictured it slipping off to drop straight down onto his foot.

"Chris," he said. "Don't mess with that."

The boy didn't answer, but kept rotating the plate on its metal post.

Nimec wondered if the steady rat-a-tat of the speed bag had drowned out his voice, called out at a louder volume.

Chris was oblivious. Or seemed to be. Ignoring Nimec, he gave the weight another turn, climbed onto the bench, and then stretched out on his back, sliding under its rack to grip the barbell resting across its uprights.

"Hey, Chris, get away from there!"

Nimec had shouted at him this time, starting toward the bench, no longer contemplating what would happen if a single plate clunked down on the kid's big toe. He'd been pressing two hundred pounds with that bar—about double Chris's weight—and didn't want to imagine the consequences of it somehow falling on his chest.

Behind him, Megan had cut short her exercise and turned to see what was going on. Standing near the bag, she watched Chris sit up, slowly toss his legs over the side of the bench, and hop off onto the floor, as if only then having become aware of Nimec.

"Chris, did you *hear* me?" Nimec stood crossly in front of him. "You know the rules."

And he did. In fact, Nimec thought, he'd always shown impressive maturity in the gym after being cautioned about its do's and don'ts, staying away from its equipment when unsupervised, earning a fair amount of latitude while hanging around to observe Nimec's workouts. This wasn't in the least bit like him.

Nimec stood waiting for an answer, instead got a blank stare and silent shrug.

He looked at Chris with equal parts anger and confusion, not knowing what to make of his unresponsiveness. And the kid's wooden attitude wasn't exclusively reserved for him. He'd gone from fawning over Meg to acting as if she wasn't there.

"Okay if I go downstairs?" Chris asked. His tone flat, not a jot of defiance or stubbornness in it.

"I think you'd better," Nimec said.

Chris went past him to the elevator, touched his index finger to the biometric access control pad beside its door, and entered like a sleepwalker.

Nimec stood alongside Megan as the car descended, tugged confoundedly at his chin.

"You have any idea what that was about?" he asked.

Megan groped for something to say that would offer a bona fide insight.

"None, Daddy-O," she replied, giving up. "But you might want to consider changing the code on that lock till after the kid is past puberty."

"Throne's all yours, Collins," Jeffreys said, and rose from his stool to make room for his young reliever.

It was nine-twenty-five according to Jeffreys's wrist-watch, which he set against the official clock in the big room upstairs at least once a week just to stay on the ball. The hour between nine and ten was when things were slowest in the building. The first wave of traders was over, these men being mostly relics around his own age who were pro-grammed to show up early, looking for some other gray-beards to bargain with in person, or maybe check their office answering machines, devices they still saw as being the lat-est in high-tech gadgets. The second wave wouldn't start till eleven, eleven-thirty, when the younger dealers came in from their home offices after they got through doing what-ever it was they did to earn money over the Internet.

A quiet time, Jeffreys thought, and a good one for him to stretch his legs for a few minutes, pick up a coffee at the cor-ner doughnut stand, argue some Middle Eastern politics with Musaf the vender, and have a smoke out on the side-walk. You couldn't do that last thing anywhere else nowa-days, not without getting slapped with a fine, or even risking *arrest* and a thirty-day jail term. Made you feel like some punk kid sneaking out of the house to toke up on happy weed, thank you Mr. Mayor, and hope your high-toned friends fancied the expensive cigars they smoked out there in those private golf clubs in Aruba, Acapulco, Hawaii, or whatever other hideaways you'd zip 'em off to on your pri-vate jet every single weekend. Ran this town like a Puritan, his personal life like an Arab sheik. According to the newspapers, his Eminence even had "sin rooms" for his guests to slink into at some of the parties he'd thrown in his Park Avenue townhouse before taking office.

Jeffreys stepped down from the guard platform, mentally praising himself for having voted for the other clown in the last election.

"Anything you want me to bring back?" he asked the relief man.

"Yeah," Collins said. "Halle Berry."

"Cream cheese or butter?"

"Butter." Collins grinned. "That much woman, you better ask for lots extra on the side."

"If I can get her for under a buck, she's yours."

Jeffreys hitched up his trousers by the belt, slipped on his jacket, and patted it down for his cigarettes. Much as he hated to admit it, he did feel a *little* conscience-stricken about smoking, not because the current boss of City Hall had done everything under the sun, moon, and stars to make him feel that way, but because his wife had asked him to quit the habit as a kind of New Year's resolution. He'd tried sticking to it for Rosie's sake, and done an okay job this past month or so. Might even have succeeded better if it wasn't for the heavy-duty stuff on his mind, having to be a tattler for that investigator from Belgium . . . which reminded him of something.

"There ought to be somebody name'a Katari showin' up any minute," he said, pointing to the note he'd jotted in the margins of the guest book. "African guy from Israel, can't speak English."

"Huh?"

"Don't ask," Jeffreys said. "He gets here, you need to page Avram Hoffman in the main room and show him along."

Nodding, Collins took his place on the stool behind the guard podium.

A moment later Jeffreys turned and left the building.

Avram was back in the main hall, his morning worship concluded, the prayer shawl and phylacteries returned to their pouch in the cloakroom. Activity seemed to be picking up at the tables, though hardly by leaps and bounds.

Avram glanced at the row of wall clocks over the glass booth near the passage from which he'd emerged. They displayed the time in each of the world's major trading centers, and served as reminders to check his cell phone, which he'd turned off before entering the chapel forty-five minutes earlier. There was a voice message from Katari, a courtesy call in jumbled English and Hebrew to say he was en route from his hotel on Madison Avenue. E-mail messages from business contacts in Antwerp, Tokyo, and Mumbai. Also a couple of missed calls in the past ten minutes, their numbers blocked to his caller ID display. Avram had a hunch about their source, and delayed checking the e-mail to wait for his unknown caller to try him again.

He heard the cell phone ring within minutes and thumbed the TALK button.

"Yes?"

"Good of you to answer."

Avram recognized Lathrop's voice in an instant.

"I was at morning services," he said. "You understand."

"Sure. A pause to cleanse your soul."

"Improve it," Avram said. "There are rabbis, Talmudic sages, who give the opinion that man is superior to the angels. In the sense that God made them as perfect as they can be, wholly spiritual beings, while we who possess dual spiritual and material natures have the ability to transcend what we are. To refine ourselves."

"Gems in the rough."

"Something like that, right." Avram shrugged. "I'm always searching for betterment on all fronts."

"Then you'll be happy to take a look at the best."

Avram's pulse quickened.

"What have you got for me?"

"I said *take a look*."

Avram stepped to the side as several of the others who'd been in the synagogue moved past.

"I have an important appointment this morning," he said.

"Cancel it."

"I can't, it's too late to postpone. The buyer's already on his way here, and I can't reach him. . . ."

"Put him off. Or have him wait for you. There's a limited window of opportunity, and you'll have customers lined up to eat out of your hand in the long run."

Silence. Avram could feel ripples of eagerness and excitement under his skin.

He found a vacant seat away from the other men sprinkled around the room, stared out at the rooftops uptown through its large glass wall.

"How and where do you want to meet?"

"You know the program, Avram," Lathrop said. "Get going and keep your phone on, I'll fill you in along the way."

"Where's the movie star babe I ordered up for breakfast?" Collins asked, watching Jeffreys approach the guard platform.

"Too expensive, plus I couldn't fit her in here." Jeffreys rattled the small white bag he'd brought from the vender's cart. "Got you a bagel instead."

"Buttered?"

"Like you wanted, my man."

Collins reached for the bag with a mock frown. "Guess I'll have to settle."

Jeffreys unzipped his jacket, shook off the outer chill that still seemed to be clinging to him.

"Any happenings to report?" he said.

"No." Collins rose from the stool. "Well, actually, that guy showed. Katari."

"You see he got upstairs okay?"

"Yeah. He's there now, but isn't too happy, let me tell you." Collins shrugged. "Came in right after the dealer he was supposed to meet left the building."

Jeffreys looked at him.

"*Left?*" he said.

"Not more than a minute or two after you did," Collins said, and tapped a slip of paper that lay beside the guest book. "Must've had somewhere important to go . . . dropped this in front of me, hustled straight out the door in a big rush."

His brow furrowing, Jeffreys reached for the paper and read what Avram Hoffman had written on it.

Goddamn, he thought.

Malisse had expected Plan A to be bungled, although not even he had thought the bungling would commence at this earliest introductory stage.

He stood on the corner of 47th and Fifth, pausing to catch his breath, feeling thwarted and foolish as he looked about the avenue. His eyes scanned the sidewalk, the intersection, the passing taxicabs and busses. According to Jeffreys, almost five minutes had elapsed since Avram Hoffman had exited the DDC building behind him, and trying to guess which direction he'd taken amid the streams of vehicular and foot traffic seemed futile, idiotic, a matter of going through the motions. Jeffreys's reliever wasn't even certain he'd noticed him turn toward Fifth, and why should he have? He knew nothing of the ongoing surveillance.

Frowning, Malisse turned right on his heels toward the IRT subway station three blocks uptown. It was an instinctive choice. Hoffman could have dropped a trail of breadcrumbs, and the filthy pigeons infesting these streets would have pecked it up by now. But he had left the DDC suddenly, unexpectedly, and with obvious haste. If he meant to get somewhere in a hurry, it stood to reason he would take the fastest available mode of transportation, and in this city that would be the train . . . assuming he hadn't simply needed to walk some short distance. And why assume that or anything otherwise? It was all a toss-up.

Malisse's frown deepened. Idiotic. Everything had been botched. Better he'd stayed in the warmth of the coffeehouse, with its pleasant wafts of the brewed and baked. . . .

The thought broke off as he noticed a man in a charcoal overcoat and light gray snap-brimmed fedora in the crowd about halfway up the block, his back to him, walking at a brisk pace. Malisse gave him a moment's look. His size matched Hoffman's. His stride. And the outer clothes resembled what he'd seen Hoffman wear the past two days. His hat had been herringbone tan, though. His coat a brown tweed. But yesterday was yesterday. Nothing said a man couldn't change his colors—and these were still well coordinated.

Malisse quickly turned to follow. Perhaps it was a stretch to hope he'd been fortunate enough to spot his quarry. But better to chase after hope than stand arrested with futility, he thought. If nothing else it would get his blood going, take some sting out of the cold.

Malisse sleeved between clots of pedestrians, dodged a
bicycle messenger, was almost struck by some cretin motoring past on a Segway at a higher speed than the cars in the
avenue—*here* was a threat to human life exceeding any
posed by tobacco.

Now he'd almost caught up with his man, who had stopped
on the corner of 58th Street, waiting for a traffic light to
change. As the red shifted to green and the man started across
the street, Malisse hustled to outstrip him and get a look at
his face, edging to his right amid the surrounding crush.

A glance over his left shoulder dashed Malisse's short-
lived flirtation with luck. The man was not Hoffman. Beard-
less, years older, wearing no glasses, he did not bear any
resemblance to Hoffman. Well, there was the hurried walk,
the style of dress. Malisse was disappointed, yes, but would
not thrash himself for having made his bid.

He slowed to a halt as the man was absorbed by the cease-
lessly kinetic crowd. Shoulders bumped his arms, elbows
poked his side. On his immediate left near a bank entrance, a
dark-haired fellow in an outback coat stood dropping coins
in one of those ubiquitous public UpLink Internet terminals
Malisse had seen springing up everywhere lately in cities
throughout Europe, including the streets of his native Brus-
sels. Malisse looked at him a second, thinking he was the
only person in sight besides himself who wasn't moving in
step with the herd. Malisse wondered with droll humor
whether he ought to tap him on the shoulder and suggest
they form a brotherhood of some kind.

Then the man turned from the terminal's screen and shot a
glance back over at Malisse, appearing to sense his attention. His face was expressionless as their eyes momentarily
touched. Malisse felt a little embarrassed—was he now to

become both an intrusive nuisance to strangers *and* partner to muddlers?

Malisse turned back downtown without lingering another second, leaving the man to his private affairs. After a few steps he began to prop up his spirits by thinking positively, and soon had recovered his optimism, deciding he might yet salvage something of practical benefit from the otherwise wasted effort of having sped from his warm, comfortable booth in the café.

Here on the street, one could at least have a good smoke.

Malisse reached into his coat for a Gitanes, girding for whatever excuse Jeffreys meant to offer for his surprising incompetence.

Standing at the public-access Internet terminal, Lathrop waited as the guy who'd briefly looked his way on the side-walk moved on uptown. He'd had the misplaced, distracted look on his face of someone that had taken a wrong turn and wasn't quite sure of his bearings—probably nobody to worry about. Still, Lathrop kept a cautious eye on him, fol-lowing his progress a bit before he turned back to the screen.

Lathrop fed the rest of his coins into the terminal's pay slot, used its touchpad to access his fictitious Hotmail ac-count, and then punched in a short message for Avram, who had stepped aboard the bus downtown on his instructions minutes earlier.

The message read: *Get off 42nd Street stop, enter Grand Central Station at Vanderbilt entrance, wait on west balcony.*

After sending it to Avram's wireless e-mail address, Lath-rop cleared the terminal's screen, shoved his hands into his pockets, and walked briskly south toward the station.

• • •

"The pinhole suns," Lathrop said to Avram over the cellular. He'd called rather than e-mailed now for reasons Avram didn't pretend to know. "You see them?"

"I see them," Avram said to his own surprise. He'd never lived anywhere but New York City—couldn't have begun to count the number of times he'd been through Grand Central Station—and now here he was again. Yet he had never before been aware of those bright circles of sunlight laid out in east-west alignment on the tiled marble floor of the main concourse. He looked up at the sky ceiling from where he stood on the west balcony, tried to locate their source, didn't find anything, and wondered if they might be projecting from the ornate window grills beneath the ceiling's mural of Zodiac constellations.

"Avram."

"Yes?"

"Admire the scenery later," Lathrop said. "I want you to go down to the concourse, head toward the east side of the terminal. Walk straight along those suns until I call back."

The phone went dead.

Avram paused before descending the staircase. His eyes moved left to the circular bars and dark wood booths of the Michael Jordan Steak House angling off in a kind of L along the terminal's north balcony, and then shifted toward the Cipriani Dolci restaurant that occupied the smaller balcony on the south wall. Avram didn't spot Lathrop in either place. He looked out over the concourse to Métrazur on the opposite balcony, where he could remember the giant Kodak Colorama billboard taking on soot for decades before the terminal's renovation, but it was too far away for him to tell whether Lathrop might be seated among the elegantly dressed professionals meeting there for coffee and pastries. And say he was. Avram didn't know how he could manage to see across to this balcony with the unaided eye. Would he be playing the role of a tourist and holding binoculars? Taking photographs with a zoom camera? Or might he find another cover for himself, a different lookout? All Avram knew for certain was that Lathrop had to be somewhere in the midst of the thousands upon thousands circulating about the great rail terminal. Somewhere nearby, watching, observing him. Maybe he was down below, blended in with the clusters of people at the ticket windows and indicator boards, or the travelers around the glassed information kiosk. But Avram could not see him. Knowing Lathrop had tracked his progress since he'd left the Diamond Exchange on 47th Street, he couldn't see him. Hadn't once caught a glimpse of him during his walk downtown. And never had while on any of their previous tangos around the city.

Avram tried not to let that bother him, but he was only human. And strangely enough the idea of being watched by Lathrop made him less uncomfortable than his sure knowledge of how much Lathrop would *enjoy* watching him. The smug confidence he would exude. He was unsurpassed in his ability to see without being seen, gliding like a phantom among the masses. And he was just as good a choreographer of others' movements. A master of the dance, with all the conceit of one. Though Avram accepted the need to follow along, and could not dispute its wisdom given the stakes, he could have very easily lived without being put through his complicated paces on this bitter winter morning—street by street, station to station. Yes, of course, the dance had been expected. But Avram sometimes wondered if Lathrop took it to excessive lengths, led him through some twists and turns for no reason other than his own amusement.

Avram did his best to suspend these thoughts, and pushed off the balustrade. Then he went downstairs and followed the path of miniature suns to where the escalators ran between the MetLife tower's lobby and the concourse.

His phone bleeped again and he stopped to answer.

"Okay," Lathrop said in his ear. "The ramp to the East Side IRT's just ahead toward Lexington. You know the one."

Avram remained at a standstill as waves of men and women parted around him, sweeping in from every direction, moving toward the escalators and various railway gates.

"I know it," he said, glancing at the passage.

"Wait two minutes after I sign off, use that big brass clock over the information booth to count down," Lathrop said. "Then walk to the ramp . . . not too fast, not too slow. When you reach the stairs—"

"You'll get back to me," Avram said.

At five minutes to eight, San Jose time, Pete Nimec zipped down from his office on the top floor of UpLink's Rosita Avenue headquarters to enter a secure conference room in its underground bowls, where he found Megan and Roland Thibodeau, one of his two Global Field Supervisors, already seated at its boardroom-style table.

"Where's Ricci?" he asked, noting the absence of Thibodeau's equal in rank with annoyance.

Megan shook her head to indicate she didn't know.

"Ain't seen him," Thibodeau said. Attired in a midnight-blue Sword uniform shirt and pants—his optional preference over a business suit—he ran a hand across his walrus mustache, the bristling remnant of a full brown beard that he had recently whittled off in obvious but unexplained correlation with his diminishing, if still considerably padded, waistline.

Nimec motioned at the room's large wall-mounted plasma screen.

"We're about to have a video hookup with New York," he said. "He knew about it Friday afternoon. I told him before we left."

"So did I," Thibodeau said. His throaty Cajun accent made the word "I" come out sounding like *ahh*. "Don't appear to have done no good."

Nimec frowned.

"Either of you try reaching him on his cell?"

"More than once," Megan said.

"Got his voicemail, that's about it," Thibodeau said.

Nimec's frown deepened. This was clearly not turning out to be his morning.

"We need him here for the meeting," he said. "It's too important for him to miss."

"Could give you plenty examples of Ricci not being around when we need him of late, except you'd know about most of 'em before I opened my mouth." Thibodeau glanced down at the table, still swiping at his mustache. "Some men does dead before they time," he said in a near undertone.

Nimec looked at him from where he stood inside the doorway.

"What are you telling me, Rollie?" he said.

Thibodeau lifted his gaze, turned it slowly and heavily onto Nimec's.

"I'm tellin' you not to wait," he said.

Avram descended the stairs to the subway, paid his fare with a Metrocard, and went over to the compass rose at the center of the mezzanine floor, a connecting hub for multiple northbound, southbound, and crosstown lines that was the second busiest in Manhattan, surpassed in usage only by the station where he was headed. Even now, past the morning rush hour, there were riders bustling around him, turnstiles clacking in his ears, trains rumbling toward and away from the platforms a level below.

He stood against the compass's round focal pillar and faced north—the only cardinal point marked on the rosette.

His cellular beeped twice—the alert tone for another e-mail. Avram called the new message up on the display and opened it.

TAKE THE UNDERPASS TO YOUR RIGHT, it read.

Back in the coffeehouse with his cell phone to his ear, Malisse was going through the requisite formality of asking how it happened.

"Help me to understand, please," he said in a quiet voice, his words carrying a faint Flemish accent. "Why would you vacate your post when you knew our man was in the building, and could *leave* the building at any time?"

"Who says I vacated?" Jeffreys replied. "Did *I* say I vacated?"

"I believe," Malisse said, "you did."

"Uh-uh, no way you heard me say it. Because that'd mean the post was unattended when I stepped out, and I can tell you it ain't so. Never been so in all my years here. Never will be, either."

Malisse sighed over his mug . . . steam rising from an ordinary but full-bodied Italian roast this time.

"I'm merely trying to determine what went wrong—"

"That's fine," Jeffreys said. "But stick to what I told you and don't twist my words around. This spy business feels lousy enough without me havin' to be insulted by your accusations."

"No disrespect was intended."

"Fine," Jeffreys repeated. And took an audible breath. "What went wrong is I went on a ten-minute break fully thinkin' our man would be up in the big room a while."

"Waiting for his appointment."

"Uh-huh. What he called an *important* appointment."

"But he didn't wait for it."

"No, he didn't. And since my spotter don't know anything about my snoopin', and you and my bosses don't want nobody told about it, I couldn't very well have him question our man about where he was goin'. Bein' none of our security team's affair, it'd make *both* of them suspicious."

"But our man did leave behind a note."

"For his customer, right."

"Katari."

"Right," Jeffreys said. "Two, three sentences. Just to apologize for runnin' out like he did, explain some emergency came up that wouldn't take long, and ask him to sit tight in the Club till he got back."

"Which he . . . Katari, that is . . . continues to do as we speak."

"Right again," Jeffreys said.

Malisse remained silent as a group of people at a nearby booth cleared out and filed past him toward the door. What was he to comment? Crude at best, Plan A was at least out of the way, albeit disposed of sooner than anticipated. Already well formulated in his mind, Plan B would be far more elegant and effective. Expensive, too, alas . . . but Lembock had put no restrictions on his budget, and his years in the *Sûreté* had left him with expert contacts even here in New York.

"I'd like to ask one more question," he said. "Without casting any blame or insult at you, but rather for future reference. So we can decide how to best adjust our methods of working together."

"Shoot."

"Is this morning break of yours something regular?"

"Regular as my sixty-five-year-old ass startin' to hurt," Jeffreys replied. "Also regular as me havin' an urge to smoke a cigarette, which the law says I got to do on the goddamn *street* here in this city."

Malisse smiled ruefully, and told himself he should have known it all along.

His ears filled with the metallic rattle and squeal of an arriving train, Avram trotted from the mouth of the underpass to the wide 42nd Street shuttle station, where the S line between Times Square and Grand Central operated on four tracks. The two trains currently waiting were on Track 1 and Track 3. Though the train on Track 1 was almost packed, its doors had been left open for additional riders to squeeze aboard. A lighted sign above the platform said it would be the next out.

Avram presumed the train he'd just heard clanking to a stop was on Track 3 to his right. It sat empty, its doors closed. The conductor would open them for passengers once its alternate was about to move, and close them again moments after receiving the signal that the other had begun its return trip from Times Square, providing a continuous and, by the standards of the Metropolitan Transportation Authority, impressively punctual service loop between the stations.

Avram reached the platform with ample time to catch the train on Track 1, but let it go without him. Lathrop had directed him to board the third car of the second train to leave the station.

And so Avram did, dancing to his lead.

Among the first of the passengers through the train's retracting doors, he saw plenty of unoccupied seats inside. A rare thing in itself, their availability was a distinct lure, but he felt too charged with nervous energy to take one. Instead he chose to stand, gripping a hand rung as the car loaded up with people. That the choice was his own, and not another shot called by Lathrop, made it all the more desirable.

The train idled with its doors wide open for several minutes. As he waited for it to get underway, Avram found himself listening to a scrawny, long-haired kid who'd strolled aboard playing an acoustic guitar riotous with decals and hand-painted decorations. A donation can in front of him, he'd launched into a Mexican-flavored instrumental that was a fierce tease to Avram's memory, something he recognized but couldn't quite place, but associated with summer nights of another, distant time. Ten, eleven years old, a portable transistor radio hidden under his pillow, he'd spent so many of those nights listening to top-forty rock and roll in violation of his father's rigid decree, alone with the secret pleasure that only came when youth came into contact with the forbidden.

WABC AM, he thought. Cousin Brucie playing all your favorite hits.

Avram almost didn't notice when the train's doors finally slid closed. He'd become captivated by the musician, who was now midway through a flawless rendition of "Sing, Sing, Sing," the Big Band standard, keeping rhythm with some kind of jangling percussive setup on his foot, beating out its extended drum solo on the body, pick guard, and edges of his guitar. As they started pulling from the station, the guitar player concluded his second piece with another radical shift in musical styles, chopping out the introductory chords to an up-tempo country-and-western tune with vocals. His singing clear and strong over the cacophonous noise of the train, he belted out lyrics about riding the rails, and having to get on out of town in a hurry without a dime for a cup of coffee.

Impressed, Avram was certain the kid had timed his set so the third song, with its loud strumming, would coincide with the train's startup—a smart, practical touch, since the complicated single-note melody lines of his other numbers would have been buried under the loud racket of its wheels moving over the tracks.

He listened with pleasure for the rest of the short ride, wholly engaged by his skill and cleverness. Lathrop, their secretive rendezvous, all of its roundabout maneuverings faded from his mind. What pure talent, he thought. What marvelous, underappreciated talent.

A squeal of brakes now, and the train jolted into Times Square.

Before making his exit, Avram waited for the crowd of discharging passengers around him to thin out, eased his way over to the guitarist, and leaned down to slip a crisply folded ten-dollar bill into the can at his feet.

"Wow," the kid said. "Appreciate it."

Avram straightened, hesitated.

"That first song," he said. "The one you played while people were getting on at Grand Central . . . what's its name?"

" 'Walk, Don't Run,' " the kid answered with a smile. "By the Ventures, that sixties group. Figure it kind of goes with the action around here, you know?"

Avram looked at him in silence. A smile flashed across his own lips only to vanish after the briefest of moments.

Then he turned, stepped onto the platform, and reached for the ringing cell phone in his coat pocket.

When dealing with her peers and superiors at UpLink San Jose, Noriko Cousins had found that an inverse logic tended to prevail over their discussions, at least from where she sat . . . which was to say the stuff Noriko felt ought to be hardest to communicate generally turned out to be fairly easy, while the easy stuff was often a gargantuan pain in the ass for her to get across. Hard-easy, easy-hard, she wasn't sure what made it so, but thought it might be some kind of East Coast–West Coast thing. People living and working out there on the edge of the lazy, hazy, crazy Pacific just seemed to have synapses that were routed along very different paths from her own.

At any rate, Noriko had decided to begin with hard-easy at this morning's video-conference, and work her way toward easy-hard, which ran contrary to her policy of always getting the most onerous task of the day out of her hair before anything else. *Yes, class, that's correct*, she thought, here again logic was coiled in on itself like the proverbial snake eating its own tail. But she figured that if you were going to start out that way, you might as well do it with total commitment. Also, she hadn't yet decided how to make her easy-hard argument to her respected SanJo colleagues— namely persuading them to keep their oversized shoes from clomping all over her turf—and wanted to buy some time in the hope that some creative ideas would burst upon her as they rolled merrily along.

"The problem with our country's export law is twofold, or maybe threefold," she said now, more or less facing the Webcam above her desktop's flat-screen display. Three thousand miles away in their SanJo conference room, their faces in perfect resolution, Pete Nimec, Rollie Thibodeau, and Megan Breen the Ice Queen waited. "First, regulatory controls change with the political and economic tides, and that makes them ambiguous to everyone except specialized lawyers," Noriko went on. "Second, we have firms selling goods overseas that instruct those hired-gun trade attorneys to search for loopholes with magnifying glasses. Then there are companies that have been slow to put comprehensive export management systems in place, resulting in decent employees throughout the corporate hierarchy . . . top executives, members of the sales force, people at every level of every division and department . . . who want to comply with the rules but are utterly lost in the muddle. *And then* there are people in those same positions who know how to exploit the confusion for a crooked buck."

"Tough shovin' an oar through those waters," Rollie Thibodeau said.

"Very." Noriko motioned toward the coffee carafe beside her. "Anybody care for some of this?" she said, and held the pot up toward the camera's eye. "It's nice and hot."

Smiles.

"Sure," Nimec said. "Cream and a pinch of sugar."

"*Yuck*. Don't allow any on premises."

"Then I'll pass."

Noriko sipped from her cup. There, class, was what we consider a prime instance of injecting a moderate dose of levity into a serious discussion, acceptable in most forums, and highly recommended for loosening up its participants.

"Dual-use items are a category that can really drive you crazy," she said after a moment. "The government has to evaluate whether a product marketed for some harmless commercial purpose could be applied in some way that threatens our national security. If there's a determination that it might, the question becomes what's going where . . . or who's okay to receive a certain product from us, and who needs to be stopped from getting hold of it. But another country with firms capable of manufacturing that same commodity, or something similar, might disagree with our assessment, or be moved by conflicting economic and political interests, and refuse to go along with a proposed international ban. There are predictable rounds of lobbying, negotiation, and compromise before any accord is reached. And say we leverage what we want. Or most of it. With the spread of existing technologies, and the arrival of new ones, any controls have practical limits . . . as we know from hard experience."

She read immediate understanding on all the faces in her display.

"That lab in Canada, Earthglow," Megan said, airing their shared recollection. "Its scientists imported the same equipment you'd find in a factory that makes powdered baby formula to create a freeze dried medium for dispersal of its gene bombs. Then they used the same microencapsulation tech that's used for perfume samplers to stabilize the agent."

Noriko nodded and drank some coffee.

"The application of export policies isn't fixed in place—and it *can't* be," she said. "For a lot of reasons, usually involving shifts in political winds. Diplomatic relationships with countries change for the better or worse. Treaties are made and nullified. Restrictions are relaxed as incentives or goodwill gestures, tightened as safeguards or penalties. Sometimes licenses are issued for products shipped to our closest allies. Sometimes a product becomes so readily available outside our borders that whatever bans we put on it become irrelevant and hurt our companies competitively unless they're modified. . . . It depends. Even when you go to the opposite extreme, embargo a country by classifying it as a denied party, it can find legal, borderline legal, or patently illegal ways to get around the prohibition." Noriko paused, lifting her cup to her chin again. "You guys really *should* try this coffee, it's my personal blend."

"Another time, thanks," Megan said. "I've already filled my morning quota."

Noriko shrugged, sipped.

"Getting back on point, I want to give you an example of dual-use hardware in action . . . and then talk about its distribution," she said. "My cute little Mini Cooper—chili red, christened Sue Marie by *moi*—has an adaptive cruise control system that automatically slows it down if I drive over a hump in the road and come up short on an overturned semi. It uses sensors that aren't too different from the ones you'd find in a cruise-missile seeker. In fact, the semiconductors that regulate electrical current through the system are Gunn diodes, which are used in thyratron switches, which have a wide range of laser-based civilian and military applications." She took a deep swallow of coffee, held a finger up in a just-a-minute gesture, freshened her cup. "As a couple of for-instances, you'll find these kickers in surgical equipment and multichannel, or tunable, lasers used for optical communications networks. You'll also find them in nuclear triggering units . . . and potentially hard-kill high energy beam weapons. UpLink makes high-capacity Gunn diodes and builds oscillators around them. Armbright manufactures its own versions . . . and loathe though I am to admit it, they're not only competitive with ours, they're *superior.*"

"The distribution angle," Megan said. "Let's stick with it, if you don't mind."

Noriko was thinking Queen Breen had reacted to her last statement a mite curtly, and doubted it was out of defensiveness over a product comparison that weighed favorably toward the competition. It was obvious everybody knew what was coming here. Aside from an exchange of information, their bicoastal klatch was definitely leading up to a staking of territorial claims. And while Noriko preferred to keep the sparks to a minimum, she wasn't about to set herself up to be taking crap from anybody either.

Breen wanted data, she'd get it in spades.

"Gunn oscillators are controlled items that require licenses for sale abroad," she said, rapid-fire. "Depending on the performance specs of a particular oscillator . . . its heat and transmission capacities to name a couple . . . it may qualify for a license exception under conditions stipulated under Part Seven-four-oh of the Export Administration Regulations. These exceptions allow sale and shipment to government agencies, private firms, and distributors in certain country groups classified by the Bureau of Industry and Security. Offhand, I know some of *our* oscillators go to Canada, Mexico, England, France, Germany, Sweden, and Japan . . . democracies that have cooperative export policies. But while the policies of these countries are guided by common principles, there's nothing that approaches unity in how they're implemented. England might allow license exemptions that differ from those of the United States. Mexico might have other variances in *its* criteria—"

"You're conjecturing here, yes?" Megan interrupted. "Just so I'm straight."

As a stick up my ass, Noriko thought.

"Yes," she said. "Only as far as which ones I've used as examples, though. I can't claim to know the intricacies of *American* export law, forget what's in some other country's rule books. And there are something like a hundred-and-fifty in BIS's 'B Group,' which puts them on its exception list for dual-use products. Nonetheless I *can* tell you that Yemen, Malaysia, Lebanon, Burma, Pakistan . . . our government doesn't love any of them for their democratic values, but they're all strategic geopolitical allies that qualify. And that's just naming a few. While I know these countries are subject to checks and restraints *other* countries on the list might not need to worry about, and I know UpLink is more selective about its shipping policies than trade law requires, it's still possible for them to gain possession of restricted items through a quirk in the exemption policies of, oh, Great Britain . . . *hypothetically* speaking. And that's legal possession. What happens to a high-performance oscillator—ours, somebody else's, it doesn't matter—after it reaches Beirut? Rangoon? Islamabad? It isn't supposed to be transshipped to someplace like North Korea or Libya under the agreements I've spoken about, but tracking re-exports is unbelievably complicated. With front companies, shady freight forwarders . . . when we're talking about illicit detours, it can come right down to a single customs inspector who's been greased in some home or foreign port of call. And I've been sticking to material freight. The kind that's packed in crates and can be measured on scales. Technological *data*'s much, much slipperier since it'll most often involve electronic transfers—"

"One thing here, Nori," Nimec said, holding up a hand. "Those oscillators Armbright's got on the market . . . you telling us they've been reaching places they shouldn't?"

"Not definitively, no," she said. "But there are indicators that warrant close attention. Steady upticks in its transnational export of oscillators, and other dual-use elements besides, including large cargoes of titanium-sapphire tubing of the same type we've purchased from the company. These could be—I stress, *could* be—related to the production of laser-based military systems." Noriko paused right there, refraining from going through her whole checklist of suspect materials. She did not want to escalate anybody's interest at present by volunteering that these elements might also include the chemicals deuterium and fluorine. Give them that, and she'd be opening the door for them to come on like gangbusters. "Some of the freight loads . . . assuming for the sake of our discussion that the shipper's export declarations filed with Customs are *legit* and we have an accurate idea of what's in them . . . some of these loads, well, if I put a graphic on the screen and tried to show you their progress from point-of-origin to end-user, you'd see lines crisscrossing all over the map. And wind up feeling as stumped as I've occasionally been since my probe got underway."

Thibodeau scrubbed his cheek and looked thoughtful.

"Suppose for a minute Armbright's into somethin' dirty," he said. "You think it's a case of the right hand not knowin' what the left's doin', or a bad that's comin' down from the top?"

Noriko shrugged.

"The upticks I mentioned appear to have started around when the Kiran Group was brought into Armbright, but that could be a coincidence," she said. "I'm leery of red herrings. It would be a mistake for us to impose a time frame on the gathering of intelligence . . . a whole lot more of which is needed before any conclusions can be drawn. We have to be careful on this—"

"But you *do* smell something fishy coming from Kiran right now," Megan interrupted.

Noriko met her gaze across the continent. Hesitated a moment. And then gave her a slow affirmative nod, knowing full well this was make-or-break time.

"I think we should talk about Hasul Benazir," she said.

Up a flight of stairs from the shuttle platform, then over to the Lichtenstein mural on the 42nd Street–Times Square station's mezzanine, a depiction of some futuristic Manhattan as it might have been envisioned in an imaginary time of innocence.

Briefcase in hand, Avram stood under the mural watching a pantomimist in silver body makeup and a robot suit do his bit for spare change—his prolonged motionlessness broken up now and then by a mechanical gesture. The shopworn routine bored Avram, and would not pry a cent from his wallet.

He remembered the kid on the train. His agile musicianship, the wit of his song selections. That rock piece especially had caused nostalgia to seep into Avram's thoughts. He didn't know why, or didn't *quite* know. He generally carried his past without mawkishness, but the feeling had been accompanied by images from the Club's heyday. Those old gemstone cutters he'd been picturing earlier. Hunched over their polishing wheels, surrounded by the tools of their trade.

It had been a very different era.

When he'd dropped his bill into the guitarist's donation can Avram had noticed a Web address painted on the front of his instrument along with its other graffiti. What had it been? *Fuzzgrenade.com? Softgel.net?* No, no. But something along those lines. Industrious kid. He must do parties, clubs.

Avram wished he'd paid closer attention to the gaudy self-promotion. One of these days, he hoped to hold a grand affair. His silver anniversary celebration, perhaps. His son's college graduation, his daughter's wedding. He would rent a huge hall, maybe sail his guests away on a cruise. Why go for the common entertainers? The wedding orchestras? How nice it would be to give the kid a break, offer him some decent pay. Hear him perform his entire repertoire. One of these days, yes. At some gala reception. When he could stop hiding his true means, show that he was a man of substance. It would be a coming-out of sorts. . . .

His cell phone rang. Avram produced a long exhale. The

dance was grinding on his nerves; he wanted it to end.

"Yes." Wearily.

At the other end, Lathrop took note of his tone of voice.

"Patience, Avram," he said. "You're almost there."

His eyes boring holes into the robot mime, Avram gave no comment.

As Megan listened to everything Noriko Cousins said about Armbright's curious shipping patterns—not yet ready to call them *anomalies*—she was thinking that Noriko had certainly done her homework, although what she'd presented to this point (without once referring to notes) didn't go very much beyond citing details already contained in the files she had transmitted to SanJo before the weekend, and, perhaps, fleshing out some of the sketchier threads of information they included. Megan was also thinking Noriko had undoubtedly touched upon matters that might well prove to be a big deal to UpLink and the entire country if her concerns—not yet ready to call them *suspicions*—about Armbright's international-trade-law breaches were developed into solid evidence by process of investigation and analysis. But compelling as Noriko's report was, Megan had *begun* to think that nothing in it was overly relevant to the core—and as yet *unmentioned*—issue they were supposed to be discussing in their virtual face-to-face this morning, which really just involved how to go about moving ahead with the boss's clearly stated wish that Sword's New York division allocate a small portion of its divisional resources to the Case of the Vanishing Husband. In fact, Megan had over the past few minutes grown absolutely convinced that Noriko's goal wasn't to add anything substantial to her previous intelligence on Armbright, Kiran, and Hasul Benazir, but instead put a deliberate and particular slant on it, using a fair amount of words to drive home a single basic message: Keep out, no trespassing, stay the hell off my block. And whereas she was patiently letting Noriko play out her string, and would continue doing so a bit longer, Megan knew that what was coming down here, sure as sunrise, was no less than the first major test of her power of authority over Up-Link's security branch since she'd been voted in as chief executive officer of the company.

True to Noriko's emerging modus operandi, her recital on Hasul Benazir, currently in progress—and again showing thorough familiarity with her subject—was both recap and subtly spun embellishment of the dossier in her e-files. A graduate of the prestigious University of Engineering and Technology in Lahore, with dual Ph.D.s in electrical engineering and chemical, mineral, and metallurgical engineering, he'd been born forty-odd years ago in Peshawar's exclusive Hayat Abad township to parents who were members of the Pakistani ruling elite—

"This in a society that brags about not having a caste system like their abhorred Indian neighbors, but has class divisions so unbreachable they amount to the same thing," Noriko was saying now. "His father's a founding partner of the second largest industrial conglomerate in the country. Mother's a British-educated academician and daughter of the *number-one* brokerage and finance firm trading on the floor of the Karachi Stock Exchange."

"Privileged," Nimec said.

"Yes," Megan said. "I'm not sure it's fair to call him blessed, though."

Noriko nodded to indicate she'd picked up on her meaning.

"As best we know, when Hasul was twenty-two or twenty-three he was diagnosed with Xeroderma Pigmentosum, an inherited genetic disorder so rare there are only a thousand documented cases in the world," she said. "Doctors say that if all the *unreported* cases were added to the total stats it would show an incidence of one in several hundred thousand, but the odds of a person carrying the mutation still falls somewhere in the area of being struck by lightning. And when you look at the ordeal of living with XP, or the chances of dying from its complications, I might prefer taking a bolt from a blue . . ."

Hearing Noriko describe the condition, none of the three individuals in the San Jose conference room would have rushed to disagree.

Characterized by acute photosensitivity due to an inability of the skin cells to repair DNA damaged by even minimal levels of ultraviolet radiation, XP in effect made its sufferers allergic to sunlight. Usually diagnosed within the first three to five years of life, XP in its classic Type A form had an astronomical childhood mortality rate because of the development of melanomas and other severe health problems linked to the defect. But Hasul Benazir had not manifested any of its pronounced, telltale symptoms—the blistering, the cancerous skin lesions and tumors, the physical weakness, impairments to sight and hearing, and premature aging—until adulthood. And that was in its own way good news for Benazir, a strong hint, later confirmed by medical tests, that his was a variant form of the condition known as Type V. With constant medical supervision and strict regulation of his lifestyle and environment, he stood a greatly increased chance of long-term survival due to XP-V's higher level of skin-cell repair mechanisms.

"Must be a determined sonuva gun," Thibodeau said. "Lookin' at all he's accomplished. Got enough *healthy* people with money and resources don't do anything with it, you know."

"I know. But where's his determination focused? What's guiding it? I suppose they'd be my main questions," Noriko said. She refilled her coffee cup from the apparently bottomless pot on her desk. "I want to get back to Hasul's college years for a minute. He isn't the only notable figure associated with UET, Lahore. Another's a professor of Islamic studies whose political discussion groups Hasul attended *and* helped organize to the extent you could've called him a true devotee. This is openly known. We also know the name Hafiz Mohammed Sayeed from his post-academic career as founder of the 'Army of the Pure.'"

Or *Lashkar-e-Tayyiba*, of which they all were, indeed, familiar. A militant fundamentalist group with thousands of fedayeen guerillas and an extensive support network, the LeT had done much to warrant being placed on the Defense Department's list of international terrorist organizations. Although based in Pakistan, Pakistan-occupied Kashmir, and western Afghanistan, it was well-financed by backers throughout the radicalized Islamic world.

Noriko talked about the outfit's principal avowed goal of driving India from *its* territorially claimed chunk of Kashmir by any means available, and its growing ties to Pan-Islamic extremist movements with broader calls for global jihad. She told how its heavily armed fedayeen were trained in insurgent tactics, and otherwise aided and abetted by sympathetic factions entrenched within the Pakistani government—most especially its powerful intelligence service, the same branch that had assisted in the genesis of the Taliban. She told of the outfit's countless acts of brutal, indiscriminate violence against both military and civilian targets in the decade-plus since it had come into existence . . . these including kidnappings, assassinations, suicide bombings, a brazen attack on the Indian Parliament that left over a hundred dead, and massacres of entire villages to their every last man, woman, and child—

"Noriko," Megan interrupted. "Are you suggesting there's evidence Hasul Benazir has any connection to the LeT? Aside from his interest in Sayeed's teachings as a student?"

"It was more than an interest—"

"It was over twenty-five years ago. Before Sayeed formed the LeT," Megan said. "I'm not sure we can assume his discussion groups were even concerned with Islamic extremism . . . such as it existed in Pakistan during the mid-1980s."

"The Kashmiri brouhaha goes back almost *sixty* years to Britain's partition of the region with the Radcliffe line, which led to the first Muslim calls for jihad there, which led to two years of war between India and Pakistan," Noriko said. "And the fact is that the idea behind the creation of Pakistan was to establish an Islamic state that would stave off a civil war brewing between Hindus and Moslems since the turn of the *century*. Ideologies like Sayeed's don't spring up overnight. We don't need to mark the exact date nationalism and religious zeal bonded in his mind—"

"Maybe not . . . but we aren't talking about him, we're talking about Hasul Benazir," Megan said. She paused. "Listen, when *I* was a college sophomore my dormie convinced me to join an Earth Day protest . . . its mission was to save the Oregon wilderness, and the plan was for a busload of us girls to head out to a logging site and strip naked—"

Nimec looked over at her.

"Naked?"

"Nude, right," Megan said. "So as to make ourselves human symbols of how the timber industry was *denuding* our forests."

"Uh-huh," Nimec said. "And that's what you did?"

"That's what we *all* did," Megan said. "In front of a crew of about fifty gawking lumbermen, that swelled into a crowd of maybe a hundred fifty."

"Bet it stopped the wood choppin'," Thibodeau said.

"Until the cops came to make us put our clothes back on and haul us away." Megan said. "After which I'm sure the log cutting resumed with increased vigor."

Thibodeau smiled at the images his mind conjured up, particularly of Megan, thinking he'd never gotten such agreeable distractions on any of *his* jobs.

On the wall screen, Noriko was deadpan.

"I'm not only divulging this to humiliate myself," Megan said, meeting her gaze across the miles. "If we were to take everything people do when they're young, and use it as a yardstick for what they become as adults, who'd ever pass muster? Hasul Benazir has a permanent resident visa that was recently renewed . . . and that's under the heavy scrutiny that's been imposed these past few years. He's resided in this country for over a decade, employs hundreds of American citizens in his business—"

"I haven't claimed Hasul's a villain," Noriko said. "I never told you I'm convinced a crime's been committed by his company, or that it would be on his shoulders if it has. What I've said is I've noticed some things that make me curious, and then noticed other things that raise questions and might or might not be related, and want to see how they fall into place. Or don't fall into place. My office is working this. But the whole bit about an absent husband . . . I'll keep my eyes open for dope on him. Anything turns up, you'll know about it. If not, you'll also know. Why let it sidetrack us, or worse, trigger alarms?"

Megan laced her fingers together on the table.

"Top executives. Members of the sales force. People at

every level of every division," she said. "Those are your words, Noriko. Describing the sort of employees who could lead a company into trouble, or be led into it. And Patrick Sullivan is a salesman in a *major* division at Armbright."

Noriko looked at her without answering, a stony expression on her face.

Megan returned the stare, her hands still folded.

"I'm making Sullivan a priority of your investigation," she said. Then surprised herself, as well as everyone else, by adding, "We'll be sending a team to help you cover it."

And that was when Sword's operatives truly became involved, though Megan could never for a moment have imagined where her decision would lead them.

Avram emerged from beneath the neon glitz and computer animations of the marquee subway entrance at the corner of 42nd Street and Seventh Avenue, walked a block north to 43rd past more flashing electronic graphics, and then turned west toward Eighth Avenue. Clinton, they called this section nowadays. Sparkling, tidy, swarmed with tourists. The MTV studios, ESPN Zone, they were all within a block or two of here. He felt as if he'd arrived at a giant outdoor theme park for out-of-towners. The corporate pitchman's idea of urban redevelopment. But where had their giant broom swept reality in its mingled beauty and ugliness?

When Avram was a boy the area had still commonly been known as Hell's Kitchen, and he'd been warned to steer wide and clear of the *shkotzim*—a Yiddish word for non-Jews with derogatory connotations of a certain ruffianism—who lived in the neighborhood. And his family's narrow prejudices aside, it truly had been a bad section of town, with its massage parlors, street-corner prostitutes, and adult bookshops, its Irish and Puerto Rican gang members hanging around outside now-demolished tenements.

On a late spring day when he was seventeen, Avram and some friends had cut classes at school, drunk two six-packs of beer in Central Park, and gotten the idea to go to the peepshows. He didn't recall who'd proposed it. One of the other boys had boasted of having done it before with an older friend or cousin, and had given graphic descriptions of his experience. Maybe the notion had arisen in all the rest as they'd listened. At any rate, it had exerted an irresistible pull on them, and they had hopped the train downtown, jittery and eager. Imagine what Rabbi Zeimann, the principal at their yeshiva, would say, somebody had commented. Hope we don't run into him, another snorted. There had been a lot of nervous talk.

The place was on Broadway or Seventh, and Avram had seen smut magazines on wall racks inside the entrance. A potbellied man sold him four tokens for a dollar. Then, in back, there were curtained booths where a slotted token played a minute-long snippet of some pornographic film reel on a small viewscreen. The air had smelled of Lysol and something sour the disinfectant couldn't cover. Avram had parted ways with his friends as each went into a different booth. Farther toward the rear were more booths with doors instead of curtains. Two tokens made a metal partition rise from a window to offer a glimpse of a nude woman gyrating on a semicircular stage. The music was loud and throbbing. The woman would go around from window to window. The panel wouldn't stay up long before it fell and you'd have to insert another couple of tokens. If a window panel stayed up longer than the others, she would spend some extra time in front of it.

Avram had used up the tokens he'd bought, and then hurried back to the counter for more, spending the rest of the ten or twelve dollars he'd originally had with him. The woman had been black, with large pendulous breasts. She had smiled, licked her lips, run her hands over herself, a vulgar burlesque with a two-minute expiration, renewable with another trip to the fat man outside, the dropping in of more tokens. His arousal rising over his mixed embarrassment and disgust over the smell of the place, Avram hadn't cared that she in all likelihood could not even see his face through the glass. Once, he'd noticed the hardened glaze in her eyes and quickly looked away from them, concentrating on her flesh, her body. Thinking it was beautiful, no matter what, beautiful.

There, in that darkened stall, taking rapid breaths of its sour air, Avram had first seen a naked woman. And he'd never forgotten it. How could he? It was one of those crossings a man remembered. The beauty of her body, her sham lust, they remained inseparable in his mind, bound together without contradiction. Granted, it had been many, many yesterdays ago. When Avram was a teenager. But he could not say that anything he'd learned since would make him believe they were mutually exclusive.

Now Avram snapped from his thoughts to discover he'd come to the Charleston Hotel down the street from the Port Authority. Among the few welfare hotels left in this neighborhood, it was a tall old building with some closet-sized private rooms fixed up to lure budget travelers . . . and hurried couples whose only interest was immediate availability and a bed, Avram surmised. The long broom still had some work to do.

He entered, crossed the lobby to the registration desk, set down his briefcase, and caught the attention of a drowsy-eyed man seated behind it.

"I'm Mr. Cartwright," he said, giving the name Lathrop

had told him to use. "You'll have a reservation for me."

Barely looking at him, the clerk rolled his chair over to his computer, lifted his hands to its keyboard. It seemed a heavy task.

"Here it is." He tapped some keys and scanned what had come up on the monitor. "Cash payment made in full last night, I see?"

"That's right."

"Then you're set." The clerk parted ways with his chair, got Avram's card key. "Room seven-oh-nine. 'Course that's on the seventh floor."

"Of course."

"When you leave the elevator, hook a right, your door's the last one at the end of the hall."

"Thank you." Avram took the card key and hefted his briefcase from where he'd set it on the carpet beside him. "A visitor should be coming to see me any minute."

The clerk gave a sluggish nod without turning his eyes toward Avram's face.

"Sure, whatever," he said. "Long as he, she, or it's of legal age."

Minutes after he entered the hotel room, Avram heard a knock at the door, opened its peephole, saw Lathrop outside, and let him in.

The room was squarish with a double bed, a combination dresser/night stand, and a single straightbacked chair against the wall. Lathrop swept past Avram with a flap of his outback coat, going straight to a window above the dresser.

"You've found some choice accommodations." Avram said to his back. "Only the best for us, no?"

"The staffers mind their business."

"Provided we're consenting adults."

Lathrop said nothing. He reached over the dresser to part the curtains, opened the blinds, and glanced out through its slats, his eyes darting from side to side. After a moment he drew the curtains back across the window, leaving the blinds as they were.

"You'll be able to see okay in here," he said, and turned toward Avram. "Plenty of sunlight."

Avram nodded.

"Northern exposure," he said. "Very considerate."

Lathrop moved the chair over to the nightstand, sat facing the bed, and produced a flat black gem case from inside his coat.

"Come on, take a look," he said. "Neither of us has all day."

Avram settled onto the edge of the bed opposite him, hoping his anticipation wasn't too close to the surface.

"So," he said. "I'd imagine what you have to show me must be very remarkable . . . worth your demanding this hasty tête-à-tête, and my wearing out a pair of shoes to make my way over here."

"Be glad I'm thorough," Lathrop said.

Avram looked at him. "Do you honestly think it's possible I'm being watched?"

"I'm saying if there's somebody on your tail I don't spot, you could wind up pacing a federal prison cell instead of the street."

Avram gave no response. Some things were better left uncontemplated.

He turned his attention to the gem case as Lathrop opened it, focusing on its contents.

Lathrop watched the avid expression spread across his features.

"There you go," he said. "I thought they might grab you."

Avram almost gaped. The case's black foam insert tray held three rows of round, transparent jars, five to a row. Each of the lidded jars was in its own snug compartment and contained a stone of a silky violet-blue. There were radiants, round brilliants, ovals. But though they varied in size, cut, and finish, their smooth purity of color remained consistent.

He tore his eyes from them with effort.

"These gems," he said. Staring at Lathrop. "They look like Kashmirs."

Lathrop shook head.

"They *are* Kashmirs," he said. "World class."

"By whose definition?"

Lathrop shrugged.

"If it looks like a duck, and quacks like a duck," he said. "You're the connoisseur, Avram. You should be able to tell the real thing from a fake."

Avram's gaze held on his face a moment, then returned to the stones, enraptured by their cool blue radiance. Whatever notions he'd held of feigning nonchalance had been laughable, but he would settle for a semblance of restraint.

"Do you know about the Kashmir sapphire?" he said. "Its history?"

"I know what I need to know."

"Then you must be aware that true Kashmirs . . . not the ones that come from Myanmar and have been given the name because of their similar color . . . *true* Kashmirs are the rarest in the world. The most prized." Avram's throat was tight. "Most of the cut, polished gems are bought from estates and collectors. And no rough has appeared on the legal market in a quarter of a century. Their only source is—was, I should say—a Himalayan mountain valley over fourteen thousand feet above sea level. Two miles in the clouds. Outside a Pakistani village called Soomjan, in the Padar region near the Indian border."

Lathrop was silent.

"The British were meticulous about their journals, their chronicles," Avram said. "There's one I read from when India was under their rule. It says how, in 1880 or so, a pair of men from the village, game hunters, found the rough sapphires littered underfoot. Right beneath the surface of the ground, where a portion of a slope had given way in a landslide. The hunters had no idea of their value. But they thought the stones might be worth something to local traders who dealt with the colonials, and picked them out of the dirt to barter them at the market for grain."

Lathrop gave him another shrug.

"You have some reason to believe I'm interested in any of this?"

"I've already touched upon a very good one," Avram said. "Kashmirs . . . those from the traditional source . . . aren't often seen except in antique jewelry settings. Most date back to the Edwardian period, in Great Britain. The mines dug near the original find were depleted within forty years. And fewer and fewer stones have turned up since the 1920s. There's been no new prospecting. The difficult terrain, its remoteness, accounts for this in part. But mostly it's the border conflict in those hills. The unending violence. India, Pakistan . . . they both claim territorial rights to the frontier, India holding it with military troops. Local tribespeople allied with the Pakistanis fighting them from hidden rebel camps in the mountain passes." Avram paused. "Once in a great while a rough will appear on the black market. Or so I've heard. It's rumored the Kashmiri separatists search for them deep down in the old mines, finance their guerilla campaign . . . their acts of terrorism, some would say . . . with profits from the illegal sales."

Lathrop leaned forward and stared him dead in the eye.

"Avram," he said, "you sound afraid."

Avram shook his head with indignation.

"I have certain well-warranted *fears*, and would think you might appreciate the distinction," he said, and took a long breath. "Put it however you want, I know the risk of trying to pass these stones off as natural."

Lathrop stared at him.

"You don't need to take me at my word," he said. "Things shouldn't be any different than before."

Avram filled his lungs with air again, exhaled. Then he pointed to one of the small round jars in the open case, letting his finger hover just above its lid.

"That oval in there . . . it's polished but unfaceted. Known as a breadloaf cabochon, a style popular eighty years ago. I'd estimate it's a ten or twelve carater. Imagine how skeptical a customer would be should I try to broker it without a certificate of authenticity. A provenance. Then compound that skepticism by the number of sapphires you've brought. Even if the mineral and crystal inclusions . . . the color zones . . . are what they should be for stones that came out of the Himalayas, my buyers would be more than a little curious about how I've managed to obtain one or two of them, forget a dozen. And unless your terms have changed, I expect you'll want me to take all or nothing."

Lathrop leaned closer, gave him a fleeting smile.

"Use your smarts, Avram, because I know you've got plenty," he said. "We're coming from different angles. I'm in for the quick kill. You need to take the long view. Don't compare the terms of our deal to whatever you swing with *your* clients."

Avram looked at him. And kept looking.

"What are you saying?" he said.

"My source is tapped out. After this last fire sale, I'm done. There'll be no more wearing down your heels to humor me. But your business is in this city. Going to the big club every morning. Showing, bargaining. You sell a couple of these sapphires, make a handsome profit, lock the rest away in a vault. Five, ten, maybe twenty years down the line, whenever you're ready to retire, they're going to make some kind of nest egg. You can set yourself up. Your kids, their kids. Clinch your family fortune—"

"Onward unto all generations forevermore," Avram said dryly. "Now it's you who's sounding biblical, my friend."

Lathrop grinned, full out. This time it took its time leaving his face.

Avram realized his fingertip was still floating perhaps a half inch over the jar that held the large cabochon.

"May I?" he said.

Lathrop gave a nod.

Avram lowered his hand to the gem case, carefully lifted out the jar, removed its lid, plucked the sapphire from inside with two fingers, and rose from his chair. At the window, he laid the stone flat in the middle of his palm and stood admiring its even depth of color, thinking it might have been a bead of frozen blue mist against his flesh, hard as ice, yet somehow at the verge of evaporating into the air, swirling away from him at any moment. Finally he got his loupe out of his pocket and examined the sapphire in the sunlight, the ten-power magnifying lens about an inch from his eye.

What he saw left him stunned. No, more than that. *Awed.* Lathrop's other parcels had been lab-cultured marvels, indistinguishable from authentic goods. But this appeared to be on a level of its own. For a laboratory to accurately replicate the visual and gemological properties of Kashmirs would require a technology—a combination of synthesizing technologies—so advanced it boggled his mind.

Lathrop watched him quietly for several seconds after he'd returned to the dresser.

"So, Avram," he said. "Approve of what you see?"

Avram sat in the chair, his mouth dry.

The sapphire back in his palm, gleaming softly.

"On first glance . . . it's quite a specimen," he said, and moistened his lips with his tongue. "Unbelievably convincing. I'd need to give it a proper look to be sure, study its characteristics thoroughly . . ."

"No obstacle," Lathrop said. "You've got a setup at home. All kinds of precision instruments, right?"

Avram nodded.

"Go ahead and take that stone, or any other one from the case," Lathrop said. "Pick it out at random. I've got some things to keep me busy over the next few days, and that should give you time to run your tests. Be as thorough as you want before making your decision."

Avram looked at him.

"An authenticated cabochon of this size could be worth three-quarters of a million dollars," he said. "What you propose, we'd call it lending on memo at the Exchange. A slip is written up, a record of the stone passing hands . . ."

"And you're curious why I don't worry about you maybe having evil inclinations, disappearing with that little beauty."

Another slow nod from Avram.

Lathrop met his gaze, held it steadily.

"Avram, you're a family man."

"The dazzle of wealth has tempted family men to run off

before. Leave everything behind and choose lives of freedom and luxury."

Lathrop nodded. Then he reached out, put his hand over Avram's open fingers, and pressed them shut around the stone in his palm.

"Between us," he said, "you ever feel that temptation creeping up, remember I know where your wife and children sleep at night."

Cold, she thought, it was so cold. And dark outside.

It hit her the instant she left her apartment condominium, smacked her hard in the face, this spiteful winter gloom. Still shy of five-thirty P.M., and you'd think it was the middle of the night—exactly what could push her to feel more depressed and heartsick than was already the case. But she had to maintain some semblance of normalcy for the sake of her daughter. The poor kid needed to keep socializing with other children. Needed some distraction from the automatic routine of school, homework, and hanging around the cheerless atmosphere of their apartment until bedtime. Waiting for her father, watching her mother wait. The two of them just hoping to hear from him, wishing Pat would call as he so often would late in the day . . . or better, so much better, imagining he'd surprise them and come walking right in the front door.

A beanie-style cap pulled down over her forehead, a wool scarf wrapped around her mouth, the collar of her ski jacket zipped high to her chin, she turned up the street from the building's entrance courtyard, glad it was only a short walk to the indoor playspace where she'd left her daughter a little over an hour before. At five hundred dollars per year, an unlimited admission pass to GoKids almost could be considered a bargain. Compared to the cost of standard daycare, it *was* a bargain nowadays, but who was she kidding? It had been a long time since money had been a concern for her, Pat wouldn't have balked if the annual tab had come to five times that amount.

In his way, he was a good family man. And in *their* own screwy way they'd made things work as parents.

She hurried along the sidewalk, bowing her head to keep the wind out of her eyes. There'd been nothing like these supervised after-school centers when she was young, she thought, especially in the working-class area where she grew up. Nowhere outside her bedroom to play with her girlfriends in the depths of winter, unless it was at one of *their* family's apartments, in one of *their* rooms . . . and after a while they'd all just felt confined, restless, and bored with the very same toys that had seemed as if they would be never-ending fun while still gift-wrapped under the sparkling lights and ornaments of a Christmas tree. Children didn't lose their need or desire to be physically active when the fall came and leaves started dropping from the trees, but in New York, or anywhere close to the city, they barely had opportunities to exercise outdoors until spring came around. To *stretch* themselves. True, her daughter had skating, and sledding if there was snow on the ground, but first you had to get her ready, and then bring her over to a park or ice rink, these being scattered far and wide across the area. The travel and preparation involved made it a project that was strictly for weekends, when they could turn it into a full-day affair. And under the circumstances, in her current state of mind . . . just getting *herself* together and in gear sometimes seemed impossible.

It was a blessing, GoKids. An absolute blessing. With slides of every type, a sandbox, climbing ladders, jungle gyms, and hideout tunnels, it amounted to a modern playground with a roof over it, and had made all the difference in the world to her daughter, giving her something bright she could look forward to every day, a level of companionship and attention that was otherwise absent from her life right now . . . and that her own mother recognized she couldn't provide.

Even trying her best to cope, aware she couldn't put her responsibilities on hold no matter what else was going on around her, she'd been unable to manufacture a smile for her little girl these past several days. Not while she constantly felt like tearing her hair out of her head by the damned roots in her worry, or medicating herself into a stupor to quiet the scared and—God forgive her—*furious* voice in her head that told her Pat had gone too far this time around, gotten too many big ideas for his own good, taken the sort of chances that she'd repeatedly warned had been bound to lead toward serious trouble . . . trouble that could swallow up everyone and everything around him.

But she didn't want to think about it right now. What was the use? It would do her a lot more good to concentrate on putting one foot in front of the other.

She walked on into the wind with her head low, hoping she didn't crash right into somebody while rushing blindly toward the intersection. Luckily there weren't many people around at the moment. In another half an hour it would be six o'clock and the street would fill with commuters returning from work, but this was the lull when most nine-to-fivers were still in transit, jammed together in crowded trains and buses.

She could almost envy them, ridiculous as that sounded. Their average routines, their common complaints . . . right now she would have traded for them in a minute.

It was so cold out here, so dark and cold.

Her daughter's playspace was about five blocks down-town, and she would need to cross the street heading toward it, walk south on the next avenue. But the parked cars along the curb were crammed so close together—bumper to bumper, almost—that it seemed impossible to find an open-ing between them, another of this city's ongoing shortages being available spots. She figured it would be better to wait till she reached the intersection than catch her coat or slacks trying to squeeze between fenders.

Those cars aside, her block rarely got too congested. Res-idential, lined with trees, it was a lot quieter than most, and could almost make you forget what a busy part of town this was in general. She supposed the corner park over on the other side of the block, Peter's Field, also helped cut down on foot traffic. In fact, she herself wasn't eager to walk past it. There were usually strong gusts kicking up all around its fences, probably something to do with how the wind sort of pooled and swirled around the park, really just a little open space with some benches where the old men and women liked to sit around feeding the pigeons, and athletic courts the basketball and tennis players claimed as their own in the summertime.

She would hate to cross the street there, but couldn't avoid it, and admittedly felt like a spoiled, selfish bitch letting a minor inconvenience of that sort enter her thoughts. These days, she had heavier concerns pressing down on her shoulders, and might have given anything in the world to see them lifted. Having an indoor center for her daughter so close to home . . . she knew she really ought to be thankful for that and leave it alone.

Still hunched forward against the wind, she was unaware of the guy who stepped from the front passenger side of the parked car on her left until he called her name, and even then almost crashed into his door as it swung open over the sidewalk. Startled, not recognizing his voice, she came to an abrupt halt and looked up at him, barely avoiding the door.

His face, what she was able to see of it in the dark, was unfamiliar to her.

"Nice to see you," he said, smiling, repeating her name as he sidled around the door, quickly moving right up in front of her.

She didn't recognize his face in the shadows, couldn't place it, didn't have a clue who he was. But his eyes . . . something about his eyes, the way they were locked in on her, made her think she probably didn't *want* to know him.

She backed up on impulse, confused, anxious, suddenly realizing there was nobody on the park side of the street, nobody else on this side.

Nobody but the two of them standing out here on the darkened sidewalk.

"I'm sorry," she said to whoever the hell he might be. Starting to get really frightened now, trying to ease forward around both his body and the door. "I'm in a hurry to get somewh—"

His gloved hand came up, clapped over the lower half of her face before she could finish her sentence. Then another had came up to her neck, something held in it, what she thought looked like a fat marker pen. As she started to scream against the hand covering her mouth, a snapping sound came from the tubular object, and she felt a sting right through her scarf, and the scream died off into a muffled in-turned whimper.

Instantly dizzy, her senses flushing away, her legs turned to soft putty, she reeled, felt herself being shoved into the car, thrown across the backseat. And then heard its doors slamming shut in what seemed some distant place behind her.

By the time the driver got back into his vehicle and pulled from the curb, she was completely unconscious.

•   •   •

His Maglite raised above his shoulder, its lens turned downward in the pitch blackness, he walked around the pile of sod, rotten leaves, and splintered branches concealing her body. The surface of the frozen bog quivered underfoot, its icy carpet of moss and tangled weeds crackling with each step he took through his slow circle, like a thick rubber mat that had been spread over an even thicker layer of broken glass.

The flash's wide, high-powered beam revealed a hint of white flesh—part of her cheek, or maybe her neck—and he knelt to scoop another clump of dead foliage into his gloved hand and toss it where he'd caught his glimpse. He recalled having seen patches of snow among the nearby brush and stunted trees, momentarily considered flinging some onto the heap for added cover, but then decided it was better to leave the snow undisturbed. More would fall to blanket her soon enough . . . unless the coyotes and bobcats arrived first. They were all over these woodlands, half starved in the bareness of winter, scavenging for whatever food would sustain them. Probably they would take care of the body before any human being had a chance to discover it. Not many people wandered this far from the beaten path, and those who did—off-trail hikers, nature watchers, that type—wouldn't get the inclination for months. Not until the wicked cold abated.

He continued to move around the corpse, frost-hardened mud crunching beneath his weight.

The auto-injector couldn't have worked any better, he thought. A little pressure was all it had taken for its needle to eject from the tip and penetrate the heavy scarf she'd worn around her neck, releasing the contents of its prefilled dispenser.

The propofol had put her out in less than a minute. He'd experimented with a wide range of sedatives, tranquilizers, and anesthetics in his solitary career, could recite a whole desk reference's worth of names from memory, and was convinced he'd never gotten hold of anything more potent. The dosage he'd pumped into the woman, eighty milligrams into the artery that fed her brain, could have put a horse on the ground in seconds. She'd already been semicomatose when he finished her in the backseat, pinching shut her nose with one hand, clapping the other over her mouth, blocking her airways until her autonomic motor system simply gave up on trying to fill them.

His take-outs weren't always as clean, but he preferred it when they were. With his best ones, the ones that went the way she'd gone, it was almost as if he was the Sandman kneeling at their sides, gentling them to sleep, making them yield to him with a soft, easy touch.

Hush, baby, he'd whispered in her ear. *You hush, and I'll see you by-and-by.*

He had kissed her goodnight—lightly, on the cheek—as she went out with hardly a shiver and a gasp.

Now he came full circle and paused to stand in silence over the body's outstretched legs. He could see filaments of vapor escaping his mouth and nostrils to scatter in the bright cast of his Mag, hear timber creaking and groaning around him in the wind.

In the unlikely event anything was left of her when the thaw arrived, it would be sucked down into the bog. The acid mire sped up decomposition, turning organic remains into food for the peat and sphagnum. There was a whole education to be gotten from being piss poor and orphaned young, and that had been among the abundant lessons he learned in the cranberry bogs where he'd toiled during the October harvests, just a kid back then, part of a large troop of strapped and exploited seasonal laborers. The pickers, most of them, were minors like himself, along with hardscrabble local women and Mexican illegals who had come thousands of miles north of the border to join them in slogging through those flooded fields for less than minimum wage, raking berries loose from the vines so they would float to the water's surface, then skimming for them with big brooms, rakes, and nets . . . and this while the foreman, their *padrone* the migrant workers had called him, sat watching with his fat ass parked high and dry in the cab of his tractor. As you tramped across the bog, it would drop down in ditches where the cranberry vines took root, and you'd wade out deeper, step by step. Start out covered in cold slime to your ankles, and later on find yourself swamped to the waist, where the dead things came stirring up from the mucky bed. Drowned chipmunks, squirrels, foxes, birds, there would be small animals and decayed pieces of animals floating all around you, leeches and wormy creatures clinging to them, feeding on their putrefied tissues.

He remembered the cranberry bogs. Remembered the dead things. But that was long ago, and he wasn't here to do any picking tonight.

He'd found this patch of spongy ground a while back, used it for another of his jobs, and hadn't had a problem locating it again. It was the ideal place to dispose of her, hidden at the end of a dirt trail among a million acres of unpopulated wilderness out here in the Jersey barrens . . . miles and miles of nothing, of nowhere, a quick shot from Manhattan. The drive had been under forty minutes, and he'd taken it slow to make sure the staties didn't get interested in him. When he was finished looking over his work, he would pull his rental back onto Highway 73, head a few exits down the 'pike to the Lincoln Tunnel, and then he would be across the Hudson, out of that underwater tube, city lights greeting him, Broadway in his face, the Empire State Building thrusting into the eastside sky like a giant multicolored glowstick. But here, right here, none of it seemed to exist.

Over the river and through the woods, amazing.

Remaining very still over the body, he switched off his flashlight on an impulse that, while not quite unconscious, arose from a chamber of his mind buried deep down at the lowermost level of consciousness.

And then the world went dark.

He could have been anywhere.

He could have been nowhere.

Nowhere, U.S.A. Riding along some unmarked road, mile after empty mile, in a big old Mack truck that was redder and shinier than a fire engine, he thought with a smile of bitter recollection, his free hand briefly touching the right side of his neck.

After a second he thumbed his flash back on, turned, and walked away from the evidence of his latest atrocity, bearing with him an indelible reminder of the many crimes of his past.

FIVE

VARIOUS LOCALES

AVRAM HOFFMAN DASHED BY JEFFREYS ON HIS way to the elevators in the DDC's ground-floor entrance hall. It was already twenty minutes past nine, late for his morning prayer session, and he couldn't afford to run even a minute later. Mr. Katari had left the Club in a huff well before Avram returned from yesterday's hastily arranged meeting with Lathrop, and his indignance over having been put off was understandable. In the competitive hustle of the jewelry trade, one's time was not to be squandered. A missed appointment could lead to another, and that might result in lost opportunities. The domino effect could be rapid and serious. All the hard, quantifiable appraisals of a gemstone's value, its cut and carat, clarity and color, scientific identification and grading—*all* of it—meant less than its tenuous hold on a potential buyer's fancy. No man or woman had ever died for lack of a precious bauble. It could sparkle with the brilliance of a thousand suns, but what did that matter if it couldn't arouse a comparable gleam in the eye of the beholder . . . or if its lure to the eye faded before a sale was closed? The true measure of its worth would be found in dreams, desires, and passions—and these were fleeting intangibles, enchantments of fickle power. *That diamond you promised me hasn't arrived? The broker was held up at an appointment? Well, I'm flying out of town tonight and will have to shop around.*

Avram had needed to shower Katari with apologies, guarantee him exclusives and special discounts, practically offer verbal supplication over the phone to convince him to come back here today. But Katari was a major client, and Avram wouldn't hang himself with a noose of pride.

He stepped into the elevator now, out of breath, bleary-eyed with exhaustion, his cheeks flushed above the line of his beard. It was the rushing. The constant scurrying to get things done. He'd been awake most of the previous night in his home laboratory examining the Kashmir with his various instruments . . . a binocular microscope, a polariscope, an immersion cell analyzer, all state-of-the-art equipment for which he had paid many thousands of dollars. At about eight o'clock, his youngest daughter, Rachael, had knocked on the door with a stack of books in her hand . . . would he read to her? Avram had sent her off to bed in a brusque, preoccupied tone for which he still felt guilty. Told her he was too busy, knowing he had broken a promise made earlier. But he'd considered it an urgent *must* to look for any signs of artifice before dropping the sapphire off at the GIA laboratory . . . a stop he had made first thing this morning, eager to get the certification process underway, hours of his own extensive tests having shown him absolutely nothing that might indicate the stone wasn't of natural origin. Though the lab was just down the block from the DDC building on Fifth Avenue, Avram's need to wait for his regular man and put in a request for prioritization had put him behind schedule. If there was a trait shared by experts of every kind, he thought, it was that they seemed to enjoy stretching the patience of those who depended on their services.

As he rose to the trading floor in the elevator, Avram remembered the hurt look on Rachael's face over his snappish dismissal, and silently pledged to make it up to her soon. Tonight, if he had the time. He would try to be better with Rachael tonight.

Meanwhile, he had to pull himself together and set his mind toward the long day of bargaining ahead.

What Anthony DeSanto usually did after walking the two blocks from his apartment to the office at Dunne Savings and Loan every morning was browse through the newspapers over a cup of spiced apple cider and a blueberry muffin, preferring the city's two major tabloids, the *Daily News* and *New York Post*, for their extensive sports coverage. There were enough hours in the day for him to get beat over his head with the stories of war, terrorism, crime, politics, and economic turmoil that dominated their front-page headlines, and Tony figured the latest developments on all those glorious subjects could wait until he was caught up on the game scores.

Tony guessed he was a creature of habit, and scanning the papers—back to front—was stage one of his ordinary routine at the bank, a chance to catch his breath after hustling uptown on the train, a comforting transitional phase to help ease him into the feverish rhythms of the workday. Right now, though, things *weren't* routine, or ordinary, and he couldn't pretend they were. For maybe two, three days after Pat disappeared, Tony had tried to go about his mornings as if nothing was wrong, thinking it would help stave off his creeping fears. He had picked up the papers at the newsstand outside the Union Square subway exit, bought his cider and muffin at the green market, and, once he'd plunked himself down at his desk, studied the sports section as though everything was the same as usual . . . although he'd been constantly and ever-more-keenly aware that it wasn't. But it seemed worth a shot trying to focus his thoughts on the previous night's monster jams and power plays—even a *half-hearted* shot—if there was any chance it could temporarily distract him from thinking about what could have happened to his best friend of twenty-five years, a guy who'd seemingly vanished into thin air.

The problem, though, at least over the past couple of days, was that all it seemed to do was remind Tony of how very wrong things were. The interest he and Pat had in the games was a huge part of their friendship —was intertwined with it, you could say. Every so often they'd sandwich an alternate topic of conversation between heated debates over stats, wins, and losses, almost as if to prove they *could*, like a couple of hardcore alcoholics trying to convince themselves they were really just social drinkers. Of course, those departures from their subject of choice were hardly what Tony considered sweeping in scope, and tended to swing between venting about their jobs and observations about female acquaintances past and present . . . juicy commentaries and footnotes often laid out in terms that might not be considered clear signs of male maturity to someone in a position to overhear them. It wasn't that they made a deliberate attempt stay away from the serious shit, and there were enough exceptions to the rule. Tony felt closer to Pat than he'd ever been to his own brother, knew he could share virtually any secret with him, open up to him when something important needed to be confided . . . and he'd always figured Pat felt the same. Twenty-five goddamned years, they'd been friends. A *quarter century*. Over that time they had trusted each other with all kinds of things, protected each other a load of different ways, but hadn't needed to waste too many words in the process. You take a couple of guys from Brooklyn who've hung out since they were teenagers, put them together at a sports bar to watch a ballgame and drink a few cold ones, they aren't all of a sudden going to turn into weepy members of the studio audience on the *Dr. Phil* show. That, Tony thought, was not what they'd have foremost in mind when they got together after work needing to shake off a million different varieties of stress . . . but it also didn't qualify them as two slobbering, jockstrap-sniffing morons.

And yet Pat had been gone a while now. Over a week. Too long, and under circumstances much too suspicious for Tony to box up his concerns for even a minute. He'd known what Pat had going on the side, of course. Wouldn't have been shocked to learn he'd been treating himself to a little something extra on *top* of it every now and then . . . can't eat the same pie every day, he always said. Tony had been originally hoping he'd decided to have his fill of *la vida loca*, celebrate some of the big new sales commissions he'd been netting these last few months with a weekend fling to the Caribbean or somewhere. God knew he'd had enough practice running cover stories to the wife.

Still, though. A week. A week and *counting*. It was way, way too long for Tony to explain away.

Tony didn't like it, not a bit.

There was missing, and there was missing. And after what Tony had heard the other night—making him frustrated enough to leave those answering-machine messages, and then get into that nasty argument only to have the phone slammed down in his ear—after all that, it wasn't doing him one iota of good to read about yesterday's Madison Square

Garden face-off between the Islanders and Rangers. To the contrary, it only got his mind veering off into dark places he wanted to avoid.

And so Tony had quit on the sports pages and started flipping through the daily rags front to back. He hadn't been aware of looking for a particular type of news article, hadn't consciously realized that he had been skimming over the world, national, and business reports, and totally bypassing the editorial columns and entertainment dish to peruse the city sections, paying closest attention to pieces about local crimes and accidents . . . his eye drawn toward any shred of information, any apparent clue, that could somehow help him figure out what could have happened to Pat.

Seated at his desk now, his hot cider steaming in front of him, Tony went through the automatic motions of peeking at the general news in today's *Post* and then once again found himself turning to the NYPD DAILY BLOTTER section. He skimmed quickly down the latest batch of dreary, depressing items scratched together by police, hospital, and morgue beat reporters every night. Listed under separate borough headers, and summarized in bulleted paragraphs, they seemed pretty typical: A trannie prostitute discovered bound and beaten to death on a Bryant Park bench. A boiler explosion in the South Bronx that had killed a couple of senior citizens and hospitalized three firefighters with acute smoke inhalation. Gang-related tensions that had erupted into shootings and stabbings in a midtown nightclub. Some Harlem kid who'd gotten nabbed while breaking into a Mercedes-Benz SUV that turned out to be owned by a hot-on-the-charts rap artist and packed to the roof with crack cocaine, heroin, and marijuana, plus a small arsenal of illegal firearms for good measure. . . .

Then Tony's eyes landed on the final piece in the column

and widened with agitated dismay. He gasped in a sharp, sudden breath, almost choking as some of the half-chewed food his mouth went down his windpipe.

The single-paragraph bulletin read:

Police are asking for help locating Corinna Banks, a 31-year-old, 120-pound woman with blond hair who was last seen at 3:30 P.M. Monday dropping off her daughter, Andrea, age 4, at an indoor playspace known as GoKids on Fifth Avenue and E. 22nd Street. Ms. Banks is said to have been wearing a black beret, a dark wool scarf, a yellow ski coat with black trim, and leather knee boots. It is thought she returned to her apartment at 333 E. 19th Street (between First and Second avenues) after leaving the playspace. Anyone with information of her whereabouts is asked to call the NYPD TIPS hotline provided at the bottom of this column, or contact Detective Ismael Ruiz, 10th Precinct, at (212) 555-4682. You will not have to reveal your identity.

Tony grabbed the napkin spread open on his desk, hacking up chunks of blueberry muffin.

"Jesus Christ," he said shakily to himself. "Oh my fucking God."

He was still trying to catch his breath as he reached for the telephone.

A yarmulke on his head, dressed in a black suit and overcoat, and carrying a hardshell black leather briefcase, Delano Malisse felt like a gross fraud as he stepped into the DDC building minutes behind Hoffman. It was not posing as one of Jewish faith that gave him, the experienced undercover investigator, a sense that he was a blatant masquerader, but rather being disguised as a person of *any* religious persuasion. He had seen too much human baseness to believe in a guiding hand on high, an almighty being in whose image the species had been molded . . . unless, perhaps, God was an ogre who enjoyed peeking down at the world between his spread, hairy toes and having himself a good belly laugh at all its warts and vulgar messes. By and large, the human species uglied things up with degenerate behavior, which wasn't to say it lacked qualities Malisse thought worth preservation. Man had proven capable of making tasty food, building durable and attractive structures, drawing some pretty pictures, spinning an occasional clever tale, and stringing musical notes together in a pleasant fashion—although at least three of the four were faded, irreclaimable skills in this day and age.

Malisse, however, had other pressing concerns right now.

He strode up to where Jeffreys sat on the guard platform, hoping his fellow dramatic player had rehearsed their little scene.

"Hello," Malisse said. "I'm Mr. Friedman, here to see Norman Green."

"Got your name right here, sir." A mediocre actor at best, Jeffreys had glanced at his guest book a touch too quickly, looking uncomfortable, betraying anticipation of his lines. Still, he was new to the craft, and his stiffening informant's guilt could have been expected to keep him out of the moment. "Go straight on up to the tenth floor. I'll buzz upstairs so he can meet you."

Malisse thanked him and exited stage left via the elevator. It had been a clumsy transition but would serve its purpose.

Green was waiting outside the car as its doors opened. His resemblance to Lembock, his first cousin, was strikingly noticeable. Ancient, bone-thin, and snowy-haired, he wore a dark pinstriped suit with a white breast-pocket handkerchief, and gold-framed pince-nez glasses on the bridge of his sharply downcurved nose. His knitted yarmulke was black with a blue trim pattern, held firmly in place with a solid gold clip.

Malisse extended his hand to Green and smiled, appreciating his lenses and careful, elegant dress as reminders of an old-world refinement that many would consider quaint. How had so much been lost nowadays? he wondered.

"You're looking well, Duvi," Green said in Flemish. Although the two had never before laid eyes on each other, he stood pumping Malisse's arm as if they were the fondest of friends. Here, now, was a fine, seasoned performer. "How was your flight in?"

"A success." Malisse shrugged. "I landed alive."

Green chuckled, put a hand across his shoulders, steered him around toward the turnstiles.

"Come, Duvi, I'll show you where to hang your overcoat." And then, dropping his voice to a bare whisper: "As well as where Hoffman has left *his* coat and attaché case while he prays."

It was a quarter past noon in San Jose as Pete Nimec stood looking out at Rosita Avenue through the window beside Megan's desk. If he'd leaned his cheek flat against the pane, bent back on his knees, and cranked his neck a bit to the right, he might have seen the very edge of Mount Hamilton's eastern flank overlooking the city skyline to the northeast. From where he stood, however, the view was fairly restricted. This had taken some getting used to, and with understandable reason. Megan's office at UpLink SanJo was catercorner to the boss's far plusher suite next door—which Gordian only visited three or four times a month, max, since his stepdown—and the great rugged heave of the slope had always seemed to smack right up against your eyes through *its* floor-to-ceiling window.

"How did things go with Ricci?" Megan asked now, drawing his attention from the office towers across the street.

"I haven't spoken to him," Nimec said. "Plan to do that in about an hour."

Megan shot him a glance.

"The conference he conveniently skipped out on was yesterday," she said.

"Meg, he accounted for—"

"I want him leaving for New York tomorrow, the next day at the latest."

"I know."

"So why haven't you already *had* your talk?"

"WOW," Nimec said.

Megan looked confused.

"Wow?" she said.

"WOW, capital letters, right," Nimec said. "It's short for Women Opposed to War."

Megan's puzzled expression had deepened.

"Are we participants in the same conversation here?" she said. "Because I'm having a tough time following it, Pete."

Nimec stepped away from the window and sat down opposite her.

"WOW's a group based in San Fran, claims to have maybe five thousand members all told. There's an Internet site for it, natch," he said. "The organizers are big into peace, and lately they've had it in for us."

"By 'us' . . . you mean UpLink."

Nimec gave her a nod.

"They've posted all kinds of negative stuff," he said. "From their standpoint, we're belligerent global agitators."

"You're joking."

Nimec shook his head.

"It's a free country," he said, shrugging. "That's what they believe."

"Because we're a DoD contractor?"

"Designing the mechanisms of carnage, right," Nimec said. "And because of the security forces . . . they call them quasi-militaristic units . . . we put at our foreign stations."

Megan gave him a look.

"You *are* kidding me," she said.

Nimec reached out and tapped the back of her computer screen.

"You want to log on to their home page?" he said. "I did it last night. What's on there comes from open sources. Newspaper reports, politicians, even our own press releases . . . the facts are accurate, but they know how to cut and paste them in ways that hurt."

Megan frowned thoughtfully.

"Context is everything," she said. "Can you give me examples?"

"Sure," Nimec said. "They're critical of how we handled our run-in with those rogue paramilitaries in Gabon last year. They say we violated Brazil's national sovereignty that time we fought off the sabotage team in Mato Grosso. The same for when terrorists came after our satcom ground station in Russia—"

Nimec saw Megan's eyes widen.

"I lived through that one and we were almost *massacred* there, Pete," she said. "They also went after the Russian president, whom our Sword ops saved from cold-blooded assassination."

"So we could sink our hooks into him and his government," Nimec said. "It's part of a grand scheme we've hatched to muscle up on vulnerable, cash-strapped societies for our own omnicapitalistic motives."

"Omnicapitalistic?"

"Don't look at me," Nimec said. "I'm still trying to figure out quasi-militaristic."

Megan shook her head.

"These WOW people," she said. "May I assume they offer their bright ideas about what we *should* do to defend ourselves against attack?"

Nimec gave a nod.

"Their position's that sharing art, music, and poetry is always the best response to violence."

"Always."

"Uh-huh."

"Against any aggressor."

"Uh-huh."

"In every instance, whatever the circumstances."

"Something about it elevating the human condition, right." Nimec shrugged. "Bongo dancing might be recommended, too, but I'd have to check online to be positive."

Megan gave him a look and then went back to shaking her head.

"We weren't being singled out alone, if that makes you feel better," Nimec said. "They've got a whole list of evildoers who are keeping everybody else from the next step in evolution. Corporations, political parties . . . there's even some writer who cranks out paperback thrillers, I forget his name."

Megan was quiet a moment. She tucked a loose tress of auburn hair behind her ear.

"Okay," she said. "How does this nonsense connect to Ricci?"

"Last week a couple of women tried to get through security at our Cupertino R and D plant," Nimec said. "No fancy tactics involved. They piggyback their way into a main entrance around lunchtime, when they know there's a lot of foot traffic. Wait for employees to get smartcard authorization, slip in behind them." He shrugged. "Our tailgate sensors picked them up at the door, tagged them as intruders. Then security watched to see what they were up to. The procedure's routine . . . we have visitors all the time who don't bother checking in at the guard desk for a pass. Act like it's an inconvenience we impose on them for no good reason, and they're in too much of a hurry. Usually it turns out the person's okay—a salesman, a staffer's friend or relative— and he or she just needs to learn that kind of thing won't wash in our facilities."

"And this time?"

"The guards caught them trying use our computers and held them for the cops."

"Do we know what they were trying to access in those machines?" Megan said.

Nimec shook his head.

"Security closed in too soon, a mistake I won't let them forget," he said. "But we did find out the women are members of a certain group I've been talking about."

Megan raised her eyebrows.

"No," she said.

"Yeah," Nimec said. "And there's more. You remember those jerk kids who got busted trying to crack our system a few months ago, plaster our Web site with smut?"

"The two UCLA students," Megan said. "Brothers, weren't they?"

Nimec nodded.

"They did recon for months," he said. "Internet port

scans, network sweeps, everything they could do to probe us. At its peak it was happening once, twice an hour. Our techies figured an attack was coming, waited for our intruder detection software to backtrace their IP signatures, fed them phony passwords and entry codes. When the college boys tried using them to compromise our system, we nailed them."

Megan looked at him again.

"Pete, are you telling me they were . . . ah, how shall I put it . . . agents of WOW?"

"Something like that," he said. "Probably less stupid than calling them Brothers Opposed to War."

"BOW," Megan said. "Cute, Pete."

Nimec shrugged. "Anyway, one of the ladies that got nabbed in Cupertino happens to be Mom," he said.

Megan sighed heavily.

"Tell me that Ricci's their dear old dad, and it's your fault if I keel over sideways with an embolism."

Nimec smiled.

"The day before yesterday, we got a phone call from the feds about the case they're building . . . this was late, after I'd let Ricci know about our conference and headed on home," he said. "What I started explaining to you before is that Ricci's the one who took the call. Spoke to the lead investigator, who told him about a meeting scheduled for early the next morning between the FBI and prosecutors from the attorney general's office. They offered to let us have somebody sit in and listen, give input, whatever—a last-minute courtesy invite. The law still hasn't caught up to computer crime, and they're looking at different statutes that are already in the books, figuring out what sort of case they can build. Ricci thought he ought to head out to the capital, and you won't hear me argue he was wrong."

Megan considered that. "He could have given you notice," she said. "Phoned, e-mailed, dropped a quick memo on your desk. Done anything but leave us in the dark."

Nimec nodded.

"Agreed," he said. "I'll talk to him and ask why he didn't."

"While you're at it," Megan said, "you might want to find out about the bruises he's been sporting on his face and knuckles since Monday morning."

They exchanged looks in the momentary silence.

"If they got there over the weekend, on his own time, I'm not sure that's any of our business," Nimec said.

"I'd like the chance to make an informed judgment," Megan said. "There's been a developing pattern of conduct with Ricci. No, scratch that. A *worsening* pattern. Whatever's behind it, you know it isn't good. And it won't help to lay cover for him."

"You think that's what I'm doing?"

"If 'looking away' is easier for you to swallow, I'll go with it," Megan said. "Let's not play word games here. We both know Tom isn't right. He hasn't been for a while."

"And so you're express-mailing him east."

Megan started to say something, appeared to reconsider.

"What precisely bothers you about my decision, Pete?"

Nimec shrugged.

"Nothing to fuss over," he said. "It's just that you making it on the spot caught me by surprise."

"The truth is, I caught *myself* by surprise . . . but I wouldn't take a do-over if I could," she said. "It was really two thoughts coming together on their own. I've been thinking a change of scenery might be in order for Ricci. That some distance might give us all a clearer perspective on what's wrong, and maybe some ideas about how to fix it. When he didn't arrive for the conference, that part of it solidified in my mind. And as things developed, and I saw there was no wearing down Noriko's opposition, I decided it would be best to send someone from our office to New York."

Nimec grunted.

"I noticed she rubbed you the wrong way," he said.

"Noriko sees the Sullivan matter as a disruption to her work. She makes no bones about resenting our interference. And I feel she needs to be kept honest."

"Doesn't change how you came off," Nimec said. "A few hours before the conference you were at my gym preaching patience. But you undercut her. Did it in front of me and Rollie."

"It isn't anything personal," Megan insisted with a shrug. "I have high regard for her abilities, Pete. But let's say there are some people who need to be shown the stick before the carrot."

Nimec looked at her a moment, pulled at his ear.

"Sounds belligerent and agitating to me," he said.

Megan smiled thinly, shrugged, leaned forward across her desk.

"Bow-wow," she said.

Which Nimec guessed was as good a way as any to call their meeting to an end.

Industrial parks with billowing smokestacks filled Zaheer's view out the windshield as he turned his leased Mercury sedan off the New Jersey Turnpike just west of Trenton, checked the route directions he'd generated with a free Internet-based mapping service, and went through a quick series of turns and traffic signals. The closeup street map guided him to his desired junction in minutes.

Zaheer drove past long bands of strip malls and fast-food restaurants interspersed with vacant weeded lots, the dead stalks piercing scales of dirty ice and snow to shiver stiffly in the wind. He soon found himself among the sprawling waterfront factories he'd spotted from the highway and read the corporate names above their entrances. The one penned onto his map was over to his left, a fenced-in employee parking area beside the plant's main building. There were between fifteen and twenty vehicles slotted inside.

Going very slowly, noting the security cameras high up on either side of its otherwise unguarded gate, Zaheer passed the factory and turned up a street that ran back along the width of its parking area. His map coordinates showed that he was headed north, cruising past the east side of the plant. Perhaps halfway down the street a chain-link divider crossed the parking area and restricted admittance to another outdoor site behind it. The perimeter fence had been hung with metal CHEMICAL HAZARD and NO TRESPASSING signs as it stretched on back.

Here Zaheer's attention was caught by a large number of cylindrical storage tanks. Thirty to forty feet tall, they rose in close groupings from level concrete support platforms, six tanks to a cluster, frameworks of galvanized-steel ladders and handholds climbing up their dull gray sides. He could see tangles of curved, narrow pipelines snaking between the rail-encircled domes of each tank cluster, with a wider pipe leading along the ground from the platform bottom to the factory's rear wall.

Zaheer slid his car down the block toward a four-way intersection.

With few other vehicles on the road, Zaheer stopped at a red light in the crossing and glanced around. He could see an abandoned gas station directly behind the yard containing the storage tanks, bounded off from it by a planted copse of evergreen trees. The trees looked withered and neglected,

their gnarled roots buried in a deep carpet of shed pine needles. Around the intersection's three opposing corners were
the type of satellite businesses that would have deliberately
sprung up near the station before it shut down, their owners
hoping to attract spillover customers. There was a small Mc-
Donald's on the far side of the exchange. Also across the
street, but running off down the sidewalk from the northwest
corner, were a coin-operated car wash, an automotive supply
shop, and a nameless bar with dark, sooty windows. On Zaheer's immediate right a U-Haul rental lot filled with trucks
and trailers of various sizes occupied the intersection's
southwest corner.

Its advantageous location prompted him to smile with
cool satisfaction.

Zaheer turned into the defunct gas station before the light
could change, then made a circular inspection of the prop-
erty. He glided around the island where its uprooted pumps
must once have stood, rolled past its empty cashier's booth
and peered into the vacant shell of its refreshment shop as he
drove by the front window. Convinced the premises were deserted, he pulled his Mercury up to the screen of evergreens
behind the shop, got out, and took a small digital camera
from his coat pocket.

Zaheer stood near the trunk of the car and took a quick series of photos of the intersection's four corners, paying special attention to the U-Haul rental lot. Then he turned toward
the dying boundary trees, paused for a cautious glance over
each shoulder, and stepped forward under their black, gan-
gly boughs.

Hidden within the copse of pines, Zaheer could see the
enormous storage tanks about a hundred and fifty feet ahead
of him. Again his camera clicked. There was no fence bar-
ring access to the factory grounds from this approach. It

would have been premature to assume the site was clear of security, he thought—a guard, or guards, might very well patrol it during certain hours. Almost beyond a doubt there would be an overnight watch in place. Men, perhaps dogs. But if anyone was on shift right now, Zaheer hadn't noticed. Were it his desire, he could have easily walked right over to the tanks before it was possible to stop him . . . and when the time came to act, he had full faith there would be no need to get that close.

Al-hamdu lillahi, God had already brought him more than close enough, he thought in silence.

Zaheer stood there in the trees a while longer, observing the site and taking more than a dozen additional snapshots of the tanks for later reference. Then he returned the camera to his coat pocket and hastened back to the car.

Hasul Benazir would be pleased with the intelligence he had gathered today; all was falling well and neatly into place.

Nimec went down to Rollie Thibodeau's office and found the door partially open. He knocked and walked through as Thibodeau looked up from his desk.

"Come right on in, why don'tcha?" Thibodeau said.

Nimec pushed the door shut behind him.

"This room been swept recently?" he asked.

Thibodeau met his gaze. He held a can of Diet Coke in his hand.

"Walls are clean, if that's what you askin'," he said.

Nimec approached him and sat. The room was windowless, as Thibodeau preferred. Stacks of paperwork hid the desktop. An old-fashioned upright balance scale stood in one corner, flaking pink paint. Thibodeau had once told him it was a memento of some kind from Louisiana.

"We have to talk," Nimec said.

"Kinda got that sense."

"Everything we say stays right here. Between us."

Thibodeau nodded.

"I need you to tell me about Ricci," Nimec said.

"You mind I use four-letter words?"

Nimec didn't smile. He watched Thibodeau sip his cola, and then nod toward the water cooler.

"Be more sugar-free in the fridge compartment, you want some," he said.

"No thanks, hate the stuff."

Thibodeau patted his reduced stomach.

"Me, too," he said. "But it works."

Nimec watched him closely.

"I want to know what happened in Big Sur," he said. "When Ricci got the boss's daughter out of that cabin where she was held hostage."

Thibodeau was silent. Nimec kept watching his face.

"Filed my report four months ago," Thibodeau said.

"And I read it," Nimec said. "Back when it was written, and a bunch of times since."

"Ain't no detail was left out."

"No?"

"No."

Nimec sat there studying his features with sharp interest.

"How about what you personally took from those details?" he said. "Nothing omitted there?"

"Like?"

"Suspicions," Nimec said. "Possible conclusions."

Thibodeau looked at him.

"I wrote down what I saw," he said. "What I knew."

"Sum it up for me again," Nimec said.

"Thought you just said you been over the report."

"Once more, Rollie."

Thibodeau lifted the soda can to his lips, took a long swallow, and shrugged.

"Place had two floors," he said. "Ricci's in the lead, takes our extraction team through the back door. We see four men downstairs, get the drop on them—"

"*We.*"

"Everybody but Ricci, yeah," Thibodeau said. "Soon's we're in, I see him run on up to the second floor, see his backup follow. Ricci knew Julia was in an upstairs room, shook it outta one of her kidnappers. Knew she was alone with *Le Chaute Sauvage,* a killer who'd snuff a man or woman's life same way you'd blink an eye."

"When you say his backup . . . this would have been Derek Glenn from our San Diego unit."

"Right."

"A guy Ricci pulled in on the operation," Nimec said. "He got tight with him since they worked together a couple years back."

Thibodeau shrugged.

"Tight as anybody can be," he said. "Or so I hear."

Nimec grunted. "Okay, give me the rest."

Thibodeau spread his hands.

"Didn't see much after Glenn went up," he said. "I hear a crash on the second floor, what I can tell is a door bein' kicked in. Can't leave the first floor till we got a clamp on it. Disarm the prisoners, cuff 'em, get 'em all together in a single room. Then check and secure the other rooms. And there are attack dogs need to be sedated. Once we get it all under control, I take some of the men upstairs—"

"This is how long after the entry?" Nimec said.

"These things, you know they move in a flash."

"*About* how long, Rollie?" Nimec said.

Thibodeau shrugged, his hands still wide apart.

"More'n five minutes, less'n ten," he said. "By the time I'm upstairs, Julia's out of the room. I see Glenn in the hall keepin' her steady on her feet . . . the Killer had her tied to a chair with ropes, and there's still little pieces of 'em hangin' from her. I order the men to get her safe away, then head toward the room where Ricci found her, but the door's propped shut."

"This is after Ricci kicked it in."

"Be better if you go over that with him," Thibodeau said. "From what I heard afterward, Ricci found the Killer holdin' a knife to Julia's throat, got a trigger on him, warned him he moved a hair, he was gonna die. There a history between them to consider. Ricci was trackin' him for over a year, after he bolted from that germ-weapon plant in Canada. That whole time, *Le Chaute Sauvage* was layin' low to ground, knowin' Ricci was breathin' down his neck. History. Ricci uses it to get into his head, offers him a deal—the Killer lets Julia go free, they both lose their weapons, face off man to man." He paused a moment. "The Killer's a hired hand. Got no personal reason to hurt Julia, knows he's dead if he uses the knife. He figures Ricci's givin' him his only chance, goes for it."

"And Ricci wedges a chair against the door as soon as Julia's out."

"Says his main reason was to put something there to block it 'case the Killer got around him, giving us a few seconds to pull her away. Used whatever he could reach, and the chair was it."

Nimec looked at him.

"But putting it there wasn't only about buying time for you," he said. "It was also part of the two of them going at it alone."

"That something to ask Ricci," Thibodeau said. He reached for his soda, sipped. "It was all over in that room before I put the ram to the door. I come in, find him on the floor, his leg bleedin' rivers from a knife cut. What I know from his report is that the two of them fought like hell, an' *Le Chaute Sauvage* grabbed the blade from where Ricci dropped it. They wound up out on a balcony, out there hundreds of feet over the canyon, and the Killer took a long fall."

Nimec sat very still, his eyes on Thibodeau.

"Took a fall, or was pushed?" he said. "Let's get it right out in the open, Rollie."

Thibodeau was quiet for a while, looking across the desk at Nimec.

"Tom Ricci never been my favorite person," he said. "You won't see me shed no tears for that killer, though. Whatever did or didn't happen in there, Julia's life was a tradeoff I gonna take any time. It's finished, and we all got to walk on."

"Doesn't sound to me like you believe Ricci's done that."

"Try'n keep what I believe to myself," Thibodeau said. He shrugged a little. "You asked what I knew for a fact, I answered based on what I saw and heard."

Nimec shook his head.

"*Some men does dead before their time*," he said. "Those were your words about Ricci, or close enough. You telling me now I got their meaning wrong?"

Thibodeau met his gaze.

"Can't say what was in his mind going into that room," he said. "Don't got any more of a clue what's on it now."

"And that's that," Nimec said.

Thibodeau nodded and sat without further comment.

The silence between them stretched on, longer than the first. Then Nimec stood, his expression sober.

"If Ricci entered intending to execute a man, blocked the door so there wouldn't be witnesses, I can't let it go," he said. "I need to find out."

Thibodeau shrugged again. He drained what was left in the soda can, crunched it in his fist, tossed it into the wastebasket under his desk.

"You do, I expect it ain't gonna come no good," he said.

Nimec looked at him.

"Maybe not," he said. "But I tell you one thing, Rollie. I don't, and none of us better kid ourselves into thinking we'll ever be able to walk on."

Stiff-necked and fatigued after almost seventy-two hours of travel through stormy weather, Khalid exited the jeep, slammed the door behind him, and strode around to the front grille against an onrushing blast of snow.

He had been far short of the mark about the length of their drive to the Neelam Valley, estimating it would take a full two days, a prospect that had made him less than sanguine at the time. In hindsight, Khalid would have gladly accepted it. With the gale having inundated the entire region they needed to cover, he and Yousaf were still over a hundred kilometers from their destination. They would be fortunate to reach the village of Halmat by dawn in these conditions, and night was not yet even half over.

They had taken shifts driving round-the-clock, Yousaf adamant in his insistence they press onward over rolling mountainous terrain that would have taxed one's endurance in the best of circumstances . . . and they had until now encountered nothing but winter at its most relentless and savage. When Yousaf did acquiesce to a stop, it would be just long enough for them to get out for a miserable, hurried piss in the cold wind and snow, or sit inside their vehicle eating sparely and hastily of meal rations appropriated from the army rangers they had disposed of behind them on the road to Chirak. Then, impatient, he would order them to move on.

The storm had eased only on occasion; Yousaf's head-strong resolve never once. Earlier in their journey the snow had blown over the ground in wildly shifting eddies, twist-ing into undulant serpentine braids that deceived and wea-ried the eye, making it impossible to be sure they were even driving in a straight line. By the second night it began to come on hard and thick with the north wind's direct frontal onslaught, piling up around them in deep rippled sheets, coating the windshield faster than their wipers could scrape it clean. Tonight's progress had been an ever-worsening struggle as the center of the storm had seemed to gather around them in a turbulent mass. The moonlight had been choked off, the shadows of the mountain peaks and cornices blanked from sight along with any waypoints Khalid had meant to use for orientation. Were it not for their GPS re-ceiver they would have certainly been lost, and might well have found themselves driving in endless, wandering cir-cles. There had been embankments around which they had needed to detour, pits and ditches that seemed to open be-neath them like sucking, toothless mouths. Even with Yousaf at the wheel, reluctant to lose a moment, they had twice needed to halt due to losses of visibility and traction. On each instance Khalid had left the jeep to remove large cakes of frozen debris from between its tires and wheel wells, and then clean its headlamps of the filmy white cataracts of snow that would collect over them, blocking their output to render them all but useless.

This, then, was their third unplanned stop in the past two hours, and it had seemed to throw Yousaf—never a talkative companion—into an especially sullen and overanxious state.

His hands locked around the wheel, he had watched in brittle silence as Khalid pushed out his door, then sat very still with the motor running, and the wipers making their ceaseless rhythmical swipes across the windshield.

He went to the back of the jeep, used a few good, hard kicks to break up the clotted snow around the mudflaps of both rear tires, and scooped whatever didn't crumble out of the well with his gloved hands. Then he returned to the vehicle's front end. A glance through the windshield revealed that Yousaf was still staring at him rigidly from the driver's seat, as if he were somehow to blame for the storm and its resultant delays.

Khalid crouched to brush off the snow-covered right headlamp. To get out of the fiendish weather and know their objective was accomplished . . . these alone were adequate reasons for his eagerness to arrive at the town of Halmat in the valley. But the thought of separating himself from Yousaf and his foul moods gave him added incentive to push on.

Finished with one lamp now, Khalid set himself toward the passenger side of the jeep to clean the second, but had barely gotten as far as the middle of the fender when he was startled by the loud rev of the engine.

He turned his head toward the windshield, thinking Yousaf must have accidentally footed the gas pedal while still shifted into PARK . . . and then was horrified to see the jeep come bounding forward, bearing down on him with a sudden snarl of acceleration. Yousaf's tightened features were visible through the windshield, his eyes locked on Khalid with a terrible, narrow intensity.

Khalid was too shocked to have a chance of getting out of the heavy vehicle's way, too shocked to do anything but scream raggedly into the wind as it struck his body—and then even screaming was beyond him. He flew backward off his feet, taking a half spin before he landed roughly in the snow, his left arm and leg twisted at a grotesque angle. Blood squirted into his mouth from somewhere deep inside him, spilled over his chin, steamed from his torn flesh in the subzero Himalayan cold.

Gagging and choking, Khalid flopped over onto his right side, felt a sharp stab of pain in the center of his chest, and knew at once that several of his ribs had been shattered. Then he realized through his pain that the jeep's lights had continued to shine on him, pinning him in their beams. The right headlamp dim with its film of snow. The one he'd cleared off harsh and blindingly bright. He somehow managed to prop himself up on his elbow, tried dragging himself through the snow out of its direct glare.

But again Khalid was given no time to move even an inch. His eyes wide, his mouth yawping with shock, he saw Yousaf stop the vehicle, shift into reverse, come to another momentary stop, and then charge rapidly toward him again.

The jeep rolled over Khalid at full speed, crushing him into the ground, its wheels dragging his limp, mangled body along for almost two minutes before finally leaving it behind in a heap of churned and bloodied snow.

Yousaf did not bother to look back. His face set with determination, he plunged on alone through the storm-tossed darkness, bearing his precious cargo to those who awaited it across the furthermost borders of night and nation.

Roger Gordian studied the pile of rocks in front of his wheelbarrow, saw one he liked for the course he'd been laying on his stone wall, picked it up with a grunt of mild exertion, and then placed it atop the last two rocks he'd stacked. Nice, he thought. A beaut, in fact. Shifting it around for the best fit, Gordian pressed down on it with his hand, noticed it wasn't quite balanced, readjusted it, pressed down again, felt it wobble some more, made another unsuccessful readjustment, scratched his chin, and knelt to investigate.

Ahh, he thought with a nod. *Elementary.*

From his crouched position Gordian could see a gap between his latest addition to the wall and its two underlying stones. He poked his finger into it, discovered it went in all the way to the middle knuckle. What he would need to do here was fill that hole.

He got to his feet, studied the rock pile for something the right size, didn't see any likely candidates, and hunted around in the grass for a minute. Then a little chunk of quartz caught his eye from a nearby patch of grass and he went on over for a closer look.

Above him at the crest of the hill that sloped down in landscaped terraces from the verandah of their Palo Alto home, Ashley stood watering her hillside plants with a garden hose, sweeping it from side to side, leaving transitory rainbows in the air as sunlight passed through the fine mist around its nozzle. A year earlier they'd spent thousands for an underground sprinkler system after Ash had decided that using the hose was ridiculously obsolete. For a while she'd given the newly installed system unqualified raves, preached the gospel of liberation from the endless dragging and snagging of hoses, and talked repeatedly about donating the evil rubber serpent—and its various carriers, extensions, and attachments—to a Goodwill shop she supported in town.

Then she'd had a spontaneous reversal of faith. Or at least it had seemed spontaneous to Gordian. Maybe she'd contemplated it long and hard in private. All he knew for certain was that Ashley had stalked in from the garden one day, complained the sprinklers weren't reaching anything close to all her "spots," and gotten the old hose out of the shed where it had languished for months—unused but surprisingly undonated. Sprinkler systems, she'd declared to him, were at best secondary aids to dedicated keepers of the green, and, at their worst, excuses for the lazy and slothful to shirk their gardening responsibilities.

Gordian hadn't personally noticed a significant difference between Ash's pre-sprinkler and post-sprinkler hillside plants. They had always looked beautiful and well-tended to him. But then, he accepted that she had superior garden aesthetics. Just as it went without question in their household—well, mostly— that he was the better builder.

Gordian plucked the stone he'd spotted from its grassy nest and inspected it in his palm. It was about four inches wide and somewhat wedge-shaped . . . just what the wall-doctor ordered.

Now he brought his new find back to the wall, worked it partway into the gap with his fingertips, took a hammer from his tool belt, and carefully chinked the stone into place. Then he gave the large rock he'd been trying to stabilize another test.

It sat steadily on the two supporting rocks beneath it.

Okay, he thought. *Very nifty.*

Gordian stood admiring the wall for a bit. There was still a lot of work ahead of him before it was finished. Two weeks' worth, maybe three. But he thought he'd gotten the hang of how to make the stones hold together, and always took satisfaction from figuring out how things worked. Simple things, complicated things, they were all enjoyable to him.

But tell me . . . are they comparable? an inner voice asked. *Not equally, mind you. I've cut you some slack there and didn't use that particular word. What I want is your overall feeling of how one stacks up against the other—excuse the pun.*

Gordian frowned at the nagging voice in his head. It didn't speak up too often, but when it did, it was with the leery, contentious tone of an attorney cross-examining a reluctant witness on the stand, always using the old courtroom tactic of never asking a question whose answer you didn't already know. It would not, however, be necessary to put Gordian under solemn oath to gain an admission that his backyard stonewalling didn't approach—never mind *equal,* counselor—the challenge of turning the failed electronics firm he'd bought at a bargain-basement price into a technological giant, or designing the GAPSFREE avionic suite that had revolutionized the U.S. military's recon and target acquisition capabilities to earn him his wealth and reputation. Nor did it quite impart the satisfaction he'd gotten from taking great strides toward the creation of a truly global telecommunications web. But Gordian had given ten years of his life to service in the Air Force, better than double that many to UpLink. The next chunk of it belonged to the wife and family that had sacrificed so much to his dream of a world made freer by the open spread of information . . . and he meant to share it with them with the same passion he'd devoted to his professional and public occupations. While it seemed he'd taken sail on his sixtieth birthday only yesterday, the line of that rear horizon was further away in fact than in his mind. Why keep looking back through a telescope to measure himself against his own past achievements? Gordian didn't know. Still, he sometimes had trouble steering away from making comparisons. And maybe, counselor, just maybe, the greatest challenge every man faced as he grew old was trying to recognize how pointless it was to compete with the younger man he'd been.

Gordian couldn't have begun to guess why this train of thought abruptly made him remember that he owed Lenny Reisenberg a phone call, but *something* in it did, and he paused as he was about to lift another rock from the pile to dial Lenny's office on his cellular.

"Boss!" Lenny said when the receptionist transferred the call. "I was hoping you'd buzz me. Wasn't sure if I should give things a little while longer—"

"I figured, Len," Gordian said. "And I apologize for not getting back to you sooner."

"Busy soaking up the joys of retirement?"

"So to speak," Gordian said. "I have to admit, though, there are moments when I feel out of my element. Like I'm playing hooky from school, I suppose."

"'Cutting class,' Boss," Lenny said. "Or 'skipping school.' You say 'playing hooky' to my kids, they won't have any idea what you mean." He paused. "Hell, *I* don't know where the term comes from."

"I think the reference is to fishing," Gordian said. "You'd hide a string and a hook in your book bag and then sneak on over to the lake to see what you could catch."

Lenny *ahh*ed.

"Wouldn't have guessed," he said. "The only lake we had in Brooklyn was this cesspool in Prospect Park. And the only thing I ever caught there was a foot fungus that lasted for a year."

Gordian smiled.

"Lenny, I have some news for you," he said. "I've gotten our security people to move on the Sullivan matter. They're either already in high gear, or will be very soon."

Lenny was silent a moment

"Boss, I can't tell you how much I appreciate this," he said.

"Forget it, Lenny."

"Really—"

Gordian glanced up the hillside at Ashley, who saw him

looking and waved. He raised his hand over his head, waved back.

"Len, please, it isn't that big a deal," he said. "Not when I consider all the favors you've done for me over the years."

"If you insist, Boss," Lenny said. "I still don't know what to say."

"Then save your words for that woman who asked for our help, Mary Sullivan," Gordian said. "Make sure she knows we'll do our best to find out what's happened to her husband."

Lenny was silent another moment before he answered.

"I will, Boss," he said. "And I'll be keeping my fingers crossed it doesn't turn out to be anything too bad."

Detective First Class Ismael Ruiz, Tenth Precinct, had decided to postpone asking DeSanto the last little question on his mind right now until after he'd reviewed what the guy already told him, making sure he'd gotten everything down right.

Ruiz sat at his desk in the squad room, glancing over his notepad, tapping it with the sharp end of his pencil.

"Okay," he said. "If I understand it, you've been Patrick Sullivan's beard while he's been conducting an extramarital relationship—"

"Hold on," DeSanto said from the chair opposite the detective. "You didn't hear me use that word."

Ruiz looked at him as if to ask *what* word.

"Beard," DeSanto said. "I never mentioned I was his beard."

Ruiz frowned, thinking it was going to be one of those afternoons. A thin, dark-skinned thirty-five-year-old whose height was generously recorded at 5' 7" on his driver's license, he was often mistaken for someone in his early twenties when people met him for the first time, including the scumbag hoods he busted, the cranky New Yorkers he was sworn to protect from them, and even other cops of junior rank. While his wife insisted he ought to be happy about his youthful appearance, pointing out there were people who would pay anything to shave a decade of wear and tear off their looks—and *did* in droves every single day with skin peelings, botox injections, and plastic surgery—it wasn't something he especially liked, since, his high rank aside, it sometimes stood as an obstacle to him getting his props on the job without having to make a muscle.

"Sorry," Ruiz said now. Whatever DeSanto's beef with his common slang, it wouldn't be courteous or productive to offend him. "Beard, it's a figure of speech. For somebody who lays cover for somebody else that's having an affair—"

"A homosexual affair," DeSanto said. "Which Pat and I absolutely aren't. *Homosexual*, you understand."

"I do, yes."

"Because when you use the word you did . . . well I guess it comes from when gay men used to wear beards so people would think they were macho, though nowadays that doesn't tell you anything." He paused. "There's a veep at the bank where I work—got a bush like an ape on his face—who just told me he's marrying his boyfriend. Which, you know, doesn't bother me. These times we live in, I think about what can happen to people, I say let them be happy any way they can, long as they don't hurt anybody."

Ruiz offered no comment. He'd actually believed the term beard had originated with *lesbians* who dated or married men to hide their true sexual preferences. But he didn't want to get off on some bullshit tangent about his choice of words. Not when there were two fresh missing persons cases Anthony DeSanto had likely tied together with the information he'd volunteered here.

"To verify, the bank where you work . . . this is the Dunne S and L near Union Square?" he said, steering things back on course.

"Yes. A couple blocks from my apartment."

"And you're a loan officer there?"

"A commercial loan manager," DeSanto said, and straightened his shoulders. He was a blunt-featured, seriously overweight man who was nonetheless very well-groomed, his thick brown hair worn in a neat layer cut, his navy-blue business suit tailored flatteringly to cover up the full extent of his bulk.

Ruiz waited a second before saying anything else. DeSanto's body language told him he'd better get the professional handle right next time. Whatever the hell distinction there was between loan officer and manager, it seemed important to the guy, who was apparently a stickler for proper terminologies.

"Talking about Patrick Sullivan and Corinna Banks," he said. "Your knowledge is that they've been carrying on an affair for some time. . . . That accurate?"

"Yeah," DeSanto said. He shrugged. "It didn't start out serious. Pat loves his wife, I can tell you. But he's in sales, travels around to different cities, even different countries sometimes."

"This is with Armbright Industries."

DeSanto nodded.

"Selling fancy techware."

DeSanto nodded again.

"The traveling bit can be hard . . . a man spends weeks away from home in strange places, it's natural to get lonely," he said. "Pat will be out of town somewhere, hit a bar, buy some woman a few drinks, share a good time with her, end of story."

Ruiz remained silent, thinking he could be apart from his wife for a thousand days and nights—no, make that a thousand times *ten*—and never consider sharing that kind of good time with another woman.

"And that's how he met Ms. Banks?" he asked after a moment, studying his notes and realizing he hadn't yet gotten that information from DeSanto. "While he was on the road?"

"No." DeSanto hesitated, smoothed his suit jacket. "The truth is somebody I was *dating* introduced them."

"A girlfriend."

"My *ex*-girlfriend," DeSanto said. "Joyce happened to know Corinna, worked with her at a cosmetic counter in Bloomie's."

"That would be Bloomingdale's here in the city."

"Right."

"On East Fifty-ninth Street."

"Right."

"So Pat's fooling around isn't *only* restricted to his long and lonely business trips."

DeSanto gave him a look.

"I'm telling you," he said, "Patty loves his wife and family, does his best for them."

Ruiz let that stand, instantly regretting his sarcasm. You were on the force long enough, you had to fight succumbing to a confrontational us-and-them mentality. This wasn't a grilling, after all. DeSanto had come forward on his own.

"Your ex have a second name?" he said.

"Breyers."

"That's B-R-E-Y-E-R-S?"

"Like the ice cream, right."

"Somewhere she can be contacted if necessary?"

"Don't ask me where she is now, it was a bad split," he

said. "Far as I know she moved down south to Atlanta a couple years ago."

Ruiz grunted, jotting the name in his pad.

"Back to Patrick and Corinna again," he said. "You told me it didn't start out serious between them."

"Right."

"That they were, in your opinion, having a casual fling."

"At first, anyway," DeSanto said. "Though Corinna got to be special to him."

"Even before she got pregnant?"

DeSanto nodded.

"Before he found out Corinna was pregnant, before she took the test."

"You mean the paternity test."

"Yeah." DeSanto produced a long, slow sigh. "It kind of shows of what I've been trying to explain about Pat. Once he found out he was the baby's father, he went out of his way to take care of Corinna."

"Never pressed her to get an abortion?"

DeSanto shook his head firmly.

"She wanted to keep the baby," he said. "Besides, Pat's a Catholic. He's against that sort of thing."

Doesn't seem to have a problem making exceptions for adultery, Ruiz thought but did not say.

He took a minute to check his notes for more points that needed clarification, eager to wrap the interview and start figuring out what it all meant.

"You've said Corinna was living in an apartment in Yonkers when Pat met her."

"Yeah."

"That she was still there when she gave birth to their little girl . . . Andrea, is it?"

"Yeah," DeSanto said.

"And that Corinna and her daughter stayed in that apartment for several years."

DeSanto nodded.

"The place was rent-stabilized, so Corinna could afford it as long as she went on working," he said. "She wasn't out to bleed Pat dry. Supported herself the best she could, and he helped out with the rest. Money for child care, health insurance, whatever expenses he could manage. He earned good money, but sometimes I still wondered how he did it. Two families to look out for, it had to be tough for him."

"Must've gotten a lot easier this past year, year-and-a-half," Ruiz said, and looked up from his pad.

DeSanto was silent a moment.

"You're talking about him moving Corinna and the girl into the city, I'd say it was a better setup for all of them," he said. "Easier for Patty, I know. Working in Manhattan, he can stop by their place in Chelsea almost every day. Lunchtime, after work, whenever he has a chance. Once a week he'll stay there until late at night. Tells Mary . . . that's his wife . . . tells her he's with me watching a ball game. Sometimes he sleeps over there, says the game ran late, or we had too much to drink, or the weather's bad."

"And you always cover for him."

DeSanto nodded.

"I'm his best friend," he said. "I cover."

Ruiz kept his eyes on him.

"Buying a Chelsea condo would've set Pat back two, three hundred grand at a bargain rate," he said. "A few months later he leases Corinna a Jaguar, which also has to cost him a small fortune. And then according to you, he tells her she doesn't have to work anymore . . . correct?"

DeSanto nodded again.

"Yeah," he said. "He did all that."

Which brought Ruiz to a very critical question.

"How?" he said. "Pat win the Super Lotto? Find a buried treasure chest in Central Park?"

DeSanto hesitated, then slowly met his gaze.

"It's like what I told you before," he said. "The big bucks started coming in for him after Armbright bought that Pak company—"

"This would be the Kiran Group."

"Yeah," DeSanto said. "When Pat was moved over to its international wholesale division, things really took off for him income-wise."

"Must've taken off in the neighborhood of a few hundred thousand dollars a *year* over what he'd been earning."

Silence. DeSanto examined his jacket, smoothed it down over his sides.

"I don't have a clue how Pat found the extra padding for his wallet," he said after a while. "Pat didn't talk about it, I didn't ask."

"Never wondered?"

"Didn't *ask* him, is what I just told you."

"Your closest friend."

"That's right," DeSanto said. "Sometimes part of being a friend's realizing what *not* to talk about."

"But you think Pat and Corinna talked about it," Ruiz said.

DeSanto looked at him for a full thirty seconds before he finally nodded.

"Became pretty damn sure after Pat disappeared," he said.

"When she phoned you looking for him."

"She calls, his wife calls, I become information central," DeSanto said with a bleak smile. "It starts one-thirty in the morning. Mary's worried, leaves a couple messages on my machine—"

"This is last Wednesday."

"Pat's usual night to spend time with Corinna, right."

"And your night to cover for him."

"Right," DeSanto said. "Pat always warns me when he plans to sleep over in the city instead of just stay late."

"So your stories jibe for Mary."

DeSanto nodded.

"Meanwhile, Pat hasn't come home, Mary's worried he might've got into an accident because of that storm, wants to know if he's staying over at my place. At first I don't pick up the phone, let her talk to my answering machine. Got no idea what to tell her."

"Since Pat didn't tip you he'd be spending the entire night at Corinna's place."

"Like the two of us have it worked out going back forever," DeSanto said.

Ruiz nodded.

"Okay," he said. "Let's hear the rest."

"Detective, no disrespect, but I need to get back to the bank—"

"Once more and you'll be on your way," Ruiz said, cutting off his objection with a firm look.

DeSanto shook his head with resignation, sighed heavily.

"Around two o'clock or so, after Mary's *third* message, I decide to call Corinna's, ask for Pat, pass on the information that the wife's upset and he'd better get in touch," he said. "What I'm guessing—this is when I call—is that he got caught up in some heavy action over there made him forget all *about* the wife for a while, you know how it goes."

Actually, Ruiz didn't. Not firsthand. Never in a *million* years, firsthand.

"And then what?" he said.

"Then the phone rings again practically while I'm reaching for it. I figure this'll be Mary again, but instead it's Corinna, who's also half out of her skull with worry."

"Looking for Pat?" Ruiz said.

"Yeah." DeSanto's voice had begun to tremble a little. "Said he'd left her place to meet somebody on business—"

"This is around ten o'clock."

"He got the Jag out of the garage around ten-ish, right," DeSanto said. "Told her he'd see her in an hour, hour-and-a-half, but never came back."

"She didn't mention who the somebody he'd gone to meet might be?"

"No."

"Didn't mention where they were supposed to be hooking up?"

"No."

"Or what kind of business he could have had at that hour? In the middle of an *ice* storm?"

"No."

"And you didn't question her about it."

"No, I didn't," DeSanto said. He shrugged. "It was one of those situations I explained to you."

"When you felt you weren't supposed to ask."

DeSanto nodded.

"The next few days I'm on Corinna's case like you wouldn't believe," he said. "Phoning her, arguing she needs to tell the cops whatever she knows. But *she* insists Pat would be against it. Says it'd ruin his marriage, bring everything about the two of them out into the open."

And maybe bring out whatever it was he'd been doing to jump about five income brackets a year as a glorified parts salesman, Ruiz thought.

"So it goes back and forth between you," he said.

"Without her budging an inch," DeSanto said. "Corinna's

all crazed. Goes ballistic on me, saying I don't know what it's like to be in her shoes, stuff like that. Meanwhile, she tells me she's checked some parking-violations page online, found out the Jag's been towed to one of those police lots on the West Side. Which to me really proves something bad's happened. Why in the world would Pat abandon it otherwise?"

"But you still held out on contacting the police yourself."

DeSanto expelled another long sigh.

"It was a mistake," he said. "Looking back now, if I'd do anything different, it'd be to call you people right away. But if Pat's marriage blew up, I didn't want the bomb that fell from the sky to have my name on its nose cone. I made a promise to him . . . I mean, years ago. Swore I'd keep his thing with Corinna secret no matter what. And stupid as it sounds, I felt it was on *her* to decide what to say about it. How *much* to say." He shook his head. "When it finally got to where I had enough of waiting for her to get off the fence, and was ready to make the call, Corinna told me she'd been in touch with somebody who could help."

Ruiz looked at him. This was one of the details that had piqued his interest during DeSanto's first rendering of his story. "You're positive that's *all* she told you."

"Yeah."

"No mention of who that somebody was."

"None."

"But you didn't get the impression it was the authorities."

"That wasn't the feeling that came across to me over the phone, no."

"What sort of feeling *did* come across?"

DeSanto shook his head, spreading his hands a little.

"I can't explain it," he said. "Just that it wasn't the police, you know."

Ruiz let his answer stand right there, seeing no point in

pressing any further. But he wondered if the somebody in question could have been the same person Sullivan had gone to meet that night he vanished, or if there were at least *two* mysterious somebodies in the picture so far.

He flipped a page in his pad, quickly read over his few remaining lines of scribbled notes, decided he was almost finished with DeSanto.

"Your final phone conversation with Corinna was yesterday?" he asked.

DeSanto nodded.

"If you want to refer to it as a conversation," he said. "It was more like I talked, she yelled in my ear, then hung up on me."

"And you didn't hear from her after that."

"No." DeSanto said. "I tried to call back later on, got her machine. Would've tried again *today* . . . but then I saw that notice in this morning's paper."

"The police blotter."

DeSanto nodded.

"I'm telling you, Detective, I almost choked on my breakfast," he said. "Thought I'd never get the air back in my lungs."

Silence. Ruiz gave himself a minute to digest it all. A man and woman having an adulterous affair disappear, you might assume they'd gone off into the rosy sunset hand-in-hand—except for their four-year-old daughter being left behind at the day care center. Plus, he himself had been in Corinna Banks's apartment for a walkaround, and there had been every indication she'd only meant to step out for a few minutes. Freezer food thawing in the sink. Clothes in her mini washer/dryer. The television on, and the cable guide's scheduler set for two different programs airing later on that night. So what to make of things?

Ruiz knew he had to act fast tracking down these two people—the longer you waited, the colder any trail they'd left would become. His first steps would be to run what DeSanto had told him by his squad commander, establish a liaison with the Nassau County detectives who were presumably on the Sullivan case . . . *and* have that Jaguar pulled out of DOT impound for inspection right away. He also wanted the okay to go wide with this thing. Call a news conference, issue regular press releases, get images of Sullivan and Banks onto the airwaves. He would personally distribute fliers and handbills all over town . . . whatever could be done to get the public's help in conducting the investigation. With two missing persons here, and no clues to either one's whereabouts, you wanted to open up as many sources of information as possible.

Ruiz sat thoughtfully for another minute, wondering if there was anything more to be gotten out of DeSanto while he still had the guy here in front of him. Then he decided he might as well recheck DeSanto's contact information—his address, home and work phone numbers, and so forth—and let him head back to the office. They were done for the time being . . . aside from that one little question he'd been meaning to ask.

"Something I'm curious about, Mr. DeSanto," Ruiz said. "You say you put off calling us because you felt obliged to keep your buddy's secrets . . . went in circles with Corinna about that for a whole *week* . . . so how come you contacted me directly instead of using the anonymous tip line? That way you could have communicated everything you know, and still not have your name on that marriage bomb you mentioned."

DeSanto didn't answer for a moment. Then he tugged and smoothed his suit jacket again and sighed.

"When I read about Corinna, her disappearing so soon after Pat . . ." He looked at Ruiz, swallowed hard. "Me being Pat's best friend, I was scared I might be next in line. And just between us, Detective, *no* damned promise is worth dying over."

Lathrop was at a desk in the furnished shoebox of an apartment on Lexington Avenue with a bottle of beer beside his notebook computer and Missus Frakes perched on the other side of it staring at him. She'd managed to spring up there without needing a lift, and Lathrop supposed that made this one of her good days. He didn't yet know what kind of day it would be for him, but some complications had emerged in the broad scheme of things, and he meant to decide whether or not he could minimize their damage to his plans, or even turn them to his advantage.

Lathrop took a drink of beer and looked at the old coon cat, his fingers around the bottle's long neck.

"I thought we could sit tight a while longer," he said. "If I'd gotten the Dragonfly keys out of Sullivan's girlfriend, we'd be in a better position. But it is what it is, Missus Frakes. It is what it is. The house of cards I built for the two of us is feeling pretty shaky right about now, you agree?"

The cat watched him. Her gleaming limpid eyes were in contact with his, and they narrowed at the sound of his voice.

"Can't pretend not to know what this thing with the girlfriend means," Lathrop said. "It doesn't leave much time, eliminates options."

The coon stared at him from the top of the desk, her eyelids rising and falling in a demonstration of serene feline rapport. Lathrop approximated it with a blink of his eyes. In front of him his computer's power was off, its screen raised but blank.

He lifted his beer bottle by its neck again, tilted it to his lips, took a long swallow.

"If I wanted to be conservative, I'd cut those options down to two," Lathrop said. "And when time's at a premium, conservative might be just the way to go."

The cat continued to watch him. Lathrop ran a fingertip around the inside of the bottle's mouth to wet it with a drop of beer and then held the finger straight out toward her face, moving it closer slowly to avoid startling her. Conditioned by past abuse, she flinched back a little anyway and straightened as if preparing for a defensive bat of her paw. Lathrop became very still, held the finger about a half inch in front of her nose until she leaned forward and sniffed it. Then she relaxed her guarded posture and licked off the beer, her tongue like sandpaper against his skin.

Lathrop let her finish having her taste, pulled back his finger, and switched on the computer.

"It's coming up on zero hour, Missus Frakes," he said. "Zero hour in the house of cards. And if we intend to come out ahead, we need to grab a joker or two out of the air, run with them fast as we can."

Lathrop thought a moment. He already knew who one of his e-mail recipients would be. The other, though . . . he wanted to give the other a spot more consideration.

He recalled an interesting night in the park a few years ago. Balboa Park in San Diego, to name the place. He'd been right in the middle of some heavy fireworks between a couple of narco barons serving payout on a blood feud, and for Lucio Salazar and Enrique Quiros, the end result had been mutually exclusive to their lives—*buenas noches, amigos*, no loss. UpLink's security ops had been in the thick of that donnybrook, too, and Lathrop's brief encounter with their man in charge had left him feeling there was a deep, rich vein of secrets running in that particular gent, secrets he might plumb and use to his advantage somewhere down the line. But that was only part of what he'd sensed, and maybe even the lesser part. For the brief moment they had faced one another in the shadows, Lathrop had felt an inexplicable kinship with him, a resonance of a sort he'd never known before or since. It had been as if he'd seen a figure on the surface of a dark, still pool that conformed so closely to his outlines it could not have been mistaken for anything but his own reflection . . . and then had looked over his shoulder and suddenly realized it belonged to someone else, someone standing right there behind him at the edge of the mirrored water. Lathrop hadn't forgotten that jarring impression, *couldn't* have forgotten it. In fact, it had driven him to find out the man's name and store it away in his mental book of people to remember.

Now Lathrop brought up UpLink International's corporate Web site on his browser, skipped the animated graphic introduction, clicked on the icon for its main American bureau, and then went through several drop-down menus until he reached the contacts list for its security staff. There was an electronic mail link to the chief of security— *peter.nimec@uplinksanjo.sword.com*—but nothing for the person in question.

Lathrop didn't think guessing it would be a problem—organizations the size of UpLink almost always used consistent user-ID–host-domain address formats. If two or more employees had the same name there might be initials or some other characters attached to the user IDs to distinguish between them. But his man's name wasn't too common . . . certainly he was no John Smith . . . and Lathrop thought the odds were low that anyone in his division would share it. Still, he'd keep his message vague enough so it would mean absolutely nothing if it reached the wrong person, and at the same time embed it with a verbal cue to assure his intended party knew full well who'd sent it. Unless, of course, it simply bounced . . . in which case he would have to do some more guesswork.

Logging on to his anonymous client server, Lathrop opened a new message window and addressed it to: *thomas.ricci@uplinksanjo.sword.com.*

Then he wrote and sent his e-mail, snapped off another to the candidate he'd originally decided to reach out and touch, and finally leaned back in his chair.

The choice was either to play the wildcards in hand or get caught holding a wasted bluff, Lathrop thought.

He was curious to see how his latest play turned out.

Tom Ricci had a face of hard stone carved in extreme, jagged contrasts. His brow formed a prominent ridge over deep hollows that trapped his eyes in shadow. His high, wide-spaced cheekbones seemed in danger of piercing the skin stretched tight over their sharp points and juts. His nose was straight except at the bridge, where it was thickened and a bit skewed from an old, badly repaired break. His long, angular chin ended in a blunt wedge, as if the hand that sculpted it had been seized by a fit of impatience, bringing work on it to a finish with an abrupt, dead blow of the mallet. These contours flouted predictability; a fine cut this way or that, a careful tap of the chisel, and it would have been easy to call them handsome. Instead one regarded them uneasily, sought balance where none could be found.

Hard stone, too, his expression. Cold and unvarying, it chilled the eye. For years Pete Nimec had been able to see a rough compassion—a stark decency—embedded within its angry lines and angles, but that had ended when the Killer did his damnable work on those young recruits in Ontario. And with the Killer dead, even the anger had been scraped away.

While Ricci had physically showed up in Nimec's office after being summoned earlier that morning, it remained an open question whether he was mentally accounted for. Sitting across the desk from him, Nimec could see nothing but distance and emptiness in his features.

There had been nothing in them as he flatly reported on his session at the AG's office in Sacramento. There had been nothing in them—except, possibly, a sort of neutral acknowledgment—after Nimec told him he'd been right to stay on top of the computer-cracking case, indicated he had no problem with his hurrying to attend, but then suggested it might have been best if he'd notified somebody about it before heading off. There had been nothing in them when Nimec turned to the Sullivan business, outlined the picture as it looked at the moment, mentioned its tangential connection to the separate probe of Armbright that Noriko Cousins had gotten underway, and then informed Ricci of the decision to have him go east, oversee things, and hopefully help get it all wrapped up to everyone's satisfaction.

When Nimec sprang the news that he'd called Derek Glenn down in San Diego and arranged for him to accompany Ricci, he finally thought he saw something.

Unsurprisingly, it wasn't pleasant.

"Why Glenn?" Ricci said. His eyes held on Nimec, unmoving. "You're going to send along another warm body, we have people here at SanJo."

Nimec had been prepared for the objection. He'd also been ready to give the unshaded, if partial, truth in response.

"The two of you've been successful together in the past," he said. "I figured you could use the help."

"Help or a baby-sitter?"

Nimec hesitated.

"You tell me," he said. "We carry a lot of weight in New York. The mayor's office, NYPD, the whole city government gives us a lot of leeway to operate. If it turns out we need them on this one, decide to ask for their assistance, you'll be there to represent us." He struggled a moment with the rest. "Those bruises on your face and knuckles . . . you'd have to admit they don't send a good message."

"Inside UpLink or out?"

"Take your pick."

Ricci looked at Nimec in silence for a long time. Nimec didn't look away.

"Shipping me off to the Big Apple," Ricci said. "This an idea somebody kicked around the boardroom?"

"I wouldn't put it that way."

"Put it any way you want," Ricci said. "I'm asking whose brainstorm it was."

Their eyes remained locked.

"I wouldn't go along with it unless I thought it made sense," Nimec said. "It's mine, it's someone else's, doesn't make a difference."

"Does from where I sit," Ricci said. "People here aren't happy with me, they're entitled to their reasons. Maybe I don't like them. Maybe I don't care enough to find out what they are." A pause, his gaze very still. "People are making decisions about me, then I have to know how they're lining up. If I'm on my own."

Nimec hesitated.

"I'm no front runner," he said after a moment. "I brought you into UpLink because I felt you could be the best. Nothing's changed that. But we can't make believe things have been working out lately . . . and I think everybody needs to take a little time to figure out how come." He paused. "You have an objection to the assignment, tell me right now."

Ricci sat. His eyes pressed flatly on Nimec's. And more than his eyes. Nimec could feel the heavy and impervious bar of his thoughts pushing up against him.

Then Ricci finally shook his head.

"No," he replied. "No objection."

And they said nothing more to each other as Ricci rose from his chair, turned his back, and left Nimec to watch him step out of the office—the door shutting behind him with a soft but noticeable click of the latch.

Ricci entered his office, locked the door, and went to his computer to clean up his hard drive. He had quickly eliminated the cryptic e-mail message he'd received a little earlier that afternoon from his INBOX and DELETED ITEMS folder, clearing cache memory at the same time, but that really just scattered everything around the hard drive instead of really getting rid of it, and he'd wanted to perform a thorough wipe as soon he was back from seeing Nimec. Although access to the machine would require biometric hand-key user authentication—coupled with the standard password ID—Ricci had no intention of taking any chances with what might or might not happen while he was gone.

Seated at the machine, Ricci opened his hard disk scrubber and chose the high-security menu option that would destroy any traces of erased e-mails scattered in the drive's free disk space and file slack. Then he leaned back in thoughtful silence and waited for the software to complete its function with multiple passes of the drive sectors.

New York City had sent out an unexpected call even before Ricci had known he was headed there.

What surprised him even more than the call itself was his interest in finding out where it would lead.

•   •   •

Turning from his computer to the aquarium in his office wall, Hasul Benazir watched the tiny blue-ringed octopus jet from its artificial cove, and then fall upon a live crab he had dropped into the feeder panel above the tank. When dormant, the nocturnal octopus was a yellowish-brown that camouflaged it against the habitat's rocks. As it struck now, blue circles flared brightly on the eight pale yellow tentacles that clenched its prey, its beak piercing the crab's shell to flood the soft meat underneath with sufficient poison to kill two dozen grown men.

The crab twitched, its legs dancing spastically over the bottom gravel as the injected toxin paralyzed it. Already it was being devoured.

Benazir studied the tank a moment or two longer and then shifted his attention to his computer's flat-panel monitor, which was encased in a contoured radiation filter to shield him from its ultraviolet emissions. When at the computer, he typically limited his sessions to an hour maximum and wore sun-block for additional protection. Since his deliberate exposure several days past, he had been applying a special lotion impregnated with Dimericine, a molecularly engineered enzyme harvested from yeast and algae enzymes that entered the skin cells through liposomal absorption and was believed from preliminary testing to repair light-ravaged DNA. While the research on its medical effectiveness was still inconclusive, Benazir was relieved that his lips and cheeks, stung by a treacherous dusk, had not become sore or blistered.

He could find no comparable relief from his trepidations, however. In his office tonight, he had spent the greater portion of his allotted sixty-minutes staring at a two-sentence message that had arrived with his e-mail, scarcely able to believe the words on his screen.

The e-mail said:

> From: One Who Knows
> To: Hasul Benazir
> Subject: Dragonfly
> I've caught one that flew from your hand.
> Stay tuned or it will come back to bite you.

Dragonfly, Benazir thought with a fresh surge of incredulity. Although perhaps surprise was a reaction that might not be entirely warranted, and logic should have dictated that he be prepared.

The message, its timing . . . the lines that connected them could only run back to Sullivan. And beyond him. But how far, and to whom?

The answers were unknown; Benazir had deliberately kept himself at a fair distance from Sullivan's demand-side linkages. But what he *did* know was that this unexpected threat to him . . . and far more importantly to his plans . . . could not have seemed any closer, immediate, or critical.

He would need to move, and do so at an accelerated pace. *Night of Fate and Power, Day of Noise and Clamor*, he thought. Soon, oh, soon, they would come rushing upon his enemies, catching them unguarded, scouring them from the earth in a great, all-consuming tide of fury.

Benazir reached for his desk phone to contact the unlikeliest of all possible agents of their arrival.

PART 2

Zero Hour
In the House of Cards

SIX

From the *New York Post* Online Edition:

AREA COPS LINK TWO MISSING PERSONS CASES— EYE PUBLIC HELP WITH INVESTIGATION

By Jake Spencer

EXCLUSIVE

Previously treated as unrelated cases by authorities, the separate disappearances last week of a Manhattan woman and a married father residing on Long Island have been tied together by a surprise tip.

Sources inside the New York and Nassau County police departments have told *The Post* they have learned of an ongoing relationship between Patrick Sullivan, 44, of Glen Cove, and Corinna Banks, 31, a single mother living in a condominium on E. 19th Street in New York City.

A high-tech equipment salesman for the Kiran Group, a subsidiary of telecom giant Armbright Industries, Mr. Sullivan was reported missing by his wife ten days ago when he failed to return home from his corporate office at Pier 14 in lower Manhattan. Ms. Banks vanished under mysterious circumstances several days later after dropping off her four-year-old daughter at an indoor playspace only blocks from her residence.

The new information connecting Sullivan and Banks has been voluntarily provided by a close mutual acquaintance who is said to have come forward out of concern for their safety. While currently protecting this individual's identity, police are satisfied what they've learned from him is credible and have already begun gathering corroborative evidence that points toward the missing persons having a long-standing "boyfriend/kept woman relationship," as one NYPD investigator characterized it.

The investigator disclosed that Sullivan is sole owner of the condo, which has been occupied by Corinna Banks—described as an attractive, thirtyish blonde—and her daughter since he purchased it sometime last year. Garage attendants in the upscale Chelsea building have further confirmed that Ms. Banks drives a late-model Jaguar X-type sedan that police have found to be leased in Sullivan's name.

"We believe Sullivan was in Corinna Banks' apartment a little while before he disappeared, and took the Jaguar when he left there to meet somebody," a source told *The Post*, adding, "That same car was towed away from a No Parking zone the next morning and has been sitting unclaimed in impound ever since."

Police said they do not know the nature of Sullivan's meeting, raising obvious questions about where it was to take place, who he had gone to see, or what might have happened to him in the hours after he left the condominium and the discovery of the Jaguar—now undergoing forensic analysis—outside the Robert F. Wagner Middle School at 220 E. 75th Street.

"We're still gathering information, chasing down leads, and doing a lot of guesswork," a police source said.

Both police departments involved with the case are committed to working closely together and may hold a joint press conference within 48 hours in hopes of gaining public attention and bringing potential witnesses to the fore. And while cops admit there is no solid evidence linking Sullivan's disappearance to that of Ms. Banks, they are convinced it will materialize as their probe widens.

"A man and woman who share a love nest drop into nowhere a few days apart, you can bet it's not an accident," said a lead NYPD investigator. "In my eyes coincidences like that just don't happen."

Noriko Cousins was already having a supremely bad day, the kind she knew had to be governed by some Bitch Goddess of the Pit who would dispense illimitable random miseries to inhabitants of the world above, tacking on one after another until you wanted to mark the date box on the calendar with a big black X and then blow your vocal cords to shreds screaming for tomorrow to hurry up and come around.

A wretched day already, no question. A day Noriko was convinced would not pass into the next before taking a fair-sized piece out of her, chewing it to a pulp, and spitting it into a particularly foul-smelling sewer . . . which was especially discouraging when she considered that it was only a few minutes past nine o'clock in the morning, and she had barely been at the office long enough to warm the seat behind her desk.

Now she slapped a hand down on her computer mouse and attacked its left button with a finger to close her Internet browser, resentfully casting the front page of *The Post Online* into cyberspacial exile. The Sullivan thing making tabloid headlines, a joint press conference in the offing from not one but two police departments . . . she needed this about as much as an epidemic of purple leprosy, which itself barely ranked lower on her wish list than the scheduled arrival later that afternoon of her supposed "help" from San Jose. One of Megan Breen's designated hitters being the notorious Tom Ricci, who wasn't *quite* a contagious leper, but did carry the rap of being an undesirable from sea to shining sea.

Noriko took a few moments to settle down and think. Maybe there was an upside here, something to console her. The news about Sullivan's girlfriend and the towaway Jaguar had come as a double-barreled revelation—and while she would rather have learned of those disclosures before they got out to the general public, they did open new lines of independent investigation for Sword. In that respect, she had to grudgingly concede things might just work out. The same probably wouldn't hold true for Camp SanJo's decrees and impositions . . . but what she needed to get into her head was the inevitability of having to accept the variables she couldn't control, and turn those she could to her benefit.

Noriko sat back, crossed her arms. Okay, she admitted, the situation could have been shaping up much worse. That still didn't mean she had to like it, or that she didn't feel it had the potential to turn into a total circus, with her having to don a polka-dotted jumpsuit and flop shoes, climb into a miniature railroad train with the rest of the performing clowns, and tumble humiliatingly out into the ring as it gathered steam. And when she thought about the guy who'd

done the most to put her in that position, arriving last week
to mention Sullivan's name in her office for the first time, it
grew hard to resist the urge to spread some unhappiness of
her own in his direction.

He'd asked a favor from her, refused to take "no" for an
answer, and then made sure he got his way regardless.

Time to see how he would appreciate a little tit for tat.

Noriko looked up his number in her company directory,
reached for the phone, and started to punch in his area
code—which had to be dialed despite being the *same* area
code as hers, thanks to some regulatory stroke of genius by
the FCC a couple of years back mandating the 1-plus-ten-
digits policy for local calls, as though New Yorkers didn't
have to contend with enough hassles besides having to re-
program the autodial features of every computer, fax machine, and telephone in the city.

Right around digit number eight, Noriko reconsidered her
original idea, stopped pushing buttons, and instead got up to
fetch her coat from the closet. Why let the phone company
and government regulators kill her fun?

Lenny Reisenberg, who had showed up as an emissary of
the Bitch Goddess, was about half an hour from finding out
there was more than one to fear in the universe.

It would be a pure and distinct pleasure for Noriko to see
the look on his face when he did.

"You know my problem with asking favors of people?"
Brian Duncan said.

"Honestly," Malisse said, "I cannot imagine."

Duncan looked at him across their table in the glass-
enclosed public plaza outside an office tower entrance on
Park Avenue and 55th Street.

"My problem with asking favors of people," he said, "is that you always wind up having to return them sooner or later."

Malisse selected a chocolate biscotti from an assortment box he'd bought at his hotel's gift shop, dipped it into the coffee he'd picked up at an amenities stand across the plaza, and ate it with a little murmur of gratification. This was, he thought, a pleasant enough space. Warm, open, clean, planted with ficus trees and giant philodendron that stood lush and green in mid-January, even while the flower beds on the traffic islands outside were dead and smothered in sooty ice. Across the tiled floor from him a fountain gurgled softly into its shallow pool, reflecting the weak winter sun and low, strung-out clouds above.

His eyes momentarily drifted to a nearby table at which a pair of chess players sat amid a scrum of observers, all white-haired senior males, casually but neatly dressed. Members of a retirement club, perhaps.

Unable to imagine the idleness of life without work, Malisse shrank from the thought that some of them might not be too much older than himself.

He returned his eyes to Duncan—but Time, stripped naked for him like an unlovely exhibitionist, continued to distract. When Malisse had first crossed paths with the FBI surveillance expert—before calling on him yesterday, that was—his hair had been thick and brown as a mink's. It had since thinned appreciably and faded to the color of rust-speckled tin . . . yet only three or four years had passed between their meetings. At fifty-three, Malisse could not help but wonder if he showed comparable signs of aging, or if his wise departure from the *Sûreté* had slowed down his own physical subtractions.

But right now there were other subjects to occupy his thoughts. What had been Duncan's last comment? Ah, yes.

"To me, favors are the pollen of generosity, allowing sweet fruits to spring forth from friendship's fertile soil," Malisse replied belatedly. He drank some of his coffee, then lowered his voice to avoid being overheard by passersby. "Have I told you, for instance, what I take as my greatest and richest reward from the case we worked together?"

"You don't have to go through this again, Delano—"

"My greatest, richest, most *heartfelt* reward has been the knowledge that furnishing you with the names of those sellers of blood diamonds from Sierra Leone—and a list of complicit money launderers in Europe and the States—has aided your efforts to dismantle their network . . ."

"Delano—"

". . . taken tens of millions of dollars from the hands of Al Qaeda and Hezbollah murderers who would have used them to purchase guns, explosives, possibly even weapons of mass destruction . . ."

"Delano, enough—"

". . . weapons that could have caused incalculable suffering to American, British, and Israeli civilians—"

"Delano, I promised I'd help you, so cut the shit before I change my mind." Duncan paused. "You brought what I need?"

Malisse nodded, dabbed his chocolate-smudged fingertips clean on a napkin, and reached into his open overcoat for the memory stick he'd popped from his digital camera. He gave the stick to Duncan and then started on a macadamia biscotti, his eyes wandering back to the chessmen.

Their board was still crowded, the match in its preliminary stages. No doubt they were skillful to a high degree . . . how to otherwise explain the rapt interest of their watchers?

For his part, Malisse was ignorant of the game beyond the basic movement of its pieces, and had never desired to learn its rules and strategies. It took enough sweat to plot his moves through the twists and turns of reality's difficult corridors, trying to keep a step or two ahead of the ignoble creatures he meant to bag, laying snares for them along the way.

"Delano, I give you credit." Duncan had snapped the memory stick into a compact aluminum-clad case and pocketed it. "You've got balls."

"For taking the photos?"

"In the *schul* at the DDC," Duncan said in hushed voice. He shook his head with appreciation. "Monster fucking balls."

Malisse absorbed the praise with what he hoped was a semblance of grace, if not humility.

"I did what you asked," he said. "There are shots of the briefcase. The hat. And many of the coat. Its lining, seams, designer and dry cleaner's tags. Closeups of every pull or flaw I noticed in its fabric. Even the lint on its sleeves."

"Buttons?"

"Front, pocket, cuff. Inside and out," Malisse said. "You stressed that would be important, did you not?"

Duncan nodded in the affirmative

"We have to decide where to put multiple power sources and signal boosters. Get some lithium microbatteries in the buttons. I figure it might be a solution to the first hurdle."

"And the second?"

"I want to try out some ideas," Duncan said. "Whether they can be practically applied depends on what the pictures show."

Malisse looked at him.

"I can't settle for trying," he said. "I need success."

Duncan sat a moment, then leaned forward on his elbows. "Exactly how much do you know about GPS systems?"

"They use satellites," Malisse said. His face was blank. "And signals from space, no?"

Duncan studied him as if trying to decide whether or not he was joking.

"Okay, pay attention," he said. "Bottom-of-the-line units lock on to three sats and provide a two-dimensional fix on position—latitude and longitude. The coordinates are arrived at by simple triangulation . . . the travel time of the satellite signals beamed to the receiver times the speed of light. If we mount a GPS tracker underneath a vehicle, that would be all we'd need to follow it from place to place in a surveillance." He paused, dropped his voice another notch. "If you want to trace a *person* with a GPS device, it's different. Especially in a city. Two-D doesn't calculate up and down. And New Yorkers live and work in multistory buildings, not straw huts. The second your man starts climbing a flight of stairs or steps into the elevator of a seventy-floor high-rise, you're going to lose him."

Malisse nodded.

"Thank you for the technical instruction," he said. "I might now await the 'unless,' were it not for the great lengths to which I was put photographing my man's coat. Or did I somehow mistake your reasons for wanting that done?"

Duncan gave him another look.

"Pinpoint homing calls for a three-dimensional GPS receiver that acquires a fourth satellite to add altitude to the calculation," he said. "And that's at minimum. The more extra channels your unit picks up, the more data from other satellites it can use to refine the accuracy of its positional fix, or back up any or all of the four primary sats if communications get interrupted." He shrugged. "This isn't spy science. Anybody can buy ninety-five-percent-accurate three-D street-point navigators for a few hundred bucks. They weigh a pound, maybe a pound and a half, and are about the size of cordless phones . . . compact, but too large and heavy to fit in Max Smart's heel."

Malisse was puzzled. "Whose?"

"Never mind," Duncan said. He leaned closer to him. "Here's your *unless*, Delano. Once more, so I know you understand. The only way I see putting a hidden three-D GPS monitor on somebody with available tech is to integrate its hardware into his clothes, turn his whole dress ensemble into a receiver. It's the same concept as smart suits, e-wear, whatever the term du jour might be."

Malisse felt a coil of impatience in his belly. Or were his ulcers simply aggravated? He crunched into another biscotti, hopeful its honeyed coating would act as a balm in either case.

"This you indeed told me yesterday . . . to my thorough comprehension," he said, swallowing. "Now tell me how fast you can do the job."

Duncan looked at him, but didn't answer at once.

Malisse waited. His stomach remained troublesome in spite of his attempted remedy, but nothing more could be done to settle it without a cigarette—and that was denied him. The smoke police could be anywhere about, waiting to pounce at the snap of the lighter's lid, the flick of a spark off its flint. While Malisse might have fantasized about letting himself be nabbed just so he could fire up in a jail cell—a warm, indoor place, after all—Jeffrcys had informed him the citywide ban extended even to penal institutions, public workplaces that they were. Woe to the convicted felon who dared a puff of tobacco!

He looked across the table, turning his thoughts back to business. Duncan had stalled him long enough.

"The job," he repeated. "How fast?"

Duncan sighed. "Banking on the premise that it works, I'd estimate—"

Malisse shook his head.

"As I often told my pupils, we mustn't skewer ourselves on the redundant," he said, his tone short. "I ask you to reach deep into your black bag and *make* it work."

Duncan released another breath.

"Give me a week," he said.

Malisse shook his head.

"No good," he said. "It has to be sooner."

"How *much* sooner are you talking?"

"Tomorrow."

Duncan blinked.

"That's impossible," he said. "I'll push for, say, four, five days—"

"I can wait two."

"Three."

"Two," Malisse insisted. "Two at the very *most*."

Duncan continued to look unbelieving. "You're sure you don't want to check the phone book for a while-you-wait snoop shop?"

Malisse snapped him a glance.

"Do not scoff at me, Brian," he said. "My man has been very active."

"Still—"

"There is an old children's tale," Malisse said. "A brother and sister enter a deep, dark forest. The boy leaves a trail of bright pebbles to mark their way home. But when they next set out, the boy forgets the stones and instead drops only breadcrumbs from his knapsack. These are eaten by hungry birds, and the trail is lost to those who might follow in search. As are the children, who, as it happens, have stumbled upon a witch's hoard, but are nowhere to be found with the jewels."

Duncan looked at him.

"You think you're onto something big," he said.

Malisse shrugged over his box of treats.

"Once, African diamonds led us to terrorists and gun runners," he said. "We must always remember a trail of shining stones can lead anywhere, and bear in mind how quickly it may turn to crumbs that are snatched away by whatever is in the air."

"You want me to do *what*?" Lenny Reisenberg said from where he sat behind his desk.

"Assist in my investigation of Kiran," Noriko Cousins said from where she stood in front of him.

He looked at her, groping for a response, his mouth a speechless O of surprise.

She looked back at him, waiting. Dressed in a black skirt, tights, boots. Black leather GI dress gloves stuffed halfway into a side pocket of her zippered black biker jacket. A leopard Carnaby hat tucked down over her straight, dark hair adding some Swinging Sixties flash to the ensemble.

It was a scant two minutes after she'd come barging into Lenny's office.

"I'm a shipping officer," he said at last, "not an investigator."

"And I'm a corporate security agent, not a volunteer for the National Missing Persons Helpline," Noriko replied. "Which, sad to say, didn't give *me* the choice to stay out of something I didn't want any part of."

Lenny felt heat rush into his cheeks, thinking he could have kicked himself. That was one great answer he'd given her there. Some mighty original words popping out of his mouth. Or was his memory playing tricks by reminding him they were the very same words he'd used when Mary Sullivan had showed up to drop *her* little burden on his lap only a week, ten days ago? And how effective had they been for him then?

He realized his mouth was hanging open and shut it. His fate might be inevitably sealed, but he could still hold on to a little dignity.

"Go ahead," he said. "Tell me how I'm supposed to help."

"You can start by tracing every one of Kiran's export shipments from point of origin to final destination," Noriko said. "Look at cargo manifests, modes of transport, travel routes, receiving terminals . . . pull together every available detail and give them a comprehensive evaluation. Any time-charters or tramp vessels should be red-flagged. The same goes for transshippers here or abroad, outfits you *remotely* suspect may be cutouts. If something smells fishy, I want to know before anyone else—meaning the police."

There was a pause of several seconds.

"I'd need access to confidential filings to get anywhere," Lenny said, then. "Nobody's going to just hand them to me—"

Noriko stopped him with a slicing motion of her hand.

"That's bullshit," she said. "I was working the case when those lunatics blew up a piece of our city. You've got sources. Friends in the Customs office. I know you reached out to them for information."

Lenny was shaking his head.

"Different circumstances," he said. "You make it sound like it was easy—"

"Wrong," Noriko said, interrupting him again. "What you hear is me sounding like I know what has to be done. *How* is up to you. Easy, hard, somewhere between, I don't care. As long as it's right away."

More silence. Lenny exhaled. He was thinking that the next time he was mulling an important decision, he might have to stay away from kosher delicatessens. He was also thinking that the next time Noriko Cousins showed up at his office without notice, he'd be sure to instruct his admin to tell her he was out sick . . . which suddenly led him to wonder why she hadn't lowered the boom over the phone.

"*Kneeesh, kneeesh,* ought to go back to school," he muttered to himself. "Damn right."

"What?" Noriko said.

"Never mind." Lenny produced a defeated sigh. "I've got one question you could maybe answer. A condition of surrender."

She nodded.

"Did you walk all the way here just to watch me squirm?"

Noriko pinned him with a look, cut a little smile.

"Of course not, Lenny," she said. "I took a cab."

His husky six-foot-four, hundred-ninety-five-pound frame outstretched in the passenger cabin of a custom Learjet 45, Derek Glenn was studying the menu on his lap, nursing his third Dewar's Special Reserve on the rocks, and musing that there were certain rare and satisfying instances when the high concentration of melanin in his skin bequeathed by his African ancestors gave him a distinct social advantage over white men, one such being that it was tough to get pinned as red-in-the-face drunk when your face just so *happened* to be darker than chestnuts roasted on an open fire.

This fringe benefit of Glenn's blackness was by no means the only enjoyable part of his flight from Santa Clara to New York. In fact, Glenn had been too busy marveling at the preposterous abundance of luxuries aboard the UpLink bizjet to even think about it until a few minutes ago. Get a little sample of its plump leather seats and expansive leg room, not to mention the fully stocked and flowing wet bar, the catered lunch of marinated chicken and greens, the hors d'oeuvre platters of fresh seafood, overstuffed finger sandwiches, imported cheese, and sliced fruit, and now the lavish dinner menu he'd just been handed with its main-course offerings of fettuccini Alfredo, rib-eye steak, veal in wine sauce, beef stroganoff, or blackened swordfish . . . get yourself a taste of *these* high-flying extravagances, and the next time some flight attendant on a commercial airliner offered you a rubbery cold-cut sandwich and pretzel nuggets from his or her food cart, you might be pushed into talking serious *smack* to the poor dupe.

Undecided between the veal and pasta dishes, Glenn glanced over his shoulder at Ricci, who had been sitting alone toward the rear of the cabin since takeoff, staring out his window into the blue. If there had been a single damper on the trip thus far, it was his complete and utter inapproachability. But Glenn was not so stupid that he didn't realize Ricci's worrisome state of mind was the reason he'd been pulled from his San Diego security detail for their current assignment, regardless of the spiel Pete Nimec had given about the two of them making a crackerjack team. For that matter, *Glenn's* entire reason for having flown from his hometown roost without too much complaint was an awareness that Ricci had been in a slide since Big Sur, maybe even longer, and that he'd once been the closest thing on earth the guy had to a friend.

Glenn sighed. He had to admit helping Ricci did fit his pattern, this goddamned masochistic compulsion to take desperate causes upon himself. Born and raised in San Diego's east side, Glenn had returned there after a decade of service with Delta's Joint SpecOps unit and been doing the community activist bit whenever he had any time to spare, working to rescue his neighborhood from the termite gangbangers and wrecking-ball public developers who'd been moving in on its solid citizens from both ends. He didn't want or need Ricci as an additional reclamation project, and yet had done nothing to stop the deal from being laid on him.

Glenn kept looking contemplatively toward the back of the plane. After coming up against a wall trying to talk to Ricci earlier, he'd figured it might be best to let him be. However, it seemed to him that now was one of those times when he ought to make another attempt at reestablishing communication. There was a lot about Ricci that he found hard to understand. A lot about him that was even harder to like. But Glenn thought he maybe understood *and* liked him more than it was convenient, or even healthy, to admit. Thought Ricci, for all the hardness that came along with him, might be the most stand-up human being he'd met in his entire life.

He expelled another breath, rose from his chair, started to take his whiskey with him, and then abruptly decided against it. The handful of times they'd hung out together at Nate's Bar in San Diego, Ricci had ordered nothing stronger than a Coke. And though it hadn't been brought up in so many words, Glenn had always figured he'd been keeping some kind of problem with the bottle in check. He didn't seem to have too much trouble with it, not then, but it wasn't the same when a man was slipping down a mineshaft, looking for anything that might slow his fall to the bottom.

Glenn knocked off the rest of his drink with one deep swallow, put his glass onto the lowered tray in front of him, slid into the aisle with the menu, and went on back past a group of four company officers, divisional COOs and CIOs who were sharing the flight east on their way to some sort of telecom industry conference. Gathered around their laptops at a circular table, they didn't seem to notice him at all.

Neither did Ricci. He was turned toward the window as Glenn approached, still gazing into the layer of turquoise sky through which they were streaking above a thin, vaporous floor of cirrus clouds.

"Got a great menu," Glenn said, and flapped it once to get his attention. "Want to come on up and order dinner?"

Ricci slowly shifted his attention from the window.

"No, thanks," he said. "There are some things I want to think about."

Glenn stood watching Ricci's impassive face from the aisle.

"You don't need to make this worse than it is," he said. "Worse than it has to be between us, anyway."

"Sure," Ricci said. "It's just a big adjustment for me, flying with a babysitter."

Glenn hesitated a moment.

"Suit yourself, man," he said. "But I didn't put you in this predicament. Didn't ask for this job. We're on it together—"

"Like it or not?" Ricci said, and looked at him.

Glenn shrugged. The plane's turbines droned smoothly on around the low conversational voices of the executives behind him.

"My only point's that talking to each other wouldn't hurt," he said.

Another moment passed. Ricci kept looking at him, his eyes as pale and blue as the untouchable sky outside.

"Something needs to be shared," he said, "we'll talk."

Glenn considered how to answer, didn't take long to conclude there was really nothing more to say. Ricci's quiet, relentless antagonism could wear you down fast.

He squared his shoulders into another shrug, but Ricci didn't see it. His eyes had instead gone again to the window and whatever separate space might have drawn their attention.

"Enjoy the view," Glenn said, his level tone betraying only a fraction of his discouragement as he turned and carried his menu back to his seat.

The sun was at its midday zenith in a cold, sickly gray sky as Hasul Benazir strode from the Kiran building's front entrance, crossing its paved and landscaped grounds on his way toward the mountain woods. He was covered in full UV gear, wearing a shielded headpiece instead of the sunglasses, hood, and draping face guard he had used on the dusk of his self-exposure. Based on the design of a motocross helmet, the headpiece with its Velcro collar ring and dark pull-down visor sealed him in more completely to provide a superior level of protection.

Hasul would not have dared remove it for a moment this time. Even the bled-out light of a winter's noon would ravage him, setting cancerous fire to his genes.

Zaheer walked with him, his face clinched with unhappiness over what he perceived as an abrupt change in their plans. Hasul understood his reaction and would not fault him for it—why else had he kept the entire truth from him, but for having anticipated his discontent?

Now they entered the forest growth, took a long slow natural path under the trees and down the slope, and after a time stepped out into a small, frost-browned knoll.

John Earl stood at the far side of the clearing in his black leather coat, a watchcap pulled down over his head, a muffler around his neck. As they appeared he reached into a pocket for a pack of cigarettes, shook one out, slid its filter between his lips, held a disposable lighter to its tip, and smoked, looking straight across the open space between them.

Zaheer turned toward Hasul as they stopped outside the treeline.

"This one, he is dangerous," he said, and tilted his head in Earl's direction.

Hasul nodded.

"What we do is dangerous, and it can only increase the likelihood of success to use him," he said. "Your contribution will not be outshone, rest assured."

Zaheer looked at him in tentative silence.

"It is not for myself that I ask you to reconsider," he said.

Hasul reached out and placed a gloved hand on his shoulder. In a ventilator compartment at the back of his helmet, a small battery-powered airflow fan whirred softly to prevent his breath from fogging its visor.

"Trust me and wait," he said. "I will only be a short while."

His face dour, Zaheer did not answer.

At that, Hasul lowered his hand, then turned and went over to Earl, the bare winter earth of the field hard and ungiving under the ridged rubber soles of his boots.

"You found your way here without trouble, it seems," he said, halting in front of him.

Earl slid his cigarette between his lips, absently holding the lighter, rotating it in his hand.

"Just an old country boy in the woods," he said. "Long as I trust my feet, they'll bring me to the right place by-and-by."

Hasul was silent, his attentive expression partially obscured by the UV helmet's tinted visor.

"Your vehicle," he said. "You left it without being observed?"

"At a gas-and-food stop about a mile down the mountain and east of here." Cigarette smoke laced from Earl's thin smile. "Thank goodness for McDonald's, don't know what anybody the wide world 'round would do without them."

Hasul looked at him. A gust of wind flapped the ultraviolet blocking fabric of his external garments. Overhead, the sun showed through a gap in the fast-moving clouds to send glancing rays off his visor.

"I have more work for you," he said.

Earl shrugged, took a deep inhale off his cigarette, held his breath a moment.

"I don't ever like to say no a job," he said, blowing smoke. "But I'm not half finished with the last thing. The little woman, you know she couldn't give me what I needed. Didn't have it in her head."

Hasul nodded.

"That is why it is crucial to move forward with added urgency," he said. "The situation is not what I thought it to be. Whether he is dead or alive, Patrick Sullivan meant to betray me the night of his disappearance."

"You're sure of it."

"Certain," Hasul said. "He had something of mine in his possession when he went to meet his contact. Items I did not suspect he knew existed."

"How'd he get hold of them?"

"They were stolen," Hasul said. "I have yet to learn how."

Earl looked at his helmeted face. A small mist of breath formed inside the UV shield and was almost immediately dried up by its airflow fan.

"Can we talk free and open?" he said.

Hasul nodded again.

"It is the reason I chose to meet out here rather than at my office," he said.

Earl stood there smoking. The field around him dimmed and brightened under the patchwork shadows of the wind-herded clouds.

"My guess is your other missing items aren't more of those sapphires," he said.

"Yes."

"Are you going to tell me what they are?"

"It will be necessary if you agree to the mission."

Earl looked at him, smoking. He seemed to just then realize he was still holding the Bic and dropped it into his coat pocket.

"Mission," he repeated. "I thought we were talking *job*."

"The word was of your choice, not mine," Hasul said, meeting his gaze from behind the darkly tinted face shield. "In comparison, the whole of what you've done for me before amounts to a string of minor errands."

Earl grunted. "What kind of risk are you talking?"

"High."

"And the money?"

"Commensurate," Hasul said. "A hundred thousand dollars, half on acceptance, the remainder upon completion. Payment in full would not be contingent upon a guaranteed outcome, but only the successful execution of your given role."

Earl looked at him. "*My* role."

"Yes."

"Who's got the other?"

"You will be assisted by Zaheer."

A few seconds fell away. Quiet, Earl remembered something Hasul had told him at the conclusion of their last appointment.

"Later's come up faster than expected," he said. "But maybe your clock does it different from mine."

Hasul had continued to regard him through the dark glass panel.

"I am the clock whose hand marks the hour," he said. "And *by* my hand it comes as it is meant to."

Earl was silent, smoking, his eyes ranging out to Hasul's sideman back over near the trees. These were some crazy people. So crazy part of him wanted to get out of whatever Hasul was talking about before he even got in. But the money . . . the money was key. With enough of it a man would be able to open any door, get in and out of any*thing*.

Earl stood there another moment as cloud shadows fled beneath the sun. Then he finally snapped away the remnant of his cigarette and gave Hasul a nod.

"Okay," he said. "Talk to me."

It was about half past noon and Avram Hoffman was at the Club, finished with Katari and going over the rest of the day's appointments in his Palm computer's date book. Farther down the long cafeteria table where he sat by the floor-to-ceiling windows, three men were bargaining over a parcel of mediocre diamonds—the Nadel brothers, who'd recently closed their retail business and moved into Internet jewelry sales, and an aging Hasidic broker named Taubman who'd come to show them his goods.

Avram could hear their obligatory back-and-forth. One of the brothers, Yussel, complaining about Taubman's asking price while pointing out deliberately concealed flaws he insisted had become visible under his loupe. Taubman insisting there *were* no such flaws. Nadel's exaggerated umbrage at the denial. "This is fracture filled, you should take a look here in the sun." "Maybe you should look at the *lab reports*." "I don't need to look at the lab reports." "How can you say I'm supposed to look at my own diamond, if *you* don't think you need to look at the reports?" "You want to hear what *I* say?" "If you're going be more reasonable than your brother." "I say my *tuchis* makes better reports every morning than that Thai grader you use—"

Avram tuned them out with a surpassing disgust that bordered on contempt. The old broker's reports, whatever artificial processing Yussel Taubman had or hadn't seen in the dull light of an overcast January day . . . it all seemed recycled and trifling to him. He was moving up and on, and had heard enough of that sort of thing to last a lifetime.

Avram took his cellular from his pocket. Besides wearing on his tolerance, the negotiations he'd overheard had reminded him of his intention to call the GIA lab and nudge things along there.

The phone rang three times in his ear before Craig Brenner, the gemologist, picked up at the other end.

"Avram," he said, "I can't talk right now."

"Was it clairvoyance or caller ID that told you it would be me?"

"You decide," Brenner said. "Look, really, I *am* too backed up to talk."

"This will only take a moment," Avram said. "The sapphires . . ."

"I promised I'd look at them right away, and that's what I'm doing," Brenner said. "Pushed you ahead of twenty other clients who are wondering if I've looked at *their* stones, and that's including *Tiffany's*—"

"It was my brother-in-law's company, not the Tiffany family, who gave your son his sponsorship at Brown University."

A pause, a sigh.

"The golden rod again," Brenner said. "You going to hold it over my head forever?"

"Forever and beyond," Avram said. "I'm in a great hurry."

"You're in a hurry, I'm in a hurry, everybody's in a hurry," Brenner said. "Listen, Av. Turnaround for an analysis is usually a two-week minimum, and I've got an expert doing a Secondary Ion Mass Spec for you in two *hours*. That's a quarter-million dollar unit I've tied up, plus his time, which isn't cheap—"

"You've already examined the sapphire yourself?"

"I have, yes."

"And your findings?"

"Obviously inconclusive," Brenner said. "I've tested for specific gravity, run color filter and immersion tests, looked at them under a stereo microscope . . . the same kind of things you probably did at home. There's no sign of heat or chemical color enhancement, and the crystallization patterns look natural, but it's possible a specialized laboratory could make fools of us. Until the SIMS provides meaningful information on trace-element concentrations, we can't be close to definitive. And even then, Avram, this isn't an exact science. This tech's so new, and the stone so rare, there just isn't the kind of comprehensive database that allows for a hundred percent accurate comparison check."

"I can settle for something less than a complete grading for now," Avram said. "Every journey begins with a small step."

"And the race is not to the swift."

Avram smiled wanly at that. "Craig . . . what do your eyes and experience tell you?"

Brenner sighed again.

"Early opinion," he said. "I mean *very* early, got it?"

"Yes."

"This stone looks like a moneymaker to me," Brenner said. "I don't know how you managed to raid the Maharajah's tomb, but it's either an authentic Kashmir, or the most magnificent fake ever produced."

Avram fell silent, his heart knocking in his chest, his hand suddenly moist with sweat around the cell phone.

"Now that I've lit up your existence," Brenner said, "is it okay if I get back to my mundane one?"

Avram still didn't say anything. A moment before he had glanced over at the Nadels, who were still quibbling with old Taubman's prices. Now, suddenly, they seemed to vanish before him. Instead, he could see the talented guitarist from the subway the day before.

Soon, Avram, thought, he would be free. As free, in his own way, as that young man had been.

"Thank you, Craig," he said at last. "I really do appreciate your help."

Then he ended the call to make another on the spot, thinking it would be none too premature of him to contact the Russian.

Leaving the shelter of the hut with its central fire pit, Yousaf accompanied the others a short distance through bitter wind and cold toward a mud-brick stable.

He entered behind them and stood watching as the pack mules were saddled, harnessed, and loaded by their handlers, four hired Bakarwal nomads who would guide him out on his final passage from his homeland . . . one that had begun long days ago with the truck convoy out of Islamabad, and was soon to lead him across the northernmost strand of the Line of Command over high mountain trails negotiable only by foot and hoof.

With Yousaf were a half dozen of the *Lashkar-e-Tayyiba* fedayeen he had met near Halmat at the outskirts of the sixteen-kilometer-wide military buffer zone between Pakistan and Indian-administered Kashmir. All but their leader, Farris Ahmad, would be climbing the steep valley slopes with him tonight.

Yousaf leaned back against the wall of the stable, thinking. On his arrival at the fedayeen encampment—was it only yesterday?—he'd found a mixed group of political and tribal confederates, their practical alliance formed under the banner cause of Kashmiri independence. There were Sunni Dogras and Gujjars. Pashtuns from the vast Northwest frontier province. A considerable number were intelligence agents who had broken with the nation's present government-by-coup and were Yousaf's principal links to the fedayeen. He'd known some well enough to have called them by their first names; others were of familiar face. But life in the rough hills had so transformed them, it had been a struggle of sorts to recognize even those with whom he'd worked closely at the Directorate's Karachi bureau.

Yousaf had been particularly struck by how much Ahmad—once his immediate superior, now a chief among outlaws—had changed in the year since his sudden desertion from the ISID. The holder of an exemplary record, he had been a robust, dashing man with a small, neatly trimmed mustache; a perfect model of distinction in his starched, pressed uniform and spit-polished shoes. But the officer Yousaf remembered was a distant cry from the hardened guerilla who had welcomed him back at the Halmat camp, and led him here to the Bakarwal enclave. Like the fedayeen under his command, Ahmad was gaunt and leathery, his lips cracked from undernourishment, his wild, shaggy growth of beard bushing down from his cheeks to his chest. Also like the other fighters, he had on threadbare combat fatigues that showed signs of frequent and hasty mending, and scuffed, worn-at-the-heel boots. And again, as did the rest, Ahmad carried a large backpack, multiple duffels, and a shoulder-slung Kalashnikov assault rifle. Distrustful of the profiteering nomads, some of his rebels had brought additional small and man-portable arms with them tonight, including RPG-7 launcher tubes.

Yousaf continued to observe the activity around the mules from his spot by the stable wall. Betrayal, he mused, could come from many unexpected directions.

This thought was still very much in his mind as Ahmad turned from the hurried preparations of the guides and approached him over the straw-covered floor.

"I expect you'll be on your way in the shorter part of an hour," Ahmad said. He angled his head back toward two of the stalls. "The laser components are transported on different mules from your provisions, you see?"

Yousaf nodded, looking past him at the splendid, barrel-chested animals. The Bakarwal had lashed wooden loading boards onto either side of their large-girthed saddles and were roping the precious cargo that would complete the Dragonfly cannon—boxed and bundled in canvas sacking—to the boards.

"Travel over the mountains is never easy, especially in winter, but night can be your best friend," Ahmad said. "The guides know the terrain walking blindfolded, and you have been favored by a three-quarter moon and starlight." He regarded Yousaf. "There is also a surplus of food should it be needed—we'd expected you to arrive with at least one other man."

"And I would have, if the rangers outside Chikar had not forced me to set out alone and in haste." Yousaf looked him in the face as he spoke his lie. "What are the chances of encountering more troops?"

Ahmad continued to appraise Yousaf, seemingly lost in a moment's thought. "An outside possibility always exists," he said. "Of late my scouts have seen no signs of either the president's forces or Indian security, however."

"And should that change?"

"They will keep their eyes open and be in immediate radio contact with you," Ahmad said. "If all goes well, you will be across the LoC and make your rendezvous with half the morning to spare. Should you be forced to leave the pass on either side, the mules have sufficient food, water, and ammunition on them to last many days. And we have amply stocked caves along the way you can quarter in for many more if the situation were to demand it."

Yousaf was silent. *The president's forces*, he thought. *How aptly put*. It was only their potential deployments that were of concern to him. For if all did indeed go as he'd planned, there would be no need to cram into some deep stone cranny and hide away like a scurrying rat. Not once his column reached the border, at any rate.

Ahmad tapped him on the shoulder now and nodded back in the direction of the hut they had left moments earlier.

"Our Bakarwal hosts have prepared some jerked lamb for us, and put fresh, spiced coffee up to brew over their flame," he said. "Given the immoderate cost of their hospitality, you might wish to join me in partaking of it in the time that remains before you leave."

Yousaf looked at him, smiled, and nodded.

"Yes, Ahmad," he said, as they started toward the barn's door of bound saplings. "That is truly something I would enjoy."

"If you're moving from a one-bedroom apartment, I usually recommend either the ten-foot truck or that cargo van over where your friend's waiting in his car," said the man at the U-Haul reservation counter. He nodded toward the wide office window behind Earl to indicate the rental vehicles out in his lot. "Which one's best depends on your needs."

Earl stood looking at him across the counter. "How's that?"

"Basic rate's the same for both—twenty bucks a day, seventy free miles, though added mileage is a few cents higher with the truck," said the U-Haul rep. "If you've got large pieces of furniture, it gives you a little more space. Van's new, comfortable, handles nice and smooth. But company policy's that it's only available for local moves—that's defined as the tristate area, and no out-of-town dropoffs. You'd have to return it to me at this center within forty-eight hours."

Earl glanced over his shoulder at the van parked near Zaheer's Mercury. Then he turned back to the U-Haul rep, took his cigarettes from his coat pocket, and flashed them above the counter.

"Okay with you that I smoke while I give it some mind?" he said.

The rep shrugged, a stubble-cheeked, potbellied man in his fifties wearing a green-and-black buffalo-plaid hunting shirt and oversized work dungarees.

"Doesn't bother me, and only brings out the summons books across the Hudson," he said, his hand appearing from under the counter with an ashtray.

Earl tapped a cigarette from the pack, lit it with his Bic, and took a drag.

"That van ought to be fine," he said. "Got enough room, and I don't expect to be running up too many of those plus-miles before I'm back to you."

The U-Haul man eyed him a minute, scratched his unshaven chin.

"Maine," he said. "Bet anything it's what I hear."

Earl plucked the cigarette from his mouth, held it between his thumb and forefingers.

"*Ayuh*," he said. A smile traced his lips. "Must be the accent, hey?"

The rep nodded.

"My sister's lived there since she got married—husband's ex-navy, used to be stationed at that base in Brunswick, bought a home and farm-equipment business a ways inland when he got out of the service," he said. "Whereabouts in the state you from?"

Earl pondered that, smoking. Whereabouts? It was a question easier asked than answered. There had been Aroostook, so near the Canadian border the geese flying by overhead would cuss you out in French when you shot at them, and then get the Royal Mounties on your ass for doing it without a license. There had been the bunch of years he'd worked at that poultry-processing plant in Belfast, renting a dump of an apartment on Union Street down the hill near the harbor, where the white trash tenants upstairs would pool their food stamps every Friday to pick up a few six-packs of cheap beer at the grocer's, start drinking after supper so they'd be bombed out of their skulls by midnight, good and lubed for the fistfights you could always expect to break out between them, and that would often as not spill out onto the road— especially on those hot summer nights when they'd get irritable, peel off their shirts, and wail on each other so hard he could hear the sound of flesh being pounded like raw slabs of beef through his open window. Brother on brother, father on son, husbands on their cheating women's boyfriends, they'd have all kinds of drunken grudge matches going on till the local cops came to dampen the entertainment.

Earl looked at the U-Haul man in silence, squinting

through the cigarette smoke streaming from his nose and mouth. Where did he consider himself from? Aroostook with its cranberry bogs and dead things? Belfast with its bloody chicken guts, and feathers blowing in the streets? Or Thomaston state penitentiary, maybe twenty, thirty miles farther south? A *dark and comfortless abode of guilt and wretchedness,* that was what the lawmakers who'd ordered it built in the 1820s had wanted for its inmates on the charter they drew up, and they'd absolutely gotten their wish. Three-foot-thick granite walls, nine-by-four max security cells with layers of stone covering them top and bottom, the yard a deep limestone pit quarried out by prison laborers. All that rock, its weight could grind the soul out of a man in no time, and Earl guessed he'd have hung himself long before his dime-and-a-half stretch there was done if not for having kept busy with his wall art. He also guessed it had gone more toward making him what he was than anything or anywhere else he could think about.

The state pen, see ya when I see ya—*ayuh, ayuh.*

"Come from a spot on the coast called Thomaston," he said now. "Quiet. Big white Yankee houses, churches, trees, and the quarry on old Limestone Hill. A town where you'd think time was standing still if it wasn't for the change of seasons."

The U-Haul man scratched his stubble again.

"Sounds like the kind of place somebody would have a hard time leaving . . . but then my brother-in-law tells me it's tough earning a decent wage up there." He slid a clipboard with an attached pen in front of Earl. "Anyway, here's the rental application. You want to show me a charge card and your driver's license while you're making it out, I can go right ahead and give you the keys to the van."

Earl took his wallet out of an inner coat pocket, removed

the two pieces of ID he'd obtained from Hasul, and passed them over the counter. He didn't know or care whether Hasul and his people had stolen someone else's identity, replacing the original photo on the driver's license with his own, or if they'd somehow had a forgery made to order. The important thing was that the license number and Visa account for a strawman who happened to look exactly like him were both valid, and that the credit line on the plastic was around twenty thou.

Earl was filling out the requested information—his newly acquired name of Gerald Donovan, his bogus address and phone number, this and that—when it occurred to him there might be a thing or two Hasul *hadn't* provided that he could pick out of the U-Haul man's brain.

"Me 'n my friend had to circle around a bit trying to find your lot, noticed all those chemical tanks behind the plant across the intersection," he said in an offhandedly conversational tone. "You know which factory I mean?"

The U-Haul rep nodded.

"That'd be Raja."

"Hmm?"

"Raja Petrochemicals," the rep said. "It's a fuel refinery . . . Indian outfit, you're wondering about its funny handle."

"Indian like Sioux and Apache?"

"Indian like an order of tandoori chicken and curried rice to go." The U-Haul man's whiskered face hung a frown. "What they've got in the tanks isn't anything you'd want on a takeout menu, I can tell you that."

Earl glanced up from the application form.

"You don't seem any too thrilled about having them for neighbors."

"Won't argue it, Mr. Donovan," the rep said, reading the name on the driver's license he'd been handed. "Not with a few hundred thousand pressure pounds of HF stored out there in those tanks you saw driving past the plant."

Earl put on a mildly inquisitive look.

"HF?" he said. "What's that?"

"Hydrofluoric acid," said the U-Haul man. His frown had deepened. "If you were from right around here, or read the same newspaper story I did a while ago, I wouldn't have to tell you."

Earl waited for more.

"Stuff's what they use to make high-octane gasoline, and it's toxic as hell," the U-Haul rep said. "Stays a gas when it's sealed in those tanks, but they ever get ruptured, let it out into the air, it would condense into clouds, even rain, that can eat through glass and concrete. And if you don't think that sounds bad enough, there's something about HF that makes human skin absorb it real easy. Soaks right up through the pores into the bone, eats away everything in between. Say it gets inside your eyes, nose, mouth . . . or you breathe it . . . I don't want to be gross, but it'd turn a person's insides to slush."

Earl's writing hand had dawdled over the rental application. "I can see how you wouldn't forget that article," he said.

The rep nodded.

"And I haven't told you the half of it," he said. "According to what I read, a couple, three years back, dozens of families had to be evacuated from some town in Texas because of a refinery fire that let HF out into the air. Also right around then, Russia had to resettle a few thousand people because it'd been leaking from a government factory . . . and add those situations together, the amount of HF I'm talking about doesn't come to a fraction of what's in Raja's tanks."

Lifting his cigarette from its ashtray rest, Earl sucked in a chestful of smoke.

"I expect there'd be some serious precautions against anything happening to the tanks," he said on his exhale.

"Should be, but aren't," the U-Haul man said. "After those psycho terrorists drew a bull's eye around New York, Homeland Security pushed through a bunch of laws that said chemical companies had to beef up their safeguards. But it hardly bothers to enforce them—you know how it goes. Time passes. Everybody bitches about costs. The cops and feds get busy with other things. Elections come and politicians move on to talking about 'the children' and teachers and classroom sizes, like they really give a damn about anybody's brats but their own. Meanwhile the chemical outfits hire shysters to find all kinds of loopholes and get their lobbyists in Washington to make sure they can relax and sit pretty. Couldn't be gladder that nobody's paying attention to them, since improvements cost money, and they'd rather gamble with people's lives . . . and I mean millions in Jersey, Pennsylvania, and New York just worrying about Raja Petro alone . . . than spend a nickel."

Earl was shaking his head in feigned disbelief.

"Sounds damned unbelievable," he said.

"It does, I know," said the U-Haul man. "But how the newspaper reporter figured it, the amount of HF gas in Raja's tanks is enough to kill off not one, two, or three, but *four* million people, depending on which direction the wind blows."

Earl had continued to shake his head as he went on writing up his paperwork. He was thinking about what Hasul had said to him earlier on that day: *I am the clock whose hand marks the hour.* He was wondering, besides, whether that made him the finger that would push the button.

He pulled the ashtray closer, crushed out his cigarette, and returned the clipboard to the man behind the counter.

"Done, I guess," he said. "Hope my questions didn't spin your wheels overmuch."

The U-Haul rep shrugged, scanning the application.

"Don't worry about it," he said enduringly. "I'm still alive and kicking, so why complain?"

Earl smiled.

"That's the attitude," he said. "All you can do's control what you can, and let the rest work itself out."

The U-Haul man nodded, glanced up from the completed rental form, and smiled back at him.

"Everything looks good, buddy," he said. "Give me a minute to process this, and I'll bring you the keys to the van."

"I don't think we should try to do too much," Noriko Cousins said. "The simpler we keep things, the better they're going to work out for us."

She looked across her desk at Tom Ricci and Derek Glenn, thinking Ricci certainly did not look like he had the slightest intention of making things complicated. If his silence was to be taken as evidence, he'd shown little or no interest in a single word she'd uttered about the Case of the Vanishing Husband—which, practically speaking, had now expanded to include hubby's vanished playmate, both for Sword and the New York and Nassau County police departments, since it seemed reasonable to assume that finding out what happened to *her* would be a big step toward solving the mystery of *his* status, be it fair or foul.

Noriko had been hoping that she was on the money about Ricci's apparent indifference, which might, just might, translate into a sign that he'd stay well out of her way, and possibly be westward bound before too long, *adios, hombre*. The read she'd gotten on Glenn, by comparison, hadn't left her as encouraged that he'd be easy to shake off. There had been too many probing questions and attentive comments from him during this afternoon's let's-get-introduced-and-up-to-snuff session. Also way too much direct eye contact, though Noriko had been around the block often enough to tell some of that was because he happened to find her attractive, and had maybe picked up on a mutuality—using a term she'd recently found in her *New York Times* crossword puzzle dictionary—that she had been struggling to nip in the bud. In both principle and practice, Noriko was opposed to mixing business with pleasure. Very often.

Now Glenn looked at her from where he stood leaning against a file cabinet, his broad arms folded over his chest, wearing a gray wool sportcoat, light blue turtleneck, and gray pleated trousers.

"When you say 'simple,' I'm guessing you really mean separate," he said. "Or am I wrong about that?"

Noriko looked at him a moment and flashed a smile that he returned at once and in full, beaming it across her office, the nice, even whiteness of his teeth an appealing contrast to the equally nice and even brownness of his skin.

"You're absolutely right," she said, and wondered what the hell kind of bud-nipping she meant to accomplish by swapping smiley faces with Glenn. "Whatever attention I've been paying to Armbright Industries, and the Kiran Group in particular, is fairly routine corporate intel. Sullivan is a woman asking for help, and the boss wanting to give it as a personal favor. I see no reason to wrap them together."

"Except when you consider he's a top salesman for a division that's maybe exporting restricted technology to foreign countries, something that would involve the kind of shady people who can do worlds of bad."

Noriko shrugged her shoulders.

"You won't get an argument from me," she said. "All I

want is to make sure we don't get our paths twisted when they really should be kept clean and distinct from each other. *Separate.* Minus conjecture, that's how they are so far. And that's how we should work them unless they naturally connect."

Glenn stood with a thoughtful expression on his face. In a chair he'd pulled up into the opposite corner of the office, Ricci maintained the virtually unbroken silence he'd brought on arrival, his hands meshed on his lap, his left foot balanced over his right knee.

"You talk to any of the cops that are looking for Sullivan yet?" Glenn said after a minute.

Noriko shook her head.

"The detective in charge is named Ruiz," she said. "I don't know him, but I have an open line to Bill Harrison, which means I can be put on to him easily enough."

Glenn raised his eyebrows.

"*The* Bill Harrison?" he said. "As in the ex–police commissioner?"

"Right."

"Impressive," Glenn said. "I read that bio he wrote after the terrorist hit. Lost his wife when it went down, almost his daughter, too, and still managed to carry this town on his shoulders while the Washington politicos were hiding out in silos somewhere under the Great North American Prairie."

Noriko nodded.

"Bill's a good guy and a friend," she said.

"What white people call a *positive role model* for us black people," he said.

Noriko looked at Glenn, catching his droll tone, noticing the smile that had reappeared on his face.

"A friend," she repeated with a shrug.

His smile grew larger and brighter.

Noriko willed herself to look away from it and cleared her throat.

"So," Glenn said. "I figure we should start by spending some time with Ruiz."

"That's what I had in mind."

"We play straight with him far as Sullivan's concerned, tell him how the whole thing came to our attention, see if he wants to share and share alike."

"Right," Noriko said. "My guess is he'll be more than helpful."

"After Harrison gives him a ring."

"Right," Noriko said again. "I just want to make sure that any inklings we have about Kiran are kept out of the conversation."

"Separate and distinct."

Noriko nodded.

"It's almost five o'clock, a little late in the day to start making arrangements," she said. "I'll get on the phone first thing in the morning. Shoot for a meeting with Ruiz as soon as possible."

At the opposite corner of the room, Ricci leaned forward in his chair and planted both feet on the floor.

"Your crew been keeping up an onsite surveillance of Kiran?" he said, lensing her with his pale blue eyes. "I mean, at its main headquarters in the Catskill mountains."

Noriko looked at him, her lips pressed together. The sudden end to his silence had surprised her, as had the change of subject that came with it.

"There was an intelligence summary in the files I e-mailed to SanJo," she said. "We do what's legal. And viable."

"And I'm asking if that includes staking a continuous post there at night," Ricci said.

Noriko sat without breaking eye contact with him.

"My practice has been to use frequent spotters," she said, then.

"But nothing steady."

"No," Noriko said. And paused. "Look, you're curious about the unusual amount of activity at Kiran after regular business hours. We've been, too. And not just since yesterday, or last week. But the fact that the company's president and head of research suffers from XP, a condition that makes him critically allergic to sunlight, might be all there is to it."

"Might," Ricci said. "Or might not."

There was another silence. Noriko shifted behind her desk.

"What happened to our staying focused on Sullivan?" she said "To not letting ourselves get sidetracked? Or weren't we as clear about that as I thought?"

Ricci shrugged.

"I just asked some questions," he said. "Didn't tell you to push anybody or anything to the side."

Glenn looked over at him from against the file cabinet, cleared his throat.

"Maybe we've talked enough for now," he said. "I figure you and me could use a chance to settle into our hotel rooms, rest up for tomorrow."

Ricci sat there for a moment, his gaze moving from Glenn to Noriko and back to Glenn.

"I'd rather walk around a while first," he said, shrugging again. "Catch you later."

And then he stood up, turned toward the door, and went out.

Noriko watched the door shut behind him, turned to Glenn.

"He always like this?" she said.

"Mostly, yeah," Glenn said. "Except when he's worse."

She pursed her lips and exhaled with a low whistling sound.

"It must've been a long, long flight for you."

Glenn looked at her.

"The food was super-duper," he said. "Drinks, too."

Noriko studied him quietly, tipped her head toward the coatrack, and pushed her chair back from behind her desk.

"You feel up to another round or two?" she said.

Glenn grinned, winked at her.

"I can only promise to try my best," he said.

Yousaf stood out behind the Bakarwal hut in the tarpaulin-covered ditch that passed for a latrine here, thinking the cold was so intense his prick was liable to freeze and break off in his hand before he finished his piss. But the need to relieve himself was only one of the reasons he'd excused himself from Ahmad. There had been a notion of sending out a radio call to those who awaited him on the mule trail, both to warn them about Ahmad's advance scouts and signal his departure from the nomadic camp . . . an idea over which Yousaf was grateful his good sense had prevailed. Though he had deceived Khalid and the rest of his men about a great many things as they'd rolled toward the Chikar roadblock, the concerns he'd expressed about intercepts had been truthful—and they had not yet left his mind. Not at all, in fact. Even in these remote regions, it was best to be on guard against eavesdroppers.

Zipping his trousers now, Yousaf started back toward the hut and his soon-to-be guides over the mountains. He had come too far now to let fear exert any pull over his decisions. Dragonfly would soon make him a wealthy man, and that prospect alone ought to steer him away from a recurrence of foolish impulses.

His customers knew the dangers of this highland frontier

better than he and would not need any warning to be on the alert.

Tom Ricci peered through the viewfinder of his digital camera, crouching amid the pines and leafless oaks of a forested ridge above the Kiran Group's company grounds. The req slip Grand Prix GTX he'd pulled out of Sword-Manhattan's downtown garage had been left some thirty or forty yards behind him in the night, at the side of an unmarked country road that ran parallel to the western edge of the grounds for several hundred yards before turning north toward an eventual dead end. Designated Rainer Lane on his map, its dark, wooded sameness was interrupted only by a long-forsaken drive climbing steeply uphill from the road's right shoulder.

Ricci had thought it an opportune spot to leave the car. The isolated drive would be easy to find when he returned, and the two separate passes he'd already made around Kiran suggested there would be a good overlook directly across the lane through the trees.

As he'd eased to a halt off the road, Ricci had noticed that a ten- to fifteen-foot-high barrier of fencing and razor coil had been erected at the foot of the drive. His headlights offered glimpses of chewed, rotted out blacktop where its sheeting of snow and ice gapped open, revealing a reflective no-admittance sign on the gate. And just beyond it, another, much older, sign. A large, weathered wooden rectangle on sagging double posts, its hand-painted lettering was chipped, peeled, and faded—but still legible. The top line said: HOTEL IMPERIAL, A FUTURISTIC RESORT. Beneath it in smaller characters were the words: DAY CARE, FILTERED POOL, AIR-CONDITIONED ROOMS, CELEBRITY NIGHTCLUB. Hanging separately from its bottom on a pair of rusted eyehole hooks, a much more slender wood banner announced: BUDDY GROOM, MASTER OF CEREMONIES, BACK AGAIN FOR THE 1969 VACATION SEASON!

Ricci had stared at the sign and wondered. Nineteen sixty-nine, Summer of Love. If that had been Hotel Imperial's last hurrah, maybe one factor in its demise had been Buddy Groom and his Celebrity Nightclub acts getting the show stolen out from under them by the Woodstock festival a handful of miles away.

Cutting the ignition, Ricci reached over to the passenger seat for the gear bag containing his flashlight, camera, and binoculars, got out, and crossed the road. He'd gone less than twenty yards into the trees before finding an advantageous hump of mountainside from which to look down on the Kiran Group's corporate development.

That was a little over an hour ago.

He had been on the look ever since.

It was now a quarter past eleven according to the virtual dial on his WristLink wearable. Everything cold, quiet, and pitch black around him under the barren treetops. Considerably brighter below him, where Kiran's groomed and level grounds were circled by high-output stadium lights on steel frame towers that dispersed an almost glareless white radiance over the entire site.

Ricci kept his eye to the camera, a fourth-generation night-vision with microelectromechanical sensors that brought its intensifier tube and ocular lens into rapid focus wherever he pointed and zoomed. He'd prepared to be out a while, dressing in a black leather cruiser jacket, thermal fabric vest, and full-finger shooter's gloves, pulling a night camo heat-exchanger balaclava over his head as he left the car. Its mouth port would help retain the heat and vapor normally lost through his exhalations, recycling them into the frigid air he breathed in to keep his internal body temperature raised.

He clicked the shutter-release button, added a fresh telescopic image of the U-Haul van parked outside Kiran's service gate to the snapshots he'd already taken. There were pictures of the van itself. Pictures of the three business-suited men he'd seen repeatedly appear from the gate and roll dollies of mid-sized packing cartons out to the van's cargo section. And pictures of the tall man in the car coat— it was black leather, like Ricci's own—who had stayed close to the van throughout their comings and goings. Blond, fair-skinned, wiry, all arms and legs, he had alternated between sitting in the driver's seat and pacing around the van in the cold, chain-smoking as he watched them climb aboard with their boxes and then emerge at different intervals to wheel what were presumably the same boxes, collapsed and emptied, back through the gate.

The operation had triggered Ricci's curiosity. He wasn't clear on what he'd expected to see here tonight. What he *was* seeing. But instinct told him none of it was meant to be seen . . . and his repeated gut checks had just strengthened that feeling. The rental van accounted for many of his questions. The activity to and from the van. And the tall man. Maybe especially him.

Ricci had read the intelligence workups on Hasul Benazir, learned all about his genetic condition and habitual night hours. He'd also gotten a related short from an outside source. Information Noriko Cousins either didn't know or was intent on holding back from him. He had no idea which it was. No idea if she might be the only one at UpLink, and by extension Sword, who was keeping secrets. Whatever the score, he found it hard to be that concerned about it. Not with a secret or two of his own tucked away in his pocket.

He steadied the camera on the tall man, clicked again. Couldn't get too many photos of him. It was a safe guess that the others were Kiran personnel. Coatless, wearing uniform dark suits, they carried swipe cards that gave access to the service gate, a motor operated rolldown that would automatically close behind them after each of their trips in and out of the building. Their distinctive South Asian features had made Ricci remember something in the Kiran files about a core group of veteran employees—executives, advisors, and techs, or so it described them—that Benazir had brought over from Pakistan on H1Bs: specialized work visas.

Tall Man was another story. The obvious outside man. And an impatient one waiting near the conspicuous U-Haul parked in a secondary parking area around the corner from the building's main entrance. The only other vehicles, a small fleet of Mercedes sedans Ricci figured for company cars used by the dark-suits, were in the regular employee parking lot in front of the entrance.

No, Ricci thought, the van didn't fit any more than Tall Man. Even granting Benazir's late schedule, its presence was very suspect. A business like Kiran would ship in freight trucks, not cheap daily or weekly rental vans. But why else would it be here? Somebody in the building choosing this time of night to clean out his desk, maybe cart his old files or office equipment off to a warehouse? A ridiculous thought. Crazier to imagine corporate professionals wheeling those things out in handcarts when they could hire other people to do the lugging for them. No explanation came close to making sense—unless it involved a transport of goods that was meant to be covered up. But what would be the point in unpacking those boxes while they were still aboard the van? *Before* they had gone anywhere?

Now Ricci watched the three dark-suits jump from the rear of the van again, and raised an eyebrow. This time instead of returning directly to the service entrance, they locked the cargo section from the outside with a key, and then went over to where Tall Man stood by its driver's door.

It seemed their loading was finished.

Ricci pulled back on the zoom for a wide angle shot of the bunch and took his picture, a vision of himself with the Boston police department briefly and inexplicably coming into his head. Five years ago, Detective First-Grade Tom Ricci would have found a way to stomach the whole checklist of authorizations needed for a surveillance warrant. Persuaded his bosses to give him their go-aheads. Met the legal threshold that would support reasonable cause. Filled out endless forms and case reports in duplicate and triplicate, while wishing he could have stood before the court and explained that he'd learned to trust his eye and follow its lead when it started paying close attention to somebody . . . the way it was paying attention to Tall Man and friends tonight.

Five years since the BPD, Ricci thought. Five years since one of the same judges he might have asked for legal approvals had been bought by a millionaire whose son he'd nailed for murder. Five years since the kid had walked out of jail on a courtroom fix, and Ricci had walked away from a badge tarnished by bogus charges that he'd mishandled evidence.

There were scars that healed with time and experience, and scars that only got thicker.

Ricci had ceased to want or need anyone's nod of approval. For anything.

He lowered his camera, switched to the binocs strapped around his neck—these also Gen-4 NVs—and watched the four men outside the U-Haul. The dark-suits appeared to be giving Tall Man instructions, one in particular doing most of the talking as Tall Man listened, nodded his stalky neck, and every so often said something in response. After a little while their huddle broke up—Tall Man hopping into the driver's side of the van, two of the dark-suits turning to reenter the service gate, the third going back around to the rear of the van and tugging at the handles of the cargo doors, apparently checking that they were securely locked before he joined the others.

Ricci considered his next move. The approach to Kiran's parking area extended up the mountain from the same local route he'd taken coming here off Interstate 87. It was the only nearby juncture with the highway, with nothing branching from it for many miles but Rainer Lane and a couple of other dead-end stretches. Which meant the U-Haul driver would have to return to that route no matter where he might be headed afterward.

If he scrambled, Ricci thought there was a better than fair chance of catching the van's tail.

A few minutes later he was doubling back along Rainer Lane in the Grand Prix. Glancing down the slope to his right, he spotted the U-Haul through frequent gaps in the trees, already out of the parking area and coasting toward the opposite end of the approach.

He tightened his fingers around the steering wheel and put on some speed.

It was a looping quarter-mile descent to the lane's intersection with the county road. Ricci angled onto it, pushing the accelerator as he bore northeast, the direction he'd seen the van take after his last glimpse of its progress.

And then he saw its taillights ahead of him in the darkness. He estimated the van's lead at ten car lengths and eased off his gas pedal, wanting to stay close, but not so close he risked being picked up by its driver. With only a smattering of other vehicles on the road—he counted three besides his car and the van, all in his rearview—Ricci could afford to give the van some space and still keep it in sight.

Ricci followed it past the entry ramp to the southbound interstate that would have taken him back to New York City, heading farther upstate into the mountains. There were patches of woods, agricultural farms on modest plots of winter-bare earth, darkened and locked-up convenience stores that must have closed for the night hours earlier. Then a commercial railyard and crossing, and what appeared to be town lights beyond.

The U-Haul bounced over the tracks, Ricci trailing it by a steady distance. He crossed the tracks, discovered the lights were actually from a small service area—a Texaco gas station on his side of the road, a McDonald's just past it, another filling station on the other side of the road farther ahead. Opposite the fast-food restaurant was a Super 8 Motel posting special discount rates for truckers and rail workers.

Ricci saw the van hook left into the Super 8's parking lot; he reached the service area and turned right to enter the McDonald's lot, positioning the car so its driver's side faced the motel.

Ricci doused his headlamps, then looked sideways out his window. The motel was two stories of rooms in an elongated L-shaped structure set back from a turnaround spacious enough to accommodate large vehicles. He saw a tractor trailer in front making ample use of that space, a couple of six-wheel flatbeds, a single automobile. Tall Man had pulled the van straight up to the deck of the farthest ground-floor unit from the check-in office and gotten out. He took a step toward the office, paused, reached into his coat pocket for something.

Then a passing car momentarily blocked Ricci's line of sight on its way toward the second filling station, where it swung up to a self-service pump and stopped. He studied it only long enough to confirm that it was one of the three vehicles he'd observed behind him on the country route . . . and to watch its driver, a man in a mackinaw and baseball cap, get out and unhook the gas nozzle. After that, Ricci returned his full attention to the Super 8's turnaround.

In Tall Man's hands now were his cigarettes and disposable lighter—answering the minor question of what he'd reached for in his pocket. He shook a cigarette out of the pack, put it in his mouth, put away the pack, and flicked the lighter. Ricci saw a spark, but no flame. Tall Man hunched against the wind by the van, cupped a palm over the head of the lighter, tried again to get his smoke going. It still didn't fire up. After a minute he ditched the exhausted lighter with an obviously annoyed shake of his head.

Ricci watched him stride across the motel's guest lot into the office, the unlit cigarette poking from his mouth, his frustration explained by a prominent no-smoking sign on the office window.

Less than ten minutes later, he walked back along the deck to his corner room and let himself through its door with a key-card.

Ricci sat for a long while, on the look again. It was about the time of night when his thoughts would start getting away from him lately, turn all sorts of wrong corners, but it helped to be concentrating on the action, to be mentally outside himself, and he was hoping he'd be okay without needing anything else to keep his head straight. He saw the driver who'd been gassing up at the pump return to his car—it was a late-model Buick, similar to his requisition—make a K-turn out of the station, drive across into the McDonald's parking lot, exit the car, and head into the restaurant. He saw the lights go on behind Tall Man's drawn curtains, and after fifteen minutes or so saw them go off—bedtime. Chances were the U-Haul didn't have a theft alarm, and Ricci visualized himself breaking into it in the darkness of the lot, getting into the cargo section with his digital camera . . . a notion he might have seriously entertained if the van hadn't been parked right outside Tall Man's window, where the chances were too great he'd see or hear something.

Ricci leaned forward, meshed his hands over the steering column. Even as he'd dismissed the one idea as wishful thinking, another had taken shape for him. There was something to what Noriko Cousins had said about not trying to do too much, though in a different sense than she'd meant it. If he couldn't find out what the dark-suits had loaded into the van, maybe he could still learn something about any personal freight Tall Man might be carrying with him.

He let another few minutes pass, keeping an eye out for anybody in the motel lot, or on its ground floor decks, or on its upper-level terraces. Watching for anybody who might be looking out the office window, or any sign of movement anywhere around or in front of the place. When none came up, he got a small brown-paper evidence bag out of his glove box and crossed the road.

The faint neon gleam of the motel sign at the lot's entrance was enough to reveal the shape of Tall Man's ditched lighter—a plastic Bic—on the ground near the left front tire of the U-Haul.

Ricci waited a second, alert. No doors opened. No lights came on. Nothing happened to surprise him.

He crouched, picked up the lighter, and dropped it into the bag. He folded the top of the bag over once, a second time, peeled off the adhesive label, and stuck it on over the double fold to seal it. Then he put the envelope in his coat pocket and quickly backtracked to the fast-food joint's parking lot.

Ricci noticed that the guy in the baseball cap and mackinaw had returned to his Buick and seemed to be dozing, leaning against the headrest with his eyes shut, his seat semi-reclined. Instead of going over to his own car, he strode over to where the guy was parked across the lot and rapped his knuckles on the Buick's roof to get his attention.

The guy opened his eyes, sat up straight, looked out his window. Ricci put on a smile, gestured toward his own car, made a winding gesture in the air, and he lowered it.

"Something I can do for you?" the guy said, shifting around behind the wheel to face him.

Ricci nodded, and as he did, moved slightly closer to the driver's door and shot a right jab through the open window, getting most of his arm and shoulder into it, connecting hard with the side of his chin. The driver grunted with pain and surprise as his head snapped back, his hand going up to his face.

"You're out of your goddamned mind," he said.

"Rather be that than the one who got made," Ricci said, and held out his palm. "Come on, show me your tag."

The driver sat there massaging his chin.

"Up yours," he said.

Ricci had kept his hand out.

"Your tag," he said. "Either show it to me, or I can run a check on you. But I have to go to the trouble, you better believe I'll have you busted down."

The guy looked at Ricci a second, frowning. Then he dropped his hand from his chin, got a cardholder out of his mackinaw, and passed it out the window.

Ricci flipped it open, studied the UpLink Security ID card inside, read the name below its holographic Sword insignia.

"Bennett," he said, repeating it aloud. "Cousins put you on me, or you pick me up on stakeout over at Kiran?"

The op stared out the window.

"You're so smart, California, figure it out," he said.

Ricci looked at him in silence.

"Atta boy," he said. "Wouldn't want a demerit on the report card."

"Yeah, well, screw you, too."

Ricci's smile was cutting.

"Here's one you can answer," he said. "That van . . . it going to stay in sight?"

"What do you think?"

"I meant after your shift ends."

"I know what the hell you meant."

Ricci looked at him another moment, reached into his pocket for the sealed evidence bag, handed it through the window with the cardholder.

"I want what's in the bag tested for prints right away . . . I'm talking first thing in the morning," he said. "You ever try tailing me again, you might want to be smarter yourself, use a car I won't have seen in the same req lot where I got mine."

Bennett looked at him, flexed his jaw.

"Thanks for the advice, hump," he said.

Ricci pulled into a public rest stop shortly before reaching the large barrier toll plaza between I-87 and the southbound Garden State Parkway to Manhattan.

In the empty parking area outside the visitor's building, he got his palmtop out of a utility pocket in his tac vest and typed out a brief e-mail, addressing it to a Yahoo mobile account:

> O.W.K.
> Ready to meet tomorrow. Where and when—preference?
> R.

He sat for perhaps ten minutes afterward, staring at the computer screen, considering whether to hit SEND or DELETE on his keyboard.

Curtain number one, curtain number two, he thought. You bet your life.

Finally, his choice made, Ricci brought up the computer's WiFi interface and zipped off his message.

He could almost feel the lion's breath as he did.

Malisse's elevator was dangerously out of control.

At first everything had seemed normal. He'd stepped inside alone, pushed the button for the tenth floor, and leaned back against the rear of the car as it rose. To his surprise, it had stopped on the third without opening either its inner or outer doors. When he'd pushed the DOOR OPEN button to get them to retract, his car had plunged down the shaft so sharply his stomach had lurched into his throat, jolted to a halt midway between the first and second floors, then reversed itself and shot up to the fifth. Again the doors had stayed shut, trapping Malisse behind them. Again he pushed ten on the number pad, repeatedly jabbing the button with his finger until his car had seemed to resume normal operation, its indicator lights telling him he'd begun to move up the shaft. Six, seven, eight, nine, and coming level with ten. . . .

Then another sudden jolt and the elevator overshot his desired floor as if on high-powered thrusters, its hoist cables screaming, sides rattling, its decorative interior panels and mirrors shuddering and crashing down around him.

Malisse had been thrown about, on the verge of panic. How fast was he moving? Twenty meters per second? Thirty? Struggling to keep his feet under him, convinced the stress of rapid acceleration would break the car apart at any moment, tear it from its cables to send it freefalling down to the bottom of the shaft, he'd staggered toward the control panel and flipped the bright red EMERGENCY STOP switch.

An alarm bell kicked in at a deafening volume, but still the car kept ascending with rocket speed. On the verge of panic, Malisse wondered if he was a certain goner. What good would it do for someone to hear the racket if the elevator didn't brake? If the alarm merely rang and rang and rang as it soared up, up, up, past the building's highest story, staying in one piece only long enough to hit the roof?

Malisse grabbed the handrail, bracing for the inevitable collision, his ears filled with the clangorous, useless noise of the alarm bell—

And then he awoke to the ringing of the bedside phone in his room at the Mayfair Hotel.

Tossing free of his blankets, Malisse yanked off the black satin sleep mask he'd worn to foil the eternal and unspeakably intrusive lights of Manhattan. A moment later he glanced at his alarm clock, blinked twice as he groped for the receiver.

It was two forty-five A.M.

What boor, he thought, would call at this mad hour?

He jammed the phone against his ear.

"Who?" he demanded angrily.

"Duncan," said the voice at the other end. "You sound kind of winded, Delano. I didn't take you from any nocturnal diversions, did I?"

"Only my blissful dreams," Malisse said. He took a calming breath. "Are you aware of the time?"

"Vaguely," Duncan said. "We cardholders in the blackbag union keep odd schedules, and I hope you don't expect any apologies. Fact is, you ought to be appreciative."

Malisse sat up, shoved his pillows against the headboard, settled back onto them.

"I assume you're about to tell me why," he said at once.

"You wide awake?"

"Yes."

"Good," Duncan said. "Because I'd hate for you to claim that I didn't remind you about our meeting tomorrow. Or later this morning, I should say. Seven o'clock, Park Plaza, our usual table near those chess players."

Malisse's pique had melted away into eager curiosity.

"I don't recall our having made the appointment," he said, taking up the tease.

"No?"

"No."

"Well, maybe we didn't have one before, come to think," Duncan said. "Anyway, D, I've been to a tailor shop that had the coat you ordered in stock. They did while-you-wait alterations after all . . . though it took a cart full of my personal chips, and had me in the waiting room until maybe five minutes ago."

Malisse straightened, drew an excited breath.

"Duncan, I truly *do* appreciate this," he said.

"Enough to treat me to breakfast?"

"Ja, ja . . . certainly!"

The FBI man chuckled at the other end of the line.

"I know you're sincere when you stutter in Flemish," he said. "Seven on the nose, Delano. And expect me to eat hearty."

SEVEN

AT A LITTLE PAST EIGHT O'CLOCK IN THE MORNING, Ricci left his hotel room, took the elevator downstairs, and, as he went past the restaurant's lobby entrance, saw Derek Glenn stepping out with a cup of takeout coffee.

Ricci would have walked on toward the street if their paths hadn't crossed.

They stopped in front of each other, exchanged glances.

"Am I early, or you late?" Glenn said with a wooden smile.

Ricci shrugged.

"I want to check on some things downtown," he said. He continued to eye Glenn flatly. "Those are the same clothes you had on when I left there yesterday."

Glenn's expression grew more awkward.

"If you're so bothered by it, I'll just hurry on up to my room and change," he said. "Meet you at HQ in a while." And abruptly turned toward the elevators.

When Ricci got to her office, Noriko Cousins was at her

desk behind her computer. She pulled her head up from an open file folder and waved him through the door.

"I've heard you had a busy night," she said, sounding anything but pleased.

Ricci went to the corner chair and sat without hanging his coat.

"Wasn't the only one," he said.

She gave him a look. "Am I supposed to guess the meaning of that?"

"We're talking work, it means your frequent spotter at Kiran better learn to be more careful. If I could pick him up, so could the guy in the van," Ricci said. He shrugged. "There's some other meaning of 'busy' you want to discuss, I'm all ears."

Noriko was quiet a moment.

"I got your advance billing," she said. "The tough-guy attitude. The lone wolf bit. But I hadn't heard what a truly pathetic human being you are."

Ricci's smile slashed at her.

"Guess we'll stick to talking work," he said.

Noriko had kept looking steadily into his eyes, and she still didn't flinch.

"I don't care how you operate in San Jose, or what you've gotten away with under people's noses out there," she said. "But this is my city, and I've got no long leashes for anybody. Heading out on a surveillance last night wasn't something you should have done without authorization. It wasn't something you had any right doing in secret . . . and just so there's no confusion, my problem isn't with you getting your neck hacked open without anybody having a clue what's happened. The important thing is that you could have put our whole investigation in jeopardy."

Ricci stared back across the desk, shrugged his shoulders.

"I was worried about keeping secrets from you, I'd have gotten myself a Hertz rental car instead of ticketing that one out of the req lot, where I knew you'd make sure somebody would notice." He shrugged again and gestured toward the file folder that had remained spread open in front of her. "What's important is if those printouts mean your boy Bennett got any results off the cigarette lighter."

Noriko looked at him.

"Your partner called to say he'd be here any minute," she said. "I want him in on this, too."

It was, in fact, almost five minutes of chilly silence before Glenn arrived at her office. He moved past Ricci with a nod, tossed his coat up on a hook, and stepped toward Noriko's desk.

"Good morning," he said to her, smiling.

"Getting there," she said, and flashed him a quick little smile of her own.

Glenn settled into a chair, waited.

"Time for us to share and share alike," Noriko said. She gave him a revelatory look, then shifted her gaze to Ricci. "Starting with what you saw last night out at Kiran, and then afterward."

Even as an expression of surprise began spreading over Glenn's features, Ricci told of his observation of the plant, the loading and apparent unpacking of boxes aboard the U-Haul van, the dark-suits who'd done it, and the Tall Man. Then he went through his tailing the van to the trucker's motel, his recovery of the tossed lighter in the motel lot, and his passing it on to Bennett for examination . . . recounting all of it in a precise but dispassionate near-monotone.

"That's what I saw," he said finally. He looked straight at Noriko. "The rest's with you."

There was no hesitation in her nod.

"We lifted quite a batch of prints off the lighter, ran them through IAFIS courtesy of the access we're permitted by the Feds," she said, using the acronym for the FBI's Integrated Automated Fingerprint Identification database. "Every one of them belongs to a man named John Earl Fletcher . . . or John Earl, as he prefers to be called."

"What kind of rap sheet's he got?" Glenn said.

"A long and bad one," Noriko said. She scanned a sheet in her folder. "It starts almost twenty years ago with a string of misdemeanors and minor felonies in Maine. Possession of illegal substances, drunk driving, public nuisance, that sort of thing. There're several juvie arrests and probations, a conviction for snatching a wallet at knifepoint. Then he does six months in county jail for assault and battery. A year later, he's slapped with a charge of third-degree murder . . . a sheriff's deputy. Convicted and sentenced to fifteen years in the Maine state penitentiary."

"That sounds kind of light for a cop killing," Glenn said

"I thought so, too," Noriko said. "Went ahead and cross-referenced the IAFIS information with other clearanced databases, found that it was ruled accidental . . . the details in the system are sketchy, but it seems they had a personal background of some sort. Knew each other from high school, the way they do in small towns. Earl was driving a truck for a local fuel company. He and the cop are involved in some kind of shouting match over a routine traffic summons, stupid affair. One thing leads to another, and soon they're in a fistfight. The cop falls, hits his head, doesn't get up. And Earl goes into the system for a major stretch, where he becomes a man."

"Gets uglier as they get older."

"Doesn't it always," Noriko said. "When we next catch up with Earl, after his release, he's changed scenes to Newark,

New Jersey, and been arrested in connection with a RICO probe. There's a charge of interstate travel in aid of racketeering . . . and worse, multiple charges of murder-for-hire. But a couple of key witnesses change their testimony prior to trial, and the case against him is dropped."

Glenn snorted. "Oh, what luck," he said with an ironic smile.

Noriko shrugged, glanced down at her folder.

"There's nothing else as far as what I've dredged out of the computers. John Earl Fletcher—a.k.a. John Earl—seems to exit stage left until he shows up at Kiran with a U-Haul."

Ricci had sat in his corner of the office without reacting to what she said, or apparently having done anything but lean back and stare into space. Now he moved his eyes to Noriko and kept them on her.

"Your lookouts ever see that van at the plant before?" he said.

"No," she said. "Last night was a first."

"And it's still at the motel."

She nodded. "The minute Earl leaves his room, I'll know about it."

"So we've got a guy who gets mobbed-up doing hard time, a pro hitter and dirty carrier, moving stuff for Kiran when the lights are off, then parking a mile away like he's in no kind of hurry to go anywhere with it. That make sense?"

Glenn scratched behind his ear.

"Not much," he said. "Unless maybe he's waiting."

Ricci turned to him.

"Waiting for what?"

Glenn shrugged.

"Somebody to meet or contact him, something to happen, no way for us to know," he said.

Silence. Noriko slowly closed the file folder she'd been holding and flipped it onto her desk.

"I've seen something this morning besides the law-enforcement material," she said. "An e-mail from Lenny Reisenberg."

Both men looked at her.

"The shipping manager who got us mixed up in the Sullivan case?" Glenn said.

Noriko gave him a nod.

"It's a long story," she said. "What might be relevant here is that Lenny's started to dig into some of Kiran's shipping records, and a standout he's already figured worth passing on is that a lot of the dual-use laser components Kiran's been sending abroad in increased quantities—parts I've been wondering about for a while—have been freighted to an off-shore distribution outfit in Singapore. That same company has major offices in Amman, Jordan, and Cairo." A pause, a shrug. "None of it necessarily tells us anything's fishy, since those countries are considered our diplomatic partners, but—"

"Those places are also major route-throughs for lots of neighborhood bad guys," Glenn said.

She nodded again, and they all sat without speaking for a minute. Then Ricci sat forward in his chair, shifting his eyes from one to the other.

"We damn well better find out what's in that moving van," he said.

John Earl got out of the shower in his motel room, dried himself off, wrapped a towel around his waist, and stood half naked and still mostly wet in front of the full-length mirror on the door. He touched the tattoo of the fire-engine-red Mack truck on his neck, thinking of the dream he'd had the night before. In that dream—more of a nightmare, truth be known—he was back in Thomaston, back in his prison cell, and working on the much larger version of the truck he'd painted on its wall over several years, after finally convincing the screws to look the other way . . . though he knew he hadn't been the only con at Thomaston they'd let amuse himself with arts and crafts, 'long as he was quiet and did as he was told.

It had been quite a scenic picture that developed behind those bars over to the right of his cot, starting with a variation of the fuel delivery truck he'd driven for Hastings Energy before his row with that son-of-a-bitch deputy in Belfast had sent him down, and then growing little by little around the truck—a long black sweep of roadway beneath the heavyweight's wheels, rolling green hills into forever, and, overhead, the wide blue sky with its bright round sun and cotton-puff clouds. Earl would work on that painting for hours every night till just before lights-out was called. He had always loved trucks. Step-frame trailers, cab-overs, tankers like the Hastings Energy rig. And all those nights he was in that cell working on his painting of the truck, or staring at it in the semidarkness after he'd turned in, Earl would imagine he was riding along in its cab with his windows rolled down, the roar of the wind in his ears blending together with the growl of its monster Detroit diesel engine and the loud chop of rock and roll guitars blaring from the radio.

Yeah, Earl thought, he would imagine himself in that big Mack truck, would dream about it when he fell asleep. All he'd need to do was close his eyes, and he'd be riding fast and free along some unmarked country road, the Mack redder and shinier than a fire engine, taking him anywhere but where he was, taking him nowhere he'd ever be found, carrying him away from that miserable old house of rock and steel as mile after mile of open, empty countryside spooled out behind him.

Earl frowned, once again remembering last night's dream. Then he went from the mirror to get his clothes from where he'd tossed them on the bedside chair. In that dream, everything had been changed—turned inside out—and he'd been in his prison cell asking one of the guards for paint and getting turned down, *begging* for paint so he could work on his picture of the truck and getting turned town, getting laughed at, unable to see the screw's face because it was hidden behind a dark mask like the kind you'd figure might belong on a spacesuit . . . which Earl now realized was a visored helmet exactly like the one Hasul Benazir had worn over his head while telling him about today's goddamned job. The insane fucking *mission* that was supposed to net him a mint, and that he knew would really get him killed if he went ahead with it as planned—the meat eaten clean off his bones, his lungs dripping from his asshole, melted into chunky soup by the same poisoned air that would take out millions upon millions of other unsuspecting dupes.

Earl put on his underwear, socks, jeans, and sweater, fetched his boots from where he'd left them by the door, and sat on the edge of the bed to get his feet into them, jerking their tops up over his ankles.

He didn't care about the millions. Not a whit. If all those people didn't make it into the next dawn, Earl would shed about as many tears for them as had been cried for him throughout his entire life . . . which came to a grand total of none.

They could fend for themselves, the same way he'd always looked out for himself.

The way he would *keep* looking out for himself today, to-night, tomorrow, and on into all the tomorrows they might or might not live to see.

"Good to see you again . . . Mr. Friedman, that right?"

Malisse stood facing Jeffreys in the entrance lobby of the DDC building on West 47th Street, a black vinyl garment bag folded over his left arm, a hard-shell briefcase in his opposite hand.

"Right, indeed," he said. "You have a knack for remembering names."

"Don't know 'bout that, unless you count bein' able to match the ones in this here book with people's faces." The security guard tapped the guest register on his podium with a finger and flashed the exaggerated grin of a silent screen performer. "Norman Green called to leave word you'd be comin' by early this morning."

"Called?"

"He's runnin' a bit behind, but you can sign in an' go right on upstairs to wait for him," Jeffreys said. He leaned forward with a pen, a shaded look on his face. "Got yourself 'least half an hour, Hoffman's sayin' his prayers," he said in a hushed voice. Then, in a still lower whisper that seemed to slip out unintended: "Hope the Lord has mercy on the sinner lookin' for repentance."

Malisse grunted, took the pen, and signed the guest book in the column beside his hand-printed alias.

"If God were obliging enough to ask my opinion, I would advise him to save his concern for the just, and piss an ocean down on the rest," he said, turning toward the elevator.

Urban Jewelers on West 47th Street was a thirty-year-old, family-run storefront business that sold mediocre but affordable jewelry to the targeted walk-in consumer. The shop's seemingly unimaginative name did, in fact, possess a certain double meaning that was not lacking in cleverness, since the bland reference to its location at the heart of metropolitan New York—*urban*—was also a shortened version of the surname belonging to its founder and principle owner, one Constantin Urban*iak*, a Georgian Jew who had come to New York at the head of a half-million-strong wave of ambitious arrivals when, under tremendous internal and international pressure, the former Soviet Union relaxed its emigration policies toward persecuted minorities in the early 1970s.

While Constantin still oversaw the store's general affairs— with a close eye on tax-time bookkeeping—he had for the past seven years left its daily management to his daughter and son-in-law, a hardworking and borderline honest couple, who, when they gypped their customers at all, preferred exaggeration and embellishment to outright deceit, following examples they'd learned growing up with a steady diet of American television, on which multibillion-dollar corporations sold sneakers as schoolyard status, soft drinks as adolescent sex appeal, and expensive cars as adult success with flashy prime-time advertising spots.

Constantin Urbaniak had never done any such straddling of the line. Not when he'd stood behind the shop's display counters from morning till night, and especially not these days. In his opinion, honesty, or relative honesty, was for the uninspired, men like his daughter's dull but diligent lug of a husband. An artisan by disposition, and a forger by heritage—his beloved uncle on the maternal side was the famed World War II counterfeiter Solomon Smolianoff—Constantin had always felt his true calling to be creator rather than seller. And in the back room of Constantin's office space on the seventy-second floor of the Empire State Building, a space whose front room housed Urban Jewelry's mail-order and Internet sales operation—the pet project of his eldest son, Mikail, who had earned a doctorate in business from Johns Hopkins University—his view of himself as a virtuoso of the sham was a conceit indulged with exacting, tirelessly unscrupulous dedication.

Among forgers of antique jewelry, Urbaniak strove to be the best of the very best.

Avram Hoffman had followed a loud trail of whispers (as if there were any such thing as quiet whispers in the trade) to Constantin many months ago, bringing with him a genuine Japanese pink pearl and a handful of brilliant-cut diamonds, and requesting the fabrication of a gold Edwardian hatpin on which to mount them and exponentially increase their already fair value.

Gathering from the frequency of his return visits, Urbaniak's work had not disappointed. Indeed, the difficulty of Hoffman's commissions had graduated by broad, bold leaps, as had his confidence that the hand of Urbaniak would render them to perfection . . . and there could have been no greater testament to this than the challenge he'd presented upon entering the office moments before.

The question before Urbaniak this time around—underscored by the photographs Hoffman had laid out for him—was whether Hoffman truly had what he'd *claimed* to have in his possession. With it, Urbaniak knew he could fashion Hoffman something memorable, a classic piece of work. Without it he could give him nothing.

"I must ask again about the sapphire, if you don't mind," he said, looking at Hoffman across his desk. "A twelve-point-eight-carat cabochon of first quality is noteworthy. An oval of that size from the old mines of Kashmir would be fabulous. A sensational *rarity* . . ."

"And why shouldn't a broker who is the son and nephew of brokers attain the fabulous and sensational?" Hoffman said. "Or don't you believe even the man in the middle can exceed his origins?"

Urbaniak shook his head, a bit confused over his snappish tone.

"Don't forget, you are talking to one who has done just that," he said. "In the USSR, I was a factory worker. Here, a shopkeeper for many years." He paused. "No insult was implied, and none should be taken. I only want to be sure we understand each other before moving ahead."

"Then consider yourself assured, though I don't see any reason it should matter to you."

Urbaniak shrugged.

"We can start with pride," he said. "You know my policy, Avram. I am not a peddler of glorified costume jewelry. Of crap. What leaves my workshop must be faithful to the past work that inspires it in all but age."

Hoffman was quiet a moment, his lips tight, his face suddenly flushing above the line of his beard.

"Avram, are you all right?"

"Yes," Avram said, sounding short of breath. "Fine."

"You're positive? I can get you a glass of water . . ."

Avram waved him off, inhaled, exhaled.

"Never mind," he said. "The stone I'm providing will be a bona fide Kashmir. With certifications."

Urbaniak had noticed the flush spreading to Avram's neck and forehead in little red blotches, but given his touchiness thought it be best to refrain from further comment. He instead considered his words in silence, inspecting the pictures of the sapphire ring spread out on his desk.

"If that's what it is," he said at length, "that's what it is."

"Will you be able to design a setting based on my photos?"

Urbaniak looked at him.

"I've been an admirer of Raymond Yard jewelry for a very long time and would be eager for the opportunity to"—he paused to choose the appropriate phrase—"adapt one of his pieces. Yard was among the greatest ever, an artist without peer among his contemporaries of the Deco period . . . and, speaking of men who are able to exceed humble beginnings, the son of a rail worker who became friend and advisor to the wealthy. His salon's clientele was a who's who of old-money society, and of the New York elite in particular. The Vanderbilts, the Goulds, the Beekmans and Astors . . . and of course the Rockefellers." Another pause. "It was for John D. Rockefeller Junior that he arranged the purchase of what may be the world's most famous sapphire from the Nizam of Hyderabad. A sixty-six carat stone that once shone atop the ring in these photos you've brought me, and it would later be remounted onto brooches by both Rockefeller's first and second wives—and after Yard died, set into an inferior ring at the fancy of a son of Raymond Yard's colleague, the gem dealer Esmerian. When it finally passed into the anonymity of a private collection several years ago, I believe the blue commanded a record auction price of three million dollars."

Avram had opened the collar button of his shirt under his necktie and taken more deep breaths.

"In excess of that sum," he said. "Constantin, let me ask *you* something now. Suppose another stone was included in Rockefeller's acquisition from the Indian Maharajah. Much smaller than the first—just under thirteen carats—but from the same source, and of comparable excellence. Then suppose Rockefeller had asked Yard to set it in a platinum ring for a woman other than his wife. A very young, very beautiful ingenue of the Broadway stage who kept her relationship with him discreet, and in her commendable discretion never revealed the identity of the gentleman who gifted the ring to her, or left documentation of its provenance . . . though it was styled after these photographs I've copied and brought you from a Christie's auction catalogue, and did bear the engraved letter 'Y' that was Yard's signature." Avram sat forward in his chair. "Do you follow me so far?"

Urbaniak met his gaze with interest, nodded.

"You present an engrossing history."

"I've been working hard to get the details right," Hoffman said with a conspiratorial glance.

Urbaniak gave another nod. Perhaps working too hard for his own well-being, he mused. Hoffman's breathing and color had gradually returned to normal, but he still looked tired and overwound.

"Jumping ahead," Hoffman went on now, "let us say this actress married after Rockefeller's death, keeping her intimate friendship with him secret throughout her lifetime, bequeathing the ring to her own legitimate heirs. That it passed from child to grandchild, grandchild to great-grandchild, and so forth. And that it eventually fell to a beneficiary of some current social prominence who wishes to sell it without opening dusty boxes of scandal, and has engaged a broker like myself to do that while leaving the ring's owner unnamed." He regarded Urbaniak across the table. "My question to you, a supreme craftsman, is this: would the ring's unique qualities be enough to satisfy a prospective buyer, and whoever he or she may hire to appraise it, that it is an authentic Raymond Yard?"

Urbaniak was unhesitating in his answer.

"The accomplishment of an expert hand always will be recognized by an expert eye," he said. "And, with or without documents, command a suitable price from lovers of beautiful finery."

Hoffman remained silent for a minute. Then he nodded and settled back in his chair, finally seeming to relax a little.

"Constantin," he said, "I'm going to propose that you make me something beautiful and fine."

Moments after leaving Urbaniak's office, Avram stood on the corner of 33rd Street and Fifth Avenue, trying not to draw attention from passersby, feeling more than a bit embarrassed by his weakness as he leaned against the metal stanchion of a streetlight and caught his breath.

It had been so close up there with the jeweler, he thought. So airless. The seeming lack of oxygen had stuffed his head, made his chest feel as if it were bound tight with leather straps.

Avram swooped down mouthful after mouthful of cold air, and soon enough thought he felt better—certainly well enough to finish the rest of his business.

He reached into his coat for his cell phone and sent the brief e-mail stored in its memory to Lathrop, then lifted the briefcase he'd set down on the pavement between his feet.

Now he only needed to hurry over to the bank while waiting for his callback.

"You're sure you don't want to head up to see Ruiz with us?" Derek Glenn asked Ricci. He raised his shoulders against an explosive gust of wind. "Whatever might be rotten at Kiran, we can't forget we came here to find Patrick Sullivan."

Ricci was silent. Along with Glenn and Noriko Cousins, he was standing on Hudson Street outside Sword headquarters, only minutes after the detective had phoned to arrange their appointment.

"Didn't know we were joined at the hip," he said. "There are some other things I want to check out."

Noriko looked at him from under the brim of her leopard Carnaby.

"Things?" she said.

Ricci nodded.

"Like the apartment building where Sullivan's girlfriend lived, and whatever's around it, and wherever she might've passed before she disappeared," he said. "Things like that, and maybe more."

Noriko kept studying his face.

"Do what you want," she said. "But if you have any intention of snowing me, I promise you'll rue the day."

Ricci shrugged.

"You want to put another truant officer on my back, make sure I don't do anything out of school, go ahead," he said. "I were you, I'd worry about getting those added snoopmobiles we talked about over to that motel—and doing it before your man there falls asleep at the wheel."

A moment passed. Noriko looked at Ricci, started to give him an answer, realized she had nothing much more to say, and scratched whatever might have been on its way to her lips.

Raising her arm into the air instead, she stepped past him to hail a taxi at the curb.

Malisse stood looking in the window of the Nat Sherman tobacconist's shop across from the library on Fifth Avenue and 42nd Street, one eye on a charming and doubtless exorbitantly high-priced beveled glass and cocobolo rosewood humidor in which he could envision his prized Dominican Davidoff cigars resting in conditions ideal for their robustly delectable preservation. On some other day his fancy might have flared at the sight of it on display, ignited a rhapsodic gleam in his captive eye, propelled him beyond any thoughts of frugality toward a bacchanalian splurge at the store's sales counter.

Yes, Malisse thought, on another day his abiding passion for the exquisite might have led him to spend without restraint, while today his fidelity to his obligations—reinforced by his deep-seated contempt for the greedy and corrupt—obliged him to earn old Lembock's advance with due diligence, and to be guided by the eye he had not turned toward the smoke shop's window display but kept owlishly watching the display of the phone-sized global positioning receiver in his right hand . . . a device he had dubbed the Duncan in tribute to his good friend for having furnished it. For an hour and more now Malisse had followed the blip on its electronic street map layout that was Avram Hoffman, shadowing him on foot from the quaint lampposts marking the diamond and jewelry district to the great mullioned tower of the Empire State Building over a half mile downtown, where he had then tracked Hoffman to the 93rd-floor office of one Urban Gem Sales on an elevator that thankfully had been in smooth control on liftoff, descent, and between floors—unlike last night's haywire elevator of his id.

Having drifted past the door to the office for a look, Malisse had returned to the landmark building's lobby, waited for Hoffman amid its continuous percolation of office workers and sightseers, and, upon Hoffman's reappearance from the elevator bank some forty minutes later, resumed his tagalong foot pursuit, getting no closer than a half block behind him even in the thickest crowds, and dropping no more than five blocks behind when he felt at the slightest risk of being noticed. This allowed Malisse to remain safely out of sight, yet well within range of the GPS signal boosters he'd slipped under the lining of Hoffman's briefcase in the coatroom of the Diamond Dealer Club's synagogue.

After he'd left the building—immediately afterward, in fact—Hoffman had paused at its near corner within eyeshot of Malisse and briefly appeared to stand against a lamppost for support, bracing himself with a hand as if he'd suffered a spell of weakness or dizziness. He had seemed to recover within moments, even to use his cellular before continuing on his way, but Malisse had committed this to his mental notepad, as he did with all observations relating to his cases. One never knew what grain of information might turn out to be important in the long run . . . though he supposed Hoffman, a very busy fellow, also must be a very tired fellow indeed. The clip of his perambulations this morning already had *Malisse's* joints aching with fatigue.

Hoffman's rapid footwork over the hard pavement had quickly resumed, leading Malisse back uptown, his Duncan in hand. Past the stone lions guarding the library entrance he had tracked his man, and then onto 42nd Street, where he had lagged behind Hoffman as he turned into the door of what Malisse's subsequent walk-by had disclosed was a Chase Manhattan bank.

And there inside that bank Hoffman was still, presumably conducting transactions that might be all or none of Malisse's affair.

Malisse sighed and gave the handsome humidor in the window another longing glance.

Perhaps when his work was completed, he would return here to inquire about its cost.

In the meantime, he would do what he did best, which was wait, watch, and weigh what he saw of Hoffman's activities.

Like Ahab on his determined pursuit, Delano Malisse was resting for the rush.

Avram had no sooner been ushered from the vault by a security guard when his cellular rang.

He pulled it out of his coat pocket, flipped it open, and moved to an unoccupied counter space on the main banking floor, keeping firm hold of his briefcase with one hand. Heavy as it had just gotten, he was not about to rest it anywhere out of his grasp.

"How's my timing, Avram?" Lathrop said in his ear.

"It's what I've come to expect." Unusually thirsty for the past few minutes, Avram ran his tongue over his lips, but it was without moisture. "I have what's called for, and now only need know where *I* am called."

"Twenty-sixth and Broadway, over by the flower market," Lathrop said.

"That far *downtown*—?"

"You'll see a place with plastic containers of spray-painted branches in front. Universal Florists."

Avram sighed. He looked around for a water cooler, didn't see one, and decided he might have to stop for a drink on the way to his destination

"The dance exhausts me," he said, expelling another breath.

"Don't bellyache," Lathrop said. "I'll do you a favor and try to keep it short today."

Having left his motel room to get some breakfast, John Earl was emerging from the McDonald's across the road with an order of scrambled eggs and hash browns to go when he noticed the guy parked in the fast-food joint's customer lot.

Earl had no clear idea what it was about the guy that

raised his suspicions. There was nothing funny about the car he was in, a new-ish Pontiac or Buick—Earl couldn't tell the difference at a glance, and didn't want to look too hard and call attention to himself. Nothing funny about how the driver looked, which was like anybody with a head, a face, two shoulders, and a winter parka. And nothing funny about what the driver was up to, namely sipping coffee through the lid of a paper cup.

Off the top, there wasn't a reason in the world Earl figured he ought to pay him a second thought.

Still, he wasn't the sort to ignore his intuition. He'd spent almost half his life in the pen with a bunch of psycho hardcases for housemates, men who'd be as apt to kill as cornhole him the minute he let his guard down . . . and spent just about all the rest of his life doing things that would put him right back inside with them if he wasn't careful. He'd been hunter and hunted, sometimes both at the same time, and you didn't fare too well at either end of the chase without having high-frequency reception on your shit antennas.

Earl strode past the car toward the crosswalk to the motel court, not once glancing straightaway in its direction.

Probably it wasn't anything he needed to be on the sharp about, but careful were as careful did, as somebody or other had told him once upon a year in Maine, and he didn't know of any words in the world with a truer ring. Careful had kept him rolling easy for a while now—*ayuh, ayuh*—and the occasional ditch, bump, and roadblock aside, he'd done okay avoiding the kind of blowout that could set you skidding out of your lane into a total loss.

Walking by the U-Haul, key-card in hand, Earl had already decided he was going to play it safe.

The minute he returned to his room, he'd give Zaheer a

buzz at Kiran and tell him to be sure to bring along reinforcements when he showed up.

To Avram's abounding surprise, Lathrop had been truthful about wanting to shorten their dance. And while he did not believe Lathrop ever did anything as a favor to anyone, he would nevertheless regard the accelerated pace of their final round a parting courtesy.

In keeping with its desirable spirit of brevity, Avram hustled toward the Benjamin Franklin Hotel on Sixth Avenue and 23rd from the flower market a few blocks north, another false sign-in name committed to memory (Mr. Landon), and another room number (twenty-seven) attached to it in his head. He was running early, or at least felt as though he was, since Lathrop never gave a precise time of arrival for himself. But perhaps that had more to do with his own state of exhilaration . . . an emotional peak that had for the moment lifted him past weariness, anxiety, and fatigue.

Soon enough—within half an hour, Avram expected—he would pay Lathrop for his entire lot of stones with the cash extracted from his safe-deposit box at Chase. And then he would be on his way. Urbaniak would set the large Kashmir in his Raymond Yard homage. Katari, charmed by blue fire, would be eagerly waiting to purchase it. And he, Avram . . .

For him there would be freedom, emancipation, liberation. Were there any better words to describe what he was gaining? Was it blasphemous to think of Lathrop's stones as his own gift of *p'solet,* holy chips of immense value bringing him a transcendence he had only ever fantasized about having in a material world?

Avram saw the hotel midway down the block ahead of him and stepped it up. Ah, *fuzzgrenade.com, softgel.net,* or whatever that guitarist's name had been, Avram thought.

Ah, yes, what his splendid music meant. Someday in the near future Avram would look the kid up on the Internet, find him aboard the shuttle, drop him a huge money bonus, and look him in the eye without a shred of envy, but rather a bond shared only by those who let themselves become *un*-bonded, who—

The pain in Avram's chest took him all at once. Seized him around the heart like a crushing vice. He stopped on the sidewalk, his briefcase dropping from his numb left hand to the sidewalk, his hands going to a throat that had suddenly locked tight against his efforts to draw breath.

Then the city spun around him and he was on his back looking into the cold blue winter sky without air, a jetliner flying high overhead, people's faces looking down at him, one man's closer than the rest. The man was shouting something to them about an ambulance . . . about calling an ambulance . . .

Avram grabbed his wrist, or thought he did, he wasn't sure, his confusion was too great. He was becoming distanced from himself, Avram and not Avram, two-dimensional, almost without substance, whatever sliver was left of him pressed between constrictive walls of pain.

He tried to remember something, couldn't, and tried to ask the man whose face had come so close to his own whether he might know the answer.

But then the face was wiped away. In Avram's eyes the blue sky above it momentarily turned a burning, searing red, then sheeted over with a bright blank flash of white.

And in the end, there was nothing but darkness.

At the northeast corner of Sixth and 23rd, waiting for his light to turn green so he could cross to the west side of the avenue, Malisse saw his quarry crumple to the pavement almost a full block up ahead.

His face a mask of dismay, he glanced over his shoulder at an approaching onslaught of headlamps, bumpers, and grilles, took a shaved moment to time his lunge, and then dashed forward across the stream of uptown traffic with a prayer to wing-footed Mercury . . . ignoring the Roman god's alternate reputation as a guiding messenger of thieves.

Horns blared, tires skidded, profanities slapped against his ears.

"Gratuitous!" a young woman shouted from the curb behind him, offended by a bus driver's particularly vile oath. But Malisse was already three-quarters of the way to the other side and feeling appreciative.

He took the corner with a bound and continued to race toward the fallen Hoffman, around whom a small crowd of pedestrians had begun to gather. Then he was pushing through them, scooping them aside with both arms to kneel over the broker's prostrate form.

Malisse saw the blue-tinged lips and fingertips and livid cheeks, heard the tortured wheezing for breath, and immediately thought *heart attack*.

"Ambulance!" he shouted, looking around at the confusion-frozen onlookers. *"Someone here call an ambulance!"*

And then Hoffman's cyanotic fingers grabbed hold of his wrist, pulling, pulling him down.

Malisse saw his lips move, heard nothing but the surrounding barrage of street noises, leaned close, close, closer.

"My father's name?" Hoffman rattled. His eyes widened, their pupils enormous. *"My . . . father's name?"*

Malisse looked down at him with a sudden pang of sorrow, wishing he could answer Hoffman's question as the eyes rolled back in their sockets and the hand slid limply from his arm.

Then he heard the sirens . . . and knowing he had done

what he could as a man, remembered that he was also an investigator and glanced around for the dropped briefcase.

Unnoticed in the confusion, it lay on the ground almost against his ankle.

Malisse grabbed its handle and got to his feet. Would anyone know it wasn't his?

A look from a man in the crowd told him at least one among them did.

Malisse met his gaze for just an instant. Dark-haired, wearing a long, cloaklike outback coat, he prompted a sudden jolt of recognition . . . and Malisse thought he saw a similar awareness in the pair of eyes that had become locked with his own. Where else besides this place had Malisse seen him? Where and when had they seen *each other?*

The man was gone, vanished into the growing crowd, before he could begin to remember.

And then, aware he too must move quickly, Malisse turned and hurried off down the street with the briefcase.

Ted Bristow swore under his breath, trying to figure out what to do about the long Ford trailer truck—the words OAK LEDGE TRANSPORT written on its side, for whatever it was worth—that had jockeyed into the Super 8's parking court about four minutes earlier, stopping lengthwise across his line of sight with its engine rumbling, completely blocking his view of the U-Haul and motel room he was supposed to keep under constant watch.

It would be way too easy for the man with the van to mark him as a spotter if he shifted his car around the McDonald's lot and shot for an angle that would let him see behind the truck. Easier yet to mark him if he actually got *out* of the car and started nosing around. Which Bristow supposed left him caught between the proverbial rock and hard place.

He didn't like it one bit, and Noriko Cousins would like it a whole lot less. Because anything could happen while he was stuck blind . . . any damned thing at all.

A frown wrinkled Bristow's forehead. He'd been on lookout in the parking lot for about three hours when Earl came across the road to buy himself breakfast, passing Bristow's Grand Prix once as he'd approached the restaurant's entrance, and then again as he'd carried his bagged Egg McSomething back to the motel room.

At the time Bristow hadn't thought he'd been made, but you never knew for an absolute certainty. Almost three years with Sword, a six-spot with the FBI prior to that, he had plenty of experience with surveillance gigs. The thing was, your evil counterparts often as not had comparable experience from *their* side of a stakeout, and the smart and competent ones wouldn't let on for an instant that they'd had their suspicions alerted.

In fact, Bristow thought, the *really* competent ones might just roll a truck up in front of their opposite numbers as convenient cover when they were going to pull a move. There were front and back exits to the motel court, and right now he couldn't see either of them.

Bristow's frown deepened. What the hell *was* he supposed to do here? The support cars he'd been expecting from Manhattan were stuck in a typical weekday morning logjam on the George Washington Bridge, and, guessing from their last radioed status report, he'd be lucky to see them pull up inside an hour, or realistically ninety minutes. Obviously, he couldn't wait that long for an assist. Couldn't wait *period* without taking some kind of action. But any action he took could blow an operation that had gained whole new degrees of urgency literally overnight, and he wasn't about to make any impulsive decisions on that score . . . which brought his hurried thought process on the matter all the way back to square one. Or did it?

Bristow lifted his third coffee of the morning to his lips and hesitated before sipping. Its loathsomeness aside, there might be another reason to put it down. He couldn't dance rings around the truck without becoming a spectacle. But he *could* step out for another cup, make a relatively inconspicuous attempt at updating the status of the man with the van on his way to and from the McDonald's. If that wideass truck still presented a complete obstruction to him, so be it. It beat doing nothing.

Bristow lowered the coffee cup to the floor of the car, got out, turned toward the restaurant, and was about to take a kind of wide, ambling path toward its entrance when the longhauler's engine suddenly throbbed into gear behind him.

Bristow froze mid-step. Five minutes that truck had sat there in the motel court. Nobody exiting to make a pitstop at the restaurant. And now it was simply leaving.

In his considered opinion that stunk to the fucking moon.

Casting off subtlety, Bristow whipped his head around, looked across the road as the truck began angling out of the lot—

And knew he'd been beat.

The U-Haul van was already gone.

They had arranged to meet at the south side of Washington Square Park on one of the benches facing the large dry fountain area and the arch, and that was where Tom Ricci sat watching him approach from between the wind-stripped trees to his right. There weren't many people around on this cold January morning, just small, scattered groups of college kids from New York University, and some pigeons and squirrels looking for handout crumbs.

He waited as the man in the outback coat settled onto the bench at his side, then half turned his head toward him and waited some more in silence.

"Ricci," the man said. "Suppose it was nicer weather last time we got together in the park."

Ricci looked at him fully.

"You've got my name," he said. "Give me one I can call you."

The man sat there a moment with his lips slightly parted, his head canted to the side.

"Lathrop," he said after a moment.

"That a first or last?"

"Yeah."

Ricci saw a smile touch his lips.

"I'm not in the mood to play games," he said. "Why the hell did you bring me here?"

"I told you in my e-mail to San Jose."

"You told me you had something about one of our competitors had to do with laser research. Some information we might want for ourselves."

"Thought I used the word *plans* instead of information," the man said. "And wrote *East Coast* competitor."

"Which one?"

"Is this for you or for UpLink?"

Ricci looked at him again.

"Which one?" he repeated.

A brief hesitation. Then a shrug.

"Kiran."

Ricci nodded.

"Okay, Lathrop," he said. "Talk to me."

"You don't really think that comes free, do you?"

"I think I need to know more about what you're selling before I worry about value."

Silence. Two squirrels with jet-black fur skittered down a tree trunk to the waterless fountain, one chasing the other. The first squirrel gained a slight lead, perched on its lip a second with its tail twitching as if to bait its pursuer, then leaped off along a flagstone path and up another tree as their capering resumed.

"This is the only place in the city they have black squirrels," Lathrop said. "Always thought they hibernated in winter, but that was before I got to New York."

Ricci's eyes shifted back to Lathrop from where they had watched the squirrels climb in excited contest.

"Maybe things are different here," he said.

"Or maybe I didn't know as much as I figured I did about squirrels."

Ricci smiled a little, waited.

Lathrop sat back with his hands in his pockets.

"I move around a lot," he said. "Been doing that for a while now. Get a little bit going, make what I can of it, move again once the going looks to be heading toward the rocks." He paused. "Always does sooner or later, you know."

Ricci considered that.

"This later?" he said.

Lathrop faced him, dark eyes meeting his pale blue ones.

"You wouldn't believe what happened to me about half an hour ago," he said. "Lost an important briefcase."

"This *later*?"

Lathrop breathed, exhaled.

"Zero hour," he said. "Time to move or crash."

Another pause. Ricci held Lathrop's gaze.

"I need more," he said.

"You're getting to where it costs."

"We can take care of that part between us," Ricci said. "Come on. Talk about the part I need right now."

Lathrop sat there for a very long moment, then finally nodded.

"There's a weapon," he began. "A serious weapon."

Ricci phoned Glenn on his cellular from a coffee shop bubbling with students on West 4th Street, opposite the broad stone steps of NYU's Tisch Hall.

"Ricci," Glenn said, his semi-distracted voice that of someone glancing at a caller ID display. "I was just gonna contact you."

"You out of the cop's office yet?" Ricci paused, absorbing Glenn's words. "Hold it, contact me about what?"

"Something's gone down upstate," Glenn said. Speaking quickly now. "Earl shook our guy at the motel before his support could get there."

Ricci took a snatch of breath.

"Shook him in the U-Haul?"

"Yeah, looks like some kind of setup," Glenn said. "Noriko got word over the phone and cut the meeting with Ruiz short—"

"You give him anything on Earl or Kiran?"

"No, not yet. We didn't know how much to share, wanted to figure out what to do next—"

"Never mind figuring," Ricci said. "Just hurry up and meet me at headquarters."

"Wait a minute, I—"

"Headquarters, both of you," Ricci interrupted. "Soon as you can."

Then he pressed the END button on his touchpad, reached into his coat for his Palm computer, and set it on the table in front of him.

• • •

It took Ricci just minutes to read the van's license-plate number off the digital photo he'd uploaded to his Palmtop, obtain a U-Haul nationwide 800 hotline from directory assistance, and, under the pretext that he was a renter who might have left his wallet inside the van, feed a customer service operator its plate number so she could search for the location where it had been picked up.

"The information's right here on my screen, sir," she said. "It's an affiliate in Trenton, New Jersey."

"You have directions from Manhattan?"

"I'm sorry, no, but there *is* an address, and a direct exchange—"

"Let me have it."

The operator did, and Ricci called an instant after he hung up on her.

Three rings later, a man's voice: "Hullo, Turnpike U-Haul."

"I'm bringing a van back to you," Ricci said. And again read off the plate number. "Want to confirm you're the same center that leased it."

The guy paused a second at the other end.

"You Mr. Donovan?" he said, sounding confused.

Ricci thought.

"A friend of his," he said. "Why?"

"Well, I explained to him that it only comes and goes from our center for two days max," the U-Haul rep said. His bewilderment seemed to deepen. "Also, he just had one driver listed on his application. Means nobody but Mr. Donovan should be getting behind the van's wheel, let alone retur—"

"He can't make it," Ricci broke in. "Got to be me or nobody."

"Look, something happens to you on the road, I'm screwed insurance-wise—"

"I told you my friend isn't around," Ricci said. "Now you want the damn thing back or not?"

The guy paused a beat, issued a resigned sigh

"You the same fella who drove Donovan over yesterday?"

"No, how come?"

"Because I'm trying to save you some time," he said. "He—your pal who isn't around, that is—mentioned that they went past the Raja Petrochemical plant coming here, saw those big acid gas storage tanks out back . . . which tells me they must've got lost off the Turnpike ramp, driven out of their way trying to find my lot."

Ricci's hand tightened on the phone.

"You better tell me how to get to you," he said.

Earl had driven the U-Haul down I-87 almost to where it ran into the toll plaza when he passed a sign that said one of those public rest stops was coming up on his left.

It would be a gem of a place to give Zaheer—who hadn't spoken a word from over in the passenger seat since they split the Super 8—his hard jolt of reality.

He rolled on for a quarter mile, saw the entrance to the stop, and grooved the van toward the access lane.

Zaheer looked at him, suddenly seemed to remember he had a tongue that worked.

"Where are you going?"

"Gentleman's room." Earl nodded at the visitors' building that had come into view. "We've got a long stretch of road ahead to our exit."

Zaheer's expression was incredulous.

"You've lost your senses," he said. "It was you who feared that a watch had been placed on the motel. We cannot pull over now."

Earl shrugged. That was almost a joke, Zaheer calling

him screwy. Here was somebody who was heading off to die as some kind of martyr, looking for paradise on the other side of a cloud that would turn everyone for hundreds of miles around into a popped, runny blister. Somebody who had to damn well know those biohazard suits they'd been given wouldn't offer squat for protection when the laser cannon in back zapped Raja's HF tanks . . . that *nothing* would be able to shield them, not at ground zero.

A real fucking hoot, all right, his fellow road warrior Zaheer. He really believed the payment he'd brought from Hasul would be worth something in the world beyond.

"There was a watch, we beat it," Earl said now. "And far as stopping, that's Mother Nature's call, not mine."

Before Zaheer could issue another squeak of protest, Earl swung into the deserted parking area outside the redbrick visitors' house and cut the van's motor, leaving the keys in the ignition.

"You waiting out here?" he said.

Zaheer gave a curt, silent nod of displeasure.

Shrugging, Earl climbed out of the van, entered the unoccupied visitors' station, and pushed through the men's room door.

In a locked toilet stall, he took a minute or two to urinate—no sense making himself a *liar*—and then zipped up and transferred his Sig-Sauer compact nine-mil from its peekaboo holster under his pant leg to his coat pocket, where he'd keep his hand comfortably around its grip and be able to bring it out fast and easy the minute he got back to the van.

Leaving the bathroom, Earl realized the only thing he hadn't remembered to do was flush after himself . . . but then you couldn't cover everything when you were in a hurry.

• • •

As Earl exited the visitors' station, hands in his coat pockets, Zaheer sat with the fingers of his right hand wrapped around the butt of a Zastava Model 70, the Russian police pistol tucked in the space between the U-Haul's passenger seat and door. He did not trust the *kaffir* for an instant, and would be prepared should he attempt any betrayal. Should no such attempt be made, Zaheer would simply release his hold on the little pocket automatic and continue with the mission as planned.

Either way, he was satisfied he'd covered every possibility.

Now Earl approached the van, took one hand out of his coat, reached out to open the driver's door.

"Now that was a blessed relief," he said the moment it swung wide.

Zaheer saw the gun appear in Earl's other hand at the same instant, faster than he would have anticipated.

He brought up his Zastava without hesitation, pulling the trigger even as Earl fired *his* weapon, both barrels crashing and spitting their loads.

His face contorted, Earl staggered backward, clutched his chest, and went tumbling into the brown grass in front of the building.

Zaheer dropped his gun onto his seat with a grimace, then, fiery pain spreading up the left side of his abdomen. He must hurry now to carry out what fate had designed for him.

Shoving himself into the driver's seat, he simultaneously keyed the ignition and slammed the door shut. Then he footed the accelerator, tearing out of the visitors' stop and back onto the Thruway as quickly as he could manage.

The motorcycles darted onto the Jersey Turnpike from the I-95 turnoff, an even half dozen of them weaving through heavy four-wheeled traffic as it eked southward from the bottlenecked George Washington Bridge. Lightweight, nimble, slender, and speedy, they were virtually the same bikes UpLink had designed for the Defense Department to equip the 75th Rangers for rapid deployment and attack, providing maneuverability where there was no real room to maneuver.

Ricci bent over the handlebars of his cycle, his eyes scouring the road from behind the visor of his molded speed helmet, looking for any sign of the U-Haul's orange-and-blue markings. Astride the cycle to his right in a narrow channel between lanes of trucks and cars, Derek Glenn was doing the same, as were the four other Sword ops in black biker jackets who had buzzed hornetlike from the Soho req lot.

"You see anything?" Glenn said into his wireless handsfree.

"No," Ricci said. He shot around a station wagon plastered with old, sun-bleached New Jersey Nets bumper stickers: RIDE THE A-TRAIN TO THE RIM! KENYON MARTIN—NEVER SATISFIED! "Not a goddamned thing."

They rode on, juicing their engines, dodging and shimmying between the other vehicles on the 'pike. Factory complexes ranged to the left and right of dented metal safety rails, speed blurring their boxy geometries at the corners of the riders' vision. They didn't know if the van was out front or behind them, though behind would be far better, meaning they would probably beat it to the chemical plant. Out front meant they needed to make up a lead, and an undetermined one. The van could be a mile ahead or five, and they wouldn't know until they saw it. The van could be parked outside those tanks filled with hydrofluoric acid, seconds away from puncturing them with a high-intensity laser beam at a distance of fifty or a hundred yards. It could be an eyeblink, a *heartbeat,* from ending any conjecture about its whereabouts, unleashing a noxious windborne cloud that would envelop every man, woman, and child in every vehicle on the road, snuffing their lives out like a corrosive fist reaching from the arm of the Grim Reaper himself.

Ricci came up on an SUV's rear windshield, slid sideways. Slipped behind the wide rump of a Greyhound passenger bus, cut sharply around it. He heard a rubber-on-blacktop screech, didn't look back, glad whatever accident was gumming things up at the bridge had seemingly preoccupied the smokies and local cops, unable to worry too much about them anyway. Instead he raced on hard, gripping his bars, the soles of his boots pressed against his footpegs—

Then Glenn in the hands-free again. *"Ricci, hey . . . look!"*

Ricci glanced over at him, saw him gesturing, a high forward sweep of his right arm.

He followed its movement as he bumped over a pothole, saw the orange and blue. A van? He thought so. It was maybe an eighth of a mile off, small in his vision, too small for Ricci to positively verify it was *the* van. But it was close to the exit that led to Raja Petro, and he didn't imagine for an instant that was coincidence.

Ricci opened his throttle and charged ahead, thinking he would at least have a chance to take his stab.

Weak from loss of blood, his shirt red and tacky where Earl's bullet had penetrated just above his waist, Zaheer leaned over the steering wheel as he neared the turnpike exit, crawling along, moving through the dense metro-area traffic at a snail's pace. He had put the full thrust of his will into reaching his objective, tunneled his concentration toward the normally automatic act of driving, and he could see that he was almost there, almost . . .

Then a sound behind him. Getting louder. At first its significance didn't register. Zaheer knew he was dying from the gunshot wound, and just as the glorious task that lay ahead had summoned whatever was left of his fleshly powers, *he* had summoned what remained of his inner life force to answer the call. Everything outside had been pushed from his thoughts as extraneous, a waste of precious strength. But perhaps he had been wrong.

Perhaps . . .

There had been the one in the car at the motel.

The one Earl had thought might be a watcher.

Zaheer listened again. Or rather focused on what he could not do anything *but* hear. That sound. No . . . *sounds*. The combined drone of rapidly accelerating engines. Revving fast in slow traffic. How could the two be reconciled?

Zaheer pulled his mind from the tunnel around it long enough to grasp what was happening, looked into his side-view mirror, and saw the motorcycles swarming up from behind.

The curve of the exit ramp within eyeshot, Zaheer slapped his hand on the wheel, blasting the cars ahead of him with his horn.

He was determined to reach the exit ramp before the infidels could overtake him.

Three-quarters of an hour late for her sales-clerk job at the Rariton Mall's Fashion Bee, a job she'd landed just a week ago in the tightest of employment markets, Johanna Hearns was already about to come apart behind the wheel over being stuck in traffic, pound the dash and scream like a madwoman in a fit of frustration, when the idiotic driver of the U-Haul behind her started in with his horn, signaling he wanted to get off at the exit a car or two up ahead of her.

Johanna shook her head, spewing a string of epithets that would have astonished her husband with their inventiveness—and *he* thought he knew them all, hardy-fucking-har. What did Chief Dirty Ballsucker in the van think? That he was the only one in a hurry? That she was deliberately holding him up because she *liked* sitting bumper-to-bumper breathing in the smell of exhaust fumes and Jersey swamp air? Or that maybe she just couldn't get enough of *Imus in the Morning* on her car radio? And while she was making with the relevant questions, here was another: that honking nut job aside, where the fuck were the cops when you needed them?

Johanna did some Lamaze to keep her cool, a holdover from courses she'd taken when her youngest was born. Mr. U-Haul was in such a rush to get to charming Trenton, she'd get her own flashers going, hope somebody in the left lane was decent enough to hang back so she could shift into it, and let him go on his merry way.

Stay cool, stay cool, Johanna thought, and slapped on her signal.

She only hoped the van driver choked on his next meal.

"That's our van," Ricci said over the radio channel linking his bike team. "I see the plate number."

"Son of a bitch." This over the radio from Cole, one of the ops behind Ricci. "He's riding his horn to the ramp, getting those people up ahead to move."

Ricci zigzagged between lanes.

"Squeeze him," he said, and shot forward.

The last of the vehicles in front of him finally out of his way, Zaheer had almost reached the exit ramp when the attack bikes began to catch up. He checked his side-views, saw several of them closing in on both sides from the rear, the two in the lead nearly at his flanks.

Gunning his engine, he took a jarring turn onto the 25 mph ramp at double the permitted speed.

Gaining, gaining, gaining.

Ricci fisted a surge of gas into his cycle's engine, took the exit ramp between the left side of the U-Haul and the concrete barrier to *his* left, roping along on the narrow shoulder.

He pulled even with the driver's window, was able to snatch a glance inside.

The dark-suit at the wheel looked back at him—and in his brief distraction started slewing from side to side on the ramp.

Ricci dropped back an instant before the van's flank would have run him into the barricade, saw Glenn do the same as the U-Haul veered to the right. Too close behind Glenn, one of the other riders lost control of his bike and took a vaulting jump over the barricade. The cycle flipped over sideways, hurling its rider from his banana seat to whatever was below the ramp.

Ricci heard his screaming begin over the wireless, heard it peak, then heard it abruptly stop.

"God almighty." Glenn's shocked voice in his ear now. "God almighty."

"Cole," Ricci said. "You hear me?"

"Yeah. That was Margolis. Shit, I think he—"

"Don't think, just pull off and stay with him. The rest of you follow me."

Ricci's temples pounded. For a millisecond he was back in Earthglow, Nichols dying in his arms, turned into a sack of blood by the Wildcat. Ricci had felt something turn inside him. Grinding like a great stone wheel. *I'm here with you,* he'd told the kid. *Be easy.*

A millisecond.

It never ended.

Ricci saw the van pulling off the ramp ahead of him, and followed.

Grappling with the steering wheel at the bottom of the ramp, trying to keep it from wrenching out of his hands, Zaheer suddenly tasted blood. Coppery blood in his mouth, coming up from deep inside his body. There was a moment of greater weakness, his consciousness fading to gray.

Then he remembered the mission, the glory, and summoned himself again.

Al-hamdu lillahi, he mouthed silently. Repeatedly. *Al-hamdu lillahi.*

Feeling God guide his hand, Zaheer swung off the ramp, and as his eyes cleared, realized he'd turned the wrong way onto the boulevard into which it fed and was shooting into oncoming traffic.

The bikes were pouring off the exit ramp behind the van when it took its wide, erratic swing against the rush of traffic, then suddenly went screeching around in a U-turn.

Ricci heard a cacophonous outburst of horns as the stream of cars and trucks skidded and parted, saw two cars sideswipe while unsuccessfully veering to avoid a collision. There were screeches, a sickening crash, and then the van looped back in the right direction, roaring toward Ricci and the others, forcing them to scatter out of its way as it plunged ahead through two red lights and then barreled down a side street.

Zaheer recalled the turns he'd made before, recognized the factories and corporate signs.

With the motorcycles behind him still, Zaheer pushed his foot against the accelerator, believing he would now have an advantage . . . if only an advantage of a few minutes. He had taken this route before—would the same be true for them?

A handful of minutes, yes. All he would need was minutes to hold them off. Minutes, and he could trigger the Dragonfly cannon.

Zaheer barreled down a street to his left, then took a right, a second right, another left, and at last saw Raja's employee lot ahead. The evil droning song of the motorcycles had briefly grown fainter at his rear as he'd left the turnpike, but he could hear it growing louder again, and knew he would have no chance to reach the intersection with the abandoned gas station.

It did not matter.

Allah would give him what he needed.

As he sped up to the parking area's entrance, he swung the U-Haul in past the factory workers' cars to the chain-link fence dividing the outdoor lot from the HF storage area.

And then they were there before him, the tank clusters with their serpentine pipelines.

Zaheer spun the van around in a full circle, backed up to the fence, slammed his brakes.

Through his windshield, he could see the motorbikes turning into the lot. A single uniformed security guard jogged toward him from the factory to his right—fat, unsuspecting, that one posed the least threat of all.

Shifting the van into PARK, Zaheer started to reach for the Zastava pistol he'd stored in the glove box, but then changed his mind, choosing instead the MP5K submachine gun under his seat.

• • •

"Yo, mister!" the guard yelled, trotting up to the driver's side of the van. "That's a restricted area, can't you read the *signs*?"

Able to hear him shouting through his window, Zaheer noticed he did not have a hand anywhere near his gun.

Fat. Complacent. They would not learn their lessons.

The guard had heard the buzzing of the cycles now. He turned his head briefly toward the parking area's entrance, saw the motorcycles, looked back at Zaheer again.

"What the hell?" he said. "What the hell *is* this?"

Zaheer had no time to waste lowering his window—the cycles were approaching. He raised the MP5 and fired two three-round bursts directly through it into the guard's face, wiping him from his sight.

Then, heedless of the shattered window glass that had blown over him in slivery piles, he slung the submachine gun over his shoulder, clambered back into the cargo section, threw himself on his stomach, and turned the cannon's turretlike beam director toward the tanks.

Cutting across the lot in a straight line, the bikes broke formation as they reached the front of the stopped van, Ricci and Glenn swooping to the left, the two other remaining Sword ops taking its right flank.

Ricci hooked his bike around toward the rear section and had time enough to see that the cargo hatch was already raised, opened from within, before fans of gunfire began pouring out of it. He wrenched his handlebars, tailing away from the van to avoid the volleys, but one of the ops on its other side was slower by a hair to react. Bullets cut into him and he went into a tailspin, spilling from his seat as his attack cycle crashed into the divider fence.

Enough, Ricci thought. *No more.*

He halted the bike at the side of the van, booted down its kickstand, and lunged off his seat, crouching low, pulling his variable-velocity snubnose automatic from under his leather jacket, switching the weapon to its lethal setting. Beside him, another motorbike also braked to a stop.

"Glenn?"

"Yeah."

"Count of three, we get around back, open fire."

"With you."

"One, two—"

"Ricci."

"What?"

"Check it out."

"Check wha—"

"Look." Pointing.

Ricci looked. And realized what Glenn had been trying to get him to notice.

The firing from the rear of the van had stopped, and a submachine gun . . . an MP5, Ricci thought . . . lay on the ground behind its back bumper, its black grip glistening wet with blood.

Ricci turned to Glenn, made eye contact with him through his visor, nodded in silent communication.

Slowly, guardedly, their weapons at the ready, they edged along the side of the van with their backs flat against it, then hooked around to the open cargo section.

The driver lay sprawled over what looked like a small cannon turret on a mount the size of a small valise. He was face down on his belly, a pool of crimson underneath him, crimson all over the turret, all over the hand hanging limply from the open bay door. Mounted inside the cargo section were three readout and control panels, their flatscreen displays blank.

Ricci looked at Glenn.

Glenn looked at Ricci.

"Done," Glenn said.

And they both lowered their weapons to their sides.

EIGHT

"GUESS IT AIN'T TOO TOUGH TO FIGURE WHY I'M here," John Earl said, trying hard to stay on his feet a little longer.

Hasul Benazir looked at Earl from behind his desk at the Kiran office.

"Our deal," he said.

Earl nodded.

"Our deal," he affirmed. "Fifty grand up front, fifty on completion—"

"Succeed or fail," Benazir said.

Earl nodded again, hands stuffed in the pockets of his coat. As always the office was silent around him except for the sounds of pumped and filtered water in the octopus tank in the wall.

He waited. Hard, hard as hell, keeping his feet under him . . . though it didn't help that Zaheer's bullet was still floating around in the red muck between his ribs, probably just about to give his heart a last cold kiss.

Hush baby, you hush.

Yeah, Earl thought, the old fire-engine-red truck he'd driven for so long would be ditching off the highway of life any time now. He had stuffed the hole in his chest with fist-fuls of gauze more than once, wrapped himself around with fresh bandage tape before showing up at the office, but all that had done was soak up the blood under his shirt and coat—well, the coat, anyway—and keep it from gushing out of him like water from a bathtub spout.

Now Benazir rose, came around the desk, stood in front of Earl.

"The money will be yours without condition," he said. "I would, however, wish to know how you managed to escape what has just begun to trickle its way into the news. Those men on motorcycles . . ." Benazir shrugged, let the sentence trail. "How?" he said.

Earl remained very still. If he took even a single step forward, backward, or sideways, he figured it would leave him flat on the floor. Of course, it wasn't his feet he had to be able to move.

"Well," he said, and pulled his Sig nine from his pocket, "it went kind of like this."

Benazir's face barely showed any reaction. After a few seconds he blinked slowly, let his eyes stay shut for another span of seconds, and released a long breath as he opened them.

"You never did think you'd have to pay up the balance, did you?" Earl said. "Never thought I'd be around to ask for it."

Hasul shook his head.

"No," he said. "I never did."

Earl looked at him with his gun between them, tightened his lips to hold back a cough. No sense messing the carpet with what would come out of him.

He motioned toward the aquarium with the pistol.

"Gonna give you a choice, Hasul," he said. "You can let your poisonous friend Legs give you a tickle or you can deal with *my* friend Siggy here. Either way, it ought to be quick."

Benazir remained nearly expressionless, staring at him with his dark brown eyes.

At length he nodded, strode toward the tank, removed the wood-veneer feeder panel from the wall above it, and set it down on the floor.

"I believe I knew," he said softly, and turned his head to look at Earl as he rolled up his shirt sleeve.

Earl grunted.

"Kinda believe you did, too," he said. He raised the gun a notch higher, his finger around its trigger. "Now go on, Hasul. Say hi to Legs for me . . . and I promise, I'll see you by-and-by."

Hasul stared at him another moment, gave him a nod, and then turned and slipped his hand into the aquarium.

Darting from its habitat cave, the octopus was quick to wrap its venomous tentacles around him.

The vid-conference between Megan Breen in San Jose and Noriko Cousins and Tom Ricci in New York took place almost immediately after the federal agents left Noriko's office.

It was no coincidence that their visit to Sword-Manhattan, and the reasons for it, were the main subjects of discussion.

"It boggles me that you let this happen," Megan was telling Noriko. "A threat of the magnitude you uncovered . . . how could you not immediately report it to the authorities? The list of protocols you violated is so long, I can only begin to list them from memory. NYPD, the FBI, Homeland Security—all of them should have been informed." She paused, shook her head. "This was a Code Red national-security emergency. Millions could have died—"

"But they didn't die, and the reason they didn't is because *we* didn't wait to move," Noriko said. Her lips tightened. "All it cost was the lives of two of my men."

Megan looked at her from across the country.

"I'm not questioning the actions you took," she said. "It's the notifications you should have—and could have—made when they were taken."

Noriko stared at the video screen from her chair at the conference table, glanced over at Ricci, glanced back at the screen. Started to say something, then stopped. And then stared at the screen some more.

"I had reasons that I can't share," she said simply.

Megan looked at her.

"Reasons," she repeated.

Noriko gave a nod.

"Reasons," Megan repeated a second time, incredulous. "Noriko, listen to what I'm saying—"

"She can hear you," Ricci said abruptly. "You want to put this on somebody, put it on me."

Megan shook her head.

"I don't understand," she said.

"My source gave me his tip on the condition that we handle everything ourselves," Ricci said. "He wanted time to get himself out of the city before it went into lockdown, and I told him he could have it. Better that than have him leave without talking."

There was a prolonged silence. Megan inhaled, exhaled.

"This mysterious source you've mentioned . . . you could have told him whatever you wanted for his information," she said. "Do you really think letting him have things his way was worth putting UpLink under fire? Our reputation, our contacts . . . were they worth jeopardizing for *him*?"

Ricci looked at her with his icy blue eyes and merely shrugged.

"No," he said. "They were for my promise."

"Yes, sir, may I help you?" the salesman said from behind his counter.

Malisse nodded.

"The cocobolo rosewood humidor," he said. "The one in your window, with the beveled glass lid . . ."

"I know which you mean," said the salesman, looking sharply down his nose at Malisse. "It is a one-of-a-kind."

Malisse tugged at his earlobe.

"I see," he said. "Well, I'd noticed it earlier, and was wondering about its price"

The salesman looked at him, and quoted a dollar amount with what appeared to be delighted scorn.

Malisse tried not to choke on the exorbitant figure. With his flight back to Antwerp booked for the morning, he had returned to the tobacconist's on a whim . . . and a foolish whim it had been to think he could afford the cigar case.

Indeed, Malisse thought, he was probably undeserving of it. Certainly undeserving. He had failed to determine anything conclusive about the sapphires. He had not learned whether they were authentic or fakes. He knew nothing more than before about their origins, or the identity of the scoundrel in the outback coat who had doubtless been set to meet the late, unfortunate Hoffman before his fall. He had done nothing, *nothing* of consequence in New York City but sample its sweets and return a briefcase full of money to Hoffman the middleman's bereaved widow.

Yes, Rance Lembock would offer to pay him despite his disappointment. And no, Malisse would accept nothing but expense money from the old survivor of genocide. How could he presume to justify the purchase of the humidor to himself?

"Ah, sir . . . if you don't mind?"

Malisse looked at the salesman, plucked from his reverie. "Don't mind what?" he said.

"I have other customers waiting," the salesman said with a wave toward some presumably invisible person at a counter where Malisse had thought himself standing alone. "So unless there's something more—"

Malisse snapped up his hand, a finger pointing skyward.

"Yes, my friend," he said. "Yes there is! Bring me the humidor, a carton of Davidoffs to fill it . . . and have the whole package gift wrapped quickly, as I have a plane awaiting to carry me away from this cold city."

The salesman's eyebrows arched. His scorn transformed to surprise, he turned to bring the valuable goods.

Malisse watched him, guiltless about the decision that had struck him like a bolt out of the blue.

Sometimes, he thought, a man must not be rewarded only for success.

Sometimes just trying one's best was worth a gift.

The seven dead bodies had been lined one beside the other on their backs, naked, stripped of their dog tags, their Indian army uniforms buried deep under the snow elsewhere on the mountainside.

Siphoned of emotion, Yousaf looked down at them. It was too late to second guess himself, yet he knew his decision not to radio out a message to his buyers had in all probability cost them their lives . . . and crushed his hopes of ending this night as a very rich man. While the border patrol uniforms the men had worn—and identification they'd carried—had gotten them past the Indians on the other side of the Line of Command, it had not stopped them from being ambushed by Ahmad's scouts here on the mountain pass.

Cold and pale under the moonlight, they might have looked like their own ghosts had it not been for the single, red, seeping bullet hole Yousaf could see in the middle of each man's forehead.

As far as he knew, bloodless spirits did not bear the marks of a gunpoint execution.

He turned toward one of the LeT scouts that had led him to the bodies, trying to maintain his presence of mind. "Tell me again when these whoresons were caught."

The scout looked at him.

"Two hours ago," he said, and gestured toward a nearby rock overhang. "We spotted them earlier. Came up the other side of the mountain and took them."

"And you say it appears they had been waiting here for some time?"

"There are signs, yes."

Silence. Several paces away, just out of earshot, a Bakarwal guide waited near his mule, holding the beast's rope in his hand as it snorted steam into the icy night air.

Yousaf glanced over at him and thought a moment. The prospect of wealth might be lost to him, at least for now. But there was still more of the game to play, another deception he must turn to assure the scout's suspicion did not instead turn his way.

"The nomads," he said in a lowered voice. "It can only be that they betrayed us. Conspired with these troops so we'd be caught before making our rendezvous across the border."

The scout continued to eye him.

"That might be easy for me to believe," he said. "India's government and military generals would pay a high price for the Dragonfly cannon."

Yousaf nodded.

"Enough of a fortune to satiate even a Bakarwal's greedy soul," he said. "My intelligence is that only two complete units have been produced. That the other remains with our brothers in Americ—"

Yousaf became aware of someone stealing up behind him far too late to avoid the arm that had suddenly locked around his throat—and the cold press of a blade across it.

A harsh voice in his ear: "Judge no one else's soul. Not when it was you who sent one of your own operatives to his death in the wastes between here and Chikar."

Yousaf tried to shake his head in denial, felt the knife press more tightly against his throat, and stopped.

The scout in front of him, meanwhile, had taken several long steps forward.

"Did you think Ahmad would not have you watched from the beginning, little pig?" he said. "That he would not have eyes among the men in your convoy? A voice to inform him that you'd started across the mountains with another? Or can it be you've already forgotten your good companion Khalid?"

Yousaf swallowed silently and the steel edge of the blade met his Adam's apple.

"Cast blame wherever you will, it was *you* who arranged for your mule train to encounter these troops . . . if actual troops they are," the scout said to him, bringing his face close. "I suspect them to be something else. Khalistani fighters disguised as soldiers. Or Nagas. Or Punjabi rebels." The scout's face came still closer. "Brothers sometimes compete most fiercely, do they not? And there has been much competition for the weapon among our professed brethren in India."

Yousaf swallowed again. The blade broke skin.

"Let me speak to Ahmad," he grated in desperation. "I can prove you're wrong—"

"Ahmad," the scout repeated. A mocking grin had spread across his face. "Tell me, little pig . . . how can you be sure that my men and I are loyal to *Ahmad*? That we do not have our own buyers for the cannon? What makes you so certain of its destination—its intended targets—in a world of constant *un*certainty?"

Yousaf looked at him, his mouth forming a circular grimace of surprise.

It had suddenly dawned on him that he had no answers. No answers to any of the scout's questions. No answers to his own. No answers to anything at all.

Nothing, indeed, to take from the world but uncertainty as the scout looked past him at whoever had come up from behind, and made a slicing gesture with his hand, and the knife sliced deeply, deeply into his throat.

Tom Clancy's Power Plays

Created by Tom Clancy and Martin Greenberg
written by Jerome Preisler